RANDOM
HOUSE
LARGE
PRINT

The Secret
Between Us

Also by Barbara Delinsky
available from Random House Large Print

Family Tree

The Secret
Between Us

Barbara Delinsky

RANDOM HOUSE
LARGE PRINT

This is a work of fiction. Names, characters, places, and incidents either are the product of the author's imagination or are used fictitiously. Any resemblance to actual persons, living or dead, events, or locales is entirely coincidental.

Copyright © 2008 Barbara Delinsky

Library of Congress Cataloging-in-Publication Data
Delinsky, Barbara.
The secret between us / by Barbara Delinsky. — 1st large print ed.
p. cm.
ISBN 978-0-7393-2652-7
1. Mothers and daughters—Fiction. 2. Family secrets—Fiction. 3. Truthfulness and falsehood—Fiction. 4. Large type books. I. Title.
PS3554.E4427S423 2008
813'.54—dc22
2007047264

www.randomhouse.com/largeprint

FIRST LARGE PRINT EDITION

10 9 8 7 6 5 4 3 2 1

This Large Print edition published in accord with the standards of the N.A.V.H.

Jacket design by Kelly Blair
Jacket photograph by Andrea Chu

To Ruby, with sparkle and love

Chapter 1

They were arguing in the seconds before impact. Later, Deborah Monroe would agonize about that, wondering whether, had she been focused solely on the road, she might have seen something sooner and been able to prevent what occurred—because the argument had been nearly as distracting as the storm. She and her daughter never argued. They were similar in looks, temperament, and interests. Deborah rarely had to tweak Grace—her son, Dylan, yes, but not Grace. Grace usually understood what was expected and why.

This night, though, the girl fought back. "You're getting hyper about nothing, Mom. Nothing happened."

"You said Megan's parents were going to be home," Deborah reminded her.

"That's what Megan told me."

"I would have thought twice if I'd known there would be a crowd."

"We were **studying.**"

"You, Megan, and Stephie," Deborah said, and, yes, the textbooks were there, damp from Grace's dash to the car in the rain, "plus Becca, and Michael, Ryan, Justin, and Kyle, none of whom were supposed to be there. Three girls study. Four girls and four boys make a party. Sweetie, it's pouring rain, and even **above** the noise of that, I could hear shrieking laughter all the way from the car."

Deborah didn't know if Grace was looking guilty. Long brown curls hid broad-set eyes, a straight nose, and a full upper lip. She did hear the snap of her daughter's gum; its spearmint shrouded the smell of wet books. But she quickly returned her own eyes to the road, or what she could see of it, despite the wipers working double time. Visibility on this stretch was poor even on the best of nights. There were no streetlights, and moonshine rarely penetrated the trees.

Tonight the road was a funnel. Rain rushed at them, swallowing the beam of the headlights and thrashing against the windshield—and yes, April meant rain, but this was absurd. Had it been as bad on the way out, Deborah would never have let Grace drive home. But Grace had asked, and Deborah's husband—**ex**-husband—too often accused her of being overprotective.

They were going slowly enough; Deborah would repeat that many times in subsequent days, and forensics would bear it out. They were less than a minute from home and knew this part of the road well. But the darkness was dense, the rain an unreckoned force. Yes, Deborah knew that her daughter had to actually drive in order to learn how, but she feared this was too much, too soon.

Deborah hated rain. Grace didn't seem fazed.

"We finished studying," the girl argued around the gum in her mouth. Her hands were tight on the wheel, perfectly positioned, nothing wrong there. "It was hot inside, and the AC wasn't on yet, so we opened the windows. We were taking a break. Like, is it a crime to laugh? I mean, it's bad enough my mother had to come to get me—"

"Excuse me," Deborah cut in, "but what was the alternative? You can't drive by yourself on a learner's permit. Ryan and Kyle may have their licenses, but, by law, they're not allowed to take friends in the car without an adult, and besides, we live on the opposite end of town from the others—and what's so bad about your mother picking you up at ten o'clock on a weeknight? Sweetie, you're barely sixteen."

"Exactly," Grace said with feeling. "I'm sixteen, Mom. I'll have my real license in four months. So what'll happen then? I'll be driving myself places all the time—because we don't only live on the opposite end of town from everyone else, we live in the middle of **nowhere,** because Dad decided he had to buy a **gazillion** acres to build a McMansion in the forest, which he then decided he didn't **want,** so he left it **and** us and moved to Vermont to live with his long-lost love from twenty-five years ago—"

"Grace—" Deborah couldn't go there just then. Grace might feel abandoned by her father, but the loss hit Deborah harder. Her marriage wasn't supposed to end. That hadn't been in the plan.

"Okay, forget Dad," Grace went on, "but once I get my license, I'll be driving places alone, and you won't **see** who's there or whether there's a parent around, or whether we're studying or having a party. You're going to have to **trust** me."

"I do trust you," Deborah said, defensive herself now, but pleading. "It's the others I don't trust. Weren't you the one who told me Kyle brought a six-pack to the pool party at Katherine's house last weekend?"

"None of us had any. Katherine's parents made him leave."

"Katherine's **parents. Exactly.**"

Deborah heard her growl. "Mom. We were studying."

Deborah was about to list the things that could happen when teenagers were studying—things she had seen both growing up, when her father was the only family doctor in town, and now, being in practice with him and treating dozens of local teenagers—when a flash of movement entered her line of sight on the right. In quick succession came the jolt of a weighty thud against the front of the car, the slam of brakes, the squeal of tires. Her seat belt tightened, holding her while the car skidded on the flooded pavement, fishtailed, and spun, all in the space of seconds. When it came to a stop, they were facing backward.

For a minute, Deborah didn't hear the rain over the thunder of her heart. Then, above it, came Grace's frightened cry. **"What was that?"**

"Are you okay?"

"What was that?" the girl repeated, her voice shaking this time.

Deborah was starting to shake, too, but her daughter was upright, belted in, clearly okay. Scrabbling to release her seat belt, Deborah hiked up the hood of her slicker and ran out to search for whatever it was they had hit. The headlights reflected off the wet road, but beyond that paltry light, it was totally dark.

Ducking back into the car, she fumbled through the glove box for a flashlight. Outside again, she searched the roadside, but saw nothing that remotely resembled a downed animal.

Grace materialized at her elbow. "Was it a **deer?**" she asked, sounding terrified.

Deborah's heart continued to pound. "I don't know. Sweetie, get back in the car. You don't have a jacket." It was a warm enough spring night; she just didn't want Grace seeing what they had hit.

"It **had** to be a deer," Grace cried, "not even hurt, just ran off into the woods—what else could it be?"

Deborah didn't think a deer wore a running suit with a stripe up the side, which was what she swore she had seen in the split second prior to impact. A running suit meant something human.

She walked along the edge of the road,

searching the low shrubs with her light. "Hey," she called out to whoever was there, "are you hurt? Hello? Let me know where you are!"

Grace hovered at her shoulder. "Like, it came from **nowhere,** Mom—no **person** would be out here in the rain, so maybe it was a fox or a raccoon—or a deer, it **had** to be a deer."

"Get back in the car, Grace," Deborah repeated. The words were barely out when she heard something, and it wasn't the idling car. Nor was it the whine of wind in the trees or the rain splattering everything in sight.

The sound came again, definitely a moan. She followed it to a point at the side of the road and searched again, but it was another minute before she found its source. The running shoe was barely visible in the wet undergrowth some four feet from the pavement, and the black pants rising from it, half hidden under a low branch of a hemlock, had a blue stripe. A second leg was bent in an odd angle—broken, she guessed—and the rest of him was crumpled against the base of a tree.

Supine, he ran no risk of suffocation in the forest undergrowth, but his eyes were closed. Short dark hair was plastered to his forehead. Scrambling through a clump of wet ferns, Deborah directed her flashlight to his head, but didn't see any blood other than that from a mean scrape on his jaw.

"**Omigod!**" Grace wailed.

Deborah felt for a pulse at his neck. It was only when she found it that her own began beating again. "Can you hear me?" she asked, leaning close. "Open your eyes for me." He didn't respond.

"**Omigod!**" Grace cried hysterically. "Do you know who that is, it's my history teacher!"

Trying to think quickly, Deborah pulled her daughter back onto the road and toward the car. She could feel the girl trembling. As calmly as she could, Deborah said, "I want you to run home, honey. It isn't more than half a mile, and you're already soaked. Dylan's alone. He'll be scared." She imagined a small face at the pantry window, eyes large, frightened, and magnified behind thick Harry Potter glasses.

"What'll **you** do?" Grace asked in a high, wavery voice.

"Call the police, then sit with Mr. McKenna until an ambulance comes."

"I didn't see him, I swear, I didn't see him," wailed Grace. "Can't you do something for him, Mom?"

"Not much." Deborah turned off the engine, turned on the hazards. "I don't see any profuse bleeding, and I don't dare move him."

"Will he **die?**"

Deborah grabbed her phone. "We weren't going fast. We couldn't have hit him that hard."

"But he got way over there."

"He must have rolled."

"He isn't moving."

"He may have a concussion or be in shock." There were plenty of worse possibilities, most of which, unfortunately, she knew.

"Shouldn't I stay here with you?"

"There's nothing you can do here. **Go,** sweetie." She cupped her daughter's cheek, frantic to spare her this, at least. "I'll be home soon."

Grace's hair was drenched, separating into long, wet coils. Rain dripped from a gentle chin. Eyes wide, she spoke in a frightened rush. "Did **you** see him, Mom? Like, why would **anybody** be walking on the road in the rain? I mean, it's dark, how could I **possibly** see him, and why didn't **he** see **us?** There are no other lights here."

Deborah punched in 9-1-1 with one hand and took Grace's arm with the other. **"Go,** Grace. I need you home with Dylan. **Now."** The dispatcher picked up after a single ring.

Deborah knew the voice. Carla McKay was a patient of hers. She worked as the civilian dispatcher several nights a week.

"Leyland Police. This call is being recorded."

"Carla, it's Dr. Monroe," she said and shooed Grace off with a hand. "There's been an accident. I'm on the rim road, maybe a half mile east of my house. My car hit a man. We need an ambulance."

"How badly is he hurt?"

"He's unconscious, but he's breathing. I'd say there's a broken leg, but I'm not sure what else. The only cut I see is superficial, but I can't look more without moving him."

"Is anyone else hurt?"

"No. How fast can you get someone here?"

"I'll call now."

Deborah closed the phone. Grace hadn't moved. Soaking wet, curls long and bedraggled, she looked very young and frightened.

Frightened herself, Deborah stroked wet hair back from her daughter's cheeks. On a note of quiet urgency, she said, "Grace, I need you home with Dylan."

"I was driving."

"You'll be more of a help to me if you're with Dylan. Please, sweetie?"

"It was my fault."

"Grace. Can we **not** argue about this? Here, take my jacket." She was starting to slip it off when the girl turned and broke into a run. In no time, she had disappeared in the rain.

Pulling her hood up again, Deborah hurried back into the woods. The smell of wet earth and hemlock permeated the air, but she knew what blood smelled like and imagined that, too. Again, she looked for something beyond the scrape on Calvin McKenna's jaw. She saw nothing.

He remained unconscious, but his pulse was strong. She could monitor that and, if it faltered, could manually pump his chest. Studying the angle of his leg, she suspected that his injury involved the hip, but a hip injury was doable. A spine injury was something else, which was why she wouldn't move him. The EMTs would have a backboard and head immobilizer. Far better to wait.

It was easier said than done. It was an endless ten minutes of blaming herself for letting Grace drive, of taking Calvin McKenna's pulse, trying to see what else might be hurt, wondering what had possessed him to be out in the rain, taking his pulse again, cursing the location of their house and the irresponsibility of her ex-husband, before she saw the flashing lights of the cruiser. There was no siren. They were in too rural a part of town for that.

Waving her flashlight, she ran back onto the road and was at the cruiser's door when Brian Duffy stepped out. In his mid-forties, he was one of a dozen officers on the town force. He also coached Little League. Her son, Dylan, had been on his team for two years.

"Are you all right, Dr. Monroe?" he asked, fitting a plastic-covered cap over his crewcut. He was already wearing a rain jacket.

"I'm fine. But my car hit Calvin McKenna." She led him back to the woods. "I can't tell how badly he's hurt." Once over the ferns, she knelt and checked his pulse again. It remained steady. She directed her flashlight at his face; its beam was joined by the officer's.

"Cal?" she called futilely. "Cal? Can you hear me?"

"What was he doing out here?" the officer asked.

Deborah sat back on her heels. "I have no idea. Walking? Running?"

"In the rain? That's strange."

"Particularly here," she said. "Do you know where he lives?" It certainly wasn't nearby. There were four houses in the circle of a mile, and she knew the residents of each.

"He and his wife have a place over by the

train station," Brian replied. "That's a few miles from here. I take it you don't treat him?"

"No. Grace has him in school this year, so I heard him speak at the open house last fall. He's a serious guy, a tough marker. That's about all I know." She was reaching for his pulse again when the road came alive with light. A second cruiser arrived, its roof bar thrumming a raucous blue and white. An ambulance was close behind.

Deborah didn't immediately recognize the EMTs; they were young, likely new. But she did know the man who emerged from the second cruiser. John Colby was the police chief. In his late-fifties, he would have been retired had he been working anywhere else, but he had grown up in Leyland. It was understood that he would keep working as long as his health allowed. Deborah guessed that would be a while. He and his wife were patients of theirs. His wife had a problem with allergens—dander, pollen, dust—that had resulted in adult-onset asthma, but John's greatest problem, beyond a pot belly, was insomnia. He worked days; he worked nights. He claimed that being active kept his blood pressure down, and since his blood pressure was chronically low, Deborah couldn't argue.

While John held a floodlight, the EMTs

immobilized Calvin. Deborah waited with her arms crossed, hands in the folds of her jacket. He made neither movement nor sound.

She followed them out of the woods and was watching them ease him into the ambulance, when Brian took her arm. "Let's sit in the cruiser. This rain's nasty."

Once inside, she lowered her hood and opened her jacket. Her face was wet; she wiped it with her hands. Her hair, damp and curling, still felt strange to her short after a lifetime wearing it waist long and knotted at the nape. She was wearing a tank top and shorts, both relatively dry under her jacket, and flip-flops. Her legs were slick and smudged with dirt.

She **hated** rain. It came at the worst times, defied prediction, and made life messy.

Brian folded himself next to her behind the wheel, and shook his hat outside before closing the door. He took a notebook and pen from a tray between the seats. "I have to ask you a few questions—just a formality, Dr. Monroe." He checked his watch. "Ten forty-three. And it's D-E-B-O-R-A-H?"

"Yes. M-O-N-R-O-E." She was often mistakenly thought to be Dr. Barr, which was her maiden name and the name of her father, who was something of a legend in town. She had used her married name since her final year of college.

"Can you tell me what happened?" the officer asked.

"We were driving along—"

"We?" He looked alarmed. "I thought you were alone."

"I am now—Grace is home—but I had picked her up at a friend's house—that's Megan Stearns's house—and we were on our way home, going really slowly, not more than twenty-five miles an hour, because the rain was so bad. And suddenly he was there."

"Running along the side of the road?"

"I didn't see him running. He just appeared in front of the car. There was no warning, no time to turn away, just this awful thud."

"Had you drifted toward the shoulder of the road?"

"No. We were close to the center. I was watching the line. It was one of the few guidelines we had with visibility so low."

"Did you brake?"

Deborah hadn't braked. Grace had done it. Now was the time to clarify that. But it seemed irrelevant, a technicality.

"Too late," she replied. "We skidded and spun around. You can see where my car is. That's where we ended after the spin."

"But if you drove Grace home—"

"I didn't drive her. I made her run. It isn't more than half a mile. She's on the track team." Deborah wrangled her phone from a soggy pocket. "I needed her to babysit Dylan, but she'll want to know what's happening. Is this okay?" When he nodded, she pressed the speed-dial button.

The phone had barely rung when Grace picked up. "Mom?"

"Are you okay?"

"I'm okay. How's Mr. McKenna?"

"He's on his way to the hospital."

"Is he conscious?"

"Not yet. Is Dylan okay?"

"If being dead asleep on the sofa when I got here means okay, yes. He hasn't moved."

So much for large eyes at the window, Deborah thought, and heard her ex-husband's **You worry too much,** but how not to worry about a ten-year-old boy who had severe hyperopia and corneal dystrophy, which meant that he viewed much of his life through a haze. Deborah hadn't planned on that, either.

"Well, I'm still glad you're with him," she

said. "Grace, I'm talking with the police officer now. I may run over to the hospital once
we're done. You'd probably better go to bed.
You have that exam tomorrow."

"I'm going to be sick tomorrow."

"Grace."

"I am. I can't think about biology right
now. I mean, like, what a **nightmare.** If this is
what happens when you drive, I'm not doing
it. I keep asking myself where he came from.
Did **you** see him on the side of the road?"

"No. Honey, the officer's waiting."

"Call me back."

"Yup." Deborah closed the phone.

The cruiser's rear door opened and John
Colby got into the backseat. "You'd think the
rain'd take a break," he said, adding, "Hard to
see much on the road. I took pictures of
everything I could, but the evidence won't last
long if it stays like this. I just called the state
team. They're on their way."

"State team?" Deborah asked, frightened.

"The state police have an Accident Reconstruction Team," John explained. "It's headed
by a credited reconstructionist. He knows
what to look for more than we do."

"What does he look for?"

"Points of impact, marks on the car. Where

on the road the car hit the victim, where the victim landed. Skid marks. Burned rubber. He rebuilds the picture of what happened and how."

It was only an accident, she wanted to say. Bringing in a state team somehow made it more.

Dismay must have shown on her face, because Brian said, "It's standard procedure when there's personal injury. Had it been midday with the sun out, we might have been able to handle it ourselves, but in weather like this, it's important to work quickly, and these guys can do that." He glanced at his notes. "How fast did you say you were going?"

Again, Deborah might have easily said, **Oh, I wasn't the one at the wheel. It was Grace, and she wasn't speeding at all.** But that felt like she was trying to weasel out of something—to shift the blame—and besides, Grace was her firstborn, her alter ego, and already suffering from the divorce. Did the girl need more to trouble her? Calvin McKenna was hit either way. No laws had been broken either way.

"The limit here is forty-five," she said. "We couldn't have been going more than thirty."

"Have you had any recent problems with the car?"

"No."

"Brakes working?"

"Perfectly."

"Were the high beams on?"

She frowned, struggling with that one. She remembered reminding Grace, but high beams, low beams—neither cut far in rain like this.

"They're still on," John confirmed from behind, "both working." He put his hat back on his head. "I'm going out to tape off the lane. Last thing we need is someone driving by and fouling the scene."

Deborah knew he meant **accident** scene, but with a state team coming, she kept thinking **crime** scene. She was feeling upset about the driver issue, but the questions went on. What time had she left her house to get Grace? What time had Grace and she left Megan's house? How much time had passed between the accident and Deborah's calling it in? What had she done during that time? Had Calvin McKenna regained consciousness at any point?

Deborah understood that this was all part of the investigation, but she wanted to be at the hospital or, if not there, at home with Grace and Dylan.

She glanced at her watch. It was past eleven. If Dylan woke up, he would be frightened to find her still gone; he had been clingy since the divorce, and Grace wouldn't be much help. She would be watching for Deborah in the dark—not from the pantry, which she saw as Dylan's turf, but from the window seat in the living room that they rarely used now. There were ghosts in that room, family pictures from a happier time, in a crowd of frames, an arrogant display of perfection. Grace would be feeling desolate.

A new explosion of light announced the arrival of the state team. As soon as Brian left the cruiser, Deborah opened her phone and called the hospital—not the general number, but one that went straight to the emergency room. She had admitting privileges and had accompanied patients often enough to know the night nurse. Unfortunately, all the nurse knew was that the ambulance had just arrived.

Deborah called Grace. The girl picked up instantly. "Where are you?"

"Still here. I'm sitting in the police car, while they check things outside." She tried to sound casual. "They're reconstructing the accident. It's standard procedure."

"What are they looking for?"

"Whatever they can find to explain why Mr. McKenna was where he was. How's Dylan?"

"Still sleeping. How's Mr. McKenna?"

"Just got to the hospital. They'll be examining him now. Have you talked with Megan or any of the others?" There was the issue of Grace climbing into the car on the driver's side, which might have been seen by her friends, reason to level with the police now.

"They're texting me," Grace said in a shaky voice. "Stephie tried to call, but I didn't answer. What if he dies, Mom?"

"He won't die. He wasn't hit that hard. It's late, Grace. You ought to go to bed."

"When will you be home?"

"Soon, I hope. I'll find out."

Closing the phone, Deborah tucked it in her pocket, pulled up her hood, and went out into the rain. She pulled the hood closer around her face and held it there with a dripping hand.

A good part of the road had been sealed off with yellow tape, made all the more harsh now by floodlights. Two latex-gloved men were combing the pavement, stopping from time to time to carefully pick up and bag what they found. A photographer was taking pictures of Deborah's car, both its general position on the road and the dent in the front. The dent wasn't large. More noticeable was the shattered headlight.

"Oh my," Deborah said, seeing that for the first time.

John joined her, bending over to study what remained of the glass. "This looks to be the only damage," he said and shot her a quick glance. "Think you can dig out your registration so I can record it?"

She slipped behind the wheel, adjusted the seat, opened the glove box, and handed him the registration, which he carefully recorded. Restowing it, she joined him outside.

"I didn't think of damage," she said, pulling her hood forward again. "I was only concerned with what we'd hit. We thought it was an animal." She peered up at him. "I'd really like to drive to the hospital, John. How long will these fellows take?"

"Another hour or two," he said, watching the men work. "This is their only shot. Rain continues like this and come morning, every-thing'll be washed out. But anyway, you can't take your car. We have to tow it."

"Tow it? It's perfectly driveable."

"Not until our mechanic checks it out. He has to make sure nothing was wrong that might have caused the accident—brake mal-function, defective wipers, worn tires." He looked at her then. "Don't worry. We'll drive you home tonight. You have another car there, don't you?"

She did. It was Greg's BMW, the one he

had driven to the office, parked in the Re-
served for President spot, and kept diligently
waxed. He had loved that car, but it, too, was
abandoned. When he left for Vermont, he had
been in the old Volkswagen Beetle that had sat
under a tarp in the garage all these years.

Deborah didn't like the BMW. Greg had
bought it at the height of his success. In hindsight, that was the beginning of the end.

Folding her arms over her chest, she
watched the men work. They covered every
inch of the road, the roadside, and the edge of
the forest beyond where Calvin McKenna had
landed. More than once, feeling useless and
despising the rain, she wondered why she was
there and not at the hospital helping out.

The answer, of course, was that she was a
family practitioner, not a trauma specialist.
And it was her car that had caused harm.

The reality of that loomed larger by the
minute. She was responsible—**she** was responsible—for the car, for Grace, for the accident, for Calvin McKenna. If she could do
nothing for him and nothing for the car, she
needed to be home with her children.

Grace huddled in the dark. Each time her
cell phone rang, she jumped, held it up, stud-

ied the panel. She answered if her mother was calling, but she couldn't talk to anyone else. Megan had already tried. Twice. Same with Stephie. Now they were texting.

WER R U? TM ME!

R U THER? HELLO??

When Grace didn't reply, the focus changed.

DUZ YR MM NO ABT TH BR? DD SHE SMLL IT?

R U IN TRBL? U ONLY HD I.

But Grace hadn't had only one beer, she had **two,** and even though they were spaced three hours apart, and she hadn't felt high and probably wouldn't even have blown a .01 if she had been breathalyzed, she shouldn't have driven.

She didn't know why she had. She didn't know why these so-called friends of hers—**alleged** friends, as in provable but not proved—were even **mentioning** beer in a TM. Didn't they **know** everything could be traced?

UOK?

Y WONT U TALK?

She wouldn't talk, because her mother was still with the police and Mr. McKenna was at the hospital and it was **all her fault**—and nothing her friends could say would make it better.

Chapter 2

It was another hour before the state agents dismantled their lights, and a few minutes more before a tow truck arrived. Deborah knew the driver. He worked at the service station in the center of town and was a frequent customer at her sister's bakery. That meant Jill would hear about the accident soon after she opened at six.

Brian drove her home, pulling into the circular drive and, at her direction, past the fieldstone house to the shingled garage. She was exhausted and thoroughly wet, but as soon as she had closed the cruiser door and was sprinting forward hugging her medical bag and Grace's books, she opened her phone and called the hospital. While she waited for an answer, she punched in the code for the garage. The door rumbled up as the call went through. "Joyce? It's Deborah Monroe again. Any word on Calvin McKenna?"

"Hold on, Dr. Monroe. Let me check."

Deborah dropped her armload and hung her slicker on a hook not far from the bay where her car should have stood. Leaving her flip-flops on the landing, she hurried inside, through the kitchen to the laundry room.

"Dr. Monroe? He's in stable condition. They're running tests now, but the neurologist doesn't see any evidence of vertebral fracture or paralysis. He has a broken hip. They'll deal with that in the operating room once this last scan is done."

"Is he conscious?" Deborah asked, back in the kitchen, drying her arms with a towel.

"Yes, but not communicating."

"He can't speak?"

"They suspect he can but won't. They can't find a physical explanation."

Deborah had run the towel over her face and was lowering it when she spotted Grace in the corner. "Trauma, maybe?" she speculated. "Thanks, Joyce. Would you do me a favor? Let me know if there's any change?"

Still dressed, Grace was hunched over, biting her nail. Deborah pulled the hand away and drew her close.

"Where **were** you?" the girl asked meekly.

"Same place."

"All this time?"

"Uh-huh."

"Why did the police drive you home?"

"Because they don't want me driving my car until they've examined it in daylight."

"Isn't the cop who drove you home coming in?"

Deborah drew back to study her face. They weren't quite the same height, but almost. "No. They're done for the night."

Grace's voice went up a notch. "How can they be done?"

"They've asked their questions."

"Asked you, not me. What did you tell them?"

"I said we were driving home in the rain, visibility was terrible, and Mr. McKenna ran out from nowhere. They'll have to go back along the road in the morning to see if there's anything they missed that the rain didn't get. I'll file a report at the station tomorrow and get the car. Where's Dylan?"

"He went to bed. He must have thought you were home. What do we tell him, Mom? I mean, he'll know something happened when he sees your car missing, and besides, it was **Mr. McKenna.** This is such my luck that it was my teacher. I mean, like, I'm so **bad** at

American history, people will think it was deliberate. What do I tell my friends?"

"You are not bad at U.S. history."

"I shouldn't be in the AP section. I don't have a prayer of placing out when I take the test in June. I **suck**."

If she did, it was news to Deborah. "You tell them that we couldn't see Mr. McKenna in the rain, and that we weren't going very fast."

"You keep saying **we**."

Yes. Deborah realized that. "I was the licensed driver in the car. I was the one responsible."

"But I was the one at the wheel."

"You were my responsibility."

"If you'd been driving, the accident wouldn't have happened."

"Not true, Grace. I didn't see Mr. McKenna, and I was watching the road as closely as if my own foot was on the gas."

"But it wasn't your foot on the gas."

Deborah paused, but only for a minute. Slowly, she said, "The police assume it was."

"And you're not telling them the truth? Mom, that's lying."

"No," she said, sorting it out even as she spoke. "They drew their own conclusion. I just haven't corrected them."

"**Mom**."

"You're a juvenile, Grace," Deborah reasoned. "You were only driving on a permit, which means that you were driving on my license, which makes me responsible. I've been driving for twenty-two years and have a spotless record. I can weather this better than you can." When Grace opened her mouth to protest again, Deborah pressed a hand to her lips. "This is right, sweetie. I know it is. We can't control the weather, and we can't control what other people do. We were compliant with every law in the book and did our very best to stop. There was no negligence involved on our part."

"What if he dies?"

"He won't."

"But what if he does? That's **murder.**"

"No," Deborah argued, though the word **murder** gave her a chill, "it would be vehicular homicide, but since we did absolutely nothing wrong, there won't be any charges."

"Is that what Uncle Hal said?"

Hal Trutter was the husband of Deborah's friend Karen, and while neither he nor Karen were actually related to the Monroes, they had known the children since birth. Their daughter, Danielle, was a year ahead of Grace.

Deborah saw Karen often. Lately, she had felt more awkward with Hal, but that was a whole other story.

"I haven't talked with him yet," she told Grace, "but I know he'd agree. And anyway, Mr. McKenna is not going to die."

"What if he's crippled for life?"

"You're getting carried away with this, Grace," Deborah warned, though she harbored the same fears. The difference was that she was the mother. She couldn't panic.

"I saw his leg," the girl wailed. "It was sticking out all wrong, like he fell from the top of a building."

"But he didn't fall from the top of a building. He is definitely alive, the nurse just told me so, and broken bones can be fixed."

Grace's face crumbled. "It was awful. I will never forget that sound."

Nor would Deborah. She could still hear it—that **thud**—hours after the fact. Seeking purchase, she clutched Grace's shoulders. "I need a shower, sweetie. I'm chilled, and my legs are filthy." Keeping an arm around the girl, she walked her up the stairs and down the hall. In addition to the three children's rooms, the third for a last child that Deborah and Greg might have had, there was a family room that had built-in desks, a sofa, matching armchairs, and a flat-screen TV. After Greg left, Deborah had spent so many nights here with the kids that she finally just moved into the third bedroom.

Grace was biting her nails again by the time they reached her door. Taking the hand from her mouth, Deborah looked at her daughter for a long, silent moment. "Everything will be fine," she whispered before letting her go.

The texting had stopped before her mother got home, for which Grace was grateful. What could she tell Megan? Or Stephie? Or Becca? **My mom is taking the blame for something I did? My mom is lying so I won't be arrested? My mom could go to** jail **if Mr. McKenna dies?**

Grace had thought the divorce was bad. This was worse.

Deborah had hoped that the shower would calm her, but warm, clean, and finally dry, she could think more clearly, and a clearer mind simply magnified what had happened. The sound of the rain didn't help. It pounded the roof much as it had the car, and she remembered another night, the one when her mother had died. It had been pouring then, too.

Creeping into Dylan's room, she knelt by the bed. His eyes were closed, dark lashes lying on cheeks that wouldn't be smooth much longer. He was a gentle child with more than his share of worry, and while she knew that there were cures for his vision problems, her heart ached.

Not wanting to wake him, but helpless to leave without a touch, she moved her hand over his sandy hair. Then she went to her room, slipped into bed, and pulled the covers to her chin. She had barely settled when she heard Dylan's steps, muted by the old slipper-socks that he wore every night. They were the last pair Ruth Barr had knit before her death, too big for him at first, now stretched so thin that they were about to fall apart. He refused to let Deborah throw them out, saying that they kept his Nana Ruth alive. In that instant, Deborah needed her mother, too.

"I tried to stay awake 'til you got home," he mumbled.

Pulling him toward her, Deborah waited only until he set his glasses on the nightstand before tucking him in next to her. He was asleep almost at once. Moments later, Grace joined them, crawling in on the other side. It was a snug fit, though preferable to lying awake alone. Deborah reached for her daughter's hand.

"I won't be able to sleep," the girl whispered, "not at all, the whole night."

Deborah turned her head in the dark and whispered back, "Here's the thing. We can't rewind the clock. What happened happened. We know that Mr. McKenna is in good hands and that if there's any change, we'll get a call. Right?"

Grace made a doubtful sound but said nothing more. In time her breathing lengthened, but she slept in fits and starts. Deborah knew because she remained awake for a long time after that, and for reasons that went well beyond the drumming of rain on the roof. She kept seeing that striped running suit, kept feeling the jolt of impact.

Sandwiched between the children, though, she knew she couldn't panic. After her marriage ended, she had made a vow. No more harm to the kids. No . . . more . . . harm.

The phone rang at six the next morning. Deborah had been sleeping for less than three hours, and the press of her children made her slow to react. Then she remembered what had happened, and her stomach clenched.

Fearing Calvin McKenna had taken a turn for the worse, she bolted up and, reaching over Dylan, grabbed the phone. "Hello?"

"It's me," said her sister. "I figured your alarm would be going off soon. Mack Tully was just in here. He said you hit someone last night."

"Oh. Jill." Relieved, Deborah let out a breath. She and her sister were close, though very different from each other. Jill was thirty-four to Deborah's thirty-eight, blonde to her brunette, five-two to Deborah's five-six, and the maverick of the family. Despite two long-term relationships, she hadn't married, and while Deborah had followed their father into medicine, Jill flat-out refused to take any science courses. After one post–high school year as a baker's apprentice in New Jersey, then a second year in New York and four more as a dessert chef on the West Coast, she had come back to Leyland to open her own bakery. In the ten years since her return, she had expanded three times—all to her father's chagrin. Michael still prayed she would wake up one day, go back to school, and do something **real** with her life.

Deborah had always loved her little sister, even more in the three years since their mother had died. Jill was Ruth. She lived simply but smartly, and, like her bakery, she exuded warmth. Just hearing her voice was a comfort. Talking with Ruth on the phone had conjured the smell of warm, fresh-baked bread. Talking with Jill on the phone conjured the smell of pecan-topped sticky buns.

The image soothed the rough edges of fear. "It was a nightmare, Jill," she murmured tiredly. "I had just gotten Grace, and it was rainy and dark. We were driving slowly. He came out of nowhere."

"Was he drunk?"

"I don't think so. I didn't smell anything."

"Vodka doesn't smell."

"I couldn't exactly ask him, Jill. He wasn't talking."

"The history teacher, huh? Is he badly hurt?"

"He was operated on last night, likely to put a pin in his hip."

"Marty Stevens says the guy is odd—a loner, not real friendly."

"Serious is the word, I think. He doesn't smile much. Did Marty say anything else?"

"No, but Shelley Wyeth did. She lives near the McKennas. She said his wife is weird, too.

They don't mix much with the neighbors." There was a brief pause. "Wow. You actually ran someone down. I didn't think you had it in you."

Deborah was a minute reacting. Then she said, "Excuse me?"

"Have you **ever** been in an accident before?"

"No."

"The rest of us have."

"Jill."

"It's okay, Deborah. This makes you human. I love you all the more for it."

"Jill," Deborah protested, but Dylan was awake and reaching for his glasses. "My boy, here, needs an explanation. I'll see you as soon as I drop off the kids."

"You're not driving the BMW, are you?" Jill asked. She shared Deborah's disdain for the car, albeit more for its cost than for memories of a marriage gone bad.

"I have no choice."

"You do. I'll be there at seven-thirty. Once you get to Dad's, you can use his car. I don't envy you having to tell him about the accident. He won't be happy. He likes perfect records."

Deborah didn't need the reminder. The thought of telling her father made her ill. "I like perfect records, too, but we don't always get what we want. Trust me, I didn't plan on this. My car was in the wrong place at the wrong time. Gotta go, Jill. Seven-thirty. Thanks." She hung up the phone and looked down at Dylan. At ten, he was more of an introvert than his sister had been at that age. He was also more sensitive, a character trait exacerbated by both the divorce and his vision.

"You **hit** someone?" he asked now, brown eyes abnormally wide behind his lenses.

"It was on the rim road, very dark, very wet."

"Was he splattered all over the road?" the boy asked with a hard blink.

"Jerk," Grace mumbled from behind Deborah.

"He was not splattered anywhere," Deborah scolded. "We weren't going fast enough to do serious harm."

Dylan rubbed one of his eyes. "Have you ever hit anyone before?"

"Absolutely not."

"Has Dad?"

"Not that I know of."

"I'm going to call him and tell him."

"Not now, please," Deborah said, because Greg would insist that Dylan put her on the phone and would then hassle her with questions. Glancing past Dylan at the clock, she said, "He'll be sleeping and, anyway, you need to get dressed. Aunt Jill is coming for us."

There was another hard blink. "Why?"

"Because the police have my car."

"Why?"

"They have to make sure it's in good working order."

"Is there blood on the front?"

"No. Get up, Dylan," Deborah said and gave him a gentle push.

He got out of bed, started for the door, then turned back. "Who'd you hit?"

"No one you know," Deborah said and pointed toward the door.

He had barely left when Grace was hovering at her shoulder. "But he's someone I know," she whispered, "and someone all my friends know. And you can bet Dylan's gonna call Dad, who's then gonna think we can't take care of ourselves. Like there's someone else who'll take care of us if we don't, not that Dad cares. Mom, what if Mr. McKenna died on the operating table?"

"The hospital would have called."

"What if you get a call today? I need to stay home."

Deborah faced her. "If you stay home,

you'll have to retake the test—**and** miss track practice, which isn't a great idea with a meet on Saturday."

Grace looked horrified. "I can't **run** after what happened."

Deborah knew how she felt. When Greg left, she had wanted nothing more than to stay in bed nursing her wounds. She had a similar urge now, but it would only make things worse. "I have to work, Grace, and you need to run. We were involved in an accident. We can't let it paralyze us."

"What if it paralyzes Mr. McKenna?"

"They said it didn't."

"You can really **work** today?"

"I have to. People depend on me. Same with you. You're the team's best hope for winning the meet. Besides, if you're afraid of people talking, the best thing is to behave as you always do."

"And say what?"

Deborah swallowed. "What I just told Aunt Jill. That it was a horrible storm, and that the car was in the wrong place at the wrong time."

"I'll flunk the bio test if I take it today. There's **another** AP section I shouldn't be in."

"You won't flunk the test. You're pre-med, and you're acing bio."

"How can I take a test when I barely slept?"

"You know the material. Besides, once you're in college, you'll be taking tests on next to no sleep all the time. Think of this as practice. It'll build character."

"Yeah, well, if character's the thing, shouldn't I go with you to file the police report?"

Deborah felt a flash of pride, followed by a quick pang of conscience. Both turned to fear when she thought of the possible fallout if she let Grace take the blame. The repercussions wouldn't be productive at all.

Very slowly, she shook her head, then held her daughter's gaze for a moment before drawing her out of bed.

As always, it hit Deborah in the shower—the second-guessing about what she was doing. Between diagnosing dozens of patients each week, helping her father run his household without Ruth, being a single mother and having to make sensitive decisions like the one she had just made, she was often on the hot seat. Now she stood with her head bowed, hot water hitting her back with the sting of too many choices, until she was close to tears.

Feeling profoundly alone, she turned the

water off and quickly dressed. The clothes she wore for work were tailored, fitting her slim frame well and restoring a sense of profession- alism. Makeup added color to her pale skin and softened the worry in brown eyes that were wide-set, the adult version of Grace's. But when she tried to fasten her hair in a clasp so that it would be neat and tidy as her life was not, it fought her. Shy of shoulder length, the dark waves had a mind of their own. Ac- cepting that there was no going back to her orderly life, she let them curl as they would and turned her back on the mirror.

Mercifully, the rain had stopped. Sun was beginning to break through the clouds, scat- tering gold on trees whose still-wet limbs were just beginning to bud. Grateful for a brighter day, she went down to the kitchen, set out ce- real for the kids, then phoned the hospital. Calvin McKenna was in recovery, soon to be moved to a room. He hadn't talked yet, but he was listed in stable condition.

Reassured, she skimmed her Post-its on the fridge: **pay property tax—Dylan dentist at 4—tennis camp deposit**. Then she logged on to her e-mail and phoned the answering service. Had there been an emergency, she would have been called. The messages she re- ceived now—the flare-up of a chronic ear infection, a stubborn migraine headache, a severe case of heartburn—were from patients the receptionist would schedule when she arrived at eight. Her nurse-practitioner would examine the earliest to arrive.

Deborah was usually at her office by eight-fifteen, after seeing the kids off to school, stopping to have coffee with Jill, and checking on her father. He was booked to see his first patient at eight-thirty. These days, it was Deborah's job to make sure that he did.

Her sister, Jill, though perennially at odds with the man, respected that. She appeared at the house this morning at seven-thirty on the nose. Having come from work, she wore jeans and a T-shirt. The T-shirt, always either red, orange, or yellow to match the bakery's colors, was red today, and her boy-short blonde hair was rumpled from whipping off her apron. She had their mother's bright, hazel eyes and the shadow of childhood freckles, but the fine lines of her chin mirrored Deborah's.

As soon as Grace and Dylan were in the backseat, she passed them each bags with their favorite pastries inside. She had a bag for Deborah, too, and a hot coffee in the cup holder.

Picking up the coffee, Deborah cradled it in her hands and inhaled the comforting brew. "Thanks," she finally said. "I hate taking you from work."

"Are you kidding?" Jill replied. "I get to have my favorite people in the car. Are you guys okay back there?" she called into the rearview mirror.

Dylan was. He ate his glazed cinnamon stick as though he hadn't just had a full bowl of cereal. Grace hadn't eaten much cereal, and she only picked at her blueberry muffin. She uttered a high-pitched moan when they passed the spot where the accident had been.

"It was here?" Jill guessed. "You'd never know."

No, Deborah realized. **You never would.** Only a small piece of yellow tape remained, tied to a pine to show the police where to look this morning. If there had been skid marks on the road, the rain had washed them away.

She tried to catch Grace's eye, but the girl refused to look at her, and, in the end, Deborah didn't have the strength to persist. Sitting back, she sipped her coffee and let her sister chat. It was a ten-minute respite from responsibility.

All too soon, they reached the middle school, and Dylan was out of the van. "I'm getting out here, too," Grace said, tugging on her jacket and collecting her things. "No offense, Aunt Jill, but, like, the last thing I want is to pull up at school in a bright yellow van with a totally identifying logo on the side. Everyone'll know it's me."

"Is that so bad?" Jill asked.

"Yes." Leaning forward in her seat, she said in a voice that was urgent and low, "Please, Mom. I'd really rather not be at school today. I mean, I've missed maybe two days this year. Can't I stay with Aunt Jill?"

"And have the truant officer after **me?**" Jill countered before Deborah could speak.

Plaintive, Grace turned on her aunt. "It's going to be so bad for me today. Everyone's gonna know."

"Know what? That your mother had an accident? Accidents happen, Grace. It's not a crime. If you're in school today, you can tell everyone how bad you feel."

Grace stared at her for a minute, muttered, "Yeah, right," and climbed out of the van, but when Jill might have called her back, Deborah put a hand on her arm and Grace stalked off. Her spine was rigid for the first few steps but steadily softened until she was hunched over her books, looking impossibly small.

Worried, Deborah said, "Should I have kept her home?"

"Absolutely not," Jill replied. "If nothing else, you need her busy." She put the van in gear and pulled away from the curb. "Are you okay?"

Deborah sighed, leaned against the head-rest, and nodded. "I'm fine."

"Truly?"

"Truly."

"Good. Because I have news. I'm preg-nant."

Deborah blinked. "Cute. A bit of humor to lighten things up."

"I'm serious."

"No, you're not, because, A, there is no guy in your life right now, B, you're working your butt off at the bakery, and, C, it would be one thing too many for me this morning, and you wouldn't be that cruel." She looked at her sister. Jill wasn't laughing. "You're serious? But pregnant by whom?"

"Sperm donor number TXP334. He has blond hair, is five-eight, and writes children's books for a living. A guy like that has to be compassionate, creative, and smart, doesn't he?"

Deborah struggled to take in the infor-mation.

"I need you to be happy," Jill warned.

"I am. I think. I just . . . didn't expect . . . a **baby?**"

Jill nodded. "Next November."

The date made it real. Loving babies and loving Jill, Deborah didn't know what else to do but open her arms, lean over, and give her sister a hug. "You really want a child."

"I always have. You know that."

"What about work?"

"You did it."

"I had Greg. You're alone."

"I'm not alone. I have you. I have Grace and Dylan. I have . . . Dad."

"Dad. Oh, boy." **Major** complication there. "And you haven't told him."

"Absolutely not."

Which meant one more secret to keep. "If you're due in November—"

"I'm eight weeks pregnant."

"**Eight.**" Deborah was belatedly hurt. "Why didn't you tell me sooner?"

"I didn't trust you'd let me do it."

"**Let** you. Jill, you do your own thing. Always."

"But I want your approval."

Deborah studied her sister's face. "You don't look different. Have you been sick?"

"A little here and there, mostly from excitement."

"And you're sure you're pregnant?"

"I've missed two periods," Jill said, "and I've seen the baby on a sonogram, Deborah, seen that little heart beating. My doctor pointed it out on the screen."

"What doctor?"

"Anne Burkhardt. She's in Boston—and please," Jill grew serious, "don't tell me you're angry that I didn't get a name from you, because I wanted this totally to be my choice. We both know Dad'll be a problem. But hey, I've already disappointed him in so many things, what's one more? But you—you had no part in this, which is what I'll tell Dad— but I'm not telling anyone until I pass the twelve-week mark."

"You just told me," Deborah argued, "so I do have a part in it, or at least in keeping the secret. What do I say if he asks?"

"He won't. He won't have a **clue** until I hit him in the face with it. He doesn't think I'm capable of sustaining a relationship with a man, much less having a baby, and maybe he's right about the man part. I've tried, Deborah, you know I have, but I haven't met a single guy in the last few years who was remotely husband material. Dad would have stuck me with someone I detest just for the sake of having a baby the traditional way. But my God, look at you. You played by all the rules, and now you're a single parent, too."

Deborah didn't need the reminder. It made her think of her failings, which brought the accident front and center again. She held her hair back from her face. "Why are you telling me now? Why in this awful minute when I have so much else on my mind?"

"Because," Jill said, suddenly pleading, "like I said on the phone, you're more human after last night, so I'm thinking that right now you'll understand and still love me."

Deborah stared at her sister. Jill had just added a complication to her already complicated life, but a new baby was a new baby. Reaching out, she took her sister's hand. "Do I have a choice?"

Grace loitered just beyond the school fence, gnawing on her cuticle until the final bell rang. Then, clutching her jacket tightly around her, she ran down the path and, joining the other stragglers, dashed up the stairs, into the high school. Keeping her head down, she slipped into her homeroom seat and barely heard the announcements until the principal said that Mr. McKenna had been hit by a car, was in the hospital, and deserved a moment's prayer. Grace gave him that and then some, but stole out of the room the instant the bell rang again and, squatting in front of her locker, tried to make herself invisible. Friends stopped for a few seconds to chat. **Did you know that Jarred has mono? Why is Kenny Baron running for student body president? Are you going to Kim's party Saturday night?** Grace only rose when it was seconds before her first class. Megan and Stephie came up and flanked her before she reached the door.

"We kept trying to **call** you," Megan hissed.

"Where **were** you?" asked Stephie.

"Kyle told me it was **your mom's** car that hit Mr. McKenna."

"Were you there? What did you see, Grace? Was it **gross?**"

"I can't talk about it," Grace said.

"I thought I'd **die** when I saw your mom sitting outside," Stephie muttered.

"How much does she know," Megan asked Grace. "Did she notice anything?"

"No," Grace said.

"And you didn't tell her?" Stephie asked.

"No."

"And you **won't** tell her," Megan ordered.

"No."

"Well, that's good. Because if word gets back to my parents, I'll be grounded 'til fall."

Grounded 'til fall? Grace could live with being grounded 'til fall. As punishments went, that would be easy.

Chapter 3

Michael Barr was revered in Leyland. A family practitioner before family practitioners had come back into vogue, he had spent his entire career in the town. He was the doctor of record for three generations of local families, and had their undying loyalty as a reward.

He owned a pale blue Victorian house just off the town green. It was the same house where Deborah and Jill had grown up, and while Michael had always run his practice from the adjacent cottage, both structures had grown over the years. The last of the work, to the cottage, was done eight years before as a lure for Deborah to join the practice.

In truth, she hadn't needed much encouragement. She adored her father and loved seeing the pride on his face when she was accepted into medical school and again when she agreed to work with him. She was the son he'd never had, and, besides, she and Greg were already living in Leyland, which made it convenient. Grace was six, born shortly before Deborah started medical school, and, by the time her residency was done, she was pregnant with Dylan. Her mother, a born nurturer, would have provided child care in a minute had Deborah and Greg not already employed the de Sousas. Lívia served as a sitter, Adinaldo a handyman, and there were de Sousa relatives to do gardening, roofing, and plumbing. Lívia still stopped by to clean and make dinner, and since Deborah's mother died, the de Sousas did similar chores for her father. He wasn't as enamored of them as she was, but then, no one could measure up to Ruth Barr.

Juggling her medical bag, bakery bag, and coffee, Deborah picked up the morning paper and went in the side door of the house. The accident would definitely be reported in the local weekly on Thursday. But in today's **Boston Globe?** She prayed not.

There was no sign of her father in the kitchen—no coffee percolating, no waiting mug or bagel on a napkin beside it. She guessed that he had overslept again. Since Ruth died, he had taken to watching old movies in the den until he was sure he could fall asleep without her.

Deborah set her things on the kitchen table and, not for the first time, wished her father would bend enough to accept a pastry from Jill's shop. People drove miles for her signature pecan buns, SoMa Stickies. But not Michael. Coffee and a supermarket bagel. That was all he wanted.

She hated the thought of telling him about Jill's pregnancy.

"Daddy?" Deborah called in the front hall and approached the stairs. **"Are you up?"**

She heard nothing at first, then the creak of a chair. Cutting through the living room, she found her father in the den, sitting with his head in his hands, still dressed in yesterday's clothes.

Discouraged, she knelt by his knee. "You never made it to bed?"

He looked at her with red-rimmed eyes, disoriented at first. "Guess not," he managed, running a hand through his hair. It had gone pure white since his wife's death. He claimed it gave him new authority with his patients, but Deborah thought he was something of an autocrat already.

"You have an early patient," she reminded

him now. "Want to shower while I put on coffee?" When he didn't move, she felt a twinge of concern. "Are you okay?"

"A headache is all."

"Aspirin?" she offered meekly. It was a standing joke. They knew all the current meds, but aspirin remained their default.

He shot her something that was as much a grimace as a smile, but took her hand and let himself be helped up. As soon as he left the room, Deborah noticed the whiskey bottle and empty glass. Hurriedly, she put the bottle back in the liquor cabinet and took the highball glass to the kitchen.

While she waited for the coffee to perk, she sliced his bagel, then called the hospital. Calvin McKenna remained in stable condition. This was good news, as was, she discovered next, the absence of mention of the accident in the **Globe.**

Hearing steps on the stairs, she refolded the paper and poured coffee. She was spreading cream cheese on the bagel when her father joined her. He was his usual well-dressed self. Putting an arm around her, he gave her a squeeze, then reached for his coffee.

"Better?" she asked after he had taken several swallows.

"Oh yeah." Other than bloodshot eyes, he

had cleaned up well. "Thanks, sweetheart. You're a lifesaver."

"Not quite," she said and took the opening. "Grace and I were in an accident last night. We're both fine—not a scratch—but we hit a man."

Her father was a minute taking it in, his face filled with concern, then relief, then uncertainty. "Hit?"

"He was just suddenly there in front of the car. It was out on the rim road. Visibility was really bad." When her father didn't seem to follow, she prompted, "The rain? Remember?"

"Yes, I remember. That's awful, Deborah. Do we know him?"

"He teaches history at the high school. Grace has him."

"Is he one of ours?"

One of their patients? "No."

"How badly is he hurt?"

She related what she knew.

"Not life threatening, then," her father decided as she had.

He sipped his coffee. She was starting to think that she'd gotten off easy, when, with marginal sharpness and a rise in color, he asked, "How fast were you going?"

"Well under the speed limit."

"But how could you not see him?"

"It was pouring and dark. He wasn't wearing reflective gear."

Her father leaned back against the counter. "Not exactly the image of the good doctor. What if someone thought you'd been drinking?" His eyes met hers. "Were you?"

I wasn't driving, she nearly said, but settled for a quiet, "Please."

"It's a fair question, sweetheart. Lord knows, you have cause to drink. Your husband left you with a huge house, huge responsibilities, huge **wine** cellar."

"He also left me with a huge bank account, which makes the huge house doable, but that's not the point. I don't drink, Daddy. You know that."

"Did the police issue a citation?"

Her stomach did a little flip-flop—possibly from the word, more likely from the increased edge in her father's voice. "No. They didn't see any immediate cause. They're doing a full report."

"That's swell," Michael remarked dryly. "Does the man have family?"

"A wife, no kids."

"And if he ends up with a permanent limp, you don't think he'll sue?"

Mention of a lawsuit, coming on the heels of the word **citation,** both evidence of her father's disappointment, made Deborah's stomach twist. "I hope not."

Michael Barr made a dismissive sound. "Lawsuits have little to do with reality and everything to do with greed. Why do you think we pay what we do for malpractice insurance? We may be totally in the right, but the process of proving it can cost thousands of dollars. Naïveté won't help, Deborah." He snorted. "This is the kind of discussion I'd expect to have with your sister, not with you."

And guess what she's done now? Deborah wanted to cry in a moment of silent panic, but she just said, "She's doing great."

"A baker?" he tossed back. "Do you know the kind of hours she works?"

"They're no worse than ours." Deborah had hired a nanny. Jill could, too—actually, Jill didn't have to. She lived above the bakery. She could set up a nursery in the back room and have the baby with her all the time. She could even have one of her employees help out. They had almost become like family.

"She can barely make ends meet," Michael argued. "She knows nothing about business."

"Actually, she does," Deborah said.

But her father had moved on. "You've called Hal, haven't you? He's the best lawyer around."

"I don't need a lawyer. I'll file a report today, and that's it."

"File a report at the police station? Put it in writing, and then have your own words come back to haunt you?" His color heightened. "Please, Deborah. Listen to me here. You hit someone; he didn't hit you. That makes **you** the offender. If you're talking with the police, you need a lawyer with you."

"Isn't that a sign of guilt?"

"Guilt? Cripes, no. It's preventive medicine. Isn't that what we're about?"

Deborah made house calls. It wasn't something she had planned to do when she was in medical school, or even when she started to practice—and when tests were necessary, it was out of the question. Those patients had to be seen either in the office or at the local hospital.

But not all patients needed tests, and one day a few years ago, when a regular patient had called with severe back spasms that prevented her from driving to the office, it seemed absurd not to help. The patient was a single mom, with a new baby and a disabled aunt. Deborah couldn't bear letting her suffer.

Seeing her at home made a difference in Deborah's diagnosis. The apartment—five rooms on the second floor of a two-family house—was in chaos. Clothes were everywhere; baby gear was everywhere; dirty dishes were everywhere. When Deborah talked with her on the phone, the women claimed that the spasms came from lifting the baby. In fact, Deborah saw a woman who was simply overwhelmed with her life. There were social services that could help, but Deborah wouldn't have known to give them a call if she hadn't visited the house.

Treating patients was like solving a puzzle. There were times when an office visit yielded enough clues, other times when more was needed. Since Deborah was drawn to this puzzle-solving, and liked being out and about more than her father did, she did all the home visits. This also gave her a lighter patient load and more flexibility, both of which were especially welcome after Greg left.

Today, desperate to busy herself, she set off shortly before nine to visit an elderly woman who had fallen out of bed the week before and hit her head. The concussion was mild compared to her fear of falling again. A pair of bed rails and a cane, both of which she showed Deborah now with pride, had restored some of her confidence.

Deborah's second stop was just down the road, at the home of a family with six children, the youngest three of whom had high fevers. The parents could have brought the kids in. But to risk infecting other patients in the waiting room? Deborah didn't see the point, particularly when she was going to be nearby anyway.

Ear infections. All three. Easily diagnosed, with a minimum of risk.

Her next patient lived one town over. Darcy LeMay was a woman whose husband, a business consultant, was on the road three weeks out of every four, leaving her alone in a beautiful home with a severe case of osteoarthritis. She was seeing a specialist, from whom Deborah received regular reports. The woman's current complaint had to do with such intense ankle pain that she wondered if she had broken a bone.

Deborah rang the bell and let herself in when she found the door ajar. "In the kitchen," Darcy called unnecessarily. She was always in the kitchen, and why not? It was a beautiful kitchen, complete with exquisite cherry cabinets, carved granite counters, a state-of-the-art cooktop, and appliances so neatly built-in that they were almost invisible. A baker's rack held earthenware plates in gold, olive, and rust, all hand-painted in Tuscany, Darcy had explained when Deborah had admired them on an earlier visit.

Darcy sat at a hexagonal table built into the breakfast nook. She wore a large cotton sweater over a pair of tights, and had her bad foot resting on the seat of the adjacent chair. The table was strewn with papers.

"How's the book coming?" Deborah asked, regarding the papers with a smile as she set her bag on the table.

"Slow," Darcy said and proceeded to blame her ankle for distraction, her arthritis specialist for unresponsiveness, and her absent husband for disinterest.

Deborah knew scapegoating when she heard it. Moreover, she didn't have to look at Darcy's ankle to see the immediate problem, though she did an appropriate amount of prodding. "No break," she concluded, as she had known she would. "Just your arthritis kicking up."

"So bad?"

Gently, Deborah said, "You've gained more weight."

Darcy gave a dismissive headshake. "I'm holding steady."

Denial was right up there with scapegoating. Taking a direct approach, Deborah peered under the table. "Is that a bag of chips on the floor behind you?"

"They're low fat."

"They're still chips," Deborah said. "We've talked about this. You're a beautiful woman who is carrying around fifty pounds too much weight."

"Not fifty. Maybe thirty."

Deborah didn't argue. Darcy had been thirty pounds overweight when she had last been to the office, but that was two years ago. Seeing a specialist was a convenient excuse not to have to face one's own doctor's unforgiving scale.

"Here's the thing," Deborah said, gentle again. "Arthritis is a real disease. We know you have it. The medication you take helps, but you have to do your part, too. Think of carrying a fifty-pound weight around in your arms all day. Think of the extra stress that puts on your ankles."

"I really don't eat very much," Darcy said with feeling.

"Maybe not, but what you do eat is bad for you, and you don't exercise."

"How can I exercise, if I can't walk?"

"Take some of the weight off, and you will be able to walk. Set yourself up in the den, Darcy. Working here in the kitchen is too convenient for snacking. Start slowly. Walk up and down stairs three times a day, or to the mailbox and back. I'm not asking you to run a marathon."

"You shouldn't," Darcy advised. "Fast is not always good. I heard about your accident."

Deborah was taken off guard. "My accident?"

"Speed does it every time."

Deborah might have informed her that speed had not been involved, but it was the wrong direction to take. "We were talking about your weight, Darcy. You can blame arthritis, or your husband, or Dr. Habib, or me. But you're the only one who can change your life."

"I can't cure arthritis."

"No, but you can make it easier to live with. Have you given more thought to taking a job outside your home?" They had talked about that at length last time Deborah had visited.

"If I do that, I'll never finish my book."

"You could work part-time."

"Dean earns more than enough."

"I know that. But you need to be busier than you are, particularly when he's gone."

"How can I work if I can't walk?" Darcy asked, and Deborah grew impatient. Taking a pad from her bag, she wrote down a name and number.

"This woman is a physical therapist. She's the best. Give her a call." She returned the pad to her bag.

"Does she come to the house?"

"I don't think so. You may just have to go there," Deborah said with a perverse satisfaction that had vanished by the time she left the house. Like so many of her patients, Darcy LeMay had issues that went beyond the physical. Loneliness was one; boredom, denial, and low self-esteem were others. On a normal day, Deborah might have spent more time addressing them. But there was nothing normal about today.

She had barely returned to the office when the school nurse called to say that Grace had thrown up in the girls' bathroom and needed to be picked up. How could Deborah refuse? She knew that Grace would have already taken the biology exam, and yes, she would miss the rest of the day's classes, plus track, but if Deborah's own stomach lurched at the thought of the accident, she could imagine how Grace felt.

The girl's face was pale, her forehead warm. Deborah was helping her off the cot in the nurse's office when the woman said, "We heard about the accident. I'm sure the talk didn't help Grace."

Deborah nodded, but didn't want to discuss it in front of her daughter. Once in the car, Grace put her head back and closed her eyes.

Deborah started driving. "Was the test bad?"

"The test wasn't the problem."

"How'd they find out about the accident?"

"There was an announcement in home-room."

"Saying that it was **our** car that hit him?"

Grace said nothing, but Deborah could piece together the answer. The school wouldn't have said it, but Mack Tully would have told Marty Stevens, who told his kids, who told the kids on their school bus, who told all the kids on the steps of the school. And that wasn't counting the phone calls Shelley Wyeth would have made en route from the bakery to work. Even Darcy LeMay, who lived in another town, had heard about the accident. Gossip was that way, spreading with the frightening speed of a virulent flu.

"Are they asking you questions?"

"They don't have to. I hear them anyway."

"It was an accident," Deborah said, as much to herself as to Grace.

The girl opened her eyes. "What if they take your license away?"

"They won't."

"What if they charge you with something?"

"They won't."

"Did they tell you that at the police station?"

"I haven't been yet. I'm going there after I drop you home." Her daughter's expression flickered. "And no, you can't come."

Grace closed her eyes again. This time, Deborah let her be.

The Leyland police department was housed next to Town Hall in a small brick structure that held three large offices and a single cell. There were twelve men on the force, eight of them full-time, which was all that the town of ten thousand needed. Domestic quarrels, drunk driving, the occasional petty theft—that was the extent of its crime.

As she came in, Deborah was greeted warmly by people she had known most of her life. There were brief mentions of kids, aging parents, and a ballot initiative concerning the sale of wine in supermarkets, but there was also an averted look or two.

John Colby led her to his office. Bright as he was, physically imposing as he could be, John was a shy man, more prone to seeking insight than to attacking investigations head-on. He was also modest, happier to be taping off an accident scene than to be hanging official commendations on his wall. Other than a large clock and some framed photographs of police outings, the office was unadorned.

John closed the door, took some forms from the desk, and passed them to her. "It's pretty straightforward," he said. "Take it home, fill it out, return it when you're done."

"I don't have to do it here?"

He waved his hand. "Nah. We know you won't be skipping town."

"Not quite," Deborah murmured, glancing through the form. There were three pages, all requiring details. Time and privacy would help. "Do you have the results of any of the tests yet?"

"Only the ones on your car. It looks like everything was in good working order. No cause for negligence there."

So much for the local garage, but Deborah's real concern was with the state's report. "When will you hear about the rest?"

"A week, maybe two if the lab is backed up. Some of the analysis involves mathematical calculations. They can be pretty complex."

"It was only an **accident**," she said.

He leaned against the desk. "This is just a formality. We're mandated to investigate, so we investigate."

"I've dedicated my life to helping people, not hurting them. I feel responsible for Calvin McKenna." That was the truth, though it did nothing to change John's assumption that Deborah was driving—and even here, with a man she knew and trusted, she couldn't mention Grace's name. Instead, frustrated, she said, "What in the **world** was he doing out there?"

"We haven't been able to ask him that, yet," John said. "But we will. In the meanwhile, you fill out that form. You have to file three copies."

"Three?" she asked in dismay.

"One with us, one with your insurance company, one with the Registry of Motor Vehicles. It's the law."

"Does this go on my driving record?"

"RMV keeps your report on file."

"I've never had an accident before. You

saw the damage to the car. It isn't much. I doubt I'll even exceed my deductible."

"You still have to file a copy with the insurance company. When personal injury is involved, you're required to do it. If Cal McKenna isn't insured, he may go after you for medical costs, and if he sues, your insurance company will have to pay."

Deborah had thought her father an alarmist when he mentioned a possible lawsuit. John Colby's mentioning it was something else. "Do you really think he'll sue?" she asked. "What with the rain? His lack of reflective gear? What kind of case could he have?"

"That depends on what the reconstruction team finds," the police chief said with a glance at the phone. "I'll let you know when the report comes in." His round face softened. "How's your daughter handling things?"

"Not well," Deborah said, able to be honest about this at least. "I had to pick her up from school a little while ago. She's traumatized, and the talk there doesn't help."

"What are the other kids saying?"

"I don't know. She won't tell me much."

"She's at that age," John said, head bowed. "It's hard. They want responsibility until they have it. By the way," he added, scratching his upper lip, then looking at her, "I should warn you. McKenna's wife called me this morning. She could be a problem."

"What kind of problem?"

"She's pretty upset. She wants to make sure we're not letting you off easy just because you're so well regarded in town. She's the reason you need to get your insurance company up to speed. She's angry."

"So am I," Deborah burst out. "He shouldn't have been running in the dark. Did she say what he was doing?"

"No. Apparently she wasn't home when he left the house. But don't worry. We'll do our investigation, and no one'll ever say we favored one side or the other." He tapped the desk and stood. "If I keep you much longer, I'll get flack from my men. You're seeing Officer Bowdoin's new baby this afternoon. He's pretty excited about the kid."

Deborah managed a smile. "So am I. I love newborn visits."

"You're good to do it."

"It'll be the highlight of my day." She rose with the accident report in hand. "When do you need this back?"

She had five days from the time of the crash to file a report, but from the minute she left the police station, she wanted to get it done. She made copies and spent several hours that night filling it out. She went through several drafts before she felt she had it right. Then she copied the final result, one for the police, one for the Registry, one for her insurance company. She put the latter two in envelopes, addressed and stamped them, and tucked them in her bag, but out of sight wasn't out of mind. Waking early the next morning, the report was the first thing she thought of.

Dylan was the second. She had barely left her room, when she was drawn to his by the soft sound of his keyboard. He was playing "Blowin' in the Wind" with such soulful simplicity that it brought a lump to her throat. It wasn't the song that got to her but her son. His eyes were closed, glasses not yet on. He had been playing by ear since he was four, picking out tunes on the grand piano in the living room long before he'd had a formal lesson. Even now, when his teacher was trying to get him to read music, he was far more interested in the tunes his dad had liked.

Deborah didn't have to be a psychologist to know that Dylan loved music precisely because he could do it without using his eyes. He had been severely farsighted by the time he was three and by seven had developed corneal dystrophy. Eyeglasses corrected the hyperopia, but the dystrophy meant that the vision in his right eye would be gauzy until the time when he was old enough for a corneal transplant.

Going into his room, she gave him a good-morning hug. "Why so sad?"

He took his hands from the keyboard and carefully fitted his glasses to his nose.

"Missing Dad?" she asked.

He nodded.

"You'll be seeing him the weekend after next."

"It's not the same," he said quietly.

She knew that. One weekend a month didn't make up for four weeks of no father. She and Greg had always known that they would have to work hard to juggle family time and their careers, but divorce hadn't been in the mix.

Sadly, she took a Red Sox T-shirt from the drawer, but Dylan's voice rose in dismay. "Where's my Dylan one?"

"In the hamper. You wore it yesterday."

"I can wear it today, too."

"Honey, it has Lívia's spaghetti sauce all over it."

"But it's my good-luck shirt."

His father had given him the shirt for his

last birthday, along with an iPod loaded with songs sung by his namesake, hence "Blowin' in the Wind" moments before. Deborah understood that it was Greg's attempt to involve his son in something he loved himself. But the shirt had to be washed.

"What does Dad think of Lívia's spaghetti sauce?" she asked.

"He hates it."

Totally. "Think he'd like it on your shirt?"

"No, but she's washing it too much. It's getting faded."

Deborah improvised. "Faded is **good.** Dad would agree with me on this," she added to clinch it, sounding more sure than she was. Though not much taller than Deborah, Greg had cut an impressive figure with his thick sandy hair and designer clothes. But all that was gone. She didn't know the man he was today—didn't know what kind of man could leave his wife and children on a day's notice.

"Can I call him now?" Dylan asked.

"Nuh-uh. Too early. You can call this afternoon." She tussled the thick silk of his hair. "Put on the Red Sox shirt for now, and we'll wash the other so it'll bring you luck tomorrow."

His eyes were sad. "Is Dad ever coming to one of my games?"

"He said he would."

"I know why he isn't. He hates baseball. He never played it with me. I hate it, too. I can't see the ball."

Deborah's heart ached. "Even with the new glasses?"

"Well, I guess. But anyway, I sit on the bench most of the time."

"Coach Duffy says you'll play more next year. He's counting on your being his right fielder once Rory Mayhan moves up a league. Honey? We need to get going or we'll be late."

Deborah was in the shower when the phone rang. Grace came into the bathroom and held the cordless up so her mother could see it. "You need to take this," she cried shrilly.

Turning off the shower, Deborah grabbed the phone. It was the hospital calling to tell her that Cal McKenna had died.

Chapter 4

Deborah felt her heart stop. When she could finally speak, her voice held panic. "Died? **How?**"

"A cerebral hemorrhage," the nurse reported.

"But he had a brain scan when he was admitted. Why wasn't it seen?"

"He wasn't hemorrhaging then. We're guessing it started yesterday. By the time the vital signs tipped us off, it was too late."

Deborah didn't understand what could have happened. She had checked the man herself on the road—no vital injuries, solid pulse. He had sailed through an initial surgery and regained consciousness. Dead didn't make sense.

Clutching the towel around her, she asked, "Are you sure it's Calvin McKenna?"

"Yes. They'll be doing an autopsy later."

Deborah couldn't wait. "Who was on duty when this happened?"

"Drs. Reid and McCall."

"Can I talk with one of them?"

"They'll have to call you back. A multiple-car accident just came in. Can I give them the message?"

"Yes. Please." She thanked the woman and disconnected.

Grace was in tears. "You said he wouldn't die."

Bewildered, Deborah handed her the phone and, wanting to cry herself, said, "I don't know what went wrong."

"You said his injuries weren't life threatening."

"They **weren't**. Grace, this is a mystery to me." She was badly shaken, struggling to make sense of it. "He was in stable condition. They saw nothing on the tests. I have no idea how it happened."

"I don't **care** how it happened," the girl sobbed. "It was bad enough when I thought about seeing him in class, knowing I was the one who hit him, but now there won't **be** any class. I **killed** him."

"You didn't kill him. Killing implies intent. It was an **accident.**"

"He's **still dead,**" Grace wailed.

Death was a sidebar to Deborah's job. She saw it often—fought it often. Calvin McKenna's death was different.

She couldn't think of a single useful thing to say. For her own comfort as much as her daughter's, she simply wrapped her arms around Grace.

Deborah didn't have the heart to make Grace go to school. The girl argued—rightly— that word would spread, and it seemed unfair to subject her to all that attention until they knew more. But neither of the doctors on call phoned back, which meant that there was little she could say to make Grace feel better.

There was no explanation for why the teacher had died—which was what she told Mara Walsh, the school psychologist, as soon as she came in. She and Mara often worked together with students struggling with ano- rexia or drug abuse, and, when a student had died of leukemia the year before, they jointly gathered a team of grief counselors.

Mara was shocked by today's news. She asked questions Deborah couldn't answer and shed little light on Calvin McKenna, other than to say that he had a Ph.D. in history—a surprise to Deborah, since he neither used the title nor listed the degree on the school website.

When Deborah hung up, she found Dylan listening. "Died?" he asked, his skin pale, eyes huge behind his glasses. Since his grandmother's death three years before, he had known what death meant.

Deborah nodded. "I'm waiting for a call from his doctor to explain why."

"Was he old?"

"Not very."

"Older than Dad?"

She knew where he was headed. The divorce, coming only a year after Ruth Barr's death, had compounded his sense of loss. "No. Not older than Dad."

"But Dad's older than you."

"Some."

"A **lot,**" the boy said, sounding nearly as upset as her parents when Deborah, at twenty-one, had married a man seventeen years her senior. But Deborah had never felt the difference in age. Greg had always been energetic and young. A free spirit through his teens and twenties, he hadn't grown up until his thirties—this, by his own admission—

which meant that he and Deborah felt much closer in age than they really were.

"Dad is fifty-five," she said now, "which is **not** old, and he isn't dying. Mr. McKenna was hit by a car. If that hadn't happened, he'd be alive."

"Are they gonna arrest you for killing him?"

"Absolutely not. It was a terrible accident in the pouring rain."

"Like the night Nana Ruth died?"

"Nana Ruth wasn't in an accident, but yes, the weather was bad." The rain had been driven by near-hurricane winds the night Ruth had died. Deborah would never forget the drive into town to be with her for those last hours.

"Are they gonna bury him?"

"I'm sure they will." There would definitely be a funeral, plus headlines in the local paper. She could see it—a big front page piece, along with a description of the accident naming those in the car.

"Will they bury him near Nana Ruth?"

She pulled herself together. "That's a good question. Mr. McKenna didn't live here very long. He may be buried somewhere else."

"Why isn't Grace dressed?"

Grace was on a stool at the kitchen counter. Shoulders slouched, she wore the T-shirt and boxer shorts she had slept in. She was nibbling on her thumbnail.

"Grace?" Deborah begged and, when the thumb fell away, said to Dylan, "She's not going to school. She's staying home while we try to learn something more." Deborah tapped her laptop. Patients would be e-mailing. Taking care of their problems would ground her.

"I want to stay here, too," Dylan said.

Deborah typed in her password. "There's no need for that."

"But what if they arrest you?"

"They won't arrest me," she scolded gently.

"They could. Isn't that what police do? What if I come home and find out you're in jail. Who'll take care of us then? Will Dad come back?"

Deborah grasped his shoulders and bent down so that their eyes were level. "Sweetie, I am not going to jail. Our **chief of police,** no less, said that there was no cause for worry."

"That was before the guy died," said the boy.

"But the facts of the accident haven't changed. No one is going to jail, Dylan. You have my word on that."

She had no sooner given her word, though, when she began to worry. She had to force herself to reply to her patients: **No need to be anxious, Kim, your daughter hasn't even been on antibiotics for a full day; Yes, Joseph, we'll call in a refill for the inhaler; Thanks for the update, Mrs. Warren, I'm pleased you're feeling better.**

The day before, when her father had suggested she call Hal Trutter, she resisted. Even now, she wasn't sure if she needed legal advice, but she did need reassurance.

"Karen," she said when her friend answered the phone. "It's me."

"Who's me?" Karen replied in a hurt tone. "My friend Deborah, who didn't bother to call yesterday, not even to say she wouldn't be at the gym, and left me to hear about the accident from my daughter, who keeps trying to call Grace and can't get through?"

Deborah was instantly contrite. She couldn't answer for Grace, who loved Danielle like a sister, but Karen was her best friend. She would have called sooner had it not been for Hal, which was another thing to fault him on. But she couldn't tell her friend about that. "I'm sorry. I didn't phone anyone, Karen. It was a bad day. We were pretty upset."

"Which was why you should have called.

If I couldn't make you feel better, Hal could have."

Deborah cleared her throat. "That's why I'm calling now. Calvin McKenna just died."

Karen gasped. "Are you serious?"

"Yes. I don't know the details. But I thought I'd run it past Hal. Has he left?"

"He's on the other line. Hold on a sec, sweetie, and I'll get him."

Hal sounded nearly as hurt as his wife. "You took your time calling, Deborah. Any reason for that?"

Deborah might have said, **Because for starters, you're apt to take it the wrong way,** but Grace had followed her into the den, and Deborah had no way of knowing if Karen was still on the line. So she said, "It was an accident. All I need is information. I don't think I need a lawyer."

"You need me," he drawled, likely winking at his wife. Sadly, he meant what he said. He had loved Deborah for years, or so he professed shortly after Greg left, and no matter that she cut him off with, **No way. I don't love you, and your wife is one of my closest friends,** he hadn't taken back the words. School meetings, sports events, birthday parties—he took every opportunity to remind her. He never touched her. But his eyes said he would in a heartbeat.

It had put her in an untenable position. She and Karen had shared pregnancies, kid problems, Karen's breast cancer, and Deborah's divorce. Now Deborah knew something about Hal that Karen didn't. Keeping the secret was nearly as painful as the thought of what might happen if she divulged it.

Hal had made her his partner in crime. She **hated** him for that.

"I don't think there's any problem," she told him now, "but I want to be sure. I went down to the station yesterday."

"I know. I talked with John. He doesn't see any cause for concern."

Deborah might have been irked that he had taken it upon himself to talk to the police, but she knew her father was right; Hal was the best defense lawyer around. And Hal regularly played poker with Colby, so his assurance carried more weight. Of course, things had changed since yesterday.

"Calvin McKenna just died," Deborah said, "and don't ask how, because I'm waiting to learn myself. Do you think this alters the picture?"

There was a pause—to his credit, the

lawyer at work—then a prudent, "That depends. Is there anything you were doing at the time of the crash to suggest you were at fault?"

There it was, a golden opportunity to set the record straight about who was driving. She knew it was wrong to lie. But the accident report was filled out, and the fact of a fatality made it even more important to protect Grace. Besides, Deborah had repeated the line often enough that it rolled off her tongue. "My car was just at the wrong place at the wrong time. If they weren't going to charge me with operating to endanger before, will a death change that?"

"It depends on what the reconstruction team finds," Hal replied, less comforting than she had hoped. "It also depends on the D.A."

"What D.A.?" Deborah asked nervously.

"**Our** D.A. A death might bring him into the picture."

She had called for **reassurance**. "What does 'might' mean?"

"You're starting to panic. Do not do that, sweetheart. I can get you out of whatever it is."

"But what **is** it?" she asked, needing to know the worst.

"When a death is involved," he said in a measured tone, "every side is examined. An accidental death can be termed vehicular homicide or even negligent homicide. It depends on what the state team finds."

Deborah took a shaky breath. "They won't find much," she managed to say. Of course, she hadn't imagined Calvin McKenna would die.

"Then you'll be clear on the criminal side," Hal added, "but a plaintiff doesn't need much to file a civil suit. The standard of proof is looser. John tells me he got a call from the wife. He says she's looking for someone to blame. And that was before her husband died."

"We weren't even going **thirty** in a forty-five-mile-per-hour zone."

"You could have been going twenty, and if she hires a hotshot lawyer who convinces the jury that you should've been going fifteen in that storm, she could recover something. But hey," Deborah heard a smile, "you'll have a hotshot lawyer on your own side. I'm giving John a call. I want to know what tests were done to register the guy's blood alcohol or the presence of drugs. John said you took the crash report home with you. Did you fill it out?"

"Last night."

"I'd like to see it before you file. One

wrong word could suggest culpability. Are you going to be home for a little while?"

"Actually, no." She was grateful for a legitimate excuse to see him away from the house. "I have to take Dylan to school and, since the police are done examining my car, I want to drop it at the body shop. Can you meet me at Jill's in, say, twenty minutes?"

Jill Barr's bakery, Sugar-On-Main, was a cheery storefront in the center of town. After leaving her car at the garage for repair, Deborah approached it on foot, her medical bag slung over her shoulder. Keeping her eyes on the sidewalk with its faux brickwork, she tried not to think of Cal McKenna's wife. She tried not to think of vehicular homicide. She tried not to think that people seeing her walking along Main Street might view her now in a different light.

The sweet scent of the bakery reached her seconds before she came to the small iron tables outside. Three of the four were taken. She nodded at several of the regulars as the familiar aroma took the edge off her fear.

The inside of the bakery was gold, orange, and red—walls, café tables, easy chairs, love seats. Deborah had a favorite grouping among the upholstered pieces, which was where she would have normally headed. But people often approached her there. She even got the occasional medical question—**Does this look like poison ivy?** It was the downside of having a local practice. Usually she didn't mind, but today she didn't want an audience.

Half a dozen customers waited in line; another dozen were seated around the shop. Head down lest one of them catch her eye, she continued on through the swinging kitchen door and went straight to Jill's office. She had barely settled into the desk chair when her sister arrived with a tray. It held three coffees and three SoMa Stickies. "I take it I'm joining you?" Jill asked.

"Definitely." Taking a mug, Deborah studied her. Pregnant? With her short blonde hair and freckles, and her cropped orange T-shirt and slim jeans, Jill looked like a child herself. "I can't picture it," Deborah said, oddly bewildered. "Are you feeling okay?"

"Perfect."

"Are you excited?"

"Beyond my wildest dreams."

Deborah reached for her hand. "You'll be an incredible mom."

"Then you're not upset with me?"

"Of course I'm upset. It won't be easy being up at night with a crying baby and no one to spell you. You'll be exhausted, and it's not like you can call in sick."

Jill pulled her hand free. "Why not? Look out there."

Deborah didn't have to look. She was at the bakery often enough to know that there were three people at work behind the front counter, rotating deftly between coffee machines and pastry bins as customers ordered from tall chalkboards that listed additional specialties like SoMa Shots, Smoothies, and Shakes. Two bakers would be in the kitchen until mid-afternoon, producing fresh-from-the-oven batches of everything from muffins to croissants to sticky buns. And then there was Pete, who came to help Jill with lunch.

Deborah got the message.

Still her sister said, "I have a great staff that I've handpicked and carefully trained. Who do you think was minding the shop when I was going back and forth to the doctor? I **do** have a life, Deborah. It's not all work."

"I didn't say it was."

"And I **love** what I do. I was back there kneading dough a little while ago. SoMa Stickies are **my** recipe. And SoMa Slaw? If you think I don't get joy making **Mom's** recipe every day, think again. Honestly, you sound like Dad sometimes. He thinks it's all drudgery and that I'm alone here. He doesn't know Skye and Tomas, who get here at three in the morning to bake, or Alice, who takes over at seven. He doesn't know I have Mia, Keeshan, and Pat. He doesn't know about Donna and Pete."

"He knows, Jill," Deborah said. "People tell him."

"And he can't say the bakery's a success? I did good at piano lessons when I was eight, so he decided I should be a concert pianist. I won a prize at the science fair when I was twelve, so he decided I should be a Nobel winner. Being me wasn't good enough—he always expected something more." She flattened a hand on her chest. "I want this baby. It's going to make me happy. Shouldn't that make Dad happy?"

They weren't talking about childbearing, but about the larger issue of parental expectations. Jill might be thirty-four, but she was still Michael Barr's child. "Tell him you're pregnant," Deborah urged, perhaps selfishly, but she hated having to keep this secret too.

"I will."

"Now. Tell him now."

By way of response, Jill asked, "Did you

know Cal McKenna taught several AP sections?"

Deborah stared at her sister long enough to see that Jill wasn't giving in. With a sigh, she took a drink of coffee. "Yes. I did know that." So did Jill, since Grace had him for AP American History.

"Some of his students were in here yesterday afternoon. There was talk."

Picking a pecan from the top of her bun, Deborah brought it to her mouth, then put it back down. "And that was before he died. I let Grace stay home today. Was I right to do that?"

"Dad would say no."

"I'm not asking Dad. I'm asking you."

Jill didn't hesitate. "Yes, you were right. The accident itself was bad enough, but now it has to be even harder for Grace, who knew the man. Any word on why he died?"

"Not yet." Deborah opened her mouth, about to blurt out the truth. She was desperate to share the burden of it, and if there was anyone in her life she could trust, it was Jill. But before she could speak, Hal Trutter appeared.

There was nothing subtle about Hal. Wearing a natty navy suit and red tie, he had

LAWYER written all over him. Realizing that, Deborah guessed every one of the people out front knew why he was here.

He took a coffee from the tray on the desk and looked at Jill. "Witness or chaperone?"

Jill didn't like Hal. She had told Deborah that more than once, without even knowing he had come on to her sister. It might have simply been her distrust of arrogant men. But in answer to his question, Jill folded her arms across her chest and smiled. "Both."

Feeling marginally protected, Deborah pulled the accident report from her bag. Hal unfolded it and began to read.

Deborah was comfortable with the first page, a straightforward listing of the spot where the accident occurred, her name, address, license number, car model, and registration number. She grew more nervous when he turned to the second page, where there was a line labeled "Driver."

Fighting guilt, she kept her eyes steady on Hal. He ate some of the sticky bun and read on.

Jill asked, "You're not gooeying up that form, are you?"

Just then, Deborah's cell phone chimed. Pulling it from her pocket, she read the message, swore softly, and rose. "Be right back," she said and headed through the kitchen. "Yes, Greg."

"I just got a message from Dylan. What's happening down there?"

Deborah wasn't surprised Dylan had called his father. She wished he had waited, but Cal McKenna would still be dead. Greg would have to know sooner or later.

Finding a spot in the shadow of a dumpster outside the back door, she told him about the accident. The questions that followed were predictable. Greg might have moved to Vermont to rediscover his inner artist, but to Deborah, he was still the CEO who had inadvertently micromanaged his business to success.

To his credit, the first questions were about Grace and whether either of them had been hurt in any way. Then came, **What time did you leave the house, what time did you get Grace, what time was the accident? Exactly where on the rim road did it happen, how far was the victim thrown, how long did it take for the ambulance to arrive? What hospital was he at, who's his primary doctor, was a specialist brought in?**

"No specialist," Deborah said. "He was doing fine. No one expected that he'd die."

There was a brief pause, then, "Why did I

have to hear this from my ten-year-old son? You were involved in a fatal accident, and you didn't think it important enough to keep me in the loop?"

"We're divorced, Greg," she reminded him sadly. He sounded genuinely wounded, so much like the caring man she had married that she felt a wave of nostalgia. "You said you had burned out on your life here. I was trying to spare you. Besides, there was nothing fatal about it until early this morning, and I've been slightly preoccupied since then."

He relented a bit. "Is Grace upset?"

"Very. She was in a car that hit a man."

"She should have called me. We could have talked."

"Oh, Greg," Deborah said with a tired sigh. "You and Grace haven't talked—**really** talked—since you left."

"Maybe it's time we did."

She didn't know whether he meant talking on the phone or in person, but she couldn't imagine proposing either to Grace right now. The girl saw her father every few months, and then only at Deborah's insistence.

"Now's not good," she said. "Grace is dealing with enough, without that."

"How long is she going to stay angry with me?"

"I don't know. I try to talk her through it, but she still feels abandoned."

"Because you do, Deborah. Are you imposing your own feelings on her?"

"Oh, I don't need to do that," Deborah said with quick anger. "She feels abandoned enough all on her own. You're her father, and you haven't **been** here for the last two years of her life. Literally. You haven't been down once, not **once**. You want the kids to go up there to visit, and that might be fine for Dylan, but Grace has a life here. She has homework, she has track, she has friends." Deborah glanced at her watch. "I can't do this right now, Greg. I was in the middle of something when you called, and I have to get to work."

"That's what did it, y'know."

"Did what?"

"Destroyed our marriage. You always had to work."

"**Excuse** me," Deborah cried. "Is this the man who put in sixteen-hour days right up until the moment he dumped it all? For the record, Greg, I **do** go to Deborah's track meets and Dylan's baseball games. I **do** go to piano recitals and school plays. You're the one who could never make time for us."

Quietly, Greg said, "I asked you to move up here with me."

Deborah wanted to cry. "How could I do that, Greg? My practice is here. My father depends on me. Grace is in high school—and we have one of the best school systems in the state, you said that yourself." She straightened her shoulders. "And if I had moved north with you, would it have been a threesome—you, Rebecca, and me? Oh, Greg, you made me an offer I couldn't accept. So if you want to discuss what killed our marriage, we could start with that, but not today, not now. I have to go."

Amazed at how close to the surface the hurt remained, Deborah ended the call before he could say anything else. Looking out over the yellow van with her sister's logo on the side—a stylized cupcake, frosted into peaks spelling **Sugar-on-Main**—she took several calming breaths. When she was marginally composed, she went back inside.

Hal had finished reading the report. He was standing with his hands on his hips. Jill hadn't moved.

"Is it okay?" Deborah asked uneasily.

"It's fine." He extended the papers. "If what you say here is exact, there's good reason for us to know what the guy was doing out there in the rain and whether he was hopped up on booze or drugs. Anyone in his right mind would have moved to the side of the road when a car came along. So the big question mark is him, not you. I don't see anything here that would raise a red flag on your end."

Feeling little relief, Deborah refolded the papers. "I'm sending copies to the Registry and to my insurance company. Are you okay with that, too?"

"You have to do it. Just don't talk with John again without me there, okay?"

"Why not?"

"Because the victim died. Because I'm your lawyer. Because I know John; John knows how to build a hand and hold it close. And, Deborah, don't talk to the media. The **Ledger**'s bound to call."

Of course they would, now that a death was involved. Deborah grew fearful. "What do I say?"

"That your lawyer advised you not to talk."

"But then they'll think I'm hiding something."

"Okay. Tell them you're stunned by Calvin McKenna's death and have no further comment at this time."

Deborah was more comfortable with that.

Nervously, she asked, "You don't see a problem, do you?"

"Well, you killed a man with your car. Was it intentional? No. Did it result from reckless driving? No. Was there negligence involved regarding the condition of your car? No. If the reconstruction team supports all of the above, you'll be clear on the criminal side. Then we'll just have to wait to see what the wife does."

Deborah nodded slowly. It wasn't quite the rosy, all-is-well picture she wanted, but a man was dead. There was nothing remotely rosy about that.

Chapter 5

❧

Deborah was late reaching her father's house. Hearing the shower, she put the coffee on and readied his bagel. When the water continued to run, she considered dashing over to the office to get ahead on paperwork, but the living room was too strong a lure.

A wingback chair stood in its far corner, upholstered in a faded rose brocade. Sinking into it, she folded her legs under her as she had done dozens of times growing up. Wingback chairs had been originally designed to protect their occupants either from drafts or the heat of a fire. Deborah had needed protection of another kind. She had used the chair to help her deal with her parents' expectations, and it had delivered for her more times than she could count. Her parents had assumed she was strong, assumed she could take care of herself in ways that her younger sister could not. But even if she looked the part, she was often scared to death. Sitting in this chair was akin to wearing blinders. It allowed her to focus on one thing at a time.

One thing she could do. If she was dealing with Calvin McKenna's death, she couldn't dwell on Jill's pregnancy, Greg's accusations, or Hal's betrayal of her best friend.

Pushing the last three from her mind, she relived the accident for the umpteenth time, trying desperately to see something she might have done differently. She replayed her talks with the police and, later, with Grace, but here there was no going back. Grace was her daughter, and she deserved protection. That's what parents did, particularly ones who had made their kids suffer through a divorce.

Upstairs, the shower went off. Getting up from the chair, she started back to the kitchen, caught herself, and returned to the den for a highball glass and an empty whiskey bottle. She put the glass in the dishwasher, the bottle in the trash, and unfolded the newspaper.

Calvin McKenna's death wouldn't have made the morning edition. Tomorrow's perhaps. But the local weekly would hit stands tomorrow, too. Deborah dreaded that. More, though, she dreaded telling her father that the man had died.

As it happened, he already knew. There was an impatience in his stride as he went straight to the coffeemaker. His white hair was neatly combed, his cheeks pale. The disappointment on his face made him look older.

"Malcolm called," he explained, filling his mug. Malcolm Hart was chief of surgery and a longtime friend of Michael's. "Looks like we have a problem."

"Does Malcolm know anything more?" Deborah asked.

"About why the man died?" Her father drank from his mug. "No. The widow is fighting the autopsy. She doesn't want her husband's body desecrated. In the end, of course, she won't have a say. Autopsy is the law after a violent death. She'll just slow things down."

"Doesn't she want to know why he died?"

He shrugged, swallowed more coffee.

"But if she's thinking of suing, she'll need to know the exact cause of death," Deborah reasoned, "unless there's some reason she doesn't want to know. Or doesn't want us to know."

"Like what," Michael said, and in that instant, Deborah was grateful for Hal.

"Like alcohol or drugs. We're insisting that they check for both."

Her father seemed unimpressed. "If I were you," he said, eyeing her over his mug, "I'd worry about insurance. Do you have enough personal coverage in the event that she sues?"

"Yes." Insurance was one of the things that Greg, the businessman, had bought to the hilt.

Michael sighed and shook his head.

Deborah knew he was thinking that this would be a very public stain on the family's reputation. Not wanting to hear the words, she said, "This is one of those instances when I'd do anything to turn back the clock."

"And do what?" he asked kindly enough, lowering his cup. "What would you do differently?"

She should never have let Grace take the wheel in weather like that. Should **never** have let Grace drive. But to tell her father that, without telling the police, would be making him an accomplice, as unfair as what Hal had done to her.

So she simply said, "Go even slower. Maybe wear my glasses."

He seemed startled. "You weren't wearing them?"

"I don't have to. There's no restriction on my license." Her glasses were weak. Occasionally she wore them watching a movie, but that was all.

"Shouldn't you have taken every possible precaution on a night like that?"

"In hindsight, yes."

"Your mother would have worn her glasses."

It was a low blow. "Did she ever have an accident?"

"No."

But Deborah knew differently. Feeling no satisfaction, simply a thread of anger, she said, "Take a look at her personal checkbook for the year I got married. You'll see a check she wrote for several thousand dollars, paid to Russo's garage. While she was driving down West Elm, she was looking for something on the passenger's seat and sideswiped a parked car."

Her father made a face. "That's ridiculous. I would have known."

"Her car needed a tune-up. It had to be in the shop anyway. Ask Donny Russo."

"Your mother would never have lied to me."

"She didn't lie. She just didn't tell the whole truth."

"Why would she do that?"

Deborah sighed. Gently, she said, "Because you want perfection, and we can't always deliver. Is Mom less lovable because she sideswiped a car? Am I less lovable because my car hit a man? I was upset when we hit Calvin

McKenna, and I'm crushed that he died. But it was an accident," she was suddenly close to tears, "—an innocent accident, but I seem to be the only one saying that. I'm saying it to my daughter, to my son, to Hal, to the police, to my ex-husband, to you. It would be really nice if someone said it to **me**—because, here's a flash, Dad, I'm not made of steel. And I'm not without feelings. Right now, I need support."

Deborah hadn't planned the outburst. But she didn't apologize.

Michael eyed her strangely. "Did you tell me that about your mother so that I wouldn't be angry about you?"

"It's not about anger. It's about understanding."

"Then understand this," he said and set down his mug. "I loved your mother. I was married to her for forty years, and during that time I never once had cause to doubt her. It sounds to me like you're trying to find fault with her **and** with me to get yourself off the hook. You killed a man, Deborah. It might be best if you accept that fact."

Deborah was startled by the attack and too long formulating her response. What she might have asked, had her father not left, was why he had endless compassion for his patients and none for her. The answer, of course, was that she was family, and that, for family, the expectations were different.

For patients, the expectations were always the same. Family doctors didn't get sick, didn't take long vacations, didn't take Wednesday afternoons off to play golf or, in Deborah's instance, to sit with Grace. Between ten in-office patients and four house calls, Deborah's Wednesday was nonstop. Her very last patient, waiting for her when she returned to the office, was Karen Trutter.

"If the mountain won't come to Muhammad . . ." her friend said with a small smile. She wore gym clothes stylish enough to blend with the diamond studs that were a gift from her husband and that she never removed.

Deborah closed the door, and, looking at Karen, was warned by the history of caring that had been given and taken for eighteen years. "I'm sorry," she finally said, crossing the small space to give her friend a squeeze. "You deserve better."

"You're busy."

Deborah pulled up a chair and sat. "What I am, is running to get as much done as possible before the you-know-what hits the fan."

"It was an accident."

"Thank you. But still . . ." Deborah knew that even aside from whose responsibility the driving had been, there was the issue of deception. The fact that Karen knew nothing of it made it even worse.

"Danielle says Grace wasn't in school."

"How could I send her?" Deborah asked. "She's distraught."

"Maybe she needs counseling."

"No. Just time. This is all so fresh. Have you heard about any funeral plans?"

"Friday afternoon. Here in town."

"Here?" Deborah was disappointed. She was hoping the funeral would be far away. "I'm surprised. He hasn't lived here very long."

"They're suspending classes so students who want to can attend. And there'll be a memorial service at the school Friday night. Was Hal a help this morning?"

"As much as he could be. There are so many unknowns. My stomach churns when I think about it."

"John Colby won't charge you with anything," Karen said. "He knows what you mean to this town."

"That could backfire," Deborah remarked. "He's already been warned about a whitewash. Precisely because of who I am, he could go after me harder."

"For what?"

But Deborah didn't want to list the possible charges again. "I'll let Hal tell you. He was very good to meet with me."

"Why wouldn't he? He **loves** you."

For the second time that day with someone named Trutter, Deborah felt like a fraud.

Karen frowned, seeming ready to say something more—and, for an instant, Deborah feared Hal had confessed his feelings to his wife. Then Karen closed her mouth, cleared her throat, and said weakly, "I'm actually here on business. My elbow's been killing me for two weeks. You said I should tell you if something lasts that long."

" 'Killing you'?" Deborah asked, quickly concerned. "Which elbow?"

When she bobbed the right one, Deborah took it in her hand and began to press. "Hurt?"

"No."

"This?"

"No."

She prodded enough, without distress to her friend, to rule out a broken bone. Cradling the elbow, she took Karen's wrist and moved it through a normal range of motion. This did elicit a cry. When Deborah repeated the offending movement, Karen protested again. Deborah probed the elbow again, this time focusing on the lateral tendon.

"There," Karen said and sucked in a breath.

Deborah sat back. "How often have you played tennis this week?"

"Every day, but—"

"And not just for fun. Karen, you have tennis elbow."

"Women on my team don't get tennis elbow."

Deborah chuckled with relief. "You have tennis elbow."

"But I always play every day. I've been doing this for five years now. Why suddenly the pain?"

"Because it's been five years of playing every day."

"I was thinking, uh, that there might have been something in the bone. Y'know, right breast, right arm—"

Deborah interrupted. "I know, sweetie. Last year it was your ribs, the year before that your shoulder. It happens every year at this time."

Karen winced. "Every year?"

"Well, for the last three. What is it, now, six years since the mastectomy?"

Karen swallowed. "Yup. And still there's the fear."

"There'll always be the fear, which is why you come to see me."

"But if it's psychosomatic, why do I feel pain?"

"Oh, K, it isn't psychosomatic. The injury is real. The tendon on the outside of your elbow is inflamed. Another time of year, you might ignore it. This time of year, it's an issue."

"I don't consciously remind myself that the anniversary's coming up."

"You don't have to. Your subconscious knows."

Karen finally seemed to relax. "Tennis elbow? Are you sure?"

"Ninety-nine percent."

"I don't need an X-ray?"

"Not until you take a couple of days off, ice the elbow, and let an anti-inflammatory go to work. If there's no improvement, we can take pictures."

"You think I'm silly to race in here."

"Absolutely not," Deborah scolded. "I **told** you to come. The beauty of surviving breast cancer is that doctors have to take you seriously, and, believe me, I do. There's good reason for that tendon to be inflamed, but I do understand where you're coming from."

"You're the only one. I can't exactly tell Dani. She has her own fears."

"What about Hal?"

"He doesn't want to hear. He gets too nervous." She chewed on her lower lip, before she blurted, "At least, that's what I always thought. Deborah, I need to ask you something. Do you think Hal would ever have an affair?"

Deborah remained neutral. "Be with someone else, you mean?"

Karen nodded. "I got a phone call Monday night. It was a woman. She asked if I knew where my husband was."

Deborah's own eyes went wider. "Did you?"

"I knew where he was supposed to be. He was supposed to be at work. There was something about this voice that said he might not have been."

"Did you ask who it was?"

"No. I hung up."

"Did you get the phone number?"

"It registered as 'Unavailable.' Hal got home an hour later. He said he'd had a good meeting. But he was drenched from the rain, so would I have known if the meeting took place in a bed at the Embassy Suites, and he'd come home straight from the shower?"

"Oh, Karen."

"This isn't the first time."

"She's called before?"

"Once, a couple of months ago. I feel like I ought to recognize the voice. Then I realize it's because I've remembered that call so often." She fiddled with one of her diamond studs. "So. Do you think Hal would?"

Absolutely not, Deborah wanted to say, but it would be an out-and-out lie. Feeling dishonest enough without that, she murmured, "I think he's the kind of man women look at. It's possible someone from the office has a crush on him and, since she can't get to first base, she gets her revenge by calling you and hoping you'll question Hal."

"I wouldn't question him. He'd be **crushed** if he thought I doubted him."

"Maybe he'd want to know about the call, so that he could speak to whoever it is."

"No, no. I just wanted to run it past you." Reaching out with her good arm, she cupped Deborah's chin fondly. "You're right. That was definitely a woman who wishes my husband was available, which he is not." She smiled broadly. "See? You've helped me **twice** today." She touched Deborah's hair, brushing at a few wavy strands. "This is the cutest cut, y'know. When I conjure you in my mind, I still think of you with long hair. This is freer."

"I feel like it's always messy."

"It has spunk. This is the new you, Deborah."

Deborah sat back. The new her was a liar. "Spunk, huh? My father thinks it's unprofessional."

"Fine. Let him take his bursitis somewhere else," Karen advised, then paused. "How's he handling the accident?"

Deborah kept her mouth shut.

"Meaning, poorly," Karen interpreted, and as hurt as Deborah had been that morning, she was quick to defend the man.

"In fairness, he's going through a rough time."

"Still missing your mom?"

"Big time."

"So are you."

"But it's harder for him. He goes home to an empty house. She was his soulmate. She was his **playmate.** Evenings, weekends—he doesn't know what to do with himself."

"He could help out at the bakery. Ruth loved that place."

Deborah sputtered. "My dad won't admit that. He never has." She wondered whether he would feel differently once he had a grandchild there.

"He could take Dylan fishing," Karen suggested.

They had discussed this before. Fishing was definitely an option for a boy with severe hyperopia. Dylan was a good sitter, a good thinker, and, being farsighted, he would enjoy the scenery. He might even be fine baiting hooks.

"I've suggested it," Deborah said, "but Dad always has a list of things he needs to do himself."

"Legitimate things?"

"Some are. Some of it's just busywork."

"Put him on call a couple of times a week. Why are you the only one who has to race to the hospital in the middle of the night?"

"I don't have to. I like to, especially with regular patients. That's when I feel best about myself as a doctor. Dad is past the point of needing that."

"Which may be all the more reason why he needs it. Maybe he forgets what it's like."

"Maybe," Deborah granted. "But hey, it's not much of an issue. I can't remember the last time I got a middle of the night call."

Naturally, after saying it, Deborah was woken at three the next morning by the an-

swering service. The patient was a twenty-
seven-year-old woman who had been to the
office twice in the past few weeks complaining of stomach pains. Michael had seen her
the first time, Deborah the second. In both
instances, blood tests had shown no elevated
white cells, hence no indication of appen-
dicitis.

Now, she sounded frantic. The pain was
excruciating. She had a fever and was vomiting.

Deborah quickly dressed, woke Grace to
tell her she'd be gone, and set off for the hospital. The patient, driven by a frightened husband, arrived just as she did. Deborah was
able to speed them through Emergency and a
set of definitive tests, then connect them with
a surgeon who would perform the appendec-
tomy. She saw the woman up in the elevator
and sat with her husband a bit. Then she went
to look for the doctors who had been on call
the other night.

One of them, Jody Reid, was monitoring
a post-op patient. She joined Deborah in
the hall. "You're inquiring about Calvin
McKenna," she surmised, gesturing Deborah
to the nearest computer. She logged on and
gestured again, this time for Deborah to look
at the screen.

It was a lab report. Deborah didn't have to give it more than a glance before one word popped out. "Coumadin? I didn't realize he was on it."

"Neither did we, and I was right there when they brought him in."

"He wasn't wearing a med alert bracelet?"

"No. He had no wallet, no identification on him at all, and he wasn't talking. We specifically asked him about meds and allergies, but he didn't respond. His wife was no help either. She shook her head when we asked, and she made no mention of a heart condition or anything else to warrant his taking a blood thinner like Coumadin."

"But there's a black box warning on the label," Deborah persisted. " 'Tell your doctor.' How could she not know?"

"Beats me. But it does explain why he hemorrhaged."

Deborah was incredulous. She and her father provided those of their patients who were on drugs like Coumadin with cards for their wallets, but that was only as good as the patient's diligence in carrying a wallet. "Was there anything else in his blood? Drugs? Alcohol?"

"No. Just Coumadin."

Chapter 6

❧

"What that means legally," Hal interpreted, when she called him soon after sunrise, "is that there may be reasonable doubt that the accident itself caused his death. This is good news, Deborah. Hey, I'd have preferred that he'd been tanked. Then I could argue that he staggered out in front of the car and caused the accident himself. But Coumadin raises other issues—like whether there was negligence on his part or that of his wife in failing to alert the doctors at the hospital that there was a danger of bleeding. What do you think?"

"As a doctor?" Deborah asked. "I think it's frustrating. It was an unnecessary death. As a wife, I'm confused."

"Ex-wife," Hal put in.

"If my husband had been on any major drug," Deborah went on, ignoring the remark, "I'd have made sure it was the first thing we told any doctor treating him."

"How do you feel as the driver of the car that hit him? Relieved?"

She considered that for a minute. "No. A man died."

"But you didn't cause it."

"I did. My car hit him. That started the whole thing."

"Couldn't the hemorrhaging have been unrelated to the accident?"

"You mean," Deborah asked dryly, "couldn't he have just happened to hemorrhage the day after he was tossed in the air by a car and thrown against a tree?"

Hal didn't yield. "That's exactly what I mean."

"The timing is suspicious."

He persisted. "You're a doctor. Medically speaking, is it **possible?**"

"I don't do trauma work."

"Deborah."

"Yes. It's possible."

He sighed. "Thank you." Satisfied with his cross-examination, he added a silky, "You're a stickler for details, Deborah Monroe."

"Definitely," Deborah said, reacting to the tone, "especially when it involves doing the right thing. Can I ask you something, Hal?"

"Anything, sweetheart."

"You said you would have an affair with me. Have you had others?"

There was a pause, then an amused, "What kind of question is that?"

"One that's haunted me since you first mentioned it."

"Are you considering my offer?"

"Absolutely not."

"Then why ask me this now?" He was all business again. "I'm the best lawyer you'll find, and, if it comes to a trial, I won't even charge for my time, which will be considerable. By the way, I talked with Bill Spelling." Bill was editor in chief of the local paper. Deborah had treated his children since they were born. "He's keeping Grace's name out of today's piece. That's the kind of thing I do for people I love."

"Coumadin?" Grace repeated cautiously when Deborah mentioned the word.

"It's a blood thinner, often used after a heart attack," Deborah explained. "It prevents the formation of clots that could then cause another heart attack or a stroke."

From the kitchen door, Dylan asked a horrified, "Did Dad have a stroke?"

Deborah hadn't heard the child approach. "No," she scolded gently, "Dad did not have a stroke. This is a medication Mr. McKenna was taking." She held out an arm and pulled Dylan close. "Blood thinners can also cause excessive bleeding," she said to Grace. "It's possible that's what caused Mr. McKenna to hemorrhage the other night. If the doctors in the ER had known he was taking it, they might have been able to prevent his death."

"How?"

"By counteracting the blood thinners with other drugs. And by monitoring him closely."

Dylan looked up at her, his eyes huge. "My doctor's doing that with me."

"Very different problem, sweetie. Your doctor is monitoring your eyes to make sure your prescription is right. There's nothing remotely life threatening about your eyes."

"But what if my cornea keeps getting worse, and nobody knows it but me. What happens then?"

Deborah felt a qualm. His glasses corrected for his farsightedness. The corneal problem was unrelated to that and would only be fixed by a transplant. "Do you feel something changing?"

"No. But what if it did?"

"You'd tell me, and we'd go to the doctor.

Do you feel something?" she asked again, because it wasn't like dermatitis, which was visible on the surface of the skin, or even like checking an ear for inflammation. She couldn't tell what was going on with his cornea.

"**No,** but what if we didn't tell the doctor? What would happen then?"

"You just wouldn't be able to see very well."

"Would I go blind?"

Deborah leaned closer. "Honey, are things more hazy?"

"I'm just **asking,** Mom. Would I go blind?"

"No. We've talked about that. In the first place, the lattice dystrophy is only in one eye. In the second place, as soon as you've stopped growing, we'll completely correct the problem."

"Mom," Grace interrupted sharply, "why was Mr. McKenna running if he had a bad heart?"

Deborah looked at Dylan, who seemed marginally satisfied with her answer, then said to Grace, "People with bad hearts run all the time. Exercise is important."

"Like you at the gym?" Dylan asked. "What does Dad do?"

Dad paces the floor, was Deborah's immediate thought, but of course it was wrong. Since he had fled corporate life, he no longer paced. "Yoga," she answered. She might have made a joke of it—it **so** fit the image of the new Greg—but she believed in yoga. She wished Grace would try it. Learning a relaxation technique might help with her nail-biting.

Gently, Deborah pulled the girl's hand away from her mouth, but she wasn't sure Grace got the message.

"Do you think Mr. McKenna was having a heart attack when he ran out into the street?" the girl asked. "Like, maybe he didn't know what he was doing, or maybe was disoriented and was trying to get help?"

"The doctors didn't see any evidence of a heart problem."

"So what does it mean to us if he was taking Coumadin?"

"It means," Deborah said, grateful for this small thread of hope, "that we weren't directly responsible for his death."

"Coumadin?" Deborah's father asked over his morning coffee. Only then did he look at her directly. His eyes were bloodshot, and he'd tossed back a pair of aspirin before reaching for his mug. The bottle of whiskey in the den—a new bottle, apparently opened last night—was easily down by a third, and while that worried Deborah, redeeming herself was a more immediate concern.

"The hospital is relieved," she said. "This shifts the issue from why he died to why no one knew he was taking the drug. Everyone there asked the right questions, but they weren't given answers. The patient wasn't speaking, and his wife didn't mention Coumadin. She didn't even list the name of a doctor he sees."

"Coumadin isn't OTC. Someone had to prescribe it. The wife must know who it was—unless the guy was hiding things from her, **like** you claim my wife did from me."

Taken off guard by the charge, Deborah hesitated. "I only told you that because you've put Mom on a pedestal that none of the rest of us can reach. She was human. People make mistakes."

"She's dead. She isn't here to defend herself."

"She wouldn't want defending, Dad. She'd come right out and fess up, and you'd forgive her on the spot. So I'm fessing up. I had an accident that I deeply regret. I wish I could be perfect for you. But I'm not."

"Oh, come on, Deborah," he grumbled. "Have I ever asked you to be perfect?"

"Not in as many words, but you have high standards. Take Jill. She can't meet those standards, but she loves what she does, Dad, she really does, and it's a great business. Couldn't you drop in there one day and just . . . take a look? Or take Dylan. He may not be a super athlete, but he'd love it if you went to one of his games."

"I will. I will."

"He's playing later today."

"Today's no good. Another time."

Deborah was familiar with the day's appointments and didn't know why today was "no good," but to ask it might just make Michael angry. "What about Jill? She'd love it if you stopped in. If you could see the people who wait in line—"

"Right now," Michael cut in, "I'm more concerned about you than about your sister. Have you talked with Hal about the Coumadin thing?"

"Hal's thrilled. He feels a case can be made that the drug, more than my car, caused Cal's death."

Michael studied his coffee.

"There's a validation in it for me," Deborah said. "I knew he wasn't fatally injured when I examined him. At least, now I understand why he died." When her father still didn't respond, she added, "Hal's in close touch with the police."

Michael lowered his mug. "That's good. He'll keep on top of them. The more answers we get, the better. Half of the patients I saw yesterday asked about the accident, and the **Ledger** hasn't even come out yet."

By noon, the paper was on every driveway in town. Deborah saw it at lunchtime, face up on the white Formica counter in the office kitchenette.

The article wasn't as bad as it might have been. It was on the front page, but under the fold, which meant that it wasn't the first thing people saw. Unfortunately, in a town as small as Leyland, most people read the **Ledger** cover to cover.

The article focused on Calvin McKenna— when and why he had come to Leyland, where he lived with his wife, what he taught. Teachers attested to his intellect, citing him as someone who spent his lunchtime reading history in the cafeteria. Students talked about how smart he was. Everyone expressed respect for his ability, though no one used the word **beloved.**

The reporter gave a rundown of the events of Monday night, a timeline, very cut-and-dried. Deborah might have liked mention of the fact that her car was going well under the speed limit and was in its proper lane, but the text stated simply that speed was not a factor, and that no citation had been issued. Funeral plans were much as Karen had said.

The wife wasn't quoted. Nor, thanks to Hal's advice, was Deborah.

The best part of the article, in her opinion, was that there was no mention of Grace. The worst was that with Deborah's name front and center for all the world to see, the lie grew.

Grace thought she would die. Her friends **never** read the **Ledger,** at least, not in the middle of school. But, naturally, since it was Mr. McKenna who had died, today was different. She didn't even know where they got the papers, but wherever she turned, someone had a copy.

"This is not bad," Megan remarked with the rustle of newsprint when she finished reading the piece. "They don't even say you were in the car."

That was beside the point, as far as Grace was concerned. Now the whole town knew it was her car that had hit Mr. McKenna. Half of the school was stopping her in the halls, saying stupid things like, **Wow, your mom hit him? Like, did she know it was him? So when did you find out? Do you feel guilty or anything?**

The only person she might have wanted to talk with was Danielle. She respected Danielle so much. But that was the problem—how could she lie to Danielle? But how could she tell the truth when doing it would get her mother in trouble?

So she held Danielle off with the same hand she held off the rest of her friends, and went to her next class with her head down, not that it kept people away for long. She spent the start of her lunch period fending off so many questions that she ended up picking up her tray, dumping most of her lunch in the trash, and hiding in the girls' bathroom until the bell rang. But then they started **texting.** No one was supposed to be doing that in class, but people always did. They broke the rules, and no one cared. **They** broke the rules, and no one cared.

She turned off her phone.

Track was more of the same—so many questions that the coach brilliantly decided to have her make a short statement—and what could she say? **It was an awful night—there was no visibility—we feel so bad.** Just words. They didn't come close to saying what she was really feeling, which was like a total liar. But there was no way she could tell the truth now without making liars of her mother, Uncle Hal, the police, the newspaper reporter, and whoever else was spreading word about what happened that night.

She ran poorly. Her first interval was bad, her second was worse, and she did the 800—**her** event—so pitifully that the coach let her leave before she finished.

She half walked, half ran to Sugar-On-Main and, with her phone still off, **secreted** herself—as in hid from view—in the bakery's back office until anyone from school who was out front—anyone she might **possibly** know, who might start asking questions—was gone. She'd have stayed there until her mother came, if she hadn't been starved. She devoured a brioche and two carrot muffins, washed them down with an espresso that she fixed when her aunt couldn't see, because, forget espresso, Jill hated her drinking coffee, period, but if she was going to stay awake long enough to do homework **and** study vocab that night, she needed caffeine, right?

Feeling guilty about going behind Jill's back—but not guilty enough not to check out the front to make sure that no one who mattered was there before she went out—she looked around for a way to help her aunt. With closing time less than an hour off and the front mostly empty, the rest of the staff had left. Dylan was already wiping down tables, which was good, because Grace hated doing that. She liked checking credit card slips, but Jill was doing that herself. So she set to work consolidating what remained of the day's pastries on a single tray. Squatting behind the display cases, she was hidden from anyone who might come in off the street.

She kept an eye on the door. Dylan was doing the same, glancing worriedly there between swipes with his rag, but for a different reason. He had a baseball game at five and was worried their mom would be late. He was already wearing his uniform, and had asked Jill three times whether she would drive him to the field if Deborah didn't get there on time. He had asked Grace twice whether **she** would watch the game if their mom couldn't make it.

Grace prayed she wouldn't have to. There was no way she could stand in public view watching a bunch of ten-year-olds swing at balls that were way out of reach.

She was lost in the horror of it, when her mother finally arrived and not from the gym, as Grace had thought, but still in her work clothes. She gave Dylan a hug, squeezed Jill's arm, and made for Grace. Hunkering down beside her, she said quietly, "I kept trying your phone. How'd it go today?"

"Fine, until the paper came out," Grace said with a sudden anger—and yes, at her mom. Deborah had started the lie. "All the kids were looking over each other's shoulders to see me. I felt like a criminal."

"They were reading about Mr. McKenna. It isn't every day that a teacher dies."

"They were reading about **you,**" Grace argued in a furious whisper, "and when they weren't asking me questions, they were looking at me funny, like they knew the truth. I barely made it through track practice. I mean, I botched my intervals and then didn't finish the eight hundred, which **sucks.** The whole **team** was staring."

"You're imagining it."

"No, Mom. They're staring, and they're talking about the funeral. They're all going. I mean, what am I supposed to do? I had Mr. McKenna in class. Do I go, too?"

"Do you want to?"

"Omigod, **no,**" she hissed, "it'd be a **nightmare** to be there knowing . . . knowing . . ." She couldn't say it. "But everyone else is going, so it'll look awful if I don't." She wilted. "This just gets worse and worse, Mom. It's like . . . **unbearable.** If I still liked Dad, I'd go live with **him** for the rest of the year," she threatened, inviting an argument. She knew how much her mother hated it when she talked about hating her dad.

But her mother was looking out through the display case glass at Dylan. He had moved on to a new table and was wiping it with large slow strokes. Though he had his back to them, the up-and-down movement of his head suggested he was watching his hand. Even Grace knew enough about his eyes to be uncomfortable with that.

She rose beside her mother, and for another minute, they both watched. Then Deborah went to Dylan and put a hand on his head. He jumped in surprise.

"Everything okay, sweetie?" she asked.

He nodded vigorously. "Everything's good."

"You're watching that rag pretty closely. Not blurring on you, is it?"

He shook his head.

"You'd tell me if it was?"

"Mom. Nothing's **blurred.** We have to leave soon, don't we?" he asked and looked worriedly at Grace. "You're coming, aren't you?"

"Oh, Dylan, I don't think—"

"You **have** to come," he cut in, sounding desperate. "See, that's why Coach never plays me, 'cause my family isn't there. He doesn't have a reason to do it."

"Wait a minute," Deborah said. "I haven't missed a game. Aren't I family?"

"One **small** part." He looked at Grace again and pleaded, "**Please** come," in a way that made her want to scream, because she couldn't say no when he looked at her that way. He was her little brother, he had terrible eyes, and he was so bad at baseball that it was painful to watch. Grace didn't know why her parents let him play.

Actually, she did. They let him play because baseball was normal, and they wanted that for him. They wanted him to have friends. They wanted him to be a typical boy. They wanted him to like sports.

"Five more minutes," Deborah told him and turned so that he wouldn't see what she mouthed to Grace. "Please come. He needs us there."

"How can **either** of us go?" Grace whispered when her mother was close again. "We just **killed** a guy."

"We didn't—"

"Won't it **look** bad if we're there?"

"Maybe, but what choice do we have? This is about Dylan. Should he be punished because Mr. McKenna died?"

Grace was torn. "Okay," she granted, "I'll go to the game, but I can't go to the funeral, I absolutely can't do that."

Jill joined them as they were leaving. "Are **you** going to the funeral?" she asked Deborah.

"I thought I would, out of respect."

"But you were driving the car that hit him."

Precisely, Grace thought.

"Isn't that all the more reason I should go?" her mother asked.

Grace held her breath. She could usually count on her aunt to side with her.

This time, Jill just frowned. "There must be protocol for this kind of thing. Maybe you should ask Hal."

In the car, Deborah phoned. Hal nixed the idea without a moment's pause. "Stay home."

"Why?" Deborah asked.

"Because your presence may upset the widow."

"But it's a graveside service, and it'll be packed. I'll stand way at the back. She'll never know I was there."

"And you don't think other people will see you? Come on, Deborah. Word'll spread."

She figured it would. With the appearance of the **Ledger,** though, the accident was public knowledge. As self-conscious as she felt driving through town, hiding would make it worse. "Would that be so bad?" she asked. "You wouldn't let me talk to the press, but I feel terrible about this, Hal. It's not like I set out to run the guy down, and it's not like I live in a city with millions of people and don't know who the man was. I feel responsible for what happened."

"The widow may play on that."

"Still, it was my car that hit her husband. Going to the funeral is the least I can do."

"As a friend, sweetheart, I understand," Hal replied patiently. "As your lawyer, I advise you to skip it. We still don't know what the widow plans to do. If your appearance sets her off, it'll only make things worse."

Deborah didn't ask Hal about going to a Little League game, because she didn't want him to veto that, too. After delivering Dylan to the field, she and Grace stood on the sidelines to watch with the other families. The air had cooled. Clusters of parents stood together wrapped in coats, always a natural barrier to conversation, but they were friendly enough to Deborah and Grace. If they thought Deborah shouldn't be there, they didn't let on.

Dylan spent the first eight innings on the bench. Finally, at the top of the ninth, with his team ahead by seven runs, the coach put him in. He came up to the plate adjusting first his helmet, then the goggles. He raised the bat and took his stance. He watched as the first pitch sailed high over his head.

"Good boy," Deborah shouted, desperate that he not embarrass himself, and when the second pitch was a repeat of the first and he still waited, she yelled, **"Good eye, Dylan, good eye!"**

Grace had no sooner murmured, "They're

going to walk him," when the third pitch came in over the plate. Dylan swung hard and missed. There was a groan from the crowd.

"It's okay," Deborah yelled, clapping her hands in encouragement.

Grace cupped her mouth. **"Wait for a another good one, Dylan!"**

It came on the next pitch. When Dylan didn't swing, it was a called strike. The next one was low. Dylan didn't budge.

Deborah prayed. He could hit the ball, she knew he could. He had done it for Hal the weekend before, and even though Hal had pitched almost directly at the bat, the boy had felt great.

The count was three and two. Deborah wasn't sure who was clutching whose arm tighter, Grace or her, but they were both shouting now, and if their energy was driven by something beyond the game, it didn't matter.

The pitcher held the ball close, wound up, let go. The pitch sailed in and hit Dylan on the arm. He spun around, momentarily shocked, then tossed the bat aside and happily ran to first base. When the next batter struck out, he stole to second base, then went on to third on a single into right field, and when the team's star hitter came up to the plate and doubled, Dylan scored.

The run was irrelevant, since the opposing team was shut out in the bottom of the ninth, but Dylan was more excited than Deborah had seen him in months. She was delighted.

Chapter 7

Her euphoria was short-lived. Waking up Friday morning, Deborah was determined to heed her lawyer's advice. She put on a black skirt suit simply because it felt appropriate for a sad day. When she shifted patients around to clear a window in the afternoon, she told herself that she would just take the time off from work out of respect for Calvin McKenna. And when she found herself driving toward the cemetery, she vowed to stay in the car.

The graveyard was south of town, on a succession of gentle hills whose shape was traced by the curve of narrow roads. It wasn't a large cemetery, which meant that when a big funeral took place, most of those narrow roads were lined with cars.

She pulled in behind the last car and watched its occupants walk off over the grass.

After several minutes with no new cars joining the line, she got out and followed. Warm air had returned, along with humidity. Ominous gray clouds reminded her of the storm Monday night, and she replayed the flash of movement that had brought Cal McKenna to this place—felt the impact, heard the squeal of tires, relived the horror. Again, she searched for something that might have given her warning, but she saw only rain.

She continued on along paths bordering patches of graves. When she crested a rise, she saw the group below, a heathery mix of grays and blacks, muted in the absence of sun. The minister stood at the head of a casket whose only adornment was a small bouqet of white flowers. The widow stood nearby, veiled in black and flanked by a man who resembled the deceased.

Deborah paused between several clusters of students, but she imagined they all saw her arrive. Uncomfortable, she moved closer to the grave. When she saw the widow look up, she walked faster, intent on hiding among the mourners. She found a spot behind a group of teachers, lowered her eyes, and listened for the start of the service.

For a minute, she heard nothing. Then came quiet whisperings, and an amorphous movement in front of her. She kept her eyes downcast until a firm hand took her elbow. Looking up, she was startled to see the man who had been with the widow. He was tall and dark-haired, and though his grip wasn't cruel, it was insistent as he drew her away from the crowd. He might have been guiding a friend, had it not been for his words.

"You need to leave. Mrs. McKenna doesn't want you here."

Too stunned to reply, Deborah let herself be led across the grass. As soon as they reached the nearest stretch of road, he ushered her between two tall SUVs and released her arm.

Shielded from the crowd, she finally said, "I'm sorry. I didn't mean harm."

His eyes were angry, his face grim. "Well, you caused it, once Monday night and again now. So please." He pointed. "Walk up that road and leave, so we can hold this funeral."

"I didn't see him Monday night." She was desperate to explain. "I've been haunted ever since."

"So haunted," he hit back, "that you hire a lawyer who's in tight with the police department? So haunted that you show up at this funeral to make people in town think that you care?"

"I'm haunted," Deborah whispered, "by

the idea that I was responsible for a man's death."

His reply was sharp. "What, were you speeding? Putting on lipstick? Talking on the phone? And now you're hoping for a free pass because you know everyone in town? Well, here's a flash. Cal McKenna was not as important as you and now he never will be. So, if you're haunted, good." He nodded back toward the grave. "Remember him every morning and every night. You stole his future. You **were** responsible."

Turning away, he strode between the cars and was gone before she could reply. Numbed by guilt and humiliation, she started back along the road. She stumbled once where the pavement was cracked, but caught herself and continued on to her car. She started the engine and left the cemetery, but once past its gates she turned off the main road, fearing she was going to be sick. Pulling over to the side, she opened her door and, sitting half in, half out of the car, tried to breathe deeply. In time, feeling more steady, she eased her legs back into the car and drove slowly home.

Lívia and Adinaldo were gone; the lawn was neatly mowed, and there was no sign of the van. In the kitchen, Lívia's dinner sat on the stove. Deborah knew it would be something good—something that she couldn't have made herself if her life had depended on it. Taking a bottled iced tea from the fridge, she went into the front hall. She had barely settled on the bottom stair when the doorbell rang.

She didn't move. Anyone who mattered had a key, and she didn't want to see anyone else.

The doorbell rang again. She looked at the bottle, raised it to her mouth, then paused and thought of Grace. The girl had been quiet this morning, barely responding even to Dylan. With track practice canceled for the funeral, the plan had been for her to spend the afternoon at Jill's. Suddenly picturing a dozen things that might have happened to her between school and the bakery, Deborah jumped up from the step and opened the door.

John Colby stood there. He looked awkward. "I, uh, got a call. I understand there was a disturbance at the cemetery."

Deborah gave herself a minute to recover, then said, "Disturbance? I'm not sure I'd call it that. He was quiet enough." She stood back in invitation and closed the door once the police chief was inside. "I take it he's a relative?"

"The brother. Tom McKenna. He stopped

by to see me yesterday. He wanted to read the police report."

"I'll bet he did," she remarked and put the cold bottle to her temple. "He's worried I'm getting away with something."

"Did he threaten you in any way?"

"No," she said with a dismissive gesture. "He just wanted me to leave. I can almost understand where he was coming from," she added, not caring that Hal had told her not to talk with him. This was important. "You know my family, John. Did my parents go to funerals?"

"All the time."

She nodded. "Whenever they had the slightest connection to the deceased, they were there. They felt it was their responsibility as prominent members of this community. My mother would have urged me to go today. She would have said it was the decent thing to do. So I went." The pain of it remained fresh. "Thank God, Grace did not."

John tugged his khaki shirt more comfortably over his middle. "How's she doing?"

Deborah waggled a hand.

"Not so good?" he interpreted.

"It's a difficult time."

"A difficult age, too," he said, frowning at the carpet. "It's hormones and peer pressure and feeling halfway adult but not there yet. And driving gives them a freedom some of 'em can't handle. Grace has her permit, doesn't she?"

Deborah wondered if John suspected something and was grateful to be able to give a truthful answer. "She does, but after this, she's refusing to drive. She didn't see the man on the road any more than I did. She doesn't know how we could have **not** hit him and doesn't trust that something like that wouldn't happen again." Thunder rolled in the distance. Deborah folded her arms. "She'll be upset when she hears what happened at the cemetery."

"She'll do okay. You've raised a strong girl."

"Even strong girls suffer when bad things happen. She's still struggling with the divorce."

"Well. She's certainly a leader. We're counting on her to place in the meet tomorrow."

"I'm not sure you should. She hasn't had a good running week." Deborah passed a hand through her hair. It was a mess, like her life.

"Is there anything I can do to help?" John asked kindly.

She could think of several things, not the least of which was turning back the clock and making her five minutes late picking up Grace Monday night. Five minutes would have done it. Cal McKenna would have been gone.

More realistically, she said, "I need answers. Can you get a rush on the state police report?"

"I keep calling. They say they haven't gotten to it yet. There's backlog. I only have so much pull."

"What about a preliminary report? Like where Calvin was on the road when we collided?"

"I'm trying. Really, I am."

"Okay," she said, because she did believe him, "then the Coumadin issue. Do we know anything more?"

"Not yet. I talked to the widow about it. She's no help."

"She must have known he had a problem," Deborah reasoned. "Someone prescribed that Coumadin."

"She says she doesn't know who it was, but we'll pursue it."

Deborah thought of the man who had ejected her from the funeral, and felt a stirring of anger. "Ask the brother. He seems like a smart guy. Maybe he knows."

———

Perhaps it was defiance. Maybe Deborah shouldn't have intruded on the funeral, but there was nothing private about the memorial service held at the high school that night. She had a right to be there, and though part of her wanted to stay home after the fiasco at the cemetery, the other part wanted to let the brother—**and** the widow—know that she believed in paying tribute to a man who had died.

The rain cooperated. It had come in torrents after John left and went on for an hour, during which time Deborah busied herself sorting through Dylan's outgrown clothes while "Don't Think Twice, It's All Right" blared from his iPod dock. But the downpour had slowed by the time she picked up the kids at Jill's, and was pretty much over when dinner was done.

Grace wasn't happy. She didn't want to go to the memorial service at all. But Deborah was adamant. They didn't have to arrive early, she said, and they could leave as soon as it was over. But being present to show their respect for a fine teacher was the right thing to do.

To Grace's relief, the auditorium was lit by candles at the front, which meant that when she and her mother and brother slid into the very back row, no one saw them. She listened to the service, all the while thinking that she alone had caused Calvin McKenna's death. And there was her mother beside her, sitting up straight, doing THE . . . RIGHT . . . THING, expecting her to do THE . . . RIGHT . . . THING all the time so that she'd grow up to be just like her.

Grace didn't want to be a doctor. She just wanted to be invisible. The instant the memorial service ended, she slithered from the auditorium.

"Grace! Grace, wait!"

She had actually made it down the hall, out the front door of the school, and halfway down the steps before being spotted. Without looking back, she knew it was Kyle. While her mother and Dylan continued on, she stopped, hung her head, and waited.

"Jeez, Grace," he said, catching up to her, "where are you going so fast?"

She raised her head. "Home. The memorial service is over."

"We're all going to Ryan's. Can't you come?"

"Not tonight."

"It isn't the same without you."

She shot him a withering glance. "I'm not

in the mood." When she caught her mother looking back, she started walking slowly.

"You told her about the beer, didn't you," said Kyle.

"No."

"You're lying."

"No," Grace said sharply. "I don't lie. Why would I lie?"

"Hell, I don't know, but you've been strange all week. What's going on?"

She regarded him levelly. "Mr. McKenna's dead."

"So's my grandfather, but nothing I do'll bring him back. I know you were in the car that hit him, but that's not **our** fault."

"I never said it was."

"Right, because you haven't had a chance to say it. You're barely talking to **anyone.**"

Grace stopped again. "Kyle, it's been hard, okay? It's been hard."

"I still think it's the beer," he said, moving in front of her. "Hey, it wasn't my idea to bring it. Stephie asked for it. How'd your mom find out?"

"She **didn't,**" Grace insisted. Sidestepping him, she started walking toward the parking lot. "It's just that I'm upset that Mr. McKenna died, and you all don't care."

He fell in step beside her. "We do care. We

were all here tonight, weren't we? We'd have saved you a seat if you said you were coming, but you didn't tell anybody you were."

"It was a last-minute decision." **Thanks a bunch, Mom.**

"So, are you helping out with the car wash tomorrow?"

"I can't. There's a meet."

"I know there's a meet," he said, "but it isn't until the afternoon, and you're supposed to help, even for an hour. I mean, like, you helped organize the thing, and the money we make is for the junior trip."

"Which isn't 'til next year, so I'll wash cars next time." If she wasn't under house arrest, or on **probation.** The junior trip was only one of the things—like getting her license and going to college—that she'd taken for granted. Her mother could try to protect her all she wanted, but somehow, someone would find out.

She had hoped it would keep raining so that she could have the hood of her jacket up. Her mom had hoped it would stop so that her hair wouldn't be so wild. Guess who won?

She walked faster, heading for the shelter of the car.

"What about Kim's party?" Kyle asked.

"What about it?"

"It's tomorrow night. You're going to that, aren't you?"

"No."

"Why **not?**"

Grace might have said that she didn't think it was appropriate so close to the death of someone they all knew. But that was only half the truth, and half the truth seemed to describe **all** of her life lately.

But she wasn't about to tell Kyle that. He would just tell all the other kids what she'd said, which would only give them reason to ask more questions.

"Because I don't want to," she finally replied. Jogging the last few steps to her mother's car, she climbed in and closed the door hard.

Subdued after the service and exhausted from a week with too little sleep, Deborah passed out on the sofa. When the phone rang, she woke with a start, so disoriented that it wasn't until a second ring that she identified the sound and grabbed the receiver.

"Hello?" she asked groggily.

"Grace?" came her ex-husband's hesitant voice, then, "Deborah?"

She sank back to the cushions. "It's me."

"Are you sick?"

"No. Sleeping."

"It's only ten-thirty."

"Some of us lead busy lives, Greg. We have kids to take care of. We have family to worry about. And please, don't tell me I work too much. I just wear lots of hats."

"One being 'bitch'?"

She swallowed hard. He was right.

Relenting, he said more gently, "You don't have to work. You don't need the money."

"It isn't about money." She put an arm over her eyes. Funny, she and Greg always used to talk at this hour. It was one of the few times when he wasn't either on the phone or at the computer. She hadn't minded it then. It bothered her now.

"Okay," he said. "I keep trying Grace. Is something wrong with her phone?"

"She's had it off. She doesn't want to talk to anyone."

"You mean to me."

"She won't talk to her friends, either, since the accident." Deborah massaged her forehead. "She's like a turtle, pulled into her shell."

"That's swell," Greg said. "What do you plan to do about it?"

Plan? Deborah might have laughed. She

was coming to think it was useless to plan. "I'm giving her time."

"Maybe she needs to talk with a therapist."

"She doesn't need a therapist. It's only been four days. There was a service at school tonight. The accident is still fresh."

"Okay. But I want to talk with her."

"Try tomorrow morning."

"How can I get through to her if she won't answer her phone?"

Deborah wondered at the man's lack of imagination. Quietly, she said, "We do have a house line, Greg. Call her on that. She's running in a big meet tomorrow afternoon. Why not call in the morning to wish her good luck?"

Chapter 8

The weekend wasn't a good one for Deborah. She had to race to the office when her father, whose turn it was to see Saturday morning patients, called at the last minute and asked her to cover. Back home worrying about him, she argued with Dylan, who didn't want to go to his piano lesson, and argued with Grace, who, in her absence, had refused to talk with her father on the phone, prompting Greg to call Deborah to complain. She snapped at Dylan when he couldn't find his baseball glove to take to practice, then felt guilty when he said he couldn't **see** where it was. She fought with Grace when she said she had cramps and couldn't run in the cross-country meet, then, after insisting she try, felt guilty when the girl dropped out halfway through and, demoralized, shut herself in her room the instant she got home.

Needing therapy from a friend, she met Karen for coffee, but, of course, since she couldn't tell Karen about Grace or her father or her sister or Hal, she ended up feeling worse.

Saturday night, she might have taken Dylan to see a movie at the mall, a perfect treat for a child who needed things large and bright. But Grace continued to insist that she didn't want to go out with her friends, and when Deborah finished arguing with her about **that,** she felt so bad that she couldn't leave Grace alone.

They had pizza delivered to the house, but it was a joyless dinner, followed by a TiVoed movie that was so violent Deborah turned it off halfway through. Dylan argued that he had seen worse. Grace insisted that **everyone** knew about the violence and Deborah shouldn't have TiVoed it in the **first** place. Both children retreated to their rooms, Dylan to play "Knockin' on Heaven's Door," over and over and over again on his electronic keyboard, until Grace went to Deborah in tears to complain. When Deborah tried to console her, she refused to talk, and when Deborah asked Dylan to stop playing—the music was depressing her, too—he grumbled that his dad would **never** tell him to stop.

After all that, it was no wonder Deborah didn't sleep well. She kept waking to a knot in her belly and the awful thought that she was losing a grip on her life. Things were going from bad to worse, and she couldn't seem to stop the descent.

She hoped Sunday would be better. It was a beautiful day to usher in May. The air was warm and clear, the oaks were beginning to leaf, and the azaleas in the front beds were swelling with buds. Contrary to the random havoc wreaked by storms, when the weather was calm there was a feeling of order. On days like these, she felt more in control.

Over the years, Deborah had taken to making Sunday brunch. She planned it as an anchor for the kids. Traditionally, Sunday was the one day of the week when she had time to cook, when Greg's presence could be counted on, when her parents came by. After Ruth died, Michael had come alone, and now that Greg was gone, the children needed their grandfather all the more.

This Sunday, Michael begged off. He sounded hungover when he called, and Deborah was stretched too thin to let it pass. "What's going on, Dad?"

"What do you mean?"

"You sound . . . bad." She couldn't get herself to say **hungover.**

Michael cleared his throat. "I must be fighting off the same bug the Burkes came in with last week."

"Is that all? I'm thinking of those mornings last week—"

"Those mornings last week had to do with your accident," he shot back, but quickly softened. "This weekend it's just a bug. Thanks for worrying, though. I'll see you in the morning."

He hung up without her mentioning his drinking, leaving her feeling like a total coward—and a complicitous one at that, when she had to tell more half-truths to the kids.

Grace was happy not to have a formal breakfast and returned to her room with half a bagel, but Dylan was upset that Poppy wasn't there. He retreated to **his** room after eating only a bite of the French toast Deborah had painstakingly made.

Alone in the kitchen with the remains of what should have been a family meal, Deborah was more discouraged than ever. When the doorbell rang and she looked out to see the man who had ousted her from the funeral, she wondered what else could go wrong. Already a coward in her own mind, she decided simply not to open the door.

That plan was thwarted by Dylan. Hoping against hope that his father had come, he bolted from his room and came running down the steps. Halfway down, he lost his footing and tumbled the rest of the way. Deborah helped him up and had to physically hold him still to make sure he was all right. But Dylan was dogged. Pulling away from her the instant she would allow it, he opened the door before she could stop him. Instantly crestfallen, he said, "Oh. I thought you were my dad." Sliding Deborah a woeful look, he plodded back up the stairs.

Resigned, she let the man in. As she remembered, he was tall and had his brother's sable hair and eyes. Yesterday's dark suit had been replaced by a pair of slacks and a lavender shirt, open at the throat and rolled at the sleeves.

"I'm sorry," he said to his credit after a glance at the now-empty staircase.

Deborah kept her chin up. "Not your fault."

"Is this a bad time?"

"That depends," she warned and, having nothing to lose, added, "It's been a bad week. Quite honestly, I'm feeling a little battered. So if you've come to say that I shouldn't have gone to the funeral, please don't. I got your message Friday."

"That was too harsh. I came to apologize."

Startled, she drew back. **I'm** the one who should be apologizing. That was what I was trying to say Friday."

"Yes."

"I really am sorry about the accident. It was a very bad driving night." In that instant, she forgot Friday's humiliation and was glad he had come. This was the condolence call she hadn't been allowed to pay. "I'm sorry for your loss. And sorry for Calvin's wife. How is she doing?"

"She's okay. Upset. Angry."

Angry made Deborah think of lawsuits, which made her think of Hal. If he hadn't wanted her talking to John, he would not want her talking to this man.

But Hal wasn't here. And Deborah wasn't entirely naïve. "Did she send you?"

"Selena? No."

"Does she know you're here?"

"No. And she wouldn't be happy if she did. I came because I'm trying to understand what happened." To his credit, he look genuinely puzzled. "I read the police report. Did you not see him at **all?**"

"Not until the second before impact. It was dark and pouring."

"But he was running. You should have seen movement. Were you and your daughter talking? Distracted somehow?"

"Like putting on lipstick?" she asked, referring to his remark at the cemetery. She pointed at her mouth. "Do you see lipstick here?"

He gave a small smile. "This is Sunday morning. You're at home."

"That was Monday night, and I was **heading** home," Deborah countered. "Why would I be putting on lipstick? I'm sorry, but I can't help you there. We were watching the road, **both** of us, which is what you do in weather like that. If Cal was running without reflective gear, we wouldn't have seen him in the rain. It's as simple as that."

The brother didn't give up. "Did you talk with him while he was lying there in the woods?"

"I kept calling his name, kept begging him to open his eyes, kept telling him to hang in there, that help was on the way."

"Did he respond in any way?"

"You said you read the police report."

"Police reports can be wrong."

His eyes were very dark. Deborah could

no more look away from them than she could keep her mouth shut. "Only if the person filing them lies about whether we talked. Why would I lie about that?"

"It's a good question."

"Here's another," she said, piqued. "Why was he running that night? Why in that rain?"

Again, that small smile. "Those are two questions."

His answer provoked her. "Here's a third. Did you know he was on Coumadin?"

His smile faded. "No. It looks like he chose not to tell me."

"Why wasn't he wearing a med alert bracelet?"

"He wasn't planning on being hit."

She touched her chest. "I wasn't planning on it either, which is why people carry medical IDs where**ever** they go. We might have saved him. His wife must have known he was on Coumadin. Why didn't she say something?"

"I can't answer for Selena."

"Then why wouldn't your brother talk? The doctors said he was conscious. I have patients on Coumadin and, trust me, they'd say that first thing. If they didn't, I'd wonder if they weren't self-destructive." She regretted the word the instant it left her mouth. "I'm sorry. I shouldn't have said that."

"Why did you?" he asked sharply.

"Because I don't understand this either, and it's wreaking havoc with my family." Pushing her hair back, she tried to find conciliatory words. None came, and when the brother did nothing to break the silence, she continued. "I keep taking responsibility for the accident, but am I the only one who is? Why didn't your brother make sure he could be seen on the road, or let the doctors know he was on Coumadin? Why didn't his wife tell the doctors if he couldn't tell them himself? Why didn't you know he was on Coumadin?"

"The answer is another question. Should I have been responsible for knowing? Are there limits to responsibility?" He was looking at her in a challenging way.

She held up a hand. "If you think I have answers, think again. In any case, my lawyer wouldn't want me talking with you."

"Why have you hired a lawyer?"

"Not hired. He's a friend. For what it's worth, he advised me not to go to the funeral. He said I might upset the widow. Apparently, I did."

The brother waved dismissively. "She was upset before the funeral."

"I can understand that." Deborah didn't know whether death was worse than having one's husband walk out on a day's notice, but there was certainly a finality to the former. "Will she stay in town?" When the brother didn't answer, she said, "They haven't lived here long, at least not by Leyland standards. Does she have friends elsewhere?"

"I really don't know."

"Does she have family?"

"I . . . don't know."

"Do you have any family besides Cal?"

The brother shook his head.

That made McKenna's death even more tragic. "He was a great history teacher," Deborah said. "My daughter liked him. He was very bright. It's a loss for the town."

"He was actually **brilliant.** It's a waste. And yes, I'd guess that Selena will stay here until things are settled."

Again, the specter of a lawsuit. Deborah realized Hal would definitely not want her talking to this man and was about to ask him to leave when she heard footsteps on the stairs. Dylan was coming down, one hand on the banister now and each foot carefully placed. Something was wrong.

"Sweetie?"

His eyes rose. "I can't move my arm."

Determinedly calm, she met him at the

bottom of the stairs and began probing his elbow.

He gasped. "Ow!"

"It's dislocated," she said in dismay.

"Again?" His eyes, magnified by his glasses, were glistening with tears. "Why does this keep **happening** to me, Mom?"

"Because you're loose-jointed. That's a good thing in most every other regard."

"Don't snap it back," he ordered. "It **hurts.**"

"Only for a split second. Come on." Deborah glanced at Cal McKenna's brother but didn't know how to tell him to go. So she simply led Dylan to the kitchen, sat him on a chair, and efficiently snapped his elbow back into place. He yelled at the pop, and whimpered while the pain faded. Bent over him, she kept his head pressed to her until she felt him relax. Then she cupped his face and kissed his forehead. "Better?"

He mumbled a begrudging, "It would have been worth it if Dad was the one at the door. Is he ever coming to visit?"

"He will. You'll see him next weekend."

"Up there, because the puppies are there, but I want him **here.**" Rebecca's golden retriever had had pups two weeks before and Dylan had been talking about them ever since, which made his comment all the more poignant.

Deborah didn't know what to say.

Dylan slid off the chair and left the room, walking right past Tom McKenna, who had been watching from the kitchen door.

"That must have hurt," he remarked when the boy was gone.

Hurt him? Or me? Deborah might have asked, but she was feeling dizzy. Suddenly clammy, she sat down and hung her head between her knees.

"Are you all right?" came a distant voice.

After a minute, when the risk of fainting had passed, she straightened up.

"You're very pale," he said.

"At least I'm still sitting here. I've been known to pass out on the floor."

"Doctors don't pass out."

"Moms do. I have trouble when my kids are in pain." She rubbed the back of her neck and took a slow, full breath. "Panicking doesn't help," she said aloud. It was a mantra of sorts. "Dylan's fine now."

"He doesn't need to ice the elbow?"

"No."

"He seems like a vulnerable child."

"He is."

"Bad eyes?"

"He's always been severely farsighted. When he was seven, he developed lattice dystrophy in his right eye. It's a disorder of the cornea where lines form on its back side. They grow thicker and coalesce, so vision in that eye gets very hazy. We can't do anything about the dystrophy until he's old enough for a corneal transplant, but the results are remarkable. If the dystrophy returns after that, it can be treated successfully with lasers." With a dry glance, she pushed herself from the chair. "Not that you wanted to hear any of that."

"I asked," he said. "It must be hard for the boy."

Taking a glass from the cabinet, she filled it with ice water from the refrigerator door. After several sips, she turned. "He has trouble with things, like stairs and baseballs."

"And divorces."

A week ago, she might have winced. Now Greg's leaving seemed minor compared to the other problems in her life. Helpless, she gestured toward the food still on the table. "Hungry? There's plenty left over. Brunch was not exactly a success."

"It smells good. You have enough for an army."

"Kind of like throwing a party and having no one come," she said.

"I find that hard to believe. To hear tell, everyone in this town loves you."

"I don't know about that. But I've lived here all my life."

"My sister-in-law says your husband wanted to move, but you refused to go."

Deborah took another small drink before saying, "That's right."

"Was that what broke up the marriage?"

"Absolutely not," she said, though for a time she had blamed it on that.

"She says your kids want you home more, but that you insist on working, and that your father sends you out to see patients at their homes, so that he doesn't have to share an office with you."

Deborah wasn't about to dignify the charges with a reply. "Your sister-in-law is upset. She's angry. But right now, my family's suffering on several fronts."

Footsteps sounded in the hall. Seconds later, Grace came through the kitchen door. One look at the man there, and she screamed.

Hurrying over, Deborah slipped an arm around her waist. She could feel the girl trembling, much as she had right after the accident. "It's okay, sweetie."

Grace was ashen. **"Mr. McKenna?"**

"Not your teacher. His brother."

She continued to stare at him. "What's he doing here?"

"He's trying to understand what happened, just like we are."

Looking at her mother, Grace whispered, "He's come to haunt me."

Deborah managed a small smile. "Absolutely not. He's come to make sure we're okay." In a roundabout way, she supposed it was true. At least, that was the outcome of his visit. If he had a lawsuit in mind, he had learned there were two sides to this story. The Coumadin made Cal McKenna's death much more complicated.

"I'll be leaving," Tom said quietly, looking at Deborah. "No need to show me out."

Breaking away from her mother, Grace ran into the hall to make sure the stranger had left. She stood at the sidelight, peering out as his car pulled away.

"That was interesting," said her mother.

"It was horrible!" Grace didn't realize she was biting her nail until her mother pulled her hand from her mouth. "He looks **just** like Mr. McKenna."

"They're definitely related. This one seems more solid."

"What do you mean?"

"Physically more solid. Your teacher was very thin. At the open house last fall, he kept doing this nervous thing with his finger, like he was scratching a bug bite on his scalp." She imitated it.

"Not scratching a bite," Grace corrected. "Picking his brain. He did that when he was thinking."

"His brother didn't do it the whole time he was here."

Grace cringed. "The **whole** time? How long did he stay?"

"Ten, fifteen minutes."

"Making sure we were okay?" Grace didn't believe it for a minute. "He knows."

"Knows what?"

"About the accident. He was staring at me."

"You were staring at him. And you screamed."

But Grace persisted. "He knows there's more to the accident than we're telling anyone. Did he ask about me?"

"No."

"I guess that would have been too obvious."

Her mother gave her a squeeze. "He does not know. In fact, he wanted to know if the reason I didn't see his brother was because I was putting on lipstick."

Grace stared at her, then actually laughed. "He asked that? I mean, he obviously doesn't know you. What a **chauvinist.**"

"Uh-huh. So. Want to take the car and drive me to Karen's?"

Grace sobered. "No."

"Danielle wants to talk."

"I can't."

"What about Megan? You could drive there."

"This isn't like getting back on a bike, Mom. People don't die when you hit them with a bike. Thanks, but I don't want to drive. It's bad enough when we pass that place on the road and you're driving."

"You have to do it sometime," her mother coaxed.

"Sometime I will."

"Nothing gets solved when you shut yourself off from the world. Your dad really wants to help."

Grace snorted. "He wants to think he's helping, because that's part of his new image."

"At least he's trying. You could give him a chance."

"Like he gave you? Did he give you even

the tiniest clue that he was planning to leave? Did he tell you he had loved Rebecca before he met you, or that they'd kept in touch? Did he tell you Rebecca even **existed?"** She felt horrid when her mother's face fell. "I'm sorry, Mom. I know it hurts, but it hurts me, too."

Her mother collected herself, spine straightening. "Maybe we need to accept what's happened and move on. Same with the accident."

"I can't forget I killed Mr. McKenna."

"You didn't kill him. He bled to death because no one knew he was on Coumadin."

"His life still ended. It's over. I **can't** forget that."

Deborah hugged her. "I'm not suggesting you forget anything, not the accident and not the divorce. I'm just saying that staying angry at Dad is as counterproductive as continuing to blame yourself for the accident. Locking yourself in your room accomplishes nothing."

"I feel safe there," Grace said quietly.

"Safe from whom?"

"The world. People staring, maybe knowing things they shouldn't."

"I'm not the world. What happened to your hanging out down here?"

"This is your space. My room is mine." The words came easily. Grace had always thought she was different from her friends, because she really **liked** her mother, but there was this thing between them now.

"Since when is there a dividing line?" Deborah asked.

"Since you decided to take responsibility for something I did and won't listen to how I feel about it. It's awful wondering when someone's going to find out the truth."

"But the truth is a technicality, Grace," her mother insisted, doing **exactly** what Grace had just said, which went to prove that she **wasn't** listening. "I was still the driver of record. There's no point in your hiding away."

"Like you're not?" Grace threw back, angry again. "You haven't been at the gym since it happened."

"When have I had time to go to the gym?" Deborah asked.

But Grace wasn't falling for that. "When do you **ever** have the time, but you're still there five days a week. You say it's good that people see you, so they'll know you're not just blowing hot air when you tell them **they** should exercise. But you haven't been there since the accident."

"I wanted to spend more time with you. You've had me worried. I wish you'd gone to the party last night."

Grace squeezed her eyes shut. "No, you don't."

"When something bad happens," Deborah said, "you need to put space and experience between past and present. Doing things with your friends will help. They were all at the party last night."

"So was a keg," Grace said, because it was the only sure way she could shut her mother up.

Deborah stared at her. Then her shoulders sagged. "You knew?"

"**All** the kids knew."

"What about Kim's parents?"

"They were taking car keys. We've talked about this, Mom. You know it happens."

"But these are **your** friends."

"And we're supposed to be different?" Grace cried in exasperation. Her mother expected her to have tons of friends, get good grades, and run faster than anyone else— which was totally delusional. Grace couldn't be perfect. Neither could her friends. "Everyone slept over at Kim's, girls upstairs, boys down."

"That doesn't make it right."

"Lots of things aren't right, but they still happen. You're saying it's okay I was driving, as long as no one knows. So if no one who wasn't at Kim's party knows about the keg, isn't that okay? If people sleep off what they drink before driving again, what's the harm? The harm," she went on, feeling a rising tightness in her chest, "is when you drive after you've had a couple of drinks and you don't tell anyone and something **happens,** like a man being killed. **That's** when it's **really** bad." Her throat closed. Head bent, hair falling forward, she covered her face with her hands and started to cry.

There it was. Out!

She wept softly, bracing for her mother's anger and disappointment. She wanted to be punished, because drinking and driving was a really bad thing to do, and keeping it a secret from her mother was like having a piece of broken glass in her gut.

"Oh, Grace," Deborah said softly.

"It's awful," Grace sobbed. "I mean, none of us meant any harm, and it wasn't anything more than beer, and it's like all the kids do this."

Her mother stroked her hair. "I know what peer pressure's like, but I still think you need to be with friends again. Maybe last night wasn't the right time. For what it's worth, sweetie, I'm glad you didn't go."

It was a minute before the words registered, and a minute more before Grace understood. Her mother hadn't heard. Her confession had gone nowhere. Deborah didn't get it. She refused to see.

And Grace couldn't say it again.

Still crying, she said, "Why did Mr. McKenna's brother have to **come** here? This is **our** house, and now it's like . . . like . . . we've been violated."

"That's being overly dramatic, sweetie. He came to our house because this is where we are, and he asked questions about that night, because, in his grief, that's one of the few things he can do. He's trying to figure out why his brother was out in the rain Monday night."

Grace barely heard the last. Feeling more alone than she ever had in her life, she turned and headed for the winding staircase that had been built with her own fairy-tale wedding in mind—or so her father had always said, right along with how much he loved his wife, his children, and his house, as he was running out the door to go to work. But now her parents were divorced and Dylan couldn't see and her mother still thought Grace was perfect, but there was still the beer—two cans—and Mr. McKenna was still dead.

She just didn't know what to do.

Chapter 9

Breakfast Monday morning was a silent affair.

"Doin' okay?" Deborah asked Dylan when he hadn't said a word, but he only nodded.

She bent down so he was forced to look at her. "Eyes okay?" He had been blinking earlier—had actually been blinking a lot lately—and no matter how many times she told herself that she had a roster of children with problems more serious than his, which would be solved in two or three years at most, it didn't help. As a mother, she couldn't bear the thought that his eyes were getting worse.

He nodded again and, though she didn't quite believe him, she couldn't let her own fear create a problem where perhaps none existed. So she simply straightened and asked, "Cereal okay?"

He nodded a third time and went back to it.

Grace was no better. She kept her head bent over her French book.

Deborah rested a hand on her shoulder. "Test today?"

"Mm."

"Tough one?"

"Mm."

Discouraged by the terseness, Deborah gave her shoulder a playful squeeze. "Anything else?" When Grace looked up blankly, she said, "In school? Today?"

Her daughter shook her head and returned to her notebook.

The drive into town was only marginally better. At first glance, Grace appeared to be still studying. Then, Deborah realized that though her head was bent over the book, her eyes weren't on the page. Deep in thought, she jumped when Deborah touched her hand.

"This week will be better," Deborah said softly.

"How?"

"Less raw."

"Do you feel less raw?" the girl asked accusingly.

Deborah considered her answer. "Yes. I do. That doesn't mean I'm not upset or that my stomach doesn't still churn when I realize Mr. McKenna is dead. It doesn't mean I'm not grieving." Desperate to open a door to discussion, she added, "You're right to be feeling what you do, Grace. You wouldn't be the sensitive person you are if you didn't."

Her daughter turned away.

"I mean that," Deborah said, but Grace didn't look up, and in the ensuing silence, Deborah wondered if she had said the right thing. She had moments when she wondered if she'd **done** the right thing the previous Monday night. Grace had always been such a happy child, always positive, always a talker. Now she was silent.

Deborah missed their former closeness.

She had wanted to validate what Grace was feeling, but the girl didn't speak again until Dylan left the car. Then she looked at Deborah and said in a cool voice, "I shouldn't have told you about the keg. Are you going to tell anyone?"

Deborah's heart ached. "I **want** you to tell me things like that. You **can** confide in me. Anything you say stops here."

"If you tell anyone, my friends will hate me."

"Have I ever violated your trust?"

"I wasn't even there," Grace cautioned, "so

I don't know for sure that there really was a keg. If there wasn't, you'd get me in trouble for nothing. Everything is hard enough without that."

"The accident was an accident, sweetie. You aren't in trouble for that."

"Will you hear about the police report today?"

"I don't know. But there **is** nothing to worry about. We were not driving recklessly."

"**We** were not driving at all. Will the report tell who was?"

Deborah pulled up at the high school curb. "I . . . don't see how."

"My fingerprints were on the wheel," Grace said.

"The police aren't looking for fingerprints," Deborah reasoned. "They assume I was driving. They haven't asked about you. Besides, I touched the wheel after you did. I held it when I reached back in to take the registration from the glove box."

"Deliberately?" Grace asked, sounding dismayed.

Deborah felt instantly guilty. "No. I only realized it afterward." She took a shaky breath. "Don't look at me like that, sweetheart. I didn't plan this. Had the police ever asked who was driving, I'd have told them.

I've always valued honesty. You know that." Grace made a sputtering sound. "The lack of it here eats at me just as much as it eats at you. I made the decision I thought was right. It may not have been, but it is what it is."

Grace said nothing at first. She looked at her book, then at the school. When her eyes finally turned back to Deborah, they held a dare. "So, are you going to the gym later?"

"Yes," Deborah promised. "Definitely."

Deborah wasn't hiding. Keeping a low profile, perhaps. But given Cal McKenna's death, this was appropriate.

Following Grace's remarks, though, she saw things differently. She made her usual morning stop at the bakery and deliberately greeted everyone by name. When a woman asked how she was doing, she said tentatively, "Gettin' there." She settled into her usual armchair, drank her coffee and ate her pecan roll while she skimmed the **New England Journal of Medicine.** She was in full public view. No one could accuse her of hiding.

"Anything good there?" Jill asked. Wearing bright yellow today, she put her own drink on the table and sat. "Anything new on what a pregnant woman shouldn't be doing? No wine. No fish. No red meat. No artificial sweetener. No caffeine. No sleeping on the right side, or is it the left? No painkiller stronger than Tylenol. Talk about a novel method of birth control—give women so many rules, and they figure having more kids isn't worth it."

Deborah smiled and glanced at the trio behind the counter filling orders. "Does anyone here know?"

"No. I just rolled out a batch of Stickies, like I do every morning, and no one can tell I'm drinking decaf instead of high-test. I'm expanding our Smoothie options, but that could as well be for summer as for me. Mango. Blueberry. Raspberry. This is definitely the season to be pregnant."

"I really wish you'd tell Dad. He could use a boost. It was a rough weekend."

"Rough how?"

"He missed his first couple of patients Saturday morning, and didn't make it to brunch yesterday."

"That's surprising," Jill remarked dryly. "Last time I was there, he was going through mimosas like he couldn't live without them."

"Maybe he can't," Deborah said. "He worries me sometimes. He spends his evenings alone."

"Drinking."

Deborah nodded. "He misses Mom."

"So do I, but I'm not getting soused to fill the void."

"You weren't married to her for forty years."

"No, but she was still my mom. **And** my business partner. We talked about having a bakery way back when I was still at school. Bet you didn't know that."

"I didn't," Deborah said in surprise.

"I thought it was the perfect thing for me, because I'd always loved helping Mom in the kitchen, and being a baker didn't require an advanced degree. Little did I know how much I'd have to learn about **business.** But Mom had faith. Poor thing, she was always walking a fine line with Dad when it came to me."

Deborah realized that Ruth Barr had walked a fine line about lots of things. Michael wasn't a tyrant. He was simply a man with definite opinions. Ninety-eight percent of the time he was right. The other two inevitably had to do with family expectations.

Deborah finished eating and wiped her hand on a napkin. "Did Mom ever outwardly lie?"

"I doubt it," Jill said. "She just didn't say what he didn't need to know."

"Right. So should we confront him with the drinking?"

"That depends. How bad is it?"

"He drinks himself to sleep at night."

"Every night?"

"Most, I'd guess." Deborah sat back. "He lacks a focus. Tell him about the baby, Jill. I think it would help."

"My baby should be a focus for his anger at life?"

"It could give him a new reason to live."

"Hey, if he doesn't have enough of that on his own, my baby won't help. It could stoke the anger."

"Maybe. Maybe not."

"Does the drinking affect his work?"

Deborah sipped her coffee, then lowered the cup. "He oversleeps. He's a little rough around the edges when he first gets up."

"Does it impair him as a doctor?"

"Not yet. And I do watch that. Can you imagine what would happen if he botched a diagnosis because he was taking nips from his desk drawer?" It was a viable fear, good reason right there for malpractice insurance. "Since last week, he's been fixated on **my** reputation. What about his? What about mine, if he does something wrong. Maybe I should talk to him. I use the word **en-**

abler with my patients all the time. Am I enabling Dad?"

Jill held up her hand and rose. "I'm not goin' there, Deborah. I don't know what Dad's doing because he keeps me at arm's length. Do you serve Dad his booze? No. Do you encourage him to drink? No. Are you denying that there may be a potential problem? In speaking to him, yes, because you're terrified of a confrontation. I would be, too, if I were in your shoes. See, that's where I'm the lucky one. Your life is entwined with his. Mine is not."

"Of course it is," Deborah argued, because fair was fair. She was thinking about Jill's rebellion at home and in school, even regarding the conception of her child. "So much of what you **do** is in defiance of him. It always has been. Talk of denial . . ."

"There's a difference," Jill pointed out with the wisp of a smile. "Deny his drinking, and you stand to pay the price. Deny his influence over me, and I pay nothing."

A short time later, Deborah pulled up at the house. If her father's behavior over the weekend was a prediction of what today would be like, she was in for a fight. Girding herself, she went into the kitchen.

And there he was, wide awake and hearty, sitting at the kitchen table. He had dressed, made his coffee, and was nursing a mug while he read the paper. Not only had he eaten his bagel, but he had toasted it first, to judge from the dark crumbs on his plate.

"Good morning," she said with relief.

"Good morning yourself," he said with a smile. "Kids get off okay?"

"They did." She leaned against the door. "You're looking good. Is that a new tie?"

He glanced down, took the tie in his hand. "Your mother got it for me shortly before she took sick. I haven't wanted to wear it." He looked up and winked. "She's telling me I need to get my act together and that this tie will help. Think it will?"

Deborah's smile grew. "Definitely." She was **so** relieved—as much to see her father his old buoyant self, as to have escaped the unpleasantness of a fight. "What else did she say?"

"That I've been wallowing in self-pity." He raised an eyebrow.

"That may be. What else?"

"That my missing those early appointments on Saturday was inexcusable."

Deborah waved a hand. "Inexcusable? I'd settle for . . . disappointing to those patients who would much rather see you than me."

"She also said I should have been at brunch yesterday."

An interesting point, that one. Had he been at brunch, Deborah might not have been able to talk with Cal McKenna's brother the way she had.

Not wanting to go there, she simply said, "We missed you. Last week was a hard one. The kids suffered as much as I did. Brunch fizzled without you."

He looked genuinely contrite. "I'm sorry. I **was** wallowing in self-pity. Your mother was right."

Deborah gave him a hug, absorbing the strength she remembered from her childhood. And it turned out to be a good morning at the office. May meant pollen, which brought a rush of patients with acute allergy attacks. Between those and the typical Monday morning emergencies, the four examining rooms accommodated a revolving door of patients, with Michael and Deborah shuttling from one to the next.

Fortunately, the receptionist was able to put off two house calls until Tuesday, allowing Deborah to see patients in the office after lunch as well. All of these were for annual wellness visits, and since Deborah liked to talk in depth with each patient, she was actually grateful when a last-minute cancellation called in. The break enabled her to finish up the last of the blood work herself before settling in at her desk.

Navigating around insurance companies was one of the least favorite parts of her job, and it was getting worse by the year. Her father, definitely old school in his approach, had even less patience filling out forms than she did. Deborah had finished the first and begun a second when Michael appeared at her door. No longer the cheery guy of the morning, he had a tense hand on the knob and an ominous look on his face.

"Dean LeMay just called," he said. "He wants to know why you blew his wife off last week."

Deborah felt a jolt. "I didn't blow her off." She vividly recalled the visit. "I simply told her she needed to lose weight."

"Dean says you were wholly unsympathetic about her arthritis. He says you told her she was imagining a broken bone just to give her an excuse not to move."

"I never said that."

"He says you told her that she needed to get off her butt and get a job."

"She does."

Michael's cheeks reddened. "Did you **say** that?"

Feeling the sting of his reproach, Deborah said, "Absolutely not, certainly not in those words. I talked gently with her, but it wasn't a discussion we haven't had before. She refuses to admit how overweight she is and that it does affect her ankles. I suggested she try walking even the littlest bit around the house, which is what the specialist suggests as well. She sits in the kitchen, Dad. Eating. I suggested a part-time job as a way to get her out of the house."

"Dean considers that an insult to his earning ability."

"That's his problem."

"It's ours, if they decide to switch doctors."

Deborah felt a spurt of anger. "Is it? I'm not paid for the time I spend driving to Darcy's house. If she doesn't like what I say, let her find a doctor who'll drive out there and say what she wants. If she thinks arthritis is bad, let her try diabetes or heart disease, because that's where she's headed."

Michael pushed off from her door. "I told Dean I'd get back to him once I knew the facts. What do you want me to tell him?"

Deborah was still smarting. "Why did he call you? Why didn't he call me directly?" She held up a hand. "Okay. I guess he's between a rock and a hard place. Darcy needs a scapegoat. I'm the nearest one." Her phone rang.

"What do I tell him?" her father repeated.

Deborah put a hand on the receiver. The incoming call was on their private line, which meant it was either the kids or Jill or one of a few friends who had the number. "That I spent a long time talking with Darcy, precisely because I **don't** blow off clients, but that her weight is an ongoing issue, and you and I would both welcome a talk with the two of them if they'd like to come in." She waited only until her father turned away before picking up the phone.

"Hello," she said with a lingering edge.

"Uh-oh," came Karen's tentative voice. "Want me to call back another time?"

Deborah let out a breath. "No, no, K. This is fine. I was just having an unpleasant discussion about one of our patients." Dean LeMay's call still rankled, but she forced herself to relax. "Are you okay?"

"Well, the elbow is better, which means you were right, but that means I have to ease up from tennis, which doesn't thrill me. Anyway, I'm really calling about two other

things. First, how's Grace? Danielle keeps trying to get her to talk, but she won't even text
message."

"She's going through a hard time."

"Dani may drive over tonight."

Deborah welcomed that. "She's an angel.
I hope Grace will give in. Tell Dani not to
give up."

Karen made a sputtering sound. "Oh, she
won't. She loves you guys." Her voice sobered.
"The second thing is Hal. Is he there?"

"Here? No. Why?"

"He said he was meeting with you to talk
about Cal McKenna."

Deborah's pulse raced. "Did he hear something from John?"

"Not that I know of."

"He didn't mention the accident report?"

"No. He just kind of said in passing that
he'd be seeing you. He didn't seem worried."

Deborah relaxed a bit. "Well then, he just
hasn't gotten here yet."

"His secretary's trying to reach him. He
isn't answering his cell phone."

"Maybe he's playing golf?"

"Not on a Monday afternoon. And not
without telling me."

Deborah knew what she was thinking. It
had nothing to do with the possibility of a car

accident and everything to do with the phone call Karen had received the week before.

"Has she called again?" Deborah asked softly.

"No." Karen's voice lowered. "But something's up. He snaps at little things I do, like putting the empty recycle bins back in the garage in the wrong order. Or separating junk mail from the rest and throwing it out. I've been doing that for years. Last night, he told me that maybe there was something in one of those ads that he wanted, and I shouldn't take it upon myself to censor his mail. **Censor** his mail?"

"Maybe something's going on at work," Deborah tried. The intercom buzzed. "A tough prosecutor? A difficult client?"

"I don't know. He hasn't said. I can only ask so many questions before he gets annoyed. Maybe he's just going through a midlife crisis. I think that's it." She paused. "Don't you?"

"Could be."

"Then that's it," Karen decided. "Thanks, Deb. You're always a help."

Deborah hadn't done a thing—and was feeling guilty for that, too. "If he shows up here, I'll have him call you." The receptionist buzzed her again. "Give him a little more time, sweetie. He may not even realize his cell phone is off."

Hal swore by his cell phone. If it was off, it was by design. Deborah guessed that Karen knew this, too, but neither woman was ready to say it aloud.

"I'm sure that's it," Karen said, "and you need to get that call. Want to have coffee later?"

"Can't. I promised Grace I'd work out at the gym," the important part being **at the gym.** "Want to meet me there and do side-by-side ellipticals?"

"Name a time."

"Four-thirty."

"Perfect. Go get that call."

Deborah punched in the button. "Yes, Carol?"

"I have Tom McKenna on line three. He isn't a patient. He says it's personal."

Personal was one word for it. There were others, like **risky,** meaning that she shouldn't be talking with him. But he had been friendly enough Sunday morning, and if he had news about Cal's Coumadin use, she wanted to know.

"I'll take it," she said and pressed the button.

His voice held a now-familiar resonance. "Bad time?"

"No. It's fine. I'm just finishing. What's up?"

"I'm afraid I shocked your daughter yesterday. Is she okay?"

Two shows of concern in as many days? Deborah was wary. She couldn't forget the scene at the cemetery, **surely** couldn't forget that it was her car that had led to his brother's death.

But he did sound sincere. So she said, "You're kind to ask. She's okay. She's still agonizing over the accident, but I think she accepts that you're not Cal's ghost. You do look a lot like him."

There was a pause, then a lighter, "We took after our mother."

"Were you close?"

"Not to our mother," he said.

"To each other?"

"On and off." He hesitated, before adding a resigned, "Mostly off. Our personalities were totally different."

Naturally curious, Deborah asked, "In what ways?"

There was a short silence. She was thinking that she might have overstepped her bounds, and that he would change the subject, when he offered a reflective, "He liked things in order. He liked knowing what was going to happen. That's why he liked history. Read a history book, and there are no surprises. You know how it's going it end. Cal liked neatness. His house was the same, spare and organized, each piece of furniture in its place, books neatly arranged, three nautilus shells evenly spaced across the mantel. He liked precision."

Encouraged by the sheer length of his response, Deborah asked, "And you?"

"I'm a slob."

It was so blunt, and unexpected, that she laughed. "Are you serious?"

"Very."

"Was that in a reaction to Cal?"

"No. I'm the older brother by four years."

"There's nothing wrong with being a slob."

"There is," he warned, "if it means you can't see through the clutter. I keep thinking I should have known my brother was taking Coumadin."

"How could you know, if he chose not to tell you?"

"We hadn't talked in a while. I shouldn't have let it go so long." His tone eased. "I'm still working on why he was taking the drug. What do you know about it?"

"Coumadin? It's an anticoagulant, most widely used after heart attack or stroke to prevent the formation of blood clots in arteries and veins."

"Do I assume Cal had a heart attack or stroke?"

"No. He may have had a blood clot, in which case Coumadin would have been prescribed to prevent another. He was actually young to have this kind of problem."

"There's a history of it," Tom said. "My father had a massive stroke at forty-eight." He paused, then asked cautiously, "Would Cal have taken Coumadin preventatively?"

"I doubt it. The risk of side effects is too great." She wondered whether he was testing her somehow. But she was a doctor, and, still smarting from Dean LeMay's call, she told Tom what she knew. "Normally, a person with a family history would simply make sure he was checked regularly. He'd keep his weight down and watch things like blood pressure and cholesterol. Did your brother do those things?"

"He was thin. I don't know about the rest."

"Was he worried about taking after his father?"

"We both were."

"Do you take preventive action?"

"No. But we slobs don't like regimentation," he said. "Taking daily pills would drive me nuts. Cal used to pop 'em like candy."

"Drugs?"

"Vitamins. If he used stronger things, I

didn't know. Could he have taken too much Coumadin?"

"Possibly, but even a standard dose can cause bleeding. That's why the warnings are so visible."

"What's the normal dosage?"

"A tablet a day in a strength that varies with the patient. Some people take it for a limited period, say, three to six months. Others take it for life. The latter are usually patients who've had repeated life-threatening episodes. I can't imagine your brother falling into that category without anyone else knowing."

"No," Tom said, then, "How do you know all this? Do you personally prescribe Coumadin? Or did you look it up after Cal died?"

She smiled. "I don't personally prescribe it, but I read journals. I talk with colleagues at conferences. I learn from specialists who see my patients. One thing's for sure. Patients on Coumadin require close monitoring. No doctor would renew a Coumadin prescription without follow-up exams and tests, and those tests wouldn't be done by a generalist like me. If your brother had a condition that warranted his taking Coumadin, he was seeing a specialist. His insurance company would know."

Tom cleared his throat. "Yes. I talked with them this morning. The problem is confidentiality. They won't give out information unless Selena signs a release."

Deborah sensed an edge in the way he said her name. It emboldened her. "Why would she not sign a release? This is information she'll need if she's planning to sue me." And if she was, Deborah reminded herself, Tom would be an adversary. "By the way, my friend, the lawyer, would not be pleased with this conversation. He'd be afraid I might say something that you'll use against me in court. I just want you to know that I'm being as honest as I can. I want answers as much as you do."

"I sense that. That's why I called."

She did hear sincerity. Either he was an amazing actor, or it was there. She figured she had to hear more to decide which it was. "How is Selena doing?"

"I don't know. I haven't talked with her today."

"Oh," Deborah said in surprise. "Aren't you staying with her?"

"God, no. I live in Cambridge."

"Cambridge." That was a surprise. She had assumed Tom lived out of state and was simply here for the funeral. Cambridge was an easy drive. But there was also that **God, no,** which indicated that he didn't adore his sister-in-law. Deborah was more interested in his relationship with his brother. "And you didn't see Cal often?"

"If I had, I might have known more about his health," Tom snapped. "If I'd known more about his health, I might have been able to alert the doctors myself. That's assuming Selena had called me sooner. She might have if Cal and I had been closer. How pathetic is it when two brothers don't know anything about each other's lives?"

Deborah sympathized. "It happens more often than you'd expect."

"Does that make it any less pathetic?"

"No."

There was a brief silence, then a soft, "Thanks."

"For what?"

"Being honest. It's easier to delude ourselves than to be blunt about the truth. I'll bet you're blunt with your family."

She was bemused. "Why do you say that?"

"You seem like an honest person."

How ironic was **that?** It occurred to her that, just possibly, she was being baited. "There's a difference between being blunt and being honest. Blunt can be hurtful. I try to be honest without being hurtful."

"A straight shooter."

Another irony. "Usually."

"When aren't you?"

She took a breath. "When being honest can betray a confidence." Deborah was thinking of this morning's discussion with Grace. "My daughter tells me things about her friends that I have to keep to myself."

"Serious things?"

"Sometimes. It can be tricky. If Grace told me that one of her friends was cutting herself, I'd have a hard time keeping still. Self-mutilation is a cry for help."

"Wouldn't Grace understand that?"

"I'd hope so. She might not want to know the details, like who I called. But she'd probably be relieved to share the responsibility."

"Because she trusts you. Who do you trust? Who do you share your responsibilities with?"

"My dad, when it comes to work."

"What about at home?"

"My sister some. Mostly it's just me."

"Is your ex-husband involved with the kids?"

Definitely, she wanted to say. **He calls**

them all the time. That would have been less humiliating for her. But talk about lies?

"Not actively," she said, trying to keep her voice upbeat. "He's at a different place in his life."

"He still has two children."

"He assumes I can handle it."

"Are you okay with that?"

"Absolutely not," she burst out. "All my **life** the assumption has been that I can handle it, so more and more is piled on. There are times when responsibility sucks!" Just then, she saw Hal at her office door. "Speaking of responsibility, I do have to run. Can I, uh, give you my cell number?" she asked.

"Please," he said, then seconds later, "Got it."

"Will you let me know if you learn anything?"

"Definitely."

Pretending she had been talking to anyone other than the man who could take her to court for killing his brother, she hung up the phone and eyed Hal. He looked somber. She felt a shot of apprehension. "You've talked with John?"

"Earlier," he said. "There's no news. I thought I'd let you know. Thanks to the flu, it may be another week. They're short of staff to interpret the data."

Deborah was discouraged. Much as she could tell herself that Grace had done nothing wrong, she wouldn't rest easy until the state police attested to it. "What if this were a case of a drunk driver plowing into a crowd and killing five people? Would illness slow up the report and allow a menace to stay on the road?"

"No. The menace would be in custody. It's like anything else. Cases are prioritized. Yours isn't particularly urgent."

"Fine for **them** to say," she mused dryly, "but I'm the one sitting in limbo. You, on the other hand, look like you've just come from the spa." His hair was damp and freshly combed, his cheeks faintly flushed.

"Not the spa," he said. "The racquetball court."

Karen's worried voice echoed in Deborah's ear. "Where's that?"

"At a gym in Boston," he smirked, "not far from **the** court."

"I didn't know you played racquetball."

"I don't. But several of my friends are really into it. I did a test run to see if it was something I wanted to do."

"And?" she asked, thinking that a gym in Boston would provide long-term cover.

"It might be," he said, looking pleasantly surprised. "I mean, did I ever sweat! As cardio workouts go, it's a good one. Whaddya think? Should I join?"

"What I think," Deborah said, "is that you should find a local place. Let K play with you."

"K plays tennis," he said smoothly. "She doesn't have time for racqetball."

"She'd make time if you asked."

"And have her beat me? No way." He tipped his head. "Did she call here?"

Deborah nodded.

"I **told** her I'd be in Boston," he complained. "She had my secretary calling all over the place. What is it with her lately?"

"Nothing that answering your cell phone won't solve. What if a client needed to reach you?"

"No client matter is so important that it can't wait an hour."

"If that's true," Deborah said only half in jest, "I may get myself another lawyer. I want to know the instant John calls."

Chapter 10

Deborah returned to the forms on her desk, but her heart wasn't in it. When she wasn't smarting from Dean LeMay's call, she was seeing Hal's slick face or thinking about Cal McKenna. Based on what his brother said, it sounded like Cal was slightly uptight. But wasn't she, too? She liked things neat and well planned. She could identify with the comfort Cal felt knowing how history books would end.

One of the hardest things she'd had to deal with in the first months after Greg left was not seeing the road ahead. Even when divorce papers were in the works, a part of her believed he would wake up and realize how foolish he was being.

She had always blamed him. But with her anger at the divorce diffused now, she could see that fault was relative. Greg and she shared it.

Lying about who was driving on the night Cal McKenna died? That was her doing alone. She felt the stark burden of it when the phone rang a short time later. It was Mara Walsh, the school psychologist. "I know you're probably busy, Deborah. The past week can't have been easy for you. But I'm worried about Grace."

Deborah swallowed. "Why?"

"The other kids are handling Cal McKenna's death quite well. We made our grief team available, but there have been few takers. Everyone liked Cal well enough, but kids didn't identify with his death on the personal level. Some teachers have that special rapport with their students. Cal didn't."

"And Grace?" Deborah asked.

"Grace has a special reason to mourn him. She saw it happen. I figured last week would be tough on her, and the race Saturday, well, that was totally understandable. But I was hoping after the weekend that she'd be better. She isn't. She's ignoring her friends and walking alone with her head down. As body language goes, that makes a statement."

"She's upset," Deborah acknowledged.

"John Colby was just here asking about her."

Deborah's heart began to thud.

"He came by to pick up his wife," Mara said. "She tutors students in reading—"

"I know that, but was he actually asking about Grace?"

"He'd heard from Ellen that she was struggling. He mentioned a party last weekend that she didn't go to."

"Kim Huber's, but how would John know that?"

"He said he talked with Kim's parents. He wanted to know if Grace was okay in school."

"What did you say?"

"Exactly what I just told you, that she was struggling. I'd like to talk with her, Deborah. Would you mind?"

"Of course not," Deborah said—what else **could** she say? "I'm just not sure she'll agree. I'm also not sure that the timing is right. You know how it is, Mara. When kids are singled out for special help, they begin feeling like something's really wrong with them. Grace is going through a rough patch, but I don't think it's anything time won't fix. I don't want her feeling like she's under a microscope."

"I could meet with her after school."

"She has track."

"Then evenings, if she's willing. I'm sure you're talking with her, so anything I say might be redundant. It's just that she was looking so unhappy this morning. I'd like her to know that I'm here if she needs me."

And what could Deborah say to that without being branded the coldest woman in the world? "That's fine, Mara. It's a comfort knowing you're there. Just make it optional, okay? If she isn't ready, she isn't ready."

Grace was on the oval in the stadium, bent over with her hands on her knees and her eyes on the track between her feet. She was dripping with sweat and breathing heavily. Her concentration was shot.

"Good run, Grace," said the coach, trotting up.

"It was terrible," she wheezed, barely looking up.

"Are you kidding? You started off beautifully. You were on your way to a personal best."

"Were. Right. But I didn't finish."

"Hey, you were sick last weekend. That makes today's run remarkable. Keep it up, Grace." He trotted off.

Keep it up, Grace. The words hurt, because she really **had** wanted to run well. She had been concentrating on her breathing and her stride, refusing to let the accident intrude, and she had felt really good. Then she saw John Colby and was ruined. At least, she thought it was him. She couldn't be sure, because he was heading away from her, and lots of guys his age wore khaki shirts and dark pants. But who else would be hanging around the oval at four in the afternoon? He was watching her, because he knew.

"Bonjour, Grace!"

She looked back. Her French teacher was coming toward her down the track.

"I'm glad I caught you," the woman said. "I didn't want to have to call the house."

In a breath, Grace was back in French class that morning, watching her pencil filling the test sheet. She was thinking that it shouldn't be so easy, when suddenly her hand froze and the answers refused to come.

"Can we talk about the test?" Madame Hendricks asked.

Straightening, Grace blinked the French teacher into focus. "Sure," she replied, feeling surprisingly little emotion.

"You didn't do very well," said the teacher.

"I didn't study," Grace lied. Once, such a lie would have been unthinkable.

"That's not like you. You're the top student in all of my sections this year. You knew the material. Even without studying, you should have scored well." When Grace didn't reply, she said, "I was worried you were sick, but you ran well just now. Was something bothering you this morning?"

"I couldn't focus."

"That's not good."

"I know," Grace said.

"Well. It's been a difficult week with Mr. McKenna's death. I've been thinking about this all afternoon. I could have you retake the exam, but we know you'd do well. So let's just set this one test aside. I won't average it in with your other grades. You're too good a student to be penalized for one bad day. Are you comfortable with that?"

Grace was **not.** If any of her friends had done what she had, there would be consequences. They would have to retake the test. They would have to meet with their advisor. Failure was unacceptable in this town. Leyland students were shining stars who would go on to lead spectacularly successful lives.

It made her sick.

But would Madame Hendricks understand this? No. So Grace simply nodded.

"Good. It'll be our little secret. We'll chalk it up to a bad day. **Au revoir, mademoiselle.**"

Looking pleased with herself, she walked away.

Grace stared after her, feeling not at **all** pleased. But it wasn't only the French test that had her upset. Her life used to have boundaries. It used to have certain expectations. But lately, all the rules were being broken. Her father had cheated on her mother. Her mother had lied to the police. Madame Hendricks had created "our little secret." And her friends were buying kegs.

Grace used to know where she stood. She used to know how her life would play out. No more.

At the gym several blocks from the high school, Deborah bobbed on the elliptical trainer. Arms and legs pushing and pulling, she was breathing hard and covered with sweat. She had been at it for forty minutes.

"What are you doing?" Karen asked from the next machine.

Deborah looked up in surprise. "Hm?"

"You look like you're fighting a war."

Deborah forced a smile and said a breathless, "The exertion feels good."

"Maybe for you," Karen said and came to a stop, "but I'm done." She turned off her machine, slid her towel off the hand bar, and mopped her face. "I wouldn't even have done it this long if you hadn't forbidden me to play tennis."

"Not forbidden," Deborah managed, pumping hard. "Advised. It's my job."

Karen ran the towel over her arms. "Want me to wait?"

Deborah shook her head. "Go ahead. I'll do a little more."

Karen blew her a kiss and left. Her machine was taken a minute later by the town librarian, who nodded briefly at Deborah as she adjusted her earphones.

Deborah continued for another ten minutes. Stepping off the machine, she took time to stretch before heading for the locker room.

At the door, she ran into Kelly Huber. A longtime patient of Deborah's, she was the older sister of the same Kim who had thrown the party last Saturday night. Kelly had been Deborah's afternoon cancellation, having called in to say she had a headache.

"Kelly, hi," Deborah said, feeling mellow as her breathing continued to settle. "Welcome home. Is the spring semester done?"

Kelly looked startled to see her, and not terribly happy. "I finished last week."

"You look wonderful," Deborah said.

"You must be feeling better than you did earlier."

"Some," Kelly replied and looked around nervously.

Her mother appeared in the nick of time. Emily Huber's hair was newly highlighted and caught back in a ponytail like her daughter's.

Deborah smiled. "You must be thrilled to have her home." When Emily didn't answer, she turned to Kelly. "Plans for the summer?"

"I'm, uh, not sure. I may be doing an internship." She darted a glance at her mother. "I'm going to start." Giving Deborah an awkward smile, she scooted past.

Deborah had barely processed the awkwardness when Emily said, "That was not a comfortable moment for my daughter."

Deborah frowned. "Because she cancelled her appointment with me?"

"I was the one who cancelled it," the mother said. "After what happened Saturday night, it would be best if she saw someone else. Kim, too. I'll be by for their records later this week."

Deborah was confused. "What happened Saturday night?"

"Did you **have** to call the police?"

"Excuse me?"

"Just because Grace didn't want to come to my daughter's party?"

"I didn't call the police."

"You told **them** it was about the noise, but we both know what it was about. You were hoping they'd send a cruiser to the house," she said, quieting fractionally when a pair of women passed them with curious looks. "But they know Marty and me. They trust us, maybe more than they trust you right now."

"What are you talking about?" Deborah asked with a disturbing thought. There was always a chance that Grace had told Kim the truth.

"The accident last week," Emily said with a hard stare. "Calvin McKenna was one of the best teachers at the high school. He wasn't the kind of man to be out there running recklessly. You must have been driving too fast in the rain—"

"Excuse me," Deborah cut in. "Speed was not involved."

Emily held up both palms. "Okay, but to pretend you did nothing wrong? You call the cops on other people, while you lie to them yourself?"

"What **lie?**" Deborah asked.

"It's classic. You have a few drinks, so you want others to have a drinking problem."

"I don't drink."

"Well, your father does, so it's only a matter of time."

Deborah felt like she'd been hit. "What?"

"Oh, come on," said Emily. "It's well known that Dr. Barr washes his lunch down with something more than a Diet Coke. I wouldn't have said anything if you hadn't called to report us on Saturday night." With a look of disdain she followed her daughter into the gym.

Any mellowness Deborah had taken from her workout was gone. Shaken, she went to her locker, and it wasn't mention of the accident that upset her the most. If her father was drinking at lunch, she didn't know it. If he was, they had a problem.

One of the women who had passed by during Emily's attack stood nearby. When Deborah raised her eyes, the woman looked away.

The accident was public knowledge. But Michael Barr's drinking? It couldn't be. Deborah had never seen as much as a suspicious glass at work, never the least unsteadiness, but how to check it out? She couldn't ask the nurse if she had seen anything, lest it plant a seed of doubt. And the business manager was a frank woman, who would surely have spoken up if she had noticed anything amiss.

Deborah told herself that Emily was only making trouble. But it was one more worry to add to the rest.

Then she checked her cell phone and found a message from Greg.

"Call me," he said.

She might have ignored the order if she hadn't been feeling so alone. Her life was unraveling. It was like she had to catch a thread—**any** thread—or the whole thing would come apart.

In the parking lot behind the gym, she punched in his number.

"Hi," he said pleasantly enough, before going on the attack. "Did you talk with Grace about not answering my call?"

She was a minute getting her bearings. "Yes. I did."

"And?"

"I'm afraid it was more an argument than a talk."

"Who took which side?" he asked.

"That was unnecessary, Greg. I'm on your side in this. I want Grace to talk with you. I just can't force her to do it."

"Why not?" he asked. "Tell her she can't

drive until she has a civil conversation with her father."

"I'm not sure that'll work. She's not interested in driving right now."

"Then take her cell phone away. Tell her she can't have it back until she talks with me."

"Same problem. She hates her cell phone this week."

"Hates her cell phone? What's going on?"

Deborah closed her eyes and pressed them. "Nothing that a little time won't cure." She prayed that was it, prayed that Grace hadn't said anything to Kim.

"Is it still about the accident?" Greg asked—to his credit—more gently.

"It's barely been a week. She knew the man. He was her teacher. She feels guilty."

"Guilty for the accident? She just happened to be in the passenger's seat."

She wasn't, but Deborah couldn't say it, and that was Grace's problem, she realized—the lie. It was the lie that was coming between Grace and Deborah, Grace and Greg, Grace and her friends. The lie had kept Grace from the party Saturday night, which had annoyed Emily Huber. **It was the lie.**

And Deborah was its source.

But what could she do now? The crash report was filed. Her story was on record in three different places, in addition to the **Ledger**'s account. Changing her facts now would only make things worse.

"Maybe Grace should be talking with a therapist," Greg said, interrupting Deborah's thoughts.

"I've been talking with her myself."

"Maybe she needs someone other than you. You may be a doctor, but you're Grace's mother, too. That limits what you can do for her professionally. If you can't get through to her, she needs a counselor."

"The school psychologist and I talked a little over an hour ago," she said defensively. "I still think it's premature, Greg. This just happened. I'm doing the best I can."

"Maybe your best isn't good enough."

Deborah wondered if he was right. She used to believe in herself, but since the accident, her self-esteem had taken a blow. Losing two patients she had really liked didn't help. Nor did it help when people she passed wouldn't look her in the eye—or when there was a suggestion that her father's drinking was a topic of public conversation.

"I had a project manager once," Greg said. "He swore he could handle everything, right up until the time his department fell apart. I don't want that happening to our family."

It was one jab too many. **"Our** family?" she asked with a burst of anger. "It seems to me that you opted out."

"I'm trying to opt back in."

"What does **that** mean?" She was suddenly furious. He had upended their lives in one broad sweep two years before. "We're divorced, Greg. You sold your business, and signed the house and responsibility for the kids over to me. You moved to another state and married another woman. What exactly are you opting back into?"

He swore.

"What?" she asked. "What did I say that was wrong?"

"Nothing," he replied, but more quietly. "You're never wrong, Deborah. You're competent to the extreme. Nothing ever sets you back. You don't need anyone. You sure as hell don't need me."

"Right now, I do. Being a single mother isn't fun."

"You just said I have no place there."

Deborah closed her eyes. "You were the one who left."

"And glad I did, if this conversation is indicative of your feelings for me."

She sighed. "I loved you, Greg."

"You loved having a husband. You loved having kids. I sometimes think that living in Leyland was my mistake. Leyland is Barr turf. If we'd gone to a place where you had no history, you might've needed me more."

Chapter 11

Once dinner was done and Dylan had planted himself in front of the TV, Deborah poked her head into Grace's room, motioned her to remove an earplug, and said, "I'm running into town to discuss something with Poppy."

"Discuss what?" Grace asked warily.

"It's a patient thing," Deborah replied, and indirectly it was.

Grace remained distrustful. "Why tonight? Won't you see him early tomorrow?"

"Yes, but it's something he needs to think about overnight."

"Like what?"

"If I told you that," Deborah chided softly, "I'd be betraying a confidence. I promised you I wouldn't do that."

Grace stared at her for a minute before returning to her iPod, effectively tuning her out.

Moments later, Deborah was backing out of the garage.

Her father had met his friend Matt for dinner, which meant that he wouldn't have been drinking on an empty stomach. Still, by the time she surprised him in the den, his eyes were glazed. The television was on. He had a glass in his hand and a bottle nearby.

Tell him you just happened to be passing by—maybe on your way home from dinner with Karen. Tell him you're just here to use the bathroom.

More lies? She couldn't. Thanks to Emily Huber, Michael's drinking had to be confronted. Taking the remote from the arm of his chair, she lowered the volume.

With an unsteady hand, he held up his watch and struggled to read the time. "Isn't it awful late for you to be here?" he asked.

Leave. He won't even remember you came.

But her father had a problem. **They** had a problem. Speaking quickly, she said, "I had a run-in at the gym earlier with Emily Huber. She was on a tear about my having called the police to report a noisy party. She says she's removing her girls from our practice."

Michael's mouth turned down. "Removing? What does that mean?"

"Transfering their primary care to her own doctor."

"Well, that doesn't make sense." He pulled in his chin. "All because you called the police?"

"I didn't call the police. She just thinks I did."

"What's she got against you?"

"It isn't just me," Deborah said. "She says she doesn't trust you."

"She doesn't trust **me?**" he shouted, sitting straighter. "Why the hell not?"

Deborah took a deep breath. "She claims you drink too much."

There was a moment's brutal silence, then an indignant, "What's she talking about?"

Deborah looked at the bottle.

"Christ, it's almost ten at night. What I do on my own time is none of Emily Huber's goddamned business."

"She says you drink at lunch, which **is** her business."

"I don't drink at work," he thundered. "Emily Huber is making things up. So I ask again, what the hell's she got against you?"

"This isn't about me, Dad. It's about you. I see that bottle here every morning, a new one every few days. That's a lot of whiskey. And you said you thought Mom would be telling you to pull yourself together."

He ignored the last comment. "How in the hell would Emily Huber know I drink? Did you tell her?"

"**Dad,** that's the **last** thing I'd say." Deborah squatted down by his chair. "It's no great mystery how talk starts. You had dinner tonight with Matt. Where'd you go?"

Michael was a minute answering. Finally, he said, "The Depot."

"That's right here in town. Did you drink with dinner?"

"I had one drink. Maybe two, but what business is **that** of anyone's?"

"When people see you drink, especially if you have more than two, it starts rumors."

"Have you ever seen me drunk?"

"No, but I see you the morning after, and you have a splitting headache."

"That headache is from falling asleep in this **goddamned chair.**"

"Which you do after drinking too much."

"How do **you** know?" he bellowed. "You're not here. You don't know what I drink. You don't know **anything** about me."

"You miss Mom," Deborah said quietly.

"Miss? Miss doesn't begin to express it," he roared. "I feel like half of me is gone."

"Drinking won't help," Deborah pleaded.

"Oh?" Defiant, he raised his glass and drained it in a single gulp, but when he went to set it down, he missed his mark. The glass tumbled to the carpet. Deborah retrieved it, but he seemed oblivious. "How could **you** know what helps? You've never been where I am. Your husband up and left you, and you were just fine and dandy, no mourning at all, no missing the guy."

"Dad—"

"Dad what?" he shot back, rising to face her and none too steadily. "You want to talk about my reaction to loss, let's talk about yours. You distance yourself from everyone."

It's the booze, Deborah thought, though the accusation stung. "I came here to talk about drinking."

"Didn't you **feel** anything when Greg left?"

"I felt plenty," she said angrily.

"You didn't show a damned thing."

"How could I?" she cried. Booze or not, he was being unfair. "I had two kids who felt abandoned. I had to play mother **and** father. Would it have been better to just sit looking at the broken pieces of our lives? Someone had to pick them up."

"Which you did without a hitch," Michael

said and looked around for his glass. When he didn't find it, he took another from the bar. "You cut off your hair," he mumbled. "That's all. Cut off your hair." He poured himself another drink.

"Please don't drink," she said.

Staring at her, he took a healthy swallow. "Greg liked your hair long, so you cut it short. That's the only reason. You **liked** your hair long."

"I needed a change."

"You wanted to look feminine," he charged, rapping his wedding band against the glass, "because your husband left you for another woman."

"He wanted another **lifestyle,**" Deborah corrected, close to tears.

"—and you wanted the world to know it wasn't your fault, but it was your fault, Deborah. Men want women who care. Your mother cared. She was always there when I needed her." He drank some more.

"Please don't," Deborah begged.

"She had long hair when I met her," he mused, studying what was left in the glass, "then it got too much to take care of, so she cut it. I liked it short, too, but she wasn't a doctor. A doctor has to be neat."

"I'm a good doctor," Deborah whispered.

"If I'd had a son, he'd have been a doctor."

She swallowed. "You didn't have a son."

"I always wanted a father-son practice."

Her heart was breaking. "You have a father-daughter practice."

He tossed back the rest of his drink. "Same difference."

"It isn't," she said. A sore that had festered for years suddenly burst. "I'm not your son."

He looked up. "What's that?"

"I'm not your son," she repeated more loudly.

He scowled. "What are you talking about?"

"The truth," she said. "I'm not your son. I'm your daughter, and I can only do the best I can. Maybe I'm not perfect, but God knows I've tried, and if I can't meet your expectations, maybe that's a truth I need to accept." She caught her breath. "Here's another truth. You drink too much."

"That's a truth?" He poured more, then turned to her and asked in a dangerously low voice, "Are you saying I lie?"

She was hurt enough to stand firm. "I'm saying you're in denial."

"Hah!" he said with a gesture that sent whiskey splashing from his glass. "Look who's in denial! You blame Greg for wrecking your marriage. Think your kids don't feel that?"

"Dad."

"And **you're** not setting a lousy example?"

"Please, Dad."

"Please, **what?**"

"You drink too much.

"See?" he said with a half smile. "That's what I mean. Here I am talking about emotional things, and all you can say is, 'Dad, you drink too much.' I don't drink too much," he scoffed. "And if I have a drink or two to take the edge off of sitting here alone? All it says is I'm human." He raised his glass in a toast. "You could take a lesson from that."

"Please, Dad."

His glass came down with a bang. "I don't tell you what to do off-hours. Don't tell me." He took another swallow and grabbed the remote. "Discussion done." Raising the volume, he sank back into his chair.

Heavyhearted, Deborah returned to her car and backed out of the drive. She didn't pass anyone during the short drive home and, once in the garage, was too exhausted to get out of the car.

In time the overhead light went off.

She sat in the dark until the door to the

house opened. Grace stood there, silhouetted by the hall light, her hair a mass of curls framing her head, her slender body visibly tense.

"Mom?" she called loudly.

Deborah opened the car door and stepped out. "Hey, sweetie," she said when she reached the landing.

"Why were you sitting there?"

"I was comfortable."

"In the garage?" Grace asked. "If there was carbon monoxide, you could die." She gave extra emphasis to the **y** sound at the end.

"The car's off. There's no carbon monoxide." Wiped out, Deborah walked past the girl. She didn't touch her. Touching hadn't seemed to help.

"Where were you?"

"Poppy's. I told you that." She took out a mug and filled it with hot water. "I had to talk with him." She opened the cabinet that held tea.

"About what?"

Chamomile? Ginger lemon? Papaya? Deborah couldn't begin to make a decision. Closing her eyes, she randomly touched a box. Papaya. Good choice.

"Mom?"

She removed a tea bag and dropped it into the mug. "Yes, sweetie."

"What did you talk with Poppy about?"

Deborah didn't have the strength left to invent a lie. Besides, her daughter was a smart girl. She would have noticed her grandfather drinking at brunch.

Looking directly at Grace, she said, "I think Poppy has a drinking problem."

The girl's eyes widened. "You think he's an alcoholic?"

"He may not be yet. Right now, he's just drinking too much."

"Like what does he drink? Wine?"

"Whiskey."

"Whiskey," Grace echoed. "Like, he drinks at a bar? He drinks at home?"

Deborah raised the mug to smell the soothing sweet papaya. "I've seen him drink at home, and here, and at restaurants."

"You drink at restaurants. You drink at the Trutters'."

"Not to the point of feeling it. I know what I can handle."

"And Poppy doesn't? What about at work? Does he drink there? I mean, like, that would be the worst, wouldn't it?"

"Yes. That'd be the worst." Deborah sipped her tea. "I don't know for sure."

"But you think he does?"

Deborah considered her options and again

chose the truth. "I saw Emily Huber at the gym. Did you hear anything about the police being called about noise Saturday night?"

"They think it was us."

"You knew that? Why didn't you tell me?" She waved a hand. "No matter. Emily is taking Kelly and Kim away from our practice."

Grace was silent. Finally, she said sullenly, "Did you call the police?" She had a finger at her mouth, not quite biting, but close.

Deborah didn't bother to scold her. "How would I know if there was noise or if there wasn't? I wasn't there."

"I told you there was a keg."

"You told me the next day," Deborah said by way of answering the accusation.

"Did you ask Danielle to come over?" Grace asked in that same sulky way.

Deborah was a minute following. "No. Did she come?"

"She drove over and asked me to go out. I told her I couldn't because I had an English paper to write, which I should have been doing, but wasn't." She said the last words with defiance and tucked her hands in the back pockets of her jeans. "Did you ask her to come?" she repeated.

"Absolutely not. Danielle adores you. Oh,

Grace, I'm sorry you didn't at least ask her in. Karen says she really wants to talk."

"Well, I don't. The only reason I'm telling you this is so you can tell Karen. Dani wants to talk about the accident, and I don't." She pushed her hair back. "What does Mrs. Huber have to do with Poppy drinking?"

Deborah let the other go. "She says that he drinks at lunch."

Grace crinkled up her face. **"Mrs. Huber** says that? **Mrs. Huber,** who's always sitting out back at their pool with a Cosmopolitan? **Mrs. Huber** is not one to be accusing someone else of drinking at lunch. But is he?"

Deborah put the warm mug to her cheek. "He says no."

"Do you believe him?"

"I don't know. He drinks at night because he misses Nana Ruth."

"He **loved** her," Grace scolded, as though Deborah was clueless.

"I know he loved her, Grace. I saw that love far longer than you. I totally understand why he's lonely at home, but . . . drinking at work? That's really dangerous."

Grace backed down. "Maybe it's just a drink or two."

"A drink or two could cloud his judgment."

"Do you really think he'd ever make a decision that could hurt someone?"

"Not knowingly. But an error in even something small, like the dosage of a prescription, could be devastating."

"You mean, he could be sued."

"I mean, someone could **die.** And he treats dozens of kids your age. How can he tell them not to drink if he does it himself?"

"Maybe abstinence is unrealistic. Maybe the Hubers are right about taking keys. I mean, if kids are going to do it anyway, maybe it's better to be safe. How can we know how much we can drink unless we try it?"

"It's not me saying this, sweetie. It's the law. And Poppy's in a position of moral authority. He's a role model. A role model doesn't drink at work."

"A role model doesn't lie," Grace said.

Deborah stared at her for a minute. "No."

The admission seemed to deflate the girl. "How'd you leave it with Poppy?"

Deborah gratefully returned to safer ground. "Not well."

"Is he mad at you?"

"I'd . . . say so. I'm hoping he'll get over it by morning."

"Get over it, like, realize you were right?"

Deborah smiled. "Wouldn't that be nice?"

Chapter 12

That was wishful thinking. Michael wasn't over it by morning. Deborah didn't know how much he remembered, but he called first thing to say that he was going out for breakfast and that she shouldn't stop by. Coincidence? Perhaps. His tone would have been a tip-off, but Deborah didn't talk with him herself. Dylan had taken the message without putting her on.

After dropping the kids at school, she went to the bakery. The outside tables were crowded with people enjoying the morning sunshine. Inside, she grabbed a SoMa Sticky and coffee, and went in search of Jill. She was in the office, affixing mailing labels to summer fliers. Not sure where to begin, Deborah put her things down and sank into a chair.

Jill glanced at Deborah and said, "You look lousy."

"I feel lousy," Deborah murmured. She could think of several other words for the way she felt, not the least of which was disillusioned, but lousy would do. "I had it out with Dad last night."

There was a pause, then a curious, "What does 'had it out' mean?"

"I told him he was drinking too much."

"You did? What did he say?"

"He said it was none of my business."

"Was that an admission?"

"It was a denial. Then an attack."

Jill frowned. "What kind of attack?"

"Don't scowl," Deborah said. "That's exactly how Dad looked when he told me I didn't know **anything.**"

Jill lightened up. "Why did he attack you?"

"Because I must have hit a nerve."

"What did he say?"

"How **dare** I accuse him of drinking, when **I** do blah-blah-blah."

"What was blah-blah-blah?"

"Lousy wife, lousy mother."

"He was drunk."

"Actually, no," Deborah said. She'd been thinking about this. "That's what made it so bad. He'd probably had more than he should have, but he was perfectly articulate. I think that the drink loosened his tongue. He was saying things he truly felt but had resisted saying before."

"You are not a lousy wife or a lousy mother."

"Actually, Jill, I'm not a wife at all. He made that point, along with his theory of why Greg left. He was probably right. I wasn't there for Greg."

"Pooh. Greg wasn't there for you."

"Maybe he would've been if I'd asked. I never did. So that's another of my faults."

"What—independence?" Jill asked. "Resourcefulness? Self-sufficiency?"

Deborah should have been flattered, but she said sadly, "I used to know where I was headed. Not anymore."

"Deborah. What **is** this?"

Deborah scrubbed at her forehead. "Yesterday was a really bad day."

"How so?"

"Where do I start? The disgruntled patient who complained about me to Dad? The call from the school psychologist who is worried about Grace? Another patient—uh, now, **former** patient—who attacked me at the gym?"

"Start there," said Jill. "At the gym."

"Good choice." Deborah eyed her levelly. "It explains my confrontation with Dad." She related her run-in with Emily Huber.

Jill listened, removing several labels from a sheet. "Emily Huber is only a patient of yours once removed." She stuck a label on a flier. "Anything she says is secondhand at best." Another label went on, then a third. "She's only picking on Dad to get back at you for knowing that she served the kids liquor last weekend."

"I told myself that, but then little things started niggling at me—like the way he closes his door at lunchtime. I always took it as a sign he wanted a few minutes of quiet, but he could be drinking there." She looked closer at Jill. "You're pale. Are you feeling okay?"

"Just tired," Jill said, "but that's normal. So did Dad confess to anything?"

"No. He just turned up the TV and blotted me out. He left a message this morning saying he was having breakfast out, and maybe he is. But I'll have to see him at work. It could be very awkward."

"Do you think he's an alcoholic?"

"Not yet."

"Will you warn him?"

"I don't know."

"I think you should."

Deborah sputtered. "Fine for you to say. You're not the one facing him. He'll be **furious.**"

"But if you don't and it gets worse, you'll never forgive yourself. You need to confront him again."

"I have an idea," said Deborah. **"You** tell him our fears."

"Hey, I'm not in practice with him."

"He's your father. Aren't you worried about his condition?"

"Is he worried about mine?"

"How can he be?" Deborah shot back. "He doesn't **know** about the baby."

Jill held up a hand. "I am not telling Dad about the baby."

"It could help," Deborah pleaded. "A baby is new life. You could tell him you're naming her Ruth."

"Her? I have no idea if it's a her!"

"That doesn't matter, Jill. It'd give him something good to think about. I mean, the last three years have been pretty bad for him." She ticked off on her fingers. "Mom's death. My divorce. Dylan's eyes. My accident." Her cell phone rang. "He needs something **good.** Tell him about the baby."

Jill looked far from convinced. "And have him disparage women who use sperm banks?"

"Tell him you want this baby. That's certainly the truth."

"Telling the truth is overrated."

Deborah wanted to argue. She used to believe in the truth. She used to believe in right and wrong. But not today.

Her cell phone rang again. Pulling it from her pocket, she looked at the ID panel. In the next instant, she rose. "Be right back," she told Jill and, bypassing potential eavesdroppers in the kitchen, went out the back door before answering.

"Hey."

"You did give me your number," Tom McKenna said, as if to excuse the call.

"I did," Deborah said. She was actually pleased to hear his voice. "Got any good news? I could use a lift."

"Selena signed the release, and without a fight."

Deborah walked out past the yellow van. "That was wise."

"It was actually selfish. She was hoping the records could prove her right. She wants to believe you gave Cal a dose of Coumadin while he was lying on the side of the road."

"So he'd bleed to death? That's sick." The word was out before she realized that bad-mouthing this man's sister-in-law was probably not the best thing to do.

"She didn't know he was on it," Tom said, seeming unoffended.

Deborah began walking again, down the alleyway now. The brick walls on either side offered a measure of privacy. "So was he?"

"Yes. The HMO just faxed me his records. Coumadin's right up there."

She was relieved to be proven innocent of this, at least—relieved, also, by Tom's forthrightness. "It was legitimately prescribed?"

"Apparently so. There are two doctors listed here—William Beruby and Anthony Hawkins. Have you ever heard of either?"

"No. Where are they located?"

"There's no address listed, but payments were made to UMass Memorial Medical Center for tests. I did a Web search. Both doctors are affiliated there."

"Specialty?"

"One heart, one stroke. I expected the stroke part, given the family history. Apparently Cal had a series of little ones."

Deborah stopped briefly. "TIAs?" she asked in surprise.

"That's what it says. Is it plausible?"

"Some might say Cal was too young to be having TIAs, but it does happen. You could talk with his doctors. A series of TIAs would certainly explain your brother being on Coumadin." She walked on. "Selena must have known about the strokes."

"No."

Again Deborah stopped. "How could she **not?**"

"My brother was secretive."

"But she was his wife. How could he hide something like that?"

"You tell me. Would it be possible for her not to see it?"

"Yes," she admitted. "It would be possible. By definition, a TIA—transient ischemic attack—is a stroke that lasts only a few minutes. Symptoms can be mild—a passing numbness or weakness on one side of the body, trouble seeing for a couple of minutes, dizziness. His symptoms could have been gone before she noticed, but the question is why he wouldn't tell her. Strokes are serious."

"Maybe he didn't want to worry her."

"Very noble, but he could have been driving and had a stroke with her in the passenger seat, and she wouldn't know what was happening."

"Same if he was hit by a car and rushed to the hospital," Tom countered.

"Yes," Deborah admitted. "I'm sorry. I didn't mean to be critical of your brother, or of his wife. People do what works for them."

He was silent for so long, she began to worry that either she had offended him or the connection was lost, when, quietly, he said, "I'm not sure it worked for Selena. She's pretty steamed. Since Cal's not here, she's steamed at me. She keeps asking why he would go all the way to Worcester, rather than Boston, which is closer. It seems obvious to me. Cal would have gone to Worcester for the sake of secrecy."

"And Selena suspected nothing?" Deborah asked. "She must have known he was making trips to Worcester."

"She thought he was visiting a friend. He told her the name was Pete Cavanaugh and that he was an old high school buddy who'd lost both legs in Iraq."

"Is it true?"

"A Pete Cavanaugh did go to high school with Cal. But he was Cal's nemesis. No way would they have been friends."

"Sometimes when someone is catastrophically hurt—"

"No. The Pete Cavanaugh who lived in our neighborhood did go to Iraq, but he died at the start of the war. Cal's been using him as an alibi since he and Selena moved here from Seattle. That's four years. Pete's been dead the whole time."

Deborah heard anger and couldn't blame him. Talk about telling the truth. "What about phone calls from Worcester, say, to confirm an appointment?"

"They'd have gone to his cell phone. Selena would never know."

"But **why?**" Deborah asked. Having reached the front of the alley, she stopped walking. "He had a legitimate physical condition. Was he afraid she'd think less of him, that maybe she'd walk out?"

"No. That was just Cal. My father was like that."

"Secretive?"

"To the extreme. He was master at compartmentalization. He saw his life in segments that never overlapped."

Deborah leaned against the brick wall. Traffic on Main Street was brisk. "Segments?"

"Family. There was the one he was born into and the one he created. The two never met."

"Seriously?" She couldn't imagine it. "You never met his parents?"

"Or his siblings. He'd visit them sometimes, but we never went."

"Didn't they ask about you?"

"They didn't know about us. And then there was work. I was twelve before I found out what my father did."

"What did he do?"

"He was a chemist. Renowned, actually. He lectured at universities across the country. He'd come back to visit us for a month or two, but he never talked about work at home. My mother would never answer our questions. I finally had to look him up at the library."

"That's incredible," Deborah said, trying to take it in. "But your brother didn't hide his work. His wife knew what he did."

"Some. She doesn't know how much he earned or whether his contract included life insurance or a retirement plan. He used their den as an office. She said he'd read there at night. I've been over every inch of it, and there isn't a single paper you'd call work-related."

"No student papers?"

"Some of it may be on his computer, but Selena doesn't know the password. We're assuming there are personal papers at his office at school. If not, I haven't a clue. I don't even know where he keeps his bills."

"Oh, they'll start coming," Deborah remarked.

Tom's voice held not a hint of a smile. If this was his personal catharsis, he was on a roll. "Not to the house. Bills went to a P.O. box. He got that from my dad, too—multiple P.O. boxes. Bills went to one, personal correspondence to another. Everything separate, everything private. Cal had multiple cell phones, too. I only saw the Seattle number. I didn't know he'd moved east until Selena called me last week. How's that for quirky?"

Quirky was one word for it. Others carried a darker connotation. "Did your brother have any friends?"

"Probably not as you or I would define them. Friendship demands communication."

"But he did have a spouse." Which was more than either she or Tom had.

"He did, though I'm not sure why. I'd have understood it better if there'd been children. But she claims he didn't want kids."

"Did you ever talk about that with him?"

"Me? No. I didn't even know he was **married** until Selena called to say he was dead." He paused. "I probably shouldn't be telling you this."

It was a stark reminder of opposing positions. Still, Deborah couldn't resist asking, "Was Cal a runner?"

"Not that I knew. But Selena says they met skiing, and I never knew he skied. So maybe he was a runner. Why do you ask?"

"The place where we hit him was more than three miles from his house. That'd be six miles round-trip. That's a good distance to run in the pouring rain. Either he was a dedi-

cated athlete, or he was . . ." **Disturbed** was
the word that came to mind, but she settled
for, ". . . eccentric."

"Eccentric," Tom confirmed. "He comes
by it honestly."

"How did you escape it?"

There was a short silence, then, "How do
you know I did?"

She tried to decide if he was serious or not.
"I guess I don't," she finally said.

There were a dozen more questions she
wanted to ask, not the least of which was why,
if Cal was taking Coumadin on the up-and-
up, he had chosen not to enlighten the doctors, when a car rounded the corner. It was
John Colby's dark sedan. Waving, she caught
his eye.

"I have to run now," she told Tom.
"Thank you for sharing what you did."

"Your lawyer will be pleased."

"My lawyer won't know." She watched
John turn into the alley. "Gotta run. Thanks
again." Ending the call, she walked over to the
car. She had an issue with Colby. "What happened Saturday night?" she asked.

"Saturday night?" he echoed, puzzled.

"Someone reported the Hubers to the
police." She stepped back to let him out of
the car.

"Ah. That. It was a neighbor. He's a chronic complainer—calls all the time about car radios blaring. He thought the party was too noisy."

"Did you tell the Hubers who called?"

"No," John replied cautiously and looked at her.

"Did they ask if it was me?"

He looked away. "Yes. I told them I hadn't talked with you at all."

"But they didn't accept that."

"No." He faced her again. "They claimed it was because Grace wasn't at the party. Wasn't she invited?"

"Oh, she was," Deborah said with a sigh and ran a hand through her hair. "She just didn't want to go. I lost two patients over this, John. Emily removed the girls from our practice."

"Oh, hey, I'm sorry." He sounded genuinely so. "I told her it wasn't you. Want me to go over and tell her who it really was?"

Deborah feared that would only raise charges that the police were favoring her. "No. If the trust is gone, it's gone."

"For what it's worth," he confided, "it's just as well Grace didn't go. The Hubers used to serve their older girl beer when she had friends over. There's no reason to think they don't do the same with Kim. I'd have gone there in person to take a look if the noise hadn't quieted down, but when I didn't get another complaint, I let it go. 'Course, I'd be kicking myself right now if one of the kids had wrapped his car around a tree. But there was only that one complaint." He ran his hand over the curve of his stomach. "It's a tough call in this town, with so many affluent parents and all. Sometimes you have to take them at their word." He propped an elbow on the roof of the car. "I saw Grace yesterday."

Deborah raised her brows. "You did?"

"At the oval. She was working out with the team. Boy, can she run. Left everyone else in the dust." He smiled. "She reminded me of you."

"I never ran."

"No, you swam, but you were fast. Still have those trophies?"

"Uh-huh. They're in a carton in the basement."

"Not on display? You should be proud of those things. You did great for the local team."

Deborah hadn't thought about the trophies in a while. The last time she had taken them out was to show the kids, and then, only because Karen had gone on about them. To Greg, they were the epitome of convention, won at a time when he had been building houses in the inner city, wearing long hair, grayed shorts, and a week's worth of sweat. By the time he met Deborah, he had started his business and was growing more conventional himself, but he never warmed to her high school trophies.

Now, in response to John's question, she shrugged. "Once I got married and had kids, the prizes didn't mean much. I don't want to live in the past."

"That's smart. It's not good for the kids. Some just can't duplicate what Mom and Dad did—not that your Grace isn't a winner on her own, but you know what I mean. You're one strong lady. Grace has big shoes to fill. She still into science?"

Deborah nodded.

"Gonna join you and your dad?"

"I hope so."

"And she wants it, like you did?"

"She says she does."

"Better be sure about that," he advised, staring at his shoes. "I know what it's like to disappoint a parent. You want to be a **what?** my dad used to ask. My family's all lawyers."

"You're the chief of police. That's not too shabby."

"There's a difference, my parents would

say if they were alive." He looked up. "Don't know what got me going on that. I guess it's still a sore spot. You're such a rock, even now after the accident. I worry about Grace. She's young. She may not be as strong."

"I think the week just overwhelmed her."

"I hope she's not isolating herself from her friends."

Deborah gave it a positive spin. "She's just lying low."

"Huh. Grace Kelly's girl should've done that."

"I'm sorry?"

"Remember Grace Kelly?"

"Of course," Deborah said with a touch of unease. "She was living out every young girl's dream. I was barely into my teens when she died."

"Remember how she died?"

"She was driving when her car left the road and crashed down an embankment."

"Mmm. Her daughter had a rough time afterward—you know, the one who was in the car with her. I always wondered about whether she was the one actually driving and they covered it up."

"But Princess Grace had a stroke," Deborah protested.

"Well. No matter," said the man. "Your

Grace is lucky. She has you." He scratched the back of his head. "Say, listen, I really am sorry about the Hubers. I probably should have just come right out and said who'd made the call. I hate thinking I made you lose two patients. If there's anything I can do . . ."

"There is," Deborah said. She was thinking of everything Tom had shared about his brother. She probably should tell John, but she felt—absurdly, perhaps—that she couldn't betray Tom's confidence. "Just speed up the accident report, John. You owe me this."

Chapter 13

Michael's car wasn't in the driveway when Deborah got to the house, which relieved her on two counts. First, she truly did want to think that he was out for breakfast. And second, she was pleased not to have to see him so soon.

Parking nearby, she carried her med bag, her coffee, and her untouched sticky bun down the driveway. Three cars were in the small lot there—those of the receptionist, the nurse, and an early patient who had caught a cold from her kids. After diagnosing bronchitis, Deborah sent her off with the proper prescription, and went down the hall. Her father hadn't arrived.

His office was neat but crowded. Books filled every shelf, relics of the day when journals weren't digital, and while he was totally addicted to the computer that sat on the side of the desk, he refused to get rid of them. Same with the presents that his youngest patients had given him over the years—Valentines added each year to a decorated board, numerous shells, rocks, and twigs, a primitive clay mug. Each held a memory. For all his dictatorial bearing, Michael was a softie at heart.

"Gone looking for a bottle in the drawer yet?" asked her father, coming up behind her. He dropped a handful of magazines on the desk and flipped on a light.

"No," she said. "I would never do that."

"Why not?"

"Because it's your desk."

His face was sober. "But you were thinking of it."

"I was actually thinking about you and Mom," Deborah said. And yes, it had crossed her mind to check the desk, though she hadn't drummed up the courage to actually do it. "I would have liked to have had a marriage like yours."

"You thought you did. I thought you were rushing. He was a hippie, for God's sake, but you said that was what made him special."

"It was."

"Arguable, given what he's done since, but back then you said you'd found the right guy and that if you waited until after med school, he'd be gone."

"He was," Deborah remarked.

"He wasn't **gone** until two years ago."

She gave a sad smile. "He was gone long before that."

"The marriage was bad all along?" Michael asked in surprise.

"Not bad. Just not the same as yours. I chalked it up to our being a two-career couple."

"You said he was fine with your being a doctor."

"I thought he was, women's rights and all. He seemed so modern, the ideal mix of free spirit and realist. At work, he was amazing. He brought unconventional ideas to a conventional field. I thought he was brilliant." She paused. "I thought he adored me the way you adored Mom."

"Maybe back then he did."

"Maybe I misjudged him."

"Maybe you were too young to judge him at all."

"Oh, Dad, I was not," she scolded. "I was no younger when I got married than you were."

"Things were different in my day. My buddies were being sent to Vietnam, and some of them weren't coming home. We didn't have the luxury of time."

But she shook her head. "Lots of kids still get married young."

"It's a socioeconomic thing now."

"But they do it, and their marriages don't always fail. So what's the problem with us?"

"Hey, don't include me in that."

"I know. Your marriage was perfect."

He reddened, his temper heating. "If you're going to start telling me all I didn't know about my wife—"

"No, that's not it. I'm serious. Your marriage **was** perfect," Deborah insisted. "I cannot remember once when you ever argued with Mom. I thought that was how all marriages were. Maybe I expected too much. Maybe I saw things in Greg that just weren't there."

Michael sat behind his desk and turned on the computer. "If you fantasized, it was your own doing. I never told you what to expect."

"No. But kids see their parents, and their relationship becomes the standard."

He reached for his glasses. "Doesn't look like your sister saw that."

"Oh, she did. She knew what you and Mom had. Why do you think she never found the right guy?"

Eyes on the screen, he muttered, "Because she's prickly."

"Not prickly. **Picky.** She wanted someone as strong as you."

He shot her a look. "Don't flatter me."

Deborah was suddenly impatient. "I'm not. This is about perception—perception and expectation. I saw a certain model and took certain things for granted. Clearly, I shouldn't have. But we were talking about Jill. The problem is, expectations can be hard on a child."

"Jill is not a child."

"She is. She's your child. She always will be."

He looked at her over his glasses. "Don't we have patients to see?"

"She can't do everything the way you did. That doesn't mean what she does is bad. The bakery is a fabulous place, and she's doing it well."

"Good."

"Doesn't that make you happy? What more do we want for our kids than to know they're happy?"

"Lots. We want security. We want growth. We want them to do better than we did."

Deborah thought of what John had said. "That may not be possible. What then? Are they failures?"

Her father straightened. "You tell me. You want your boy to play baseball, but he can't see. Does he actually get satisfaction from those games?"

Deborah thought about her son and fear twisted her heart. "It's about being part of a team."

"Sure, that's what we say. Only, is it? Is he better off being the worst kid on the team—"

"He isn't the worst kid."

"He can't **see**, Deborah. He can't see to hit the ball, and he can't see to field it. He is, on the other hand, a good little musician."

"He'll never be a concert pianist," Deborah said, thinking of what her father had done to Jill. "I refuse to pressure him that way."

"And you don't think forcing him to play ball isn't as bad? Come on, Deborah. You can't see what's right in front of your nose."

"I guess that makes two of us," Deborah said, just as the intercom rang.

Michael jabbed at the speakerphone. "Yes."

"Jamie McDonough is in Room One, Dr. Barr. Would you tell Dr. Monroe that the Holt children are in Room Two?"

"Fine." He punched the off button and got up. "They expect us to be there. They expect us to have answers. They **expect** us to cure their ills." Taking a lab coat from the back of the door, he pushed his arms through the sleeves. "Who cures us?" He glared at Deborah. "We are all we have."

Technically, Deborah agreed. Wasn't that the philosophy she had lived by since the divorce? **We do what we have to do, because no one else is going to do it. It may not be right, but it's the best we can do.**

Coming from her father, though, it was depressing. Drinking cured nothing. If aloneness was the problem, drinking only made it worse. The question was whether what she was doing was any better.

She might have obsessed about it if her morning hadn't been filled first with office visits, then house calls. Her afternoon wasn't much better. By the time she reached the gym, she was desperate for distraction, and pushing herself helped.

Later, pulling into a diagonal spot in front of the bakery, she phoned Greg. "Hi. It's me. Is this an okay time?"

There was a pause. "An okay time for what?" he asked.

"To talk."

"About . . . ?"

"Us. The kids." **Can't see what's right in**

front of your nose. "Maybe what went wrong."

There was dead silence. Then a curious, "What went wrong when?"

"With our marriage."

"You want to talk **now?**"

He wasn't making it easy. "If this isn't a good time, I can call back."

"That's not the point. For months after we split, I wanted to talk. You never let me."

"I couldn't. I was hurt. You had turned into someone I didn't know."

"Not true. I went back to being the man I was when we first met."

"Maybe," she conceded. "But it had been a long time, and I found the change threatening."

"Because I wanted to talk?"

"Because you wanted to tell me why you didn't want to be married to me."

"It wasn't you, Deborah. It was the whole of my life—"

She cut in. "I heard **me.** Right or wrong, Greg, I took it personally. I couldn't satisfy you as a wife, so you left. I couldn't satisfy you as a woman, so you married Rebecca. Had you been in touch with her all along?"

"No. Only at the end of our marriage."

"Did you leave me **specifically** to marry her?"

"No. Once I was gone, it just . . . fit."

"And I didn't. Do you understand why I couldn't talk? I didn't want to hear all the things I'd done wrong."

"So I was the bad guy."

"Yes."

"What's different now?"

She looked out the windshield. The afternoon sun shone on the bakery window, blocking her vision, but she knew that Grace and Dylan were inside. "The anger isn't working. I'm not sure it's the best thing for the kids. I'm not sure it's the best thing for me either."

"You're older and wiser now?"

Hearing a note of sarcasm, she said, "There were times in our marriage when I felt so much younger and dumber than you."

"You never told me that."

"I didn't like discussing our age difference."

"You threw it at me plenty when I left."

"No, Greg. All I said was that you were having a midlife crisis. Maybe you heard more than I said."

There was another silence, then a surprisingly conciliatory, "Maybe."

"I expected my marriage to last forever," Deborah said. "I wasn't prepared for what happened. I was humiliated."

"I'm sorry for that. I probably could have handled it better."

"How?" she asked. "By giving me a week's warning?"

"I'd been unhappy for a while."

"So unhappy that you couldn't discuss it?"

"I wasn't supposed to be unhappy at all. That wasn't in the plan—and I'm not being sarcastic. You weren't the only one with expectations. It occurs to me that I needed those plans to convince myself that what I was doing with my life was right. Our life together was a show. We did what was expected of the perfect couple." His voice softened. "I'm not blaming you."

Absurd as it was, her eyes filled with tears. "I couldn't move up there with you. I couldn't, Greg."

"I knew that."

"I made calls. There were too many doctors there already."

"Deborah, you don't need to explain."

"I do," she insisted. "I've always felt guilty. I felt like I chose my house and my career over my husband."

"It wasn't a black-and-white choice."

But she went on, desperate that he understand how she had felt toward the end of their marriage. "We hadn't talked about anything substantial for years."

"Deborah."

"If I let you down, I'm sorry. I thought I was doing everything right. But how do we know? How can we see down the road and know what'll work and what won't? It's like driving at night in a torrential rain. You think you know the way, but you just can't be sure."

"Are you all right, Deborah?"

She was about to say she was not, when John Colby pulled into the space beside her. Something about his expression said that he had news.

"What's happening?" Greg asked.

"Lots, I'm afraid. But I've just run out of time."

"Is it something to do with the kids?"

"Nothing that won't wait another day or two."

"This is a good time for me to listen," he said meaningfully.

She heard him. "I appreciate that. Thank you. But I'll have to call you back."

She closed her phone before he could say

another word, and rolled down her window as John rounded the front of his car and leaned in.

"I talked with the folks at the state lab," he said. "They don't like to say anything until they're done, but so far as they can see, you're in the clear."

Deborah was afraid to breathe. "In the clear?"

"There's no evidence of wrongdoing—no speeding, no reckless driving, no vehicle malfunction. It's pretty much what we said. There's no grounds for charges. They're focusing on the victim now. The preliminary report says he ran straight out of the woods."

Deborah was a minute following. **"Out** of the woods?"

"He wasn't jogging along the road. He was in the woods and ran directly out onto the road."

"There's no path through the woods."

"I know. But his footprints were there."

"Bizarre," Deborah murmured, not for the first time associating that word with Calvin McKenna.

John went on. "They took pictures of the footprints, but they haven't finished analyzing them. Could be he went into the woods to take shelter from the rain. Could be he went in to relieve himself. People at school never knew he was a runner. Looks like he kept a lot to himself."

John didn't know the half of it, Deborah thought, but to say it would lead to more questions, and to answer them would be a betrayal of Tom.

"I tried to call Hal," John added, "but he's off playing racquetball." He squinted at the bakery. "Grace inside? Oh, there she is." He grunted. "No. She's off again. Guess she didn't want to talk to me."

Deborah was relieved enough by the report to say, "Don't take it personally. She hasn't wanted to talk to me, either."

"The accident's thrown her."

"I'd say that." Deborah reached for her bag.

John opened the door and stood back. "Well, you tell her what I told you. Maybe it'll cheer her up some."

Deborah found Grace in the back office, slouched in the chair behind Jill's desk. Her feet were up, flip-flops braced against the edge of the desk.

"You shouldn't have run," she said softly. "John had good news. The state team found nothing."

Grace didn't blink. "Mr. McKenna's still dead."

"Yes," Deborah said. "He is. I'll always feel badly. I'll always feel badly about Jimmy Morrisey, too. Did I ever tell you about him?" When Grace shook her head, she said, "He was a fixture in Leyland—didn't live here, but was a handyman who worked at practically every house in town. Early one morning—I was seventeen—he was up on our roof replacing shingles when he fell. We were having breakfast and heard his cry. Poppy did what he could, but Jimmy was dead before the ambulance arrived. Poppy and Nana Ruth took it personally. They criticized themselves for rushing him onto the roof in March, when there was still morning frost. They criticized themselves for letting him work alone. But this was what Jimmy did. He'd been on a roof down the street the day before. He saw the frost when he climbed the ladder. He could have waited an hour for it to melt."

"You're saying it was his fault."

"I'm saying it wasn't entirely our fault."

"Sorry, Mom. The analogy doesn't fit. Mr. McKenna would not be dead if I hadn't been driving that car."

"Oh my," Jill said, stopping mid-stride

two feet from the door. Hand on the still-smooth belly of a buff-colored apron, she looked from Deborah to Grace. "The plot thickens?"

Grace's face crumbled. "This isn't funny," she cried, hugging herself. "I keep seeing the road in the rain . . . I **can't see** more than two feet in front of the car. It **was** my fault. If I hadn't been driving home from Megan's, Mr. McKenna would still be alive."

Knowing Jill had heard the truth—and from Grace's own mouth—Deborah felt a weight slip from her shoulders. "The point of my story," she told Grace, "is that Mr. McKenna may not have been any wiser than Jimmy Morrisey. We didn't **see** him on the road, because he wasn't **on** the road. He came out of the woods just as we went by."

"And ran right into us?" Grace asked with a horrified look.

"What kind of idiot would do that?" Jill asked, seeming horrified on more than one count as she eyed Deborah. "You lied to the police?"

"No." Deborah still thought she looked pale. "Are you feeling all right?"

"Please don't change the subject."

Deborah relented. "They assumed I was driving. I didn't correct them."

"You filled out that report, Deborah. I was right here when Hal read it."

Deborah might have made the argument about being the driver of record that night, but she was already having so many doubts about her own behavior, that she simply asked Grace, "Did you know Mr. McKenna was a runner?"

"No. But he had every right to be running that night. We don't own the road."

"Deborah," Jill persisted, "you signed your name to that form."

Deborah didn't have the strength to argue. Besides, she was making a point for Grace. "If we were doing everything right—if **you** were doing everything right and a man ran out of the woods and into the path of the car—"

"Sounds suicidal," Jill muttered.

"—it means he shares the blame."

Grace wilted. "He can't share the blame. He's dead. Besides, why is it always someone else's fault?"

"Deborah," Jill said loudly, clearly still stuck on the lie, "do you know what you've done?"

"How could I **not?**" Deborah shouted. "But what was my choice? The repercussions would have been far worse for Grace."

"Like this is easy now?" Grace cried. "You want to take the blame, only now the police say you were fine, so you want to put the blame on Mr. McKenna. What about **me?** I run lousy in a meet, and everyone says, 'Oh, poor thing, she's had a rough week.' I fail a French test, and the teacher says, 'Oh, poor thing, she had a rough day.' She erased the F from her book. She doesn't do that for everyone. Why's everyone sorry for me?"

Deborah hadn't known about the French test. More upsetting was the fact that Grace hadn't told her. Her daughter used to confide in her.

"Know what I'm doing now?" Grace asked with a nod at the laptop. "This is an English paper I handed in this morning. It was so bad that Mr. Jones caught up with me before I left school and asked for a rewrite—and that was **after** Ms. Walsh caught up with me and asked if I wanted to talk, which I do not, so please do not ask her to approach me again. And Mr. Jones? He says computers allow for as many drafts as we want, and that if students choose not to do more than one, they're making a statement."

Deborah pressed a hand to her chest. "What was your statement?"

"That grades are meaningless. They're scribbles on a page. They have nothing to do with real life."

"They do," Jill said, an unlikely supporter of high school. "They measure attitude. Bad attitude limits choices."

Which is what I don't want for my daughter, Deborah thought, **which is precisely why I did what I did after the accident.**

But Grace was eyeing her aunt. "You've done well. This place is a **huge** success."

"But it's hard work, and it's lots of worry, and maybe if I had a business partner to split the weight, I would do better. This may have nothing to do with my getting lousy grades in high school, but it's something to think about, isn't it?" She turned back to Deborah. "Obstruction of justice. Perjury. Filing a false report."

"Jill," Deborah protested. "This is **not** what I want to hear right now. I want Grace to learn about limited choices."

"So do I," Grace said. "I mean, why do I have to be a doctor?"

Deborah felt a hitch in her chest. "Don't you want to be one?"

"I don't know. But what happens if I want to be something else?"

"I thought you loved biology."

"No, Mom. Bio isn't even my best course, and I have to take the AP exam next month, which I will probably not do well on. But you said your dream was you and me practicing together."

"It is my dream," Deborah conceded, "but I thought you wanted it, too."

"Well, it may be impossible now. No one wants a doctor who commits vehicular homicide. I may not even get into medical school."

Deborah darted Jill a glance before saying, "That's why I filled out the form the way I did."

"But it'll get **out,** Mom," Grace wailed, "like with Pinocchio, it always gets out, just shows up right there on your face, whether you like it or not. You're the one who taught me that, and look what just happened. Now Aunt Jill knows."

"Aunt Jill won't tell," Jill said.

"You may not plan to," Grace accused, "but you are totally unable to lie. You say what you think, just blurt it right out. You're the most honest person I know."

Jill leaned forward, hands on the desk. "Well, I have been keeping one secret. I'm pregnant."

Grace gasped. "You **are?**"

"Definitely."

"Do we know the guy?"

Jill shook her head.

Grace's eyes opened wider. "Does Poppy know you're pregnant?"

"Not yet. And don't tell him. He'll be furious."

"But it's a **baby,**" Grace said and turned to Deborah. "You knew? And you didn't tell me?"

Deborah was guilty of lots of things, but she wasn't taking the fall for this. "Jill asked me not to. I do know how to keep secrets."

Grace wasn't impressed. "And you think that was **smart?** I mean, I'm sitting here doing homework every afternoon, while she lifts and pulls things, and you didn't think I should **know?**"

"Put that way, you should have," Deborah said and turned to her sister. "Jill, why didn't you tell her?"

"She couldn't," Grace argued, "because it's obvious she's still in her first trimester, because she's still so thin, and no one announces they're pregnant so soon, because it's bad luck."

"Who told you that?"

Grace made a face. "Do you think **no** one in my school is pregnant? It happens to rich people, too, Mom."

Deborah didn't reply. She wasn't as surprised by what her daughter said as by the fact that Grace had never said it before. They had discussed pregnancy many times in biological terms, never in terms of who was and who wasn't. Deborah had always prided herself on having an open relationship with Grace. Could be she'd been deluding herself about that.

Grace made a sound and looked away.

Deborah turned to Jill, but her sister had a strange look on her face. "Are you okay?"

Jill seemed to consider it, then gave a small smile. "I feel pangs every so often."

"Any spotting?"

"No."

"Think you should call your doctor?"

Jill sighed. "If I thought that, Deborah, I'd have already done it. I'm not taking chances with this baby."

"What baby?" Dylan asked from the door.

Deborah looked from Jill to Grace and back. It was Jill's secret. Deborah kept her own mouth shut, watching now as Dylan made his way into the room. He was touching everything he passed—doorknob, coat rack, the back of Jill's chair—with such nonchalance that only someone looking would notice. Being his mother, Deborah worried.

It took a minute for Jill to speak. Then she told Dylan, "No baby you can even **imagine.** Did you finish your homework?"

Dylan nodded—so easily satisfied? Deborah reflected. He pushed his glasses up on his nose. "I'm hungry, Mom. Are we going home soon?"

Deborah was ready to leave. She'd had enough of revelations and confrontation. Even reheating Lívia's dinner was good for regaining a sense of control. "I think we can."

"I want to stay here with Aunt Jill," Grace said.

Jill's apartment over the bakery was bright, spacious, and delightfully open, and had more square footage than that of many a town house, but Michael had found fault with the apartment and had been particularly annoyed when Jill used the bequest she'd received from her mother to buy the whole building. But Jill was Jill.

"Stay for dinner?" Deborah asked Grace.

"Overnight. Aunt Jill'll drive me home for clean clothes. Won't you, Aunt Jill?"

"Sure," Jill shot a hesitant look at Deborah, "but it's a school night. You don't usually stay over on a school night."

"Can I stay, too?" asked Dylan.

"No," Grace stated. "I want a girls' night."

Dylan's face fell.

Eager to lift his spirits, Deborah said, "Tell you what. How about you and I let them have their girls' night, and we'll have a mother-son night. Maybe Pepper's Pies?" Pepper McCoy made **the** best pizza. Her shop was only a ten-minute drive from Leyland.

Dylan brightened. "Can I stay over here another time—not this weekend, 'cause I'm going to Dad's, but another one?"

Deborah's own spirits rose at Dylan's sense of hope. "You can. I'll hold your aunt to it."

Chapter 14

Deborah was on the family room sofa with Dylan. He was reading **Where the Red Fern Grows** and appeared to be engrossed in it. She was reading a study on the overprescription of antibiotics, but her mind barely took in the words. It kept returning to the issue of a non-runner who was running in a place runners didn't run.

"I want a dog," Dylan said, looking up from his book.

"You're just saying that because you're reading a book about dogs."

"Dad has a dog," the boy reasoned.

"It came with Rebecca, and Dad has acres of land and oodles of time."

"I have oodles of time," Dylan said. He was looking up at her with a beseechfulness that was magnified right along with his eyes.

"And we have acres of land, too. I could take care of a dog."

Deborah knew he could. She worried that she couldn't.

"I **could,** Mom, and it doesn't matter **how** bad my eyes are, I'd see a dog. Rebecca's dog had eight pups."

"Uh-huh." She humored him. "You've told me that."

"Why can't I have just one itty-bitty little one?"

"Because it won't **stay** an itty-bitty little one."

"Please, Mom?" Dylan begged, sliding an arm around her neck. "I would be really **good** with a dog."

"I'm sure you would be," she said and kissed his cheek.

"Tom?"

"Yes."

"It's Deborah." She kept her voice low, not so much because Dylan was asleep with his bedroom door open, but because she felt duplicitous making the call. "I, uh, got your number from my phone, from when you called earlier," she explained. "Were you still up?"

He made a sound that might have been a chuckle. "It's only ten."

"You've obviously never had kids."

"Wear you out, huh?"

"Some days more than others." She pushed a pillow between the headboard and her back. "Tonight, I'm tired."

"Have you talked with John?" he asked.

"Yes. That's why I'm calling."

"It's pretty disturbing. The part about Cal running out from the woods."

"Do you think it was deliberate?"

"I don't know. But if he was only making a pit stop in the woods, they'd have seen his footprints going from the road, into the woods, and back."

"Wouldn't the rain have washed the road clean?" she asked.

"Not with someone Cal's size. It would've taken a while for them to be totally erased. Besides, you'd be amazed at what cameras can catch with specialized filters."

"You sound like a camera buff."

"I'm not. But I know people who are. And I read. And I ask questions."

"About cameras?"

"Other things, too." He paused. "That's actually what I do for a living." He paused again, and for a minute she feared he would end it there. Then he explained, "I write position papers for large organizations. Say a government wants to make an argument for a particular health care delivery system. I'm hired to put together a document they can use to make their case. The only way I can do a good job is by interviewing people on both sides of the issue."

"What if what you hear isn't what the government wants?"

"I compromise myself."

"Excuse me?"

He chuckled. "It isn't really that bad. If you look hard enough, you can find what your client wants. Sometimes I'm part of a propaganda campaign, but I try to keep those jobs few and far between."

"Do you work from home?"

"Yes."

"Ever tire of it?"

"No chance of that. I'm out on the road half the time interviewing people and gathering data."

Deborah was intrigued. She knew that talking with Tom was dangerous, but it had started to rain, and, with the steady patter on the roof, she didn't want to let him hang up.

Tucking her bare feet under the top of the sheet, she asked, "How'd you get started doing this?"

"I was halfway through college and needed money. A professor connected me with a friend of his who needed work done."

"So do you consider yourself a writer?"

"More an investigative journalist."

She hesitated. "Do you have any theories about your brother?"

"Based on his prints, I'd say he was in the woods before the accident."

"Do you have any idea what he was doing?"

"Hell, no. I never did." He took a quick breath. "I blame myself for that. I was older."

"Why blame you and not your parents?"

He was silent for a time. Finally, he said sadly, "I'm not sure they were capable. They were preoccupied with their own lives. When it came to us, they saw only what they wanted to see."

"They must have had reports from teachers."

"They sure did. Cal was the best student in the class."

"How was he socially?"

"Weird, but that was my own observation.

If the teachers ever mentioned it, my parents ignored them."

"He never had professional help?"

"Not back then."

"Has he since?"

"Hey, if I didn't know he was on Coumadin, would I know if he was seeing a shrink?"

Deborah didn't reply.

"Sorry," he said more gently. "You hit a nerve. But you're wondering."

Deborah couldn't pretend not to know what he meant. When a smart man ran through the woods in the driving rain and came out right into the path of an oncoming car, though its headlights couldn't have been missed, when he then refused to tell the ER doctors that he was on a drug that could cause serious bleeding—anyone would wonder. When the same man was obsessive about segregating every little part of his life, to the extent that his wife didn't know he'd had a series of strokes and his brother had no idea he'd moved east, someone like Deborah had to think that Cal McKenna might have wanted to die.

"It takes a lot of pain to throw oneself in front of a car," she said. "Was Cal depressed?"

"Selena says no."

"I take it he didn't leave a note?"

"We haven't found one. Is your lawyer wondering if it was suicide?" Tom asked. It was an unwelcome reminder to Deborah that they could be adversaries in court.

"No," she replied. "I don't tell him what you tell me."

"But he's friends with Colby, isn't he?"

Another reminder. "They play poker together."

"Is that why Colby pushed for an early report?"

"No. That was my doing. I begged."

He made a sound that might have been a laugh. "Is he a friend, or just a patient?"

"Both. In a town like this, patients are friends, too."

"Does John know we talk?"

"Absolutely not. And my lawyer would have a fit if he knew."

Tom was silent.

"Does your sister-in-law know we talk?" Deborah asked.

"No. It would upset her. She's determined to prove that Cal's death was in no way his fault. She wants a scapegoat. She'll be upset when she gets the report."

"Would she ever wonder whether Cal was responsible for his own death?"

"I doubt it. She wouldn't have seen anything pathological in what Cal did. She'd say that everyone has idiosyncracies."

"What're yours?" Deborah asked.

"I already told you. I'm a slob. What're yours?"

"I hate rain. Bad things happen when it rains."

"Like the accident?"

"Yes, but long before that. It was raining the night my mom died. It was raining the day my husband left."

"Do you get edgy every time it rains?"

"No. It's raining now, and it just feels like noise."

"But when you were out in it last week. Were you upset then?"

Deborah sensed she shouldn't have begun this conversation. But she answered anyway. "I had to pick up Grace, which isn't to say I wouldn't have rathered stay home."

"She'll be driving herself around soon."

"Uh-huh. She'll have her license in four months. That could be good or bad."

"Bad when it rains. You'll worry."

"I will."

"Well, then you should be grateful. If she'd had her license now, she might have been the one driving last week."

"Aunt Jill?" Grace whispered. "Are you asleep?"

"With my eyes open?"

"I can't see that they're open. It's too dark." Grace sat up, turning to face the half of the big bed where Jill lay. The only light came from the street and was blurred by rain. Not that Grace minded the dark. She didn't want to see her aunt's face. "I have to tell you something. Last week? At Megan's? We were drinking."

"Last week?"

"The night of the accident. The night I was driving the car that hit Mr. McKenna."

Jill moaned. "Ohhh, Gracie. I'm not sure I want to hear this."

"We were drinking beer," Grace said, knowing she could be getting into trouble by naming her friends, but needing to tell someone, and Jill had secrets of her own. "Megan's parents were out. And when Mom came to get me, I didn't even think not to drive. I wasn't drunk. Not even a buzz—well, maybe a little."

"How much did you have?"

"Two cans. But one of those was when I first got there, and the other was, like, almost three hours later. Mom's gonna hate me when she finds out."

"She doesn't know?"

"How could I tell her?" Grace cried. **"She** wouldn't do anything like that. I mean, drinking and driving is the worst thing you can do."

"You didn't tell her, even after you hit the guy? Didn't she smell it on your breath?"

"No," Grace cried. "I was chewing gum, but she wouldn't have ever thought to smell my breath. She thinks I've never had a drink in my life."

"So did I," Jill said.

Unable to interpret the remark, Grace said, "You hate me."

"I don't. I guess I just didn't realize how old you're getting."

"Don't tell me you never drank in high school," Grace scolded.

"I didn't. I smoked pot."

Grace was surprised only by the bluntness of the admission. "Pot?" That opened up a whole other can of worms. "Did Poppy know?"

"Of course. That was the point."

"Why?" Grace asked, because she had often wondered. "What started it for you?"

"My rebellion? Oh, lots of little things. Take birth order. I was a second child following on the heels of your mom. From my earliest memories, I was expected to do what she did, but I always came up short. So I decided not to compete. I wanted to be me. Acting out was a way of telling that to my father."

"What did he do when he found out about the pot?"

"He was furious."

"Like, did he take away the car keys? Take away your allowance?"

"His disappointment was enough—you know, that **look** every day when he came home from work. In our house, it was all about good behavior and reputation. It was about making parents proud."

Did Grace ever know that! She felt it every day, but magnified a **hundred** times since the accident. "Nana Ruth, too?"

"In theory. But she was a mom. A mom has a soft spot in her heart." Jill's voice held a smile. "She often talked about the soft spot babies have on the top of their heads when they're born. It allows the skull to shift a little during the birthing process, and it closes up during the first year. She used to say that it doesn't really go away, simply transfers to the mom, who holds it in her heart for the rest of her life."

"That's the sweetest thing," Grace said.

"Are you thinking of things like that now that you're pregnant?"

"I am."

"Do you wish Nana Ruth were here?"

"I do."

"To help break the news to Poppy?"

Jill shifted under the sheets. "No. I'll tell him once the first trimester is done. I'll tell everyone then."

"**No** one knows?"

"Just your mom and you."

"So, is it hard not telling? Don't you feel like everyone can see?"

"There's nothing much to see yet. My apron's a good cover."

"But don't you feel like they can guess? Like they know you're lying when you go around doing everything you normally do?"

"No."

Grace sighed. "I wish I could be more like you. I feel like everyone knows I was drinking and there's this big lie, like a bird, sitting on my shoulder. I mean, part of me wishes everyone did know." She had a thought. "If **I** got pregnant, Mom wouldn't be able to hide it."

"That'd be a bad idea, Grace."

"But what if I did? At least she'd have to tell the truth about that." She got her aunt with that one. It was rare when Jill didn't have a comeback. "What would Mom say if I got pregnant?"

"She'd be disappointed."

"Like Poppy was when you smoked pot? See? She's as bad as he is. You're right. It's all about good behavior and reputation. Their lives are a show."

"Hold on, Grace. I may have my gripes, but your mother and grandfather work hard. They perform a service to this community. Give credit where credit is due."

"Fine. But that doesn't mean it's easy being their child."

"No."

"So, what do I do?"

"You can't change being their child."

"About my **lie.** It wouldn't have been so bad if I'd told Mom about the beer right away, but now all this time has passed. Mom's taking the fall for me, but she doesn't even know about the drinking."

Jill found her hand in the dark. "Y'know, sweetie, from everything I've heard, **whoever** was driving that car did nothing wrong. Your having had a beer didn't cause the accident."

"I had two," Grace reminded her.

"That didn't cause the **accident."**

"Okay, but I'm still feeling guilty about it, and I can't tell Mom."

"What about your dad?"

"Excuse me? I don't **talk** to my dad."

"Maybe you should."

"Are you kidding? He'll be worse than Mom. I mean, like, Poppy will be disappointed, but he's only my grandfather." She paused. "He drinks too much anyway. So maybe he'd understand."

"Oh, Gracie, there's a difference between having a beer with your friends—"

"Any of whom will **kill** me if I tell," Grace interrupted.

"Can't discuss that yet," Jill said. "Stick to my first point. There's a difference between having two beers at a party and sitting alone every night drinking half a bottle of whiskey. But let's not talk about Poppy. We were talking about your dad."

"Okay," Grace said, tucking her legs under her. "Let's talk about him. He says he loves us, but he walked out without any warning."

"Your mother had warning. She may not have recognized it for what it really was, but the issues were there."

"How can you side with him?"

"I'm not. I'm saying she may have closed

her eyes to what was going on in her marriage. I have good instincts about people. I always liked your father."

"But I don't trust him. That's my problem. I don't know what he'll do if he learns what really happened the other night. He might call the other parents. He might call the police."

"He won't call the police."

"He could, and it would ruin my life, not that it's going to be great anyway, because I'm a total pariah in school. I can't be honest with anyone, because I'll get someone else in trouble. And Dad? He'll probably be just as disappointed as Mom, because he expects me to be a star, too. So I have to live with that, and with knowing a man died after the car I was driving hit him. That's the worst."

"I know."

Grace felt better. "No one else does."

Her aunt moaned in agreement—at least, that was what Grace thought the sound meant, until there was a sudden thrashing of legs. Throwing the sheet back, Jill sat up on the edge of the bed.

"What's wrong?" Grace asked.

"Be right back." Pushing herself to her feet, she headed for the bathroom. She was walking more slowly than usual, Grace thought, but it was hard to tell in the dark, and by the time a small sliver of light fell across the carpet, Jill was out of sight. Grace barely had time to get out of bed when Jill called her name.

She was at the bathroom door in a flash. Jill was on the toilet. Her face was ashen. "I'm bleeding."

"Bleeding?" Grace swallowed hard.

"I need paper towels."

Grace ran to the kitchen, unwound a bunch, and ran back. "Bleeding a lot?"

"I don't know," Jill said and took the paper towels. "I think I need to go to the hospital."

"Shouldn't you call your doctor?"

"Uh, yes." She looked more frightened than Grace had ever seen her. "Get me the phone, sweetie?"

Grace got the phone, then stood there, feeling totally helpless, while Jill struggled to remember the number—which underscored the raw fear in her eyes.

"Is it written down somewhere?" Grace asked.

"I know it, I know it," Jill breathed and, after a final hesitation, punched in the last two numbers. "I'll get an answering service," she said and, peering at the paper towels she'd been pressing against the bleeding, swore softly.

"Much?" Grace asked, heart pounding. Much would be bad.

"Enough. Uh, yes, hello. This is Jill Barr. I'm a patient of Dr. Burkhardt's. I'm nine weeks pregnant, and I'm bleeding. . . . No. Not massively. . . . No. I don't see clots." She listened, then shot a frustrated glance at the wall. "I really think I don't want to wait twenty minutes for someone to call me back. I've waited too long for this baby. I'm going to the hospital. Would you pass that message on to the doctor on call?" She hung up and, holding the paper towels in place, pulled her panties over them. "I'm sorry to do this to you, sweetie, I know it's a school night, but we're going out." Walking gingerly, she left the bathroom.

Grace followed. "Is this from the pain you felt earlier?"

"I don't know," Jill said. Even her voice sounded scared.

"Are you miscarrying?"

"God, I hope not." She unhooked a sweatsuit from the closet door. "I need you dressed, Gracie."

Grace pulled on the clothes she had worn that day. Jill was still tying her sneakers. "Can I help?"

"No. I'm okay."

"It may be nothing," Grace tried.

Jill didn't answer.

"There's always something they can do, isn't there?"

"Sure, but it may not be what I want."

Grace knew about D&Cs. Dani told her about a girl who'd had one the year before. At least, the girl called it a D&C. Everyone else called it an abortion. "I mean, aren't there things they can do to save the baby?"

Jill looked frantically around. "Keys." She set off for the kitchen.

Grace hurried after her. "I can get them, Aunt Jill. Tell me what to do. That's why I'm here."

"You're here," Jill said, "to drive me to the hospital."

Grace faltered. "I can't do that. I don't have my license."

Jill grabbed the keys and made for the back stairs. "I do, and you have a permit. We're good to go."

Grace felt faint. Sheer momentum kept her on her aunt's tail. "I can't drive."

"I can't either. I don't want to hemorrhage."

"Call Mom."

"She's ten minutes away, and that's not counting getting dressed. Besides, who'd stay with Dylan?"

"Then Poppy. He's just down the block."

Jill reached the bottom of the stairs and turned back. "No, Grace. You're here. You know how to drive."

"Last time I did, I killed a man."

"Here's your chance for redemption." She pressed the keys into Grace's hand, opened the back door, and went out.

"It's raining," Grace cried as she followed. "It's **raining.** I can't do this."

Jill turned back. She took Grace by the shoulders. Looking stern but desperate, she said, "I need you, Gracie. Right now, you're all I have."

"But it's . . . but it's the **van.**"

Jill smiled. "Automatic shift. Piece o' cake."

Chapter 15

Deborah's phone rang at dawn. Less than ten minutes later, she had Dylan up and dressed, and they were on their way to the hospital. Fortunately, he slept most of the way, so he didn't ask questions she couldn't answer.

Everyone in the emergency room knew why she was there. One of the nurses took Dylan to the cafeteria, while another guided Deborah to the right cubicle. Eyes closed, Jill lay on a gurney, her skin the color of the sheets. Biting her nails, Grace was watching her aunt's every change of expression.

Deborah touched her daughter in passing and went on to take Jill's hand. "Hey."

Jill smiled tiredly. "Hey," she said without opening her eyes.

"Grace said the baby's okay."

"I told her not to call you at this ungodly hour."

"She was right to phone. Is the baby really okay?"

"The baby's fine," Jill said. "It was only spotting. I panicked." She seemed vaguely embarrassed. "When was the last time I did that?"

Deborah couldn't remember. But Jill had never been pregnant before. "I'm glad Grace was with you."

"She didn't get much sleep. We've been here since two."

Grace looked exhausted. There were dark circles under her eyes. This time, Deborah didn't say anything about sleepless nights building character.

"Have they ordered bed rest?" she asked Jill.

"Just for a day or two."

"Are you okay with that?"

"No, but I want this baby. Skye and Tomas will have been baking for a few hours already. They won't even know I'm not upstairs. If one of you can call Alice—"

"I'll call," Grace said, pulling her hand from her mouth and standing straighter. "I can meet her there."

Jill moved her head on the pillow. "You need to sleep. Alice is good. She'll know what to do. Besides, I'm out of here as soon as they give the okay."

"Maybe you should stay a day," Deborah told her sister.

"Insurance won't pay."

"I know, but I'll pay."

"No way," Jill said firmly. "I only came here because it was close and I was scared. The longer I stay, the more people know why I'm here. If Grace hadn't called you, one of the nurses would have. Not much is sacred for a Barr in this place." Her eyes flew to the curtain that separated her cubicle from the rest of the unit. She made a defeated sound.

Michael Barr stood at the edge of the curtain. His clothes were mussed, likely from sleeping in the chair in his den. His eyes were bloodshot, his jaw stubbly.

As a doctor with visiting privileges, he had every right to look at a patient's chart, so he had helped himself to Jill's. When he was done reading, he looked at her in dismay. "Did I have to find out about this from strangers?" When Jill didn't reply, he turned on Deborah. "Did you know about it? Is that what all that please-talk-to-Jill crap was about?"

"It's not crap," Deborah said.

"Let me guess," he told Jill. "You have a boyfriend and forgot to **use** something."

"Wrong," Jill said quietly.

"Then you're carrying someone else's child? A surrogate mother? Doing it for money to support the bakery?"

"Please, Dad," Deborah tried, but Jill spoke more boldly.

"Wrong again. I **paid** to have this child and used my very own egg, which means that this is your biological grandchild."

"You went to a sperm bank? Then you don't know the father."

"I know everything but his name. I know his age, his medical history, his education, his occupation, his looks. I also know that he has other healthy children."

Grace was suddenly all eyes. "How do you know that?"

"Is this anyone's business but Jill's?" Deborah asked, but Jill overrode her again.

"I know of two children, actually, because their mothers used the same registry. That's partly why I went there myself. I wanted to know any half-siblings. I've talked with the two women. They're in touch with each other. They see each other as extended family. They get their kids together several times a year."

"That's **amazing,**" Grace breathed, clearly impressed. "Do the kids look alike?"

"They're two little boys, and no. One

looks just like his mother. But their temperaments are compatible, and they both love playing with cars and blocks."

Michael snorted. "Isn't **that** unique for boys."

Deborah was about to protest when Grace said, "Poppy, you're missing the point."

"They're also very verbal, very athletic, and very creative," Jill went on with remarkable poise for someone flat on her back. "Their dad went to Harvard. Don't you love that? He went to Harvard and rowed Varsity Crew, and now he writes children's books."

"Which no one probably reads," Michael said.

Jill had a comeback for that, too. "His all hit the bestseller lists, and he donates a portion of his profits to children's cancer centers. How can you not love a guy like that? See, Dad? I made sure to pick someone you'd approve of."

"Your mother would be thrilled," he remarked in a voice thick with sarcasm.

Mention of Ruth ended Jill's composure. Tears sprang to her eyes. "She **would** be thrilled. She'd be thrilled because I'm happy, and because she knows I'll make a good mother." She raised her voice as Michael turned to leave. "And she wouldn't be surprised like you are, because she'd have known all this from the start!"

Michael was gone.

Deborah leaned over Jill. "Mom would have been thrilled, you're **entirely** right about that, and she'd have been furious with him." She looked at Grace. "I need to talk with Poppy. You'll stay here with Jill?"

"Don't talk with him," Jill ordered. "There's no point. He won't change his mind."

"Maybe not, but enough is enough, y'know?"

"Dr. Monroe?" said a nurse, opening the curtain.

Dylan was close behind her, with two fingers under his glasses, pressing his eye. "Was that Poppy?" he asked before seeing everyone else in the room. "What's wrong with Aunt Jill?"

Deborah pulled him close and whispered. "She's going to have a baby." Enough was enough with that secret, too.

"Now?"

"No, but she wasn't feeling well, so she came here to make sure everything's okay."

Shutting the eye he'd been pressing—the left eye, the good one, Deborah realized—he looked up. "Is that why Poppy came?"

"Yes."

"Is that why he was angry?"

"He wasn't angry. He's just worried."

Putting his fingers to his left eye again, he mouthed something she couldn't make out.

"What?"

In a rush, he whispered, "Don't tell him about my eye."

"What about your eye?" she said, but suddenly she knew. He had been blinking too often, pressing it too often. Heart heavy, she took his shoulders and looked directly at him. "What about your eye?"

"It **kills,**" he said with a woeful look. "The same way the other one did."

It was all Deborah could do not to cry. "Does the light bother it?" He bobbed his head. "Since when, sweetie?"

"I don't know, but I couldn't say anything because there was all this stuff happening with you and Grace, and I **need** to be with Dad this weekend."

Deborah pulled him close again. "You will be with Dad," she said and met Grace's eyes over the top of his head. "Can you help Aunt Jill?"

Grace seemed torn between anger and worry. "I got her here, didn't I? Where are you going?"

"To see Dr. Brody."

"Nooo, Mom," Dylan wailed.

But Deborah had known there was a problem. Deep in her heart she'd known it but had looked the other way, and all the while Dylan had known what was happening and kept it all to himself.

Deborah didn't want to hear the diagnosis any more than Dylan did, but she did love his eye doctor. Aidan Brody specialized in pediatric ophthamology, and was so good with Dylan that Deborah was doubly sorry she had waited to bring him in. Aidan opened his office early to see them, and did the kind of thorough exam that said he was thrilled to help.

"This is nothing more," he told the boy calmly, "than what you have in the other eye, and it's just as curable. The pain you feel comes from tiny cracks in the surface of the cornea. There are little nerve endings under those cracks. When they are exposed, you feel pain."

"But now I won't be able to see at all," Dylan cried.

"Not true, not true," Aidan said. "You will not lose your sight. In another couple of years, once you stop growing, we'll take care of that."

"Will the transplant cure the farsighted-ness, too?"

"No. You'll continue to wear glasses for hyperopia until laser surgery can cure it. The corneal transplant is only for your lattice dys-trophy."

"But what if it keeps getting worse 'til then?"

"Did the other eye do that?"

"No."

"Right. It stabilized. This one will, too."

"But what if it doesn't?"

"It will, Dylan," he insisted with such gen-tle conviction that Deborah fully believed him. "Tell you what," he said, grabbing a card from the corner of his desk. "I'm going to write down my phone numbers at the office and at home. Any time you get scared, I want you to call." He wrote the numbers large enough for Deborah to see from where she sat. "Now, would I give you my home num-ber if I thought you'd be calling me every two minutes? No, sir. You're going to be too busy with school and your friends. But I bet you've been real worried."

"Yeah," Dylan said, clutching the card.

"Bet you were worried you were going blind."

"Yeah," he admitted sheepishly.

"Now you know you're not, right?"

"Yeah," he replied, worried again, "b-but what if I lose your card?"

Aidan Brody smiled. "Your mom knows my number. She went to medical school with my wife." He nodded at Deborah and smiled. "You can ask her. She'll write you a new card."

As Deborah drove home from Boston, her emotions ran the gamut from relief to fear. Aidan Brody had made it sound easy, but **two** corneal transplants involved **two** separate procedures, neither of which was as simple as removing a wart and both of which involved risk.

Conversely, Dylan was upbeat, the weight of worry off his shoulders and onto hers. But that was what mothers were for.

She stopped home so that they could shower, and when Deborah would have left Dylan there with Lívia to sleep, he wouldn't hear of it. She drove him to school, walked him inside to explain his tardiness, then went to the bakery.

Jill was already home sleeping. Alice had

things under control downstairs, and Grace had collapsed on a sofa in the small third-floor loft.

Deborah stretched out on her back beside Jill, who wakened with the weight shift of the mattress. "What's the story with Dylan's eye?" she asked groggily.

"Same as the other."

Jill came fully awake. "Oh, no. Oh, Deb. I'm sorry."

"Me, too. My heart breaks for Dylan. He'll have surgery in a couple of years, but there's not much to be done until then."

"How's he feeling?"

"He's great. Relieved that it's nothing worse. How are you feeling?"

"I'm okay, too. The spotting stopped. Where's Grace?"

"In the loft. Asleep."

"You need to talk with her, Deborah. She feels very guilty."

"I try, but she isn't biting."

"Try again. She's a fabulous kid. She was the one who drove me to the hospital and back."

Deborah turned her head. "She did?" When her sister nodded, she didn't know whether to be pleased or hurt. "Well, thank you. She wouldn't do that for me."

"She had a choice of driving or letting me bleed to death."

"You weren't bleeding to death."

"We didn't know that at the time. She did what needed to be done. She is like you that way."

Deborah rolled onto her side. "I always assumed she was like me in **every** way. I may have been wrong."

"She's like you in what counts."

"I thought she wanted to be a doctor."

"Is being a doctor what counts most?"

Deborah didn't have to think for long. "No. Look at me, lying here without so much as a call to the office. Jill, I'm sorry about Dad. You know how wrong he is."

"Yeah, well, I guess we always harbor a little hope."

"He'll change," Deborah said. "He just needs time to get used to the idea."

"Spoken by someone who's always been on his good side."

"Not lately."

Jill frowned. "Speaking of which, you do have patients to see."

"I'm tired."

The words hung in the air. After a minute, Jill laughed. "That's something."

It was, Deborah realized. "I've never in my

life let that be an excuse not to work. But I'm tired."

"Of work?"

"Of being good. Of **trying** to be good."

"Of trying to please Dad," Jill added.

"That, too."

"What happens if you don't show up at the office?"

"I don't know, since I've never not shown up before."

"Your patients will understand."

"Do I **care?**" Deborah shot back, then quickly said, "Yes, I care—but, my God, I've **always** been there for them. If they can't understand that just for once I need a little time, well, too bad."

"And Dad?"

"Dad'll be angry. But he'll cover for me. He'll be thinking of last Saturday, when **he** didn't show up, or maybe of this morning when he behaved like an asshole. He's probably feeling guilty. He hasn't called my cell." She had a thought. "Maybe he's writing me out of the practice. Wouldn't **that** be something?"

"Deborah. You don't want that."

She smiled sadly. "No. The practice works for me."

"It works for him, too. If he can't understand that this is a rough time for you and that you need him right now, shame on him."

"Dad? Can we talk?" Deborah asked from the door of his office.

Michael was at his desk reading. One hand held the pen that was filling out forms, the other half a calzone from the Italian restaurant down the street. A bottle of Diet Coke stood nearby, half-filled with what was clearly a dark liquid. If he was drinking something else, there was no evidence of it.

Eyeing her over his glasses, he asked in a reasonable enough tone, "Where've you been? It's been a zoo here."

"I'm sorry. I had an emergency with Dylan's eyes. I had to take him into Boston."

Michael put down the calzone. "What's the problem?" When Deborah explained, he was visibly upset. **"Both** eyes now?"

"Aidan says it happens."

"His eyesight will get worse before it gets better?"

"Looks that way," Deborah said. "Dylan's great. He insisted on going to school. Me, I'm barely beginning to process what it means. If I'm in denial, so be it. There's absolutely nothing I can do about it right now. I just . . . need to talk with you."

Michael tossed the pen aside. "If you want to talk about your sister, save your breath. I don't know what to say. I never have when it comes to Jill."

"Then let's talk about Mom," Deborah suggested.

His mouth thinned. "If you're going to say she'd be pleased, you can save your breath there, too. This wouldn't have happened if she'd been alive."

"Dad, Jill's thirty-four. She'd have done this with or without Mom's blessing."

"No. Your mother knew how to deal with you girls." Removing his glasses, he sat back. "Good God, Deborah, how could you not tell me about this?"

"I didn't know." How lovely it was to be able to honestly say that! "Jill wanted to do this on her own."

"But I'm her father **and** a doctor. By the way, do we know the doctor she used?"

"Burkhardt. She's good."

He gave a grunt. "At least your sister's learned that much."

"She's learned a lot more, Dad. She knew that she wanted a family. That's what the whole half-sibling thing is about. She wants her child to have family."

He grunted again and looked away. "That doesn't say much for her opinion of us."

"I don't take it personally," Deborah said. "My kids are older than Jill's will be, and, besides, the moms will be a support group for her."

Michael frowned. "We can't be that?"

"Dad," Deborah reminded him, "you weren't exactly jumping for joy."

"Are **you** okay with this?" he asked.

"Now that the initial shock has worn off? Yeah, I am. I always knew Jill loved kids. She's been fabulous with mine. I always knew she wanted her own. I let myself think of the bakery as her baby, but it isn't."

Michael looked down and pursed his lips.

Deborah knew what he was thinking, but she didn't have the energy to get into that argument again. Besides, the issue of the bakery was old news. "Jill does things her own way."

"Every child needs a father."

"In an ideal world, yes. But maybe our definition of 'ideal' needs to change. Look at our practice. We've seen physical abuse. We've seen emotional neglect. A bad dad can be worse than no dad. Besides, it's not like Jill's baby will be unique. Half the families in town are either blended or made up of a single parent."

"And that," Michael declared, "is why humans, like me, live only so long and then die. The world changes too much for us to accept. The beliefs we've lived by for decades become obsolete. If you'd ever told me both of my daughters would be raising children in non-traditional homes, I'd have said you were crazy." He opened his arms as if to hold a dream, then let them drop. "I wanted better. For both of you. What's happening? Since your mother's been gone, it's all fallen apart."

"Nothing that's happened since she died wouldn't have happened anyway," Deborah pointed out.

"You're wrong, missy. She'd have held things together."

"How?" Deborah argued. "What would she have done? Asked Greg not to leave and, shazam, he'd have stayed? Found a man for Jill and, presto, Jill would have fallen in love? Mom would have been a buffer, that's all. She would have helped you over the bumps in our lives."

"Since when do I need help?" he asked indignantly, but Deborah refused to back down.

"Since she died. Mom was always there for you. She filtered things. Now that you don't have her, things seem worse."

He shook his head. "She'd have held it together. I mean, Christ, look at your sister. Look at **you.** I got a call this morning from an investigator wanting to know what our relationship is with John Colby."

Deborah tensed. "What kind of investigator?"

"He was from the district attorney's office," Michael said, "which is apparently investigating your accident."

If the state police report had cleared her of criminal wrongdoing, the involvement of the district attorney had to do with civil charges. Definitely **not** what she wanted to hear. "Was it just a phone call, or did they stop by?"

"Why does it matter?"

"I don't know. I'm just trying to figure out what it was about." Likely nothing, she told herself. Just a question or two. But why ask about John?

"I'm afraid I can't help you," Michael said sweetly. "Polite as the fellow was, I didn't have the time to chat with him, because I was running from one patient to the next trying to cover for you."

"But he did mention the D.A.'s office?"

"Yes, and not once in my entire life have I had a call like that." He went on the attack—eyes flashing. "This family doesn't **do** things that bring the D.A.'s office snooping. You said it was a simple accident. You said you weren't doing anything wrong. Why in the hell would the D.A.'s office be wanting to know about our relationship with John? Our medical files are privileged. If our patients think that we're talking, we could lose half our caseload."

Deborah was more worried about Grace than about their practice. Calls from the D.A.'s office would increase the burden the girl was carrying.

Wondering what the chances were that the call to her father would be the end of it, Deborah said, "We won't lose patients. The D.A.'s office isn't asking for medical information."

"They're asking for something, and maybe it's just the start. I don't know what happened that night, but I'm telling you, if your mother had been alive—"

"—nothing would be different!" Deborah cried. **"Enough,** Dad. Mom could not have done a single thing to prevent that accident!"

His eyes were wide. "She left me with a mess. What was she thinking?"

"She didn't **plan** to die," Deborah shouted, beside herself.

"Damn right she didn't plan it, but she died, and where did that leave me? We were supposed to grow old together. We were supposed to travel and enjoy the benefits of working for so long. She was supposed to live longer than me." He seemed suddenly bewildered.

In that instant, distracted as she was, Deborah understood where Michael was coming from. Anger was a stage of grief.

Leaning over his desk with tears in her eyes, she said, "Listen to me, Dad. When Dylan's first cornea went bad, I grieved for the perfect child he should have been. I told myself that the diagnosis was wrong. I bargained with God—you know, make his eyes right and I'll do anything. When that didn't work I was absolutely **furious** that my child had to face this. In the end I had no choice. I had to accept it, because that was the only way I could help Dylan." She straightened. "Grieving is a process. Anger is part of it." She paused. "Right now, you're angry that Mom left you alone. But you're taking it out on Jill and me, and we both need you. You can drink all you want—" she raised a quick hand when his eyes darkened, "but it doesn't help, Dad. We **need** you."

Chapter 16

Deborah phoned John, but he knew nothing about the D.A.'s investigation. She called Hal, was told he was in court, and left a message. Having no information, she said nothing to Grace when she called to check on Jill. She called Greg, but had to leave a message there, too.

She saw patients through the afternoon, and each one, it seemed, had an ongoing issue with loss, from the woman who had lost her job, to the one who had lost her house, to the one who had lost her husband and wasn't able to sleep, or work, or enjoy her grandchildren. Deborah found herself talking repeatedly about unresolved anger.

Just as she was getting ready to head to the bakery, Karen called. Her voice held an element of fear.

"I think something's wrong," she said.

Deborah felt a split second's panic. "What kind of something?"

"I have a headache that isn't going away. It's been a week now."

·A symptom not to be dismissed; still, Deborah had seen her during that time. Her panic eased. "A week?"

"Well, maybe not a week. Maybe three or four days."

"Why haven't you told me?" Deborah asked. She put the strap of her bag on her shoulder and picked up her paperwork.

"Because I hate reporting every little ache and pain, and I told myself it was nothing. I do forget about it when I'm busy, but as soon as I stop, it's right there again. It isn't debilitating, but it nags." She raced on. "You're right about what happens every year around the anniversary of my mastectomy, so I've been telling myself it's nothing, but what if it isn't?"

Deborah left her office. The door to her father's was open. He had already left. "Where is the pain?"

"It kind of wanders, sometimes around the back, sometimes around the front."

"Is it causing you nausea or vomiting?" Deborah asked as she put the papers on the business manager's desk.

"No.

"And I know you've been doing the elliptical, so we can assume there's no loss of feeling in your arms or legs." She flipped off the lights. "I truly don't think it's anything serious, K," she said as she punched in the alarm. "You can always have an MRI, but let's see if there might be another cause."

"Like **what?**" Karen asked. Clearly, she could think of one cause and one cause alone.

Deborah understood that. "Eye strain. Those new sunglasses you bought. Maybe the prescription is wrong." She went out and locked the door.

"The prescription's the same. I only got new frames."

"Okay, if it's not eye strain, it could be muscle strain. Are you feeling any tightness at the back of your neck?"

"Yes."

"That would do it," Deborah said as she got to her car. It was the only one left in the lot.

"Even when the headache's at the front of my head?"

"It may be hormonal."

"My period ended a week ago."

"Could be that your cycle is shifting."

"Shifting—as in **menopause?** I'm too young!"

"Not as in menopause, just shifting, but it could also be from fatigue." There were more causes for headache than Deborah could count. "How are you sleeping?"

"Poorly." Sounding discouraged now, Karen added, "I spend half my night looking at Hal."

"Why?" Deborah asked, but she knew what was coming. Her gut had told her that this was the root of the problem.

"He sleeps like a log. He never used to, Deborah. He used to be the one who was up a lot during the night. He said he was always thinking about work—just couldn't turn it off. Is he suddenly **not** thinking about work? And it's not like he's exhausted from making love. We rarely do it. And today? I haven't been able to reach him. Lately, I **never** can reach him. I've been testing him, calling for little reasons, just to see, and I leave messages. I don't necessarily ask him to call me back—he hates nagging—but you'd think he'd feel that at least some things I'm asking deserve an answer. Either he's legitimately busy, or he doesn't want to talk to me."

Deborah wanted to say, **fuck him,** which was fine and dandy for her, but didn't help

Karen. So she said, "I don't think you need to worry about a brain tumor. Your headache's from tension."

"This isn't a joke."

"Neither is cancer, and that's always a concern, but I don't think that is what's causing your headache."

"You think it's from Hal," said Karen. "But I'm probably being ridiculous. You said it yourself—he's a good-looking man. It's just that I keep in shape and color my hair to hide the gray and spend a fortune on moisturizers to make my skin **glow,** and when he doesn't seem to notice, I imagine something's wrong. It's not like there've been any more calls. I'm sure you were right about that, too—just some woman who wishes she could have him and, since she can't, she wants to cause trouble." Her voice changed. "I'm imagining this. Absolutely." She sighed. "Okay, I feel better. Thanks, Deb."

Deborah felt slightly ill. She knew Hal was having an affair, knew it as much as she could without hard evidence, but she couldn't say anything to Karen. What good would it do? And if she was wrong?

Hal didn't return her call, either.

Greg did. His response to Dylan's diagnosis was to repeatedly ask how Deborah could have missed the signs of trouble. He was upset. He needed someone to blame. But she was feeling guilty enough on her own. **I asked; he denied it. I asked again; he denied it again. I kept a close eye on him, but at what point does my own concern cause his? And what harm was the small delay? Dylan's glasses address his hyperopia. There is nothing to be done about corneal dystrophy until he's old enough for a transplant.**

"All valid points," Greg acknowledged, "except that if you'd told me sooner, I could have talked with him. You need to share these things, Deborah. I'm still his father."

"Well, now you know," she said, frustrated. "By the way—not that you asked how I could talk so freely—Dylan and Grace are at Jill's. I'm on my way to pick up Lívia's dinner and bring it back there. Jill's pregnant and has to be in bed."

"**Jill's** pregnant?" he asked. "Good for Jill. Not getting married, I gather? She's some free spirit. Maybe I married the wrong sister."

Deborah was tired enough to explode. "She was sixteen when we met, which means that you'd have been charged with statutory rape." She couldn't resist adding, "You'd have been labeled a dirty old man for life—and besides, you didn't **want** a free spirit back then. You wanted a very stable woman, or so you told me, unless you were lying through your teeth. And what makes you think my sister would have even wanted **you?**"

Deborah stopped herself, realizing that the anger was still there—that her divorce was yet another unresolved issue in her life—when she turned a corner and spotted a gray car parked in front of her house.

"Can we discuss this another time?" she asked tensely. Before Greg could answer, she said, "Gotta run," and ended the call. She studied the car as she cruised slowly down the street. There were two men in the front. She pulled into the driveway, but didn't open the garage door. Cell phone in hand, she climbed out. She waited while the two men did the same.

Both wore suits. The man in the lead was slightly older and heavier. "Dr. Monroe?" he asked in a pleasant enough voice.

"Yes?"

"My name's Guy Fielding. My partner's Joe McNair. We're detectives with the D.A.'s office. Wonder if we could talk with you for a minute?"

Deborah swore silently. She didn't want to talk with them. Grace would absolutely **lose** it when she found out. But her options were few. She could refuse to talk, but that would be a sign of guilt. She could get back in her car and lock the doors, but that was childish. She could try to drive off, but then they might follow her.

"Do you have ID?" she finally asked.

Both reached into their jackets and produced badges. The pictures matched the faces.

Politely, she asked, "Could you tell me what this is about?"

"There was an accident last week. We have a few questions."

"I believe I answered everything that the police asked me at the time."

"That's correct. We've read the report you filed. We just have a few more."

She nodded. Without asking permission, she opened her phone and tried calling Hal. His office was closed, and he didn't answer his cell. She ended the call without leaving a message, and tried John. Carla patched her through to him at home.

"Hey, it's Deborah. I have two men here at my place. They say they're with the D.A.'s office."

"State police detectives assigned to the D.A.'s office," Guy Fielding put in.

Deborah repeated it for John. "Do I have to talk with them?"

"No, but you probably should," John said. "I checked with the D.A. after you called me before. You can be honest with them. There's nothing to hide."

If only he knew. The thought of talking with the state police was frightening.

Raising a hand to keep the detectives where they were, she went to the far side of the driveway and said quietly into the phone, "I don't understand why they're here. I thought the accident report cleared me."

"The widow went to the D.A. and made a complaint."

A civil suit. Deborah hadn't wanted to think about it when her father mentioned their call. "A complaint about what?"

"She's upset the local police haven't filed charges, so she went to the D.A. She was waiting at his office when it opened this morning. He told her he was familiar with the case since it involved a death, but that the decision to charge anyone is made at the local level. She's claiming a cover-up. No surprise there."

"There was no cover-up."

"We know that," John said, sounding uncharacteristically perturbed, but how often had he been at the wrong end of an investigation, Deborah wondered? "It was the state team that cleared you."

"Yet on her say-so alone the D.A. can file charges?"

"No. That's getting ahead of things. He won't do anything unless there's cause. His job is to take a fresh look at the case. If we had found you negligent, she'd likely have been satisfied. With the recon team just now clearing you, the timing is pretty coincidental."

There was another coincidence Deborah didn't want to think about. She had talked with Tom last night, and the widow had run to the D.A. this morning. "What about her husband's bizarre behavior?" Deborah asked John. "The D.A. should be wondering about **him.**"

"He is. But talking with you is part of the process. His men'll be talking with me and will probably want to talk with Grace."

Dread settled in the pit of her stomach. "Why?"

"She was in the car. We didn't interview her, so this is probably good."

Deborah didn't think it was good at all.

Grace was shaky enough without official questions.

"Do I need Hal here?" she asked. For all his faults, Hal did know the law.

"Can you reach him?" John asked.

"No."

"Then talk with the men now. You can be honest."

Deborah nodded. "Okay." She would gladly talk with them if they would spare Grace.

Ending the call, she walked back to the men.

Guy Fielding gestured toward the house. "Would you like to go inside?"

Absolutely not, Deborah thought. She wasn't opening **her** home to men who were looking to prolong an agony that was very personal in so many ways.

"This is fine," she said and, pushing her hair off her face, leaned against the car. "It's a nice night." And while the sun had dropped low enough to silhouette the trees, there was still a lingering warmth.

"I take it that was John Colby," the lead detective said.

Too late, she realized that she had spoken his name into the phone, not a wise move if the charge was a cover-up. That said, she hadn't done anything wrong, not where John was concerned.

"He's our police chief," she explained. "He's been in charge of the investigation here. He verified that you are who you say."

"Do you talk with him often?"

"No more so than anyone else in a town this small."

"But you have talked with him about the accident."

"Yes," she said. "He was at the scene right after it happened. He asked questions. I answered them. I saw him again the next day when I went to the police station to file an accident report."

"And you talked then?"

"About filing the report. He gave me the form and told me how many copies I needed to file."

"Has he been here at your house since the accident?"

"We're not social friends."

"No, but has he been here?"

She tried to think back. The days since the accident were starting to blur. "He came here on the day of Calvin McKenna's funeral. There had been an . . . incident at the cemetery. He wanted to know what happened."

"Your presence upset the widow," the second detective put in.

Deborah guessed that Mrs. McKenna had given them quite an account. "The funeral was open to the town. I wanted to go."

"So John Colby came here afterward," Fielding went on. "How did he find out what happened?"

"This is a small town. And anyway, one of his men was at the service."

"You didn't call him yourself?"

"Absolutely not. It was a humiliating experience. I didn't want to talk about it. All I wanted to do was climb in a hole." Tom's visit had helped. Then, and in every subsequent talk, he had been reasonable. But he had been asking about John last night. More than simple curiosity?

"Were you angry?" the second detective asked.

She returned to the day of the funeral. "At John?"

"At the McKennas."

"No. I was embarrassed and hurt. They were grieving. I could understand what they were feeling." She frowned. "Excuse me, but I'm confused. Where are you headed with these questions?" John had told her. She wanted them to confirm it.

But the first detective simply asked, "Were there other times you talked with John since the accident?"

"Yes. I was anxious about the reconstruction team's report. I called him several times to see if it was in."

"Couldn't your lawyer have done that?" asked the second detective.

"My lawyer?"

"Hal Trutter. Did he call John, too?"

"You'll have to ask him that," Deborah said. She wasn't speaking for Hal. "And he **is** a personal friend," she specified to differentiate their relationship from the one she had with John. "I haven't hired a lawyer."

"He's also a friend of John Colby's."

"They play poker together."

The lead detective said, "Let's get back to the chief of police. I understand he's a patient of yours."

"Yes. He and his wife. My dad's been practicing in Leyland for more than thirty-five years. I don't know exactly when John and Ellen signed on, but they go back a ways. John sees my dad, I see Ellen."

"Why's that?" asked the second detective, the bad cop of the pair.

Deborah looked at him. "Men are often

more comfortable being examined by a man, women by a woman."

"Then you've never examined John?"

Again she frowned. "What does this have to do with the accident?" She relented, but not to the point of discussing medical issues. "I understand that the widow is upset. She wants to blame someone for her husband's death."

"Did Colby tell you that?"

He had. But so had Tom—Tom, whom she had told about the poker connection; Tom, whom she had told about begging John for the accident report; Tom, whom she'd thought she could trust.

"John didn't have to tell me," she said. "I'm good at connecting the dots. Calvin McKenna's brother was the one who led me away from the funeral. He accused me of hoping for a free pass."

"Have you gotten one?" asked the second detective.

Deborah's patience was wearing thin. She was disappointed in Tom, frightened by a civil suit, terrified for Grace. She only wanted to get Lívia's dinner and head back to Jill's. "You wouldn't be asking that if you'd seen the state police team at the accident scene that night.

They looked at everything. They **photo-graphed** everything. Don't you trust their report?"

"Their report wouldn't reflect possible collusion between you and the police chief."

"And is that your conclusion?" she asked. When Guy Fielding raised a mediating hand between them, she moderated her voice, but only slightly. She was furious. "The state team found no wrongdoing on my part. The report also states that the quote unquote **victim** wasn't running on the road before my car came along. He came straight out of the woods and into the path of my car. Are you investigating that? Frankly, I'm starting to wonder who the victim is. My daughter and I have been through hell—because a man ran irresponsibly on a night when visibility was nil. My opinion," she said and looked from one to the other, "is that you're barking up the wrong tree."

"And where should we look?" the lead detective asked with what Deborah chose to think was respect.

"The widow. Ask her what her husband was doing there that night. Ask her why he wasn't wearing reflective gear, and why he wasn't carrying ID saying he was on a drug that could cause lethal bleeding. Ask her why

she's **so desperate** to pin his death on someone else."

The gray car had barely turned the corner
when Deborah called Karen. "Is Hal home?"

"Not yet, but he did call. One of his
clients is being indicted. He's been working
with the prosecutors for months to avoid this,
but now the client has panicked. Hal's with
him." She paused. "When I hear stories like
this, I feel so guilty imagining the things I did.
Tell me I'm stupid, Deborah."

"You are not stupid," Deborah said. "You're
human."

Her voice must have held more urgency
than the words warranted, because Karen
asked, "Is something wrong?"

All Deborah could say was, "Cal McKenna's
widow went to the D.A. Will you have Hal
call when he gets in?"

"Oh, sweetie, I'm sorry. I will."

"On my cell."

"Definitely," Karen said.

Hal's excuse to Karen might be totally
valid, Deborah realized, but she wasn't in the
mood for excuses. She phoned his cell again.
This time, she left a message. "I don't know
where in the hell you are, Hal, or who you're

with, but if I don't hear back from you within an hour, I'm getting another lawyer."

With her anger focused on Hal, she went inside, grabbed Lívia's pot of chicken stew, carried it to the car, and put it on the floor. She drove back to Jill's with an eye on the clock, determined not to say anything to Grace until she'd spoken to Hal. One hour. That was all she would give him.

He took forty minutes, and the timing couldn't have been worse. Deborah was re-heating the stew in Jill's kitchen, distracted enough to have asked Dylan three times how he was feeling. Grace happened to be nearest the phone when it rang. She saw Hal's name.

"What's he want?" she asked, passing Deborah the phone.

Deborah couldn't lie. She had done that once, and it had become a wedge between Grace and her. "The widow is making trouble," she told the girl, then asked Hal, "Where've you been?" She sounded bitchy and didn't care.

"Client emergency. What's up?"

Walking into the living room, she told him about the detectives. In response to his prodding, she related as much of the conversation as she could.

"They're fishing," he said.

"For **what?** The accident team report clears me, doesn't it? What more could they possibly find?"

"The widow claims the local police monkeyed with the evidence."

"But **John** didn't collect it. The **state** team did."

"Cool it, Deborah," Hal said. "A man died. They need to reassure themselves that the investigation was conducted properly. They're only doing their job."

"They're wasting my time!"

He sighed. "Don't tell them that. You don't want to rile them up. Obstruction of justice is a felony."

"A felony?"

"But hey, it doesn't sound like you told the detectives anything you shouldn't. I just wish you'd called me."

A **felony?** She swallowed a moment's panic. "I did call you. You weren't there. You never are." A felony charge was **bad.** "Where've you **been?**"

"You sound like my wife."

"Maybe she has a point. What's up, Hal?

People need you, and you're not around. You're playing an awful lot of racquetball these days."

There was a pause, then a cautious, "Are you suggesting something, Deborah?"

"That depends. Are you guilty?"

"Me, no. Let's talk about you. A felony conviction is serious. Hell, if the D.A. files charges, you could be prevented from practicing pending the outcome of a trial. Is that what you want?"

"No. I don't want **any** of this," Deborah cried.

"Then you don't want to rile me, either. I know the D.A. I can negotiate. I may just be your best bet at putting this case to bed."

She might have lashed back, arguing that there was **no** cover-up and that he was changing the subject, but she saw Grace watching her from the kitchen. She forced herself to calm down. Hal was right. She didn't want to rile him. "Okay," she said. "Thanks for calling. Can we talk tomorrow?"

"Your choice, sweetie. You want me, you call." He hung up.

If Deborah had any doubts, they were gone. Hal was a two-timing bastard.

But Grace was staring straight at her with

terrified eyes. "It's not over, is it," she said. "It won't ever be over."

"It will," Deborah vowed. Pushing her hair back, she tried to think straight. "We always knew this was a possibility. The widow is angry. She feels she has to do something."

"Tell them," Grace whispered.

Deborah went to her, but when she would have taken her daughter's hand, Grace crossed her arms. Deborah felt the loss. She was the one who had needed the comfort of a human touch.

Feeling on the edge of a panic that she could not let her daughter see, she asked, "What good would telling them do? It won't change the widow's case. She doesn't care who was driving, Grace. She's saying that John didn't do a thorough job investigating, but the **state** team investigated, so she doesn't have a case. The D.A. will never press charges."

"Like Mr. McKenna won't die?" Grace asked and quietly turned away.

Deborah didn't know whether it was mention of the name McKenna, or simply a natural progression of thought, but having told off both the detectives and Hal, her focus settled on Tom. Her anger built slowly, almost without her realizing it, simmering all through Lívia's dinner and the ride home. She didn't know if Tom was a friend, but she felt betrayed. It was absurd, she knew. But there it was.

Dylan fell asleep. She tried to talk to Grace, using Jill's pregnancy as an icebreaker, but Grace gave dismissive, one-word answers, finally pleading that she had to do homework, study flash cards for her PSATs, and cram for a biology AP exam. If she'd had more strength, Deborah would have discussed Grace's terseness, because there had been accusation in the listing.

But she was tired of fighting. Leaving Grace alone, she climbed into bed, but sleep wouldn't come. After an hour of tossing and turning, she kicked back the covers, went down to the kitchen, and made tea. When that did nothing to soothe her, she turned on a light in the den and tried to think who she could call. She didn't want to wake Jill, and Karen didn't answer. In desperation, she called Tom.

He had been asleep. She was upset enough not to care. Nor did she care about pleasantries. She had lived her life on pleasantries, and, like so many other things lately, they seemed a waste of time. As soon as he said that groggy hello, she said, "I trusted you."

There was a pause, then, "Deborah?"

"I trusted you," she repeated, suddenly on the attack. She was angry. And hurt. "I told you things I shouldn't have about my family. I actually thought we were friends, but now I'm wondering why a pair of detectives confronted me with all the information I told you last night. Were you working with Selena all along? Is that what the conversations we've had were about?"

There was silence, then a quiet, "No—"

"Maybe it was my fault," Deborah interrupted before he could say more. "Maybe I imagined a bond where there wasn't one. I mean, we were both agonizing over family crises, and even though they were different, I thought we understood each other. Was I wrong? Was I seeing something that wasn't there at all?"

He started to speak, but she raced on. "And besides, why would I have ever thought we could be friends? One look at you, and my daughter **freaks out.** We just want this over, Tom. But now, another investigation? You know there was no crime committed. Dragging things out won't bring your brother back." With the worst of her anger spent, she added, "I trusted you. Maybe I was a fool for that. I thought the trust was mutual." When he didn't reply, she said softly, "Are you still there?"

"Yes."

"You're not saying anything."

"You needed to vent."

"See?" she cried. "That's what I mean. Why are you being so nice?"

"Was I wrong?"

"**No.** But your reaction is very misleading given everything that's happened. Do you think I've tried to cover up anything? Are you helping Selena?"

"No to both."

"But you didn't stop her from going to the D.A."

"I didn't know she was going."

"Does she know what the report says about Cal?"

"She knows," he said with feeling.

"And what does she say? I mean, his behavior was **bizarre.** Doesn't she **see** that there was no way we could have avoided hitting him if he just darted out of the woods in front of us?"

"She can't admit that. She's too emotional."

"Well, so am I," Deborah cried, because, when it came down to it, Cal's behavior was too suspicious to ignore. "Your brother sounds disturbed. Maybe he **caused** the accident."

"Don't you think I've asked myself that question?" Tom burst out.

"We can come up with lots of other theories, like that Cal was disoriented by the glare of my headlights, or that he wasn't feeling well, or that he had a bad reaction to some other medication his wife didn't know about. When you put all the clues together, though, they suggest your brother was suicidal."

"You don't think I've wondered about that, too?" said Tom loudly. "I can't do this on the phone," he muttered almost to himself, then asked, "Can we talk tomorrow? Not on the phone, in person?"

"You're suing me," Deborah reminded him.

"I'm not. I have nothing to do with it, but we have to talk. I do trust you, Deborah. That's why I keep speaking with you. You understand what I'm saying. I need your help with this."

Put that way, what could she say?

Once they agreed to a time and a place, Deborah ended the call and returned to bed. She awoke Thursday morning to the sound of Dylan's keyboard. "Mr. Tambourine Man" was so lighthearted after the dismal news that had come the day before that she smiled all through breakfast.

Then she drove the kids to school, with her daughter as distant as ever, and she felt like a fraud again. She could yell and scream all she wanted on the phone, but if the issue between Tom and her was trust, she was abusing his. He didn't know about Grace.

Chapter 17

Deborah left the bakery with a warm sticky bun and the desperate wish that her father lived two hours away. Being thirty-eight years of age didn't seem to count for anything when it came to fearing a parent. Parking behind his car, she entered the house quietly. His coffee was ready, his bagel set out. She put her bag on the table and was mustering the courage to go looking for him when she heard him come down the front stairs.

He gave her a brief glance—more uncomfortable than angry, she realized with some relief—and went straight to the coffee urn. "You have yours?" he asked without turning.

"I'm all set."

He fixed his coffee and took the bagel to the table. Once seated, he saw the bakery bag. "Is your sister all right?" he asked quietly.

Curiosity was a good sign, Deborah decided. Subdued was better than belligerent. "She's fine. Not happy, though. I forbade her to go downstairs for at least one more day."

"And she'll listen to you?" he asked with a wry twist of his mouth.

She took the question for the rhetorical one it was and said, "Dad, I need your help this morning."

"Don't ask me to call her. I'm the last one she'll listen to."

"Not Jill," Deborah said. "It's something else. I need to take off for a couple of hours. It's about that call you received yesterday." As succinctly as she could—while his humor held—she told him about the suit the widow wanted to bring, the detectives from the district attorney's office, and what the report said about Cal running out of the woods in front of her car. She ended by telling him about Tom.

Drinking his coffee, he listened without interruption. When she was done, he asked, "Why meet with him?"

"Because he asked," she said simply, then added, "He knows his brother was suicidal. He's trying to deal with that."

"Throwing oneself in front of a car doesn't guarantee death."

"For a Coumadin user, it might."

"Was he depressed? Did he leave a note?"

"No note. And Tom doesn't know if he was depressed."

"Was he under unusual stress?"

"I don't know. Tom might. I'd like to ask him."

"Would he tell you the truth?"

"Yes. We have a good rapport. I think he sees me as a resource. When he learned his brother was on Coumadin, he asked me lots of questions about it."

"Think it's a setup?"

"No. I think he likes to bounce things off me."

"Why you?" her father asked. "There must be other people in his life."

Deborah was sure that there were, but whether Tom confided in them was something else. "I think it's just that I live in the town where his brother lived. My daughter had him in school. Tom says he trusts me."

Michael arched a brow. "His sister-in-law is suing you."

Deborah didn't need the reminder. "He says he didn't know she was. He hadn't met her until last week."

"That's odd."

"It's an odd family. Or was. Tom is all

that's left. He's struggling with what's happened."

"That's natural," Michael granted. "But should you be the one helping him?"

"It feels right to me."

"Like redemption?"

"Maybe," she acknowledged. Whatever was proven about Cal's intentions that night, the fact remained that he had been hit by her car.

Her father swallowed the last of his bagel. "I think Hal should go with you."

For the first time in the discussion, Deborah disagreed. "Hal would inhibit the conversation."

"It's not like this guy's your friend. What if he's wearing a wire?"

"He won't be," Deborah said. "If we're discussing his brother, he has more to lose than I do. He won't want any talk of suicide on tape. Suicide would jeopardize a life insurance payment. Besides, he is kind of a friend."

"A friend who gives redemption."

Deborah didn't know whether Michael was being facetious, but chose to take him seriously. "I can talk with him. He listens."

"Hal should be with you."

"I trust Tom."

Michael was quiet. Then he raised guarded eyes. "Why are you telling me this?"

"I need you to cover for me this morning."

"You could have called. Or walked in here and said you had a conference with one of the kids' teachers. You could have just not shown up, like yesterday."

She felt duly guilty. "I'm sorry for that. I didn't have much advance warning."

"And today you do? I think you want my blessing for this, but I can't give it, Deborah. You walk in here talking about being sued, and now you're going to meet with the man who's suing you? That's crazy."

"Is it?" she asked, because there was a very practical side to her meeting with Tom. "He's not the one suing me. The widow is. He may be able to control her."

"You said he barely knows her."

"But if anyone can influence her, he can. He'll tell her the down side of a suit. I need to do this, Dad. Grace and I won't rest easy until the case is resolved."

He stared at her for a minute. "It doesn't matter what I say. You'll do what you want." Turning his back on her, he went to the sink.

Deborah sat for another minute. She had come for her father's approval, but suddenly that seemed sad. "I'm an adult," she said. "I have instincts. Sometimes I have to follow them."

"What do you want from me then?"

She stood. "Respect. Acknowledgment that maybe what's right for me wouldn't be right for you."

He half turned. "You girls exasperate me."

"We can't always live up to your expectations, but that doesn't necessarily make us wrong. Times change. I need you to understand why I'm doing what I am."

"I'm trying, Deborah, but it's hard."

"It's hard for me, too," she replied. The hollow feeling inside wasn't new, but finally she had an inkling where it came from. "You keep saying you miss Mom, but don't you think I do, too? She was always in my corner, and I'm in a tough place right now. I need you to support me. If she'd been here . . ." Throat tight, she stopped.

Gruffly, Michael said, "Well, she isn't. You're right. Times change."

Deborah's eyes filled with tears. "She was a good listener," she managed to say, but that was all. Leaving her father at the sink, she returned to her car. She had driven barely a block when she pulled over, put her forehead to the wheel, and wept.

She missed her mother. Thirty-eight years old, and she might have been five, but too much had happened in her life of late. Deborah hadn't even cried like this when Ruth died. She'd had to hold things together for her father and everyone else then. Now she sobbed until she ran out of tears.

That made her late for her meeting with Tom at the park. His black car was the only one in the dirt lot. As she parked beside it, she spotted him standing by a stream some thirty feet away.

Putting on sunglasses to hide her eyes, she crossed the grass. "I'm sorry. I meant to be here on time."

"I thought you'd decided not to come," he said. "Your lawyer must have advised against it."

She waved dismissively and looked down at the stream. The soft sound of its movement was soothing. "Funny. I have no problem with water like this. I love the ocean. Love lakes. Love taking a shower or bath. It's just rain that upsets me."

For a minute, he didn't reply. Then he said, "You sound like you have a cold."

So much for wearing dark glasses. "No. I

just had a long crying jag." There seemed no point in denying it. "That's why I was late. I just sat there on the side of the road crying. Totally helpless."

She could feel him studying her. "What caused it?"

She shrugged. "Life. It overwhelms some-times."

"But you cry and recover. Some people don't. Why is that?"

She looked up at him then. He wore a wrinkled shirt, tails hanging over his jeans. His hands were in his pockets. His eyes met hers.

"I could say we are born with survival skills," she said, "but it's experience, too. Life treats each of us differently."

A pair of chickadees flitted by. She watched them disappear into a willow on the opposite bank.

"But what about the person who refuses to acknowledge his emotions?" Tom asked.

"Is that what Cal did?"

The birds were joined by others in the tree, loudly calling to each other.

"Pretty much," Tom admitted. "I was talk-ing with Selena after we saw the medical records. She kept asking how he could have had those little strokes and still risked her life by driving with her in the car, like she was expendable. She kept asking how he could have kept so much of himself from her, as if he didn't need her at all. But Cal always hid what he felt."

"Always?"

It was a minute before he said, "My parents didn't encourage emotional expression. My mom didn't like crying, and once we were old enough to take care of ourselves, she just wasn't there. What's the point of crying, if there's no one to hear?"

Having just stopped sobbing herself, Deborah said, "Catharsis."

He shot her a look. "You know that and I know it, but Cal? He never saw the point, I guess."

"Why wasn't your mom there? Did she travel with your dad?"

"That was the official story, but the truth was, she was off doing her own thing. I never knew what that was, only that she didn't like being tied down any more than my father did."

"But they chose to have children," Deborah argued and would have said something about the responsibility inherent in that if he hadn't spoken first.

"They didn't actively choose to have us.

She used to tell me that we were both little surprises. I always believed she was relieved when Cal came along, so that she wouldn't feel so guilty leaving me alone. By the time I was in high school, it was just Cal and me for days at a time."

"Where was Social Services?" Deborah asked in alarm.

"Not at our house." He qualified that. "In fairness to my parents, we had food and clothes and heat. We never lacked in the physical sense."

"Only in the emotional. But why would it take a greater toll on Cal than on you?" Deborah asked, because Tom was clearly steady, solid both physically **and** emotionally.

Taking his hands from his pockets, he said, "Maybe I was a lousy parent to him."

Deborah wondered if that was why he didn't have a wife and kids of his own. "You were a child yourself."

"I was old enough. I saw how normal people lived. I had friends. Their parents showed me kindness and warmth. Cal never had those kinds of friends. People never reached out to him."

"He was very good-looking."

"But he didn't smile. He couldn't converse easily. He didn't have friends like mine, so I tried to give him what those parents gave me." His eyes met hers. They looked haunted. "I did what I could. I guess it wasn't enough. Cal closed himself off so he wouldn't have to feel—at least, that's what I chose to believe. It was easier for me to think he didn't feel anything, than that he was in pain."

He began to walk along the bank, eventually stopping at a bench. It had been green once, but was faded to a soft gray. Deborah doubted he even saw it. He was preoccupied.

She followed him along the shore. When she reached the bench, he said, "Cal fell in love once. He couldn't have been more than twelve, but he was crazy about a girl in his class, and for a couple of weeks, she was crazy about him. For the few weeks they were together, he was a different kid. Then she fell in love with someone else."

"He must have been crushed."

"That's what I'd have been, but who knew with Cal? He clammed up. No expression of sorrow at all. Except he barely ate. When he decided he'd had enough and started packing in his meals again, it was like he had never met her. He had grown an even harder shell." Tom looked at her, bewildered. "Does this sound like a person who would **feel** enough to attempt suicide?"

Deborah wanted to deny it, but couldn't. "The unhappiness was there."

Tom slumped down on the bench. "My parents must have known it, but none of us did anything. We could have gotten him help. But we didn't."

"Was that your job?"

"Maybe not when I was a kid, but it's been a while since then." He looked at her, clearly agonizing. "He was my brother. I was supposed to love him, but how can you love someone who keeps so much to himself? We weren't ever really friends. So do you love your brother **because** he's your brother? And if you do love him, don't you owe it to him to keep in touch and see if he's okay?"

Deborah had no answers. She sat down beside him. "You said you were Cal's only family. Does that mean your parents are dead?"

"Yes."

"Your dad died of that stroke?"

"No. He recovered. But he lost his taste for life. He decided to go out in a blaze of glory. Drove off a bridge in the middle of the night with his wife at his side."

"Suicide?"

"No. The autopsy said he had another stroke." He made a wry sound. "You can imagine what Selena said when I told her that.

All this time, she had thought they were killed by a drunk driver. Apparently, that was what Cal told her. Maybe she feels she's avenging Cal's death **and** theirs by suing you." He looked at Deborah. "I knew she was upset when the accident report didn't find you guilty, and I knew that she was thinking of suing. When she finally told me, I tried to talk her out of it, because I had this feeling that Cal was partly responsible for his own death, and I didn't think she'd want that to come out. I did not know until last night that she had actually gone to the D.A. We had a huge argument about it then and another one this morning. When I used the word **suicide,** she went beserk."

"She hadn't seen anything different in him in the days before his death?"

"No."

"Had he ever tried it before?"

"Not that I know of, but there was all that deep unhappiness. Could be it finally just got to him."

Deborah was silent. Then, quietly, she asked, "Do you think it was suicide?"

He studied her for a minute before looking downstream. "In my dark moments, I do, and I blame myself."

She reached for his arm. "You can't do that

to yourself, Tom. At some point your brother was responsible for himself. I think you feel you should have been able to stop him, but there **is** a limit to responsibility. Cal made choices. At some point you have to respect those choices." She caught herself and frowned. "I'm sorry. Maybe that's not applicable. But I just said it to my dad."

"About?"

"Meeting you. He didn't think it was a good idea."

Tom held her gaze. Her hand was still on his arm. Before she could remove it, he took it in his own. "It probably isn't," he said in a voice so low that if she hadn't been sitting close, she mightn't have heard.

His fingers linked with hers. "What are we?" he asked quietly.

She swallowed. "I don't know."

"This is bad timing."

"Very."

He drew her hand to his chest, pressed it to a heart whose beat she felt, then slowly, deliberately, put it down on the bench. Deborah gently entwined her fingers with his.

She wanted to get up and walk away—thought it the safest thing to do—but she had played by the rules for so long that safe didn't appeal. There were too many reasons why she shouldn't be holding Tom's hand, not the least of which was Grace. Still, his skin was warm and his fingers strong. She needed their comfort.

"The thing with suicide," he said, "is that there's no way to prove it without a note."

She didn't remove her hand. "Is there a note?"

"No. Not yet. I'm looking."

"If Selena found one, would she tell you?"

"I think I'd see it on her face. She's not the kind of woman who can hide much."

"Is there anywhere other than the house where he might have left something?"

"I checked his office at school. It's not there. There are all those P.O. boxes. I'm in the process of getting everything forwarded to me. He also had half a dozen safety deposit boxes. I've only located two. He did have some investments. They'll give Selena a kitty, and if she sells the house, she'll have money from that."

"Did he have life insurance?"

Tom rubbed his thumb against hers. "There's a small policy that came with his job."

"Not one he took out for Selena if he died?"

"No, but null and void if suicide is proven."

He looked at Deborah. He didn't have to say that a suicide note would be good for her and not good for him. The irony of it was in his eyes.

She nodded in acknowledgment, then whispered, "I have to get back to work."

Reaching with his free hand, he raised her sunglasses. He didn't say anything, just looked at her for a long minute before replacing them. Then he brought her hand to his mouth and kissed her fingers.

Deborah returned to her car feeling nearly as bereft as she had driving there. Then, she had been mourning something that was. Now, she mourned something that might have been.

And the irony of **that?** She hadn't known she wanted it.

Chapter 18

Grace decided that if she didn't become a doctor, she'd write TV scripts, which was what she'd been doing in her head all morning. They were all crime shows, and she had conjured up a dozen different scenarios. All started with an accident, a death, then a police investigation. Each involved different evidence and produced a different result.

A **civil** suit. Everything was supposed to be **over.** She had actually been feeling better. Jill knew the whole truth and still loved her, which meant Grace had an ally. And Grace had driven Jill's van without incident, even though she didn't plan to ever drive again.

Then her mother had casually mentioned that the D.A.'s office might want to interview **her.**

Labyrinthine—that described the accident—

labyrinthine, as in being intricate, complicated, or elaborately involved. She hated
studying flash cards, hated thinking of
PSATs, **hated** the words that kept echoing
in her mind. But labyrinthine fit.

She hadn't called around to get the assign-
ments she missed yesterday, so she sat in class
zoning out. And it was amazing. None of her
teachers called on her. But then, she was
Grace Monroe, honor roll student going
through a tough time, so she was let off
the hook.

That freed her to obsess over the D.A.'s
investigation. She avoided meeting people's
eyes and walked from class to class with her
nose in a book, as good a prop as any while
her mind went from one awful scenario to
another. Her friends had stopped bugging
her, but rather than feeling relieved, she felt
guilty and very alone. She tried to think
about her aunt, pregnant and single, and
about her brother, cut off because of his bad
eyesight. They were alone, but in different
ways from her. There was a solution for
Dylan's eyes, just as there would be an end to
Jill's aloneness.

Grace was digging through books at the
foot of her locker, not sure what she was look-

ing for but content to let everyone pass by, when a warm body crouched close beside her.

"Hey."

She jumped and might have slid away if Danielle hadn't put an arm around her waist. "Don't," the older girl said. "Please. I need to talk."

Grace shook her head. "I can't, Dani. I have a test next period." It was a lie, but what was one more?

"At lunch then."

"I **can't,**" Grace said, and, for the first time, it hurt her to turn away her friend. Danielle was the sister she'd never had. Once Grace would have told her anything.

"I know about the beer," Dani murmured, "so if you think I'm asking about that, I'm not. I mean, your stupid friends have been telling everyone about it, so it isn't a secret anymore."

"They **told? Who?** Who knows?"

"I don't know, but word got around—"

"Did they tell parents?"

"I don't know, but that isn't what I want to discuss, Grace. I need to discuss the accident."

The accident **was** about beer, Grace might have screamed. All she said was, "I can't talk, Dani."

"It's about your mom and my dad. Is something going on?"

Grace was confused. "What are you talking about?"

"He was so angry at her last night. He told my mom she wasn't a friend, but my mom needs her, and, anyway, something's going on with my dad. I really need to talk, Gracie. Please?"

Grace knew what was going on between her mother and Hal, and it had to do with John Colby. Hal was furious because Deborah had talked to John without him, and now detectives were showing up at the door, and it was all Grace's fault. If she hadn't been driving that night, none of this would have happened.

And Danielle wanted to talk about **that?**

Grace hung her head. "I can't. I **can't.**" If she talked with Dani, she would break down and tell her who was driving that night, and then she'd have to worry whether Dani would tell Karen, who might tell Hal, who would be even more furious with Deborah, and then things would be ten times **worse.**

Jill knew. Grace trusted her, but couldn't risk telling anyone else. If her mother learned about the beer, she would go crazy.

"But you're a part of my family," Danielle insisted. "I **need** you."

Grace lifted her head. "I'm not a good person for anyone to need right now."

"That's **bullshit,**" Danielle whispered. "You're as good a person as I know. The accident just messed you up."

"Fine. It messed me up," Grace whispered vehemently, "but if I can't help myself right now, how can I help you?" She went back to looking for whichever book she was looking for. The bell rang. Danielle's arm fell away.

Grace half turned and pleaded, "Please understand. If I talked to anyone, I'd talk to you, but I just **can't.**"

She almost gave in then, because Danielle looked ready to cry. But someone called her name. Danielle looked down the hall and back to Grace for a second. Then she was gone.

Grace didn't plan to run well, but once she got going, it was like all her fear drove her on. She ran a personal best. The coach, who acted as though she'd been gone for a month, couldn't stop congratulating her. She felt like a phony. Avoiding her friends, she changed and walked the short distance to the bakery.

The day was warm, which meant that every sidewalk table was taken, even this late in the afternoon. Keeping her head down, Grace passed them and went inside to find

Jill. She was with a customer. From the looks of the papers fanned out between SoMa Smoothies, they were planning a catered event.

When Jill saw her, she gave her a thumbs-up with a buoyancy that left no doubt she was not only feeling better, but didn't want **anyone** telling her she should be upstairs in bed, which was precisely what Grace loved about her aunt. She knew what she wanted and what was best for her, and she did it. She took control of her life.

Dylan was at a table not far away. His math book was open, but his arms were stretched across the orange tabletop. He was wearing a grin as he looked at Grace through those thick glasses of his, and a tiny piece of her melted. She might hate herself and the world, but she couldn't hate Dylan.

Dropping her backpack to the floor, she sat down beside him. "You look happy. Ready for the game?"

His grin widened. "I'm not going."

For her little brother, who not only needed **two** eye surgeries now, but repair to that grin in the form of braces on his teeth, Grace played along. "Why not?" she asked.

"I'm quitting baseball."

"You are? Does Mom know?"

He nodded. "She said it herself. She stopped by when I got here, and I thought she was going to say she couldn't come to the game, but all she wanted to talk about was how I felt and whether I really wanted to play." His grin faded to worry. "Think Dad'll be angry?"

"Why do you care?" Grace asked but rushed on, because she knew what her brother's answer would be, and she couldn't agree with him less. "I can't believe Mom is letting you quit."

"I can't **play,** Grace. I just **suck** at it, because I can't see."

"She hates quitters."

"That was when it was only one eye. She kept saying I could do it, but now that it's both eyes, she knows I can't."

"Did she say that?"

He nodded.

"She said you **can't?**" Grace was shocked. Her mother liked to say that everything was possible. She also liked to say that ten-year-old boys needed to play sports.

"She said I could choose. She said that it wasn't fair of her to expect something that isn't right for me, and that she didn't want me to feel pressure to do something I hated. I chose to be off the team. She was gonna call the coach, so I don't even have to go tonight."

Grace didn't ask if he was pleased. It was written all over his face. She envied him that. It was nice being able to choose. It was nice being **included** in decisions. It was nice when people saw the kind of pressure you felt and realized that what was right for them wasn't right for you.

So was that weird? Something bad, like Dylan's second cornea, produced something good.

"I'm hungry," she decided and, leaving the table, went out to the kitchen. The baking was done for the day, but what wasn't out front was stacked on storage racks. She helped herself to a cupcake, ate the frosting off the top, and tossed the cake part in the trash. She did the same to a second and was about to reach for a third when she realized that cupcakes wouldn't make things better. Her aunt wouldn't care if she ate the frosting off **ten** cupcakes. She might not even notice.

Lately, it was like Grace was invisible, like she could do the worst possible thing and no one cared. But that wasn't right. There had to be rules.

Heading out the back door, she passed the

van and went up the alley. At the street, she turned left and started down the sidewalk. She passed the first store, stopped, and backed up. It was perfect. She went inside.

Sole Singer was a shoe store of the upscale variety that could only exist in a suburb wealthy enough to draw other top-notch stores, which Leyland did. It had been open for barely a year, its owners a pair of gay guys who had great taste in shoes. The brands they sold ranged from exclusive to designer, and were usually Italian. None were cheap.

Grace had been inside many times browsing with friends, and had even bought a pair of Reefs. She saw no one she knew now, just a pair of girls who were totally absorbed in themselves. Jed, one of the owners, was at the front of the store running a credit card through for a woman. He smiled and raised his chin to acknowledge her arrival, then returned to the task.

There weren't aisles. The store was too small and too chic. Shoes were arranged on tiered shelves, with boxes of different sizes stacked artfully beneath.

Grace had been eyeing a particular pair of Pradas since they had arrived several months before. They were hot pink metallic leather sandals. She went over to them, took the ap-

propriate box from under the shelf, and settled into a nearby chair, but she didn't need to
try them on. She'd done that before. She knew
they would fit.

The woman at the front shouldered her
bag and left. One of the girls wanted to try on
a pair of Marc Jacobs flats, but couldn't find
her size, so Jed went out back to look there.
When the other girl got a call, both put their
ears to the phone.

Grace slipped a sandal in each of her pockets and stood. Thinking twice, she knelt
again, closed the shoe box, and slid it into the
spot where she'd found it. Then she stood and
turned to leave, but froze. John Colby was
standing at the open front door with a hand
on the elegant brass handle. She had no idea
how long he'd been there, but he was watching her.

This was what she wanted—to be held ac-
countable for doing something wrong—but
the reality of it was so foreign to the old Grace
Monroe that she was scared.

Colby left the door open and came to her.
In a voice quiet enough not to be heard by the
girls, he said, "Please sit down and put those
back."

She considered asking what he meant,
only that would have been pathetic. She con-

sidered lying—**I was just going up to the register to pay**—only she didn't have money or a credit card and, besides, the shoes were in her **pockets.**

Docilely, she sat, removed the empty box from its stack, took first one, then the other of the sandals from her pockets and put them back. When the box was in its place, she looked up at the police chief.

That was when Jed came from the back. "John. Hey. How're you doin'?"

The chief smiled. "Not bad. You?"

Jed shrugged. "Can't complain." His gaze slid to Grace. "Did you get your mom to spring for them?"

Grace shook her head.

"Maybe another time," Jed said.

Grace nodded and started for the door, knowing that John would follow. Once on the street, she had a wild impulse to flee. But that would be stupid. Definitely. And besides, she wanted to be punished.

"This way," John said and guided her down the alley. When they reached the parking area, he released her shoulder. She went to the van, crossed her arms, and turned to face him. She expected to see anger, surely disappointment, but he simply looked sad.

"What were you thinking?" he asked.

She said nothing.

"Grace?"

"Have you been following me?" she asked.

He shook his head. "No. I've been worried, so when I see you, I take notice. I saw you go in the shoe store and was only planning to say hello. Then there you were, pocketing a pair of, what, three-hundred-dollar shoes?"

"Two ninety-five," she corrected.

"That's bad enough."

"There was a pair of wedge espadrilles for four ninety-five, only they wouldn't have fit in my pocket."

He looked at her, disappointed now. "Do you know what would have happened if I hadn't been there, and you'd stolen those shoes? Jed knew you'd been eyeing them."

"All my friends have been eyeing them. He wouldn't have found the empty box for days. He wouldn't have known it was me."

John smiled sadly. "He saw you. And we both know his stuff flies off the shelves. He'd have found the empty box in no time." He ran a hand around the back of his neck and said, "That's shoplifting, Grace. It's a crime. People go to jail for shoplifting—six months, a year." He paused. "You don't want to go to jail."

"I deserve to," Grace said, doubly disgusted with herself because, no, she didn't want to go to jail.

The police chief sighed. "I have to call your mom."

Grace uncrossed her arms, then crossed them again. "You don't. She'll be here any minute."

He glanced at the street. "You want to wait inside?"

She shook her head. She didn't want to see Jill. She didn't want to see Dylan. More to the point, she didn't want them to see her.

"Wait here," he said and walked back up the alley, leaving her all alone with no one to make sure she didn't run off—and the disgusting part of **that** was that she wouldn't. Running off wasn't the point. What good was breaking the law if you escaped? What good was breaking the law if there was no one to tell you how bad you really were?

Sinking down against the van's tire, she pulled her knees to her chest, put her chin on them, and closed her eyes. She heard cars passing on Main. She heard squirrels nosing around the dumpster. She heard the rattle of the air conditioner that Jill refused to replace, and she wondered whether anyone would come out, find her here, and ask questions. If they did, what would she say?

She was suddenly totally confused. Pressing her face to her knees, she wrapped both arms over her head and held on tightly, then more tightly again, because it was like her whole world was crashing down.

She didn't hear anything now. The noise in her head drowned everything out, but suddenly someone was touching her hair, and calling her name in a voice that was frightened and urgent and gentle all at the same time. Grace started to cry.

Deborah pulled her up and held her.

"Shoplifting?" she cried. "What is he **talking** about?"

Grace couldn't answer. All she could do was sob.

"What **happened,** Gracie?"

Grace exhaled pitiful little wails.

Deborah rocked her, much as she'd done when Grace was a child. "It's okay," she murmured. "It's okay. Nothing is that bad. Nothing is that bad."

"**I'm** that bad, I **am,**" Grace wept.

"It's been a hard time for all of us, but nothing is lost forever. Tell me, Gracie, what did you **do?**"

"I drank two beers." The words were muffled, but her mother must have heard, because she made no noise at all.

Finally, sounding confused, she asked, "At **school?**"

"At **Megan's** that night."

Deborah froze.

"I'm so bad!" Grace cried.

"The night of the **accident?**"

"You must hate me," she wailed, and she wanted that, wanted it because she deserved it—but she didn't want her mother to leave. She wanted to be a child again, like Dylan, innocent even when she did things wrong.

"I don't hate you," her mother said and, incredibly, the arms around her tightened. "I could never hate you. You're **part** of me."

"The bad part!"

"The **best** part! You are, Gracie. I don't know what happened today, but I know there's an explanation. You're a good person, and you're not a thief."

Grace couldn't stop crying. "I stole . . . a man's life . . . it's my fault."

"Absolutely not," Deborah insisted, whispering now as she pressed Grace's head to her chest. "We would have hit him regardless. My eyes were on the road, and I didn't see him either. Did I scream out to warn you? No. He came from the **woods,** Gracie. He ran into us!"

"But I was **drinking,"** Grace cried.

"You walked a straight line to the car, and talked like you always do. I'd have seen if you were drunk."

"That doesn't **matter.**"

"You drove perfectly. I was watching."

Grace tried to pull away so that she could **see** her mother, somehow make her **understand,** but Deborah wouldn't let her go. "I **drank and drove.** Why do you keep **denying** it? I should have been able to see Mr. McKenna, but I didn't. I'm **not** you, Mom. I blew a track race and failed a French test and handed in what I **knew** was a lousy English paper, and everyone is making excuses. The **whole world** is disappointed in me, only no one will come right out and say it. A man is **dead.**"

Her mother didn't argue. And suddenly Grace couldn't fight. Arms going limp, she just seemed to melt into Deborah. Here was a safety she hadn't felt in days. Her mother was warm and strong; she had answers; she was a shield, and Grace needed that now, because there was so much she didn't understand, so much she didn't know how to handle. It no longer mattered if Deborah had lied, it just didn't matter anymore.

Grace's sobs gradually stopped, but she didn't move. She didn't want to talk, didn't want to think, just wanted to be held and protected, there with her mother on the gravel in the shadow of the bright yellow van.

Deborah stroked Grace's hair. Newly washed and still damp, it smelled of mango shampoo. It was nine at night, and the girl was asleep beside her on the sofa. Seeming to need constant reassurance, she hadn't let Deborah out of her sight for more than a minute since they had left the alley. Deborah realized that between worry and fear, Grace had worn herself out. She suspected that the girl hadn't slept a full night since the accident.

Suspected? Knew. Hadn't she seen those dark circles under Grace's eyes?

But so much had been going on. Deborah had been so fixated on her own worries, many of which had to do with Grace, that somehow she hadn't understood. She had thought she was acting in her daughter's best interest, but she hadn't realized how the lie would hurt Grace. When a child feared she wouldn't be loved, that was bad. When a child had to resort to theft to get the punishment she thought she deserved, **that** was bad.

John couldn't have been more understanding. He had given them privacy, staying at the mouth of the alley until Deborah had walked Grace into the bakery. Deborah didn't know what he had heard of their conversation, but she didn't care. What mattered was Grace.

At that moment, she was feeling selfish, savoring the closeness, wanting it never to end. It had to, of course. Grace had to grow up, separate, and make her own life. **I'm not you, Mom,** she had said. The words echoed in Deborah's mind. She had to accept that maybe, just maybe, Grace's needs were different from hers.

The weight of that hit her. It was easier to think she knew everything than that there might be things about her own daughter she didn't know, precisely because she might not like some of those things. But she couldn't control Grace. She could only raise her in a way that gave her the tools to live her own life well.

Deborah wasn't sure she'd done that. Grace had to start feeling better about herself.

Gently, she eased herself out from under the girl, who continued to sleep. Taking the phone, she went to the top of the stairs. She didn't want to go farther, didn't want to let Grace completely out of her sight, but she turned half away and called Greg.

"It's me," she said when he picked up.

Then, not knowing quite where to begin, she blurted, "Greg, I think I need you to come here."

"To the house?" He sounded surprised, which was understandable. He hadn't been to the house since he had walked away. They exchanged kids at a rest stop on the highway, halfway between their homes. She hadn't once asked him to visit.

"Yes," she replied, feeling her way along. Establishing a relationship with her ex-husband wasn't something she had planned. "It needs to be here."

"Dylan has his heart set on seeing the puppies. I can't bring them down."

"Maybe you can come here Friday and take him back Saturday?" It was a lot of driving, but it couldn't be helped.

He didn't argue. Rather, he asked, "What's going on?"

Unexpectedly, her eyes filled with tears. "We need to talk."

"About?"

"The accident. Grace." She swallowed. "How we handle things."

"What is it, Deborah?" he asked, suddenly sounding so much like the man she had married that she started to cry. "Are they okay?" he asked, frightened.

It was a minute before she could speak. She pressed her hand to her mouth, feeling like Grace, overwhelmed, confused, and needing to lean on someone she loved. Because she did love Greg. She didn't want to be married to him any longer—she knew that for sure, could finally think it without anger—but there had been feelings once, feelings strong enough to evolve into something more appropriate for what they needed to do now.

Chapter 19

Dylan was ecstatic. "He's coming **here?** Oh, **wow!**" Seconds later, his face fell. "But what about the puppies? I was supposed to see them."

"You will," Deborah said. She would find a way, even if it meant that Greg drove Dylan back to Vermont and she drove there Sunday to pick him up, which probably wasn't a bad idea, especially if Grace went, too. Car time could be good time.

Grace, though, was not pleased hearing that her father was coming to Leyland. She seemed more nervous than anything else that Friday morning, and sat in the kitchen biting her nails.

"I haven't done any homework," she said.

As far as Deborah was concerned, it was no wonder that Grace couldn't focus on work.

Between yesterday's incident and now Greg's pending visit, Deborah was having trouble thinking about work herself.

"Want to stay with Aunt Jill today?" she asked Grace.

Grace did. Confession was exhausting, and she couldn't deal with school. But she did feel better. A weight was gone from her chest. She still had to tell her dad what she'd done, but it helped knowing that her mom was on her side.

She slept for much of the morning but was downstairs in the bakery when Dylan came in after school. He went back and forth between Jill and the buttercrunch donut holes, and never stopped grinning, which was pretty amazing for a guy who'd had the kind of bad news he had received barely two days earlier. Grace wanted to know his secret.

"Doesn't your eye hurt?" she asked after fixing them both SoMa Shakes.

He stirred the drink with his straw. "Yeah, but only once in a while. It's okay. It explains things. Like why I'm not as good in school as you are."

Grace might have told him that his eyes

had nothing to do with brains, which, being a Monroe, was something he would soon learn.

But he went on. "It explains why I **trip** all the time and why I was **so** bad at baseball. Even Dad agreed. He wasn't mad that I quit the team. Neither was Poppy."

Grace felt a little twist inside. Poppy was another worry. Being a Barr was nearly as bad as being a Monroe. "When did you talk with Poppy?"

"I called to tell him about my eyes. I told him that once they're fixed, I'd hit him a home run." He frowned at his drink and bobbed the straw more. "Maybe I'll hit it for Nana Ruth." He looked up again. "No. For Poppy. He wants it more."

Grace felt something akin to sympathy. She knew exactly how Dylan felt. Poppy was about expectations, which were awful when you couldn't meet them. It was nice to have a ready-made excuse.

When Deborah called to say that she was heading out to make house calls, Grace made a decision. She wanted to tell Poppy herself what she'd done.

Leaving the bakery, she started down the street. After two blocks, her grandfather's house came into view. It didn't look as big to her now as it had when she was a child, and she hadn't even included the office back then. Little had she known how big a part that office would play in her mother's life and, indirectly, her own.

Heading there now, she quietly let herself in. The waiting room was empty. The receptionist waved her in but kept talking on the phone. Grace was trying to decide whether to sit down when the nurse, Joanna Sperling, came out, wearing pink scrubs and exuding a confidence that Poppy's expectations had never been able to dent.

She opened her arms and gave Grace a hug. "I haven't seen you in ages. Are you getting too busy for us?" When Grace smiled and shook her head, Joanna added, "Your mom just left. Want to try her on her cell?"

"I'm here to see my grandfather. Is he with a patient?"

"Last one, and he's nearly through. Go on down and wait in his office. They're finished in there."

Grace didn't look at her mother's office as she passed. She didn't look much at Poppy's either, just sank into a chair and waited.

"How's my girl?" Michael said, entering the room with less than his usual energy. He seemed subdued. **Older.** "You just missed your mom," he said.

"I came to see you."

He rested against the edge of the desk. "You look very serious."

She might have said no. But she couldn't lie anymore. "I have to tell you something."

"Something about the accident?"

She caught a breath. "You know?" She would be furious if her mother had told him.

He smiled kindly. "Everyone knows. It was in the **Ledger.**"

"Not everything," she said. When he frowned, seeming truly puzzled, she realized that her mother hadn't told after all. She would have to do it herself.

But that was why she had come. It was a test. "I was driving that night, Poppy. It was me." She saw her grandfather sit back in surprise. "It was me," she repeated to make sure he knew. When he didn't react, she stated it even more clearly. "I was the one who was driving the car when it hit Mr. McKenna."

"Your mother **lied?**" he asked.

"The police never asked, so she didn't tell. Now there may be a civil suit, and if there is, the truth will come out. I just wanted you to know that I didn't mean to hit him. I didn't see him."

His cheeks reddened. "Why didn't your mother tell me this?"

"She was trying to protect me."

"From **me?**"

"From everyone." Grace felt very small. "You're disappointed in me. I know you are."

"I'm disappointed in your mother."

"It wasn't **Mom,** it was **me,**" Grace cried, because she was tired of people making excuses for her, "and that isn't even the **worst** of it, the **worst** is that I was drinking."

This time he gasped.

"Don't get mad at Mom, because she didn't know it until yesterday. My dad doesn't yet, but he'll find out tonight. I just wanted to tell you myself. You drink, so I thought maybe you'd understand." When he looked stricken, she quickly added, "That came out wrong."

He lowered himself to the chair beside hers, bringing Grace immediate relief. He was more imposing standing up, more approachable sitting. "Why were you drinking?" he asked quietly.

It was an interesting question. Neither her mother nor Jill had asked it. "There was a group of us. It seemed like a fun thing to do. My friend's parents were out."

He sat back. "At least you weren't alone. If

you were with friends, it's social. Kids experiment."

Grace's eyes filled with tears. "They don't do it and then drive."

"Sure they do. Sometimes they kill each other in the process."

"So I killed **Mr. McKenna,**" she cried. "How can you excuse it?"

He frowned. "I'm not. I'm—" he paused, then said, "rationalizing." He studied her for an agonizing minute, before saying, "I wouldn't want you to drink because I do. It is **not** a good thing. It can hurt every other part of your life. And it just hides the real problem."

Grace had overheard enough to know what he meant. "Your problem is Nana Ruth."

"My problem is **no** Nana Ruth," he replied. "What's yours?"

"Pressure," she said. Curious, she asked, "When you drink, what does it do for you? Do you feel light-headed?"

"I hate myself."

"No, Poppy. While you're doing it. What do you feel?"

"Lonely."

"But is it better once you've had a couple of drinks? I mean, does it make you forget?"

He looked at the credenza and a photograph of his wife, taken several years before her death. "It blurs things," he said, seeming so sad that Grace reached for his hand.

"I'm sorry. I shouldn't be talking about this."

He closed his hand around hers. "Yes, you should. Maybe you should have asked me about my drinking sooner. I keep forgetting you're big enough to notice these things."

"You miss Nana Ruth a lot."

"A lot. But drinking is no solution."

"Then why do you do it? For the blur?"

He thought about that. "I don't know. I tell myself it won't hurt, but it does. I tell myself it's just one night, but it isn't." He looked at Grace with shame-filled eyes. "Maybe I drink because I know she'd hate it."

"What kind of reason is **that?**"

"A bad one. One I shouldn't be telling my granddaughter."

"I'm sixteen."

"Mm. That's old."

"Old enough to kill a man with a car."

He freed his hand to point at her. "Do not, young lady, use that accident as an excuse for making other mistakes. See, that's one of my problems, as your mother so kindly made clear. I'm blaming everything that goes wrong in my life on your grandmother's death. But that's pure denial."

"Denial of what?"

"Responsibility. My own ability to make things better. Some things I can control, like not drinking, doing my job well, having brunch with my grandchildren. Blaming Ruth's death for not doing those things is a crock of you-know-what. There are too many things that I truly can**not** control, like your aunt and your mom. Hell, I couldn't even control your grandmother. She loved that bakery, just like your aunt does. And as for your mother, I'm not sure she likes practicing with me. Maybe she needs space."

"She loves you."

"That may be the problem. She feels obliged."

"Obliged to do what?"

"Be what I want. Maybe not **see** that I'm doing something wrong, like drinking."

"Are you an alcoholic?"

He considered it. "Not yet."

"Do you think you'll become one?"

"I don't want to."

"How do you keep from becoming one?"

"First, face the truth. That can be hard."

"Not always," Grace said. "When the truth comes out about the accident, I don't think they'll send me to jail, but there will be things on my record forever. That may make my life **easier.**"

"How so?"

"Once you mess up, expectations lower. I hate always having to be the best." Her cell gave a muted jingle.

"Who expects that?" her grandfather asked.

"Mom. You. And my father. If anyone hates me for what I did, he will." The jingle came again.

"Do you think he never drank?"

"I know he did, but he's totally into pure living now. He and Rebecca are vegetarians. They grow most of what they eat." There was a third muted ring.

"It's a pastime. Grace, get that phone, will you?"

"It's not important."

"Get it, please."

Grace pulled the phone from her pocket, glanced at the panel, and opened it. "I'm with Poppy," she told her mother.

Deborah sounded frightened. "I got here, and no one knew where you'd gone."

"We're talking. I'm okay, Mom. Really."

"How long will you be?"

"Not long. Poppy's gearing me up to see Dad. I'm okay. Really." And she was. Her grandfather wasn't lecturing. He wasn't ignoring how she felt. He was talking to her like she was an adult. It helped that he had problems of his own. He wasn't perfect, either.

"Why do you need to be geared up to face your dad?" Poppy asked when she closed the phone.

"I have to tell him what happened the other night, too. But I don't know how he'll react. I mean, like, he flipped out, didn't he? He just picked up one day and left. If a father loves his children, he wouldn't do that, would he?"

"I drink. Your father left. Some would say there isn't a lot of difference."

Grace shook her head. "People don't just throw away everything they have unless those things aren't worth having. So either Mom, Dylan, and me aren't worth having, or he threw away something good."

"Your father is obsessive, is all. When he does something, it totally takes over his mind. Before he met your mother, he was totally into alternative lifestyles. Then he was totally into being a businessman. Now he's totally into dropping out."

"Except when he talks with us," Grace groused. "He wants to know if I'm doing well in school. He wants to know if I'm studying vocab flash cards and taking practice PSATs. He wants me to keep running personal bests. But I can't do that all the time. What if I do lousy in school? What if I do badly on my SATs, and have a police record, and can't get into a good college?"

"You'll still get into a good college."

"Will you love me even if I don't?"

"Of course I'll love you."

"Poppy, there's no **'of course.'** Look at Aunt Jill. You're still furious at her for not going to college."

That got him. He thought for a bit and said, "That doesn't mean I don't love her."

"How can you love her and never even taste what she bakes?"

His cheeks reddened, and he looked sheepish. "Your mother left a sticky bun at the house yesterday morning. I ate it."

Grace was a minute taking that in. "Did you call Jill and tell her it was good?" When he didn't answer, she said, "See? That's what'll happen to me. Once my dad learns the truth about the accident, he won't want to talk with me at all. He'll **really** hate me then."

"He doesn't hate you now."

"Look who's in denial," she cried, but her grandfather was pointing at her again.

"Grace, you're making a mistake. It's easier

to pretend he hates you than to acknowledge that he might have had a legitimate reason for doing what he did."

"But he **left**," Grace said, needing to make her point. "If he left when everything was going great, what's he going to say now?"

Her grandfather smiled. It was a while since she'd seen that gentle, only-for-Grace smile. "You'll have to ask him that, pumpkin. The best medicine for denial is talk."

Chapter 20

Deborah had a perfect excuse for watching the street. She wanted to be with Dylan, who was at one of the bakery's window tables, looking for his dad. Greg had said he would be there by five. He claimed that he wanted to miss the Friday afternoon traffic, that he had no taste for traffic at all anymore, but the truth was that he had never liked it. More accurately, Deborah found herself thinking, he had never encountered it. He left home very early and returned very late.

But that, she reminded herself, was irrelevant. Bitterness was self-defeating. Anger had outlived its usefulness.

"Where **is** he?" Dylan asked impatiently. He was straddling one of her knees, with his elbows on the table and his eyes on the street.

"On his way," she replied, momentarily

distracted by her son. Dylan had always been a cuddler, but those days were numbered. In another year or two, he would refuse to be seen close to his mom. Making the most of the moment, she slid an arm around his waist.

"Do you think Rebecca will be with him?"

Deborah hoped not. She and Greg needed to talk without anyone listening, particularly not Greg's new wife.

"Are you okay with Rebecca?" she asked Dylan.

"She's cool." He looked back at her through eyes magnified with worry. "What if he was in an accident?"

"He'd have called."

"What if he couldn't?"

"The police would have called. Your eye seems better." He had been doing less squinting and blinking.

"It's okay. But what if Dad doesn't carry our number around anymore, just Rebecca's?"

"**She** would have called." Deborah squeezed his middle. "Sweetie, he's **okay.**"

Dylan turned back to the street just as a blue Volvo wagon pulled up at the bakery. Other than a faint coat of road dust, it looked new. The boy, still searching the end of the street for the Volkswagen, was slow seeing his father climb out. Then, with a cry of surprise, he was off Deborah's lap in a flash and out the door. Seconds later, he was on the curb, clinging to Greg like a monkey, just as he had done when he was three.

"Whoa," Jill said at Deborah's elbow, "you do all the work, take all the responsibility, do all the worrying, and your ex is welcomed like he's the Messiah? Why are you smiling?"

"I love seeing Dylan happy. He's been through so much."

"Is that a new car?"

"Looks it."

"Maybe it's Rebecca's."

"No. She drives a truck."

"Greg looks different."

Deborah agreed. He wore his usual jeans and Birkenstocks, but he did look different. "It's his hair," she decided. "He cut it." Last time, it had been straggling on his shoulders. Now it stopped at his collar.

"And combed it," Jill remarked. "And stopped coloring it. Look who's gone gray all of a sudden."

"He never colored it. Sandy to gray isn't far. You just haven't seen him in a while."

"Who's he trying to impress?" Jill asked.

Deborah snorted. "I don't think he's into that anymore."

"Then why cut his hair? Why buy a family car? And why are you defending him? He's still the guy who walked out on you."

"He's still the father of my kids." She shot her sister a glance. "I asked him to come here, Jill. Maybe he fixed his hair as a gesture of goodwill, maybe it's an acknowledgment that life is different here, I really don't know. But Dylan needs him, Grace needs him, **I** need him."

"What about independence?"

"I am independent. Right now, though, I need the help of my kids' father."

"What about all your anger?"

Deborah sighed. "Oh, Jill, it's just worn me down." On that note, she followed Dylan outside.

Greg had been saying something to the boy. Now he looked at Deborah, and she was at a loss for what to say. For the last few years, bitterness had colored her speech. Anger had given her strength. Now it seemed to have disappeared.

Greg gave her a tentative smile. "Hi."

She returned the smile. "How was the drive?"

"Not bad."

Excitedly, Dylan said, "It's a new car, Mom. Dad got it to use in Vermont." He looked up at his father. "I'm getting in, okay?" Without waiting for an answer, he ran to the driver's side, opened the door, and climbed in. His head barely hit the top of the seat, but he set his hands firmly on the wheel.

"He looks good," Greg remarked. "How's the eye?"

"The minute it was diagnosed, he stopped complaining," Deborah said. "He can deal, as long as he knows. That's pretty much where we all are right now."

"Any more word on the lawsuit?"

"Not yet." She hadn't seen the detectives' car today.

"Where's Grace?"

"She's talking with my dad."

"About how bad I am?"

"Actually," Deborah said, "she hasn't seen him since the accident. I suspect she's telling him about it."

"Mom," Dylan called with his head half out the window, "come in here!" He jabbed a finger toward the passenger's seat.

Eager to please, she joined him in the car.

"Do you **love** this smell?" he said excitedly. "And look, look at the **wood** here, is this cool?" He moved a reverent hand over the panel. "There's leather even on the **steering** wheel. And this gear shift is like a **race car.**"

Deborah didn't think a Volvo wagon was anything like a race car, but she wasn't popping his bubble.

"Watch this," he ordered and made his seat rise. "And this." He put the back of the seat down, then up, then leaned over to study the music system. "Dad says there's an antitheft device just for the audio. This is so neat." He yelled out the window, "Can we go for a ride, Dad?"

Greg came over to the car. "We'll go for a ride later. Right now, I need a drink. Is there anything in your aunt's bakery that's cool?"

Dylan listed the offerings as only a boy who spent afternoons at the bakery could do. His father named a variety of iced latte and said, "Bet you can't fix it yourself."

"Bet I can," Dylan replied and was instantly out of the car. Greg took his place behind the wheel and closed the door.

"It may take him a while," Deborah warned.

"That's the point." He turned to her. "You look okay."

"So do you."

"I wasn't the one crying on the phone last night. Why did you want me here?"

He wasn't wasting time. This was the Greg

she had lived with for the final years of her marriage. All business. Brusque to the extreme.

"The accident is a problem," she said, pushing her hair away from her face. "I need your help deciding what to do."

"What's the latest?" he asked.

But Deborah wanted to wait for Grace. It was her story to tell. Deborah also wanted a more private setting. Looking out at the crowded sidewalk tables, she said, "This isn't the best place to talk."

He turned on the car and rolled up the windows. Air-conditioning blew from the vents. "There. No one can hear." He looked away. "You asked me to come, so I'm here, but it isn't easy, Deborah. I knew it wouldn't be. The closer I got, the more I felt the pull of the life I had here." He leaned his head against the headrest. "It wasn't all bad."

She felt a glimmer of her anger return. "You said you were **miserable.** You said that you'd sold out, that what you were doing was immoral, and that if you didn't make a change, you'd die."

"I believed all those things."

"And now you **don't?**" she asked, her anger growing.

"Those things were all true." He turned

toward her. "I'm just saying that back then, they were **all** I could see."

Deborah wanted him to continue. "Why did you marry me, Greg?"

He didn't blink. "I loved what you stood for."

"Did you love me?"

"Yes, because you were what you stood for. Stability. Constancy. Family."

Pushing her hair back again, she tried to understand. "I was a lifestyle."

He considered that. "Basically. I wanted to be what you were. The business was starting to build. You fit the life that went with it."

"You used me," she said, hurt in spite of herself.

"No more than you used me," he returned. "You knew you'd be coming back here to practice, and you wanted a part of the experience to be different. My past worked for you in that regard. Even my age worked for you. You knew I wouldn't be cowed by your dad."

Deborah wanted to say he was wrong, only he wasn't. She might not have been conscious of all of those things when she had agreed to marry him, but they were true. That left the issue of what had gone wrong.

"Were you unhappy from the beginning?" she asked more quietly.

He frowned. "I don't know. Maybe after three or four years. Probably when the business took off." He looked at her. "But it wasn't you, Deborah. It was me. My work. My competitive edge just got sharper and sharper."

"I never pushed you."

"You never did," he acknowledged. "I was the one who pushed. I came to expect things of myself that I couldn't deliver."

"But you **did** deliver," Deborah argued. "You were successful beyond our wildest dreams."

He was shaking his head. "Maybe I earned more money than we'd ever expected, but remember that dream I had of blending idealism and capitalism?" He laughed. "There was always more to do, always one more challenge. I was sucked right in like the worst of the businessmen I despised. I became manipulative and demanding. I was impossible to work with. I was impossible to **live** with." He smiled. "Aren't I right?"

Deborah said wryly, "You weren't impossible to live with, because you were never around."

"Touché," he said, his smile fading. "Well, I saw me, and I didn't like what I saw. But it had become an addiction. The only way I knew to break the cycle was to leave." He touched her arm. "It really **wasn't** you, Deborah. I needed to leave the man I'd become. You just happened to have been married to him."

Deborah was about to say something about vows and responsibility and **love,** when Dylan knocked on the window. Greg rolled it down, took the drink, and promptly passed it to her. "Now one for me," he told Dylan. "Can you make it?" The boy nodded eagerly and ran off.

Deborah didn't want an iced latte. She was keyed up enough without it. Setting the cup in a holder, she turned to Greg. "You threw the baby out with the bathwater. Do you know how much that hurts?"

"I'm sure you'll tell me."

She took a breath to do just that but felt herself deflate. "Actually," she said sadly, "I won't. I can't do the anger anymore. It isn't helping the kids, and it isn't helping me."

His eyes went past her. "There's Grace," he said and was out of the car in an instant.

Grace didn't notice the blue Volvo until she spotted her father. She stopped short and held her ground. Though she didn't return Greg's hug, she let herself be guided to the car.

He opened the rear door and settled her

behind Deborah, then returned to the driver's seat. Turning sideways to see them both, he said, "Okay. What's going on?"

Grace was appalled. "You want to talk **here?** In the **car?"**

"Why not?" he replied.

"Can't we drive to the house?"

"I wasn't a very nice person there. This car is more who I am."

"I thought the VW was."

"The VW was me thirty years ago. Today I want heated seats. So that's an honest response. Tell me what's troubling you."

"Dad, Dad," Dylan called outside the car.

Greg opened the window and took the drink. "Now one for your sister?"

Dylan's shoulders sagged. **"Another** one? She doesn't drink lattes."

"She does," Grace declared loudly.

Dylan stared at her, then turned and trudged back inside.

What was troubling her? Grace didn't know where to begin. But her father was here, and her grandfather had told her to ask, so she said, "I want to know why you left. I want to know what was wrong with us and what's so great about Rebecca. I want to know why you talked about forever if you didn't mean it."

"Grace," her mother began, but her father held up a hand.

"This is okay. She just said more to me than she has in the last six months."

That set Grace off. "What did you **expect?** Did you think we'd just make the switch from Leyland to the farm without blinking? Did you think we'd just accept that Rebecca was taking our mother's place, like **she** didn't matter anymore?"

"Grace—"

"It's okay, Deborah." To Grace, he said, "I didn't think about those things at the time. I just knew I had to leave."

"That was totally **selfish.**"

"If I'd thought of you, I wouldn't have been able to leave."

Grace covered her ears. "Don't say that. Don't **say** that. A father is **supposed** to think about his kids. He's supposed to be there for them. He's supposed to **love** them."

"I do love you," Greg said.

Taking down her hands, she said, "Then I don't know how you define that word."

He looked at Deborah. "Is this you talking?"

"**No,**" Grace cried before her mother could respond, "**it's me—your daughter— who thought you'd be here for all the good things that were supposed to happen. I expected that, because you told me that, and I believed what you said.**" Hearing her shrillness, she lowered her voice. "Only you didn't come through. So you have no right to expect things from me. If I lie, that's fine. If I drink, that's fine. If I steal a pair of shoes, that's fine."

"You wouldn't do those things."

Her eyes opened wide. "I did. I did all of them. I was the one who was driving the car that night. Didn't you guess that?" He looked stunned. "But no, you wouldn't have guessed, because I'm your perfect child. Only here's a flash, Dad. I'm not. I make mistakes, and I mess things up, and sometimes I hate what I'm supposed to be doing with my life. But everyone expects it, so I do it. What about my feelings? Am I going to get to the point you were and chuck it all away?"

Her mother was looking at Grace with something akin to respect. And though Greg was staring, she refused to take back her words.

But just when Grace was feeling like she had done something right, a gray car pulled in next to the Volvo. She watched enough TV to know that the men staring at her were probably cops.

"Omigod," she said softly. "Mom?"

"They're from the D.A.'s office, Greg," Deborah said. Her voice was calm enough, but Grace knew she was frightened.

Her father got out of the Volvo and talked with the men. Terrified, Grace looked at her mother, who shushed her.

Grace waited only until he was back in the car. "What do they **want?**" she cried.

"To talk with you." He slammed the door.

"I can't talk with them."

His voice was firm. "Routine questions, they said. I told them that if they wanted to talk with my daughter, who is a minor, they'd have to arrange a time through our attorney." He turned to Deborah. "Hal's coordinating this, isn't he?"

"He will," Deborah said. The gray car pulled out as Dylan returned with the drink Grace didn't want. Her father took the drink, passed it to Deborah, and gestured for Dylan to get in the back. Then he drove home.

Deborah tried to appreciate how difficult returning there was for Greg, but she was more concerned about Grace. As soon as the car stopped, the girl jumped out and disappeared into the house.

Dylan had Greg's hand and was pulling him forward. "You have to see my keyboard, Dad—and my iPod dock."

Deborah followed them up the stairs and down the hall, but when they turned into Dylan's room, she went to see Grace. The girl was on the window seat, looking out at the street. "Do you think they'll come here?" she asked.

"The detectives? No. They heard your father."

"Can they force me to talk?"

"No," Deborah said, trying to sound nonchalant. "They're just digging around to see if they come up with anything. They must be realizing there's no case. They may just skip you and go home." Wishful thinking? She hoped it was more than that. Motioning for Grace to make room, she sat beside her. "I'm glad you told your dad."

"**I'm** glad those men showed up after I did. It's giving him a chance to cool off."

"He didn't seem angry to me."

Grace snorted. "He was shocked. The anger would have come next." She stopped and listened. Dylan was playing his keyboard. "Does he **know** what he's playing?"

Deborah smiled. " 'The Times They Are A-Changin' '? He knows the name of the song and the tune. Does he understand that there may be a deeper meaning? I doubt it."

Grace looked out the window. "I wish they were. The times changing, I mean."

Not so long ago, Deborah would have said they already had, but now that smacked of wishful thinking, too, so she just asked, "How would you like them to change?"

Grace didn't hesitate. "I want the widow to drop her suit. I want my friends back. I want . . ." She stopped.

"Please," Deborah begged. "Say what you're thinking."

"You'll be upset."

"More than I am already? Impossible."

Grace still hesitated. "This has to do with Dad."

"You want him back here for good," Deborah said. "Oh, sweetie, that won't happen. He and I are divorced. He's married to someone else."

"It's not that." She looked out the window again. "I want to know what Dad thinks of me."

"He loves you. He told you that in the car."

"But does he mean it?" the girl asked with such longing that Deborah's heart nearly broke.

She stroked Grace's hair. "You think he doesn't? Oh, sweetheart, he does. He loves you. He's **always** loved you. And why would I be upset about that?"

"Not about his loving me," Grace said, seeming uncomfortable. "About my wanting it."

Deborah caught her breath. "You thought I wouldn't want that?"

"He left you to marry another woman."

"Which was something he had to do, and maybe something that will prove right for me, too. But it had nothing to do with you and your brother. I **want** you to love your father, and I want you to know he loves you. He's your **father,** Gracie. That will never change."

"I feel disloyal."

"Oh, sweetie. I'm sorry if I've made you feel that way." Greg had been right. She had been so hurt—so **angry**—when he left that she had wanted the kids to feel the same. Pathetic.

Taking Grace's face in her hands, she said, "I want you to love your father."

"Right now," her daughter said brokenly, "I guess that isn't the issue. Now that he knows what I've done, will he still love **me?"**

Deborah stood in the kitchen a short time later watching Greg and Dylan shoot hoops. Dylan didn't sink many, not because of his eyes as much as his lack of experience. There were no town teams yet for children his age, and though Greg had shown him the basics in Vermont, he claimed he couldn't practice alone. With his father here, he was trying again. Greg was showing him how to free himself up to shoot.

Basketball would be better than baseball, Deborah thought. The ball was bigger and the goal well-defined. This might be something Dylan could do. If he wanted it. She was going to have to ask, and then listen to what he had to say. It wouldn't do to make the same mistake twice.

She made a pot of coffee—strong, the way Greg liked it—and sipped some from a mug. Over its lip, she watched Greg toss the ball to Dylan again and again, for Dylan to shoot. He snagged rebounds and sent them back to the boy. He also caught the ball when it missed the backboard and tipped it in when it was close. He was good. He was patient. He was encouraging.

He wouldn't have done this three years before, Deborah realized. Sad that a father had to leave to be a better dad. But if patience and understanding came with distance, she was grateful. She and Grace needed both.

Greg gave an appreciative sniff when he came in from the garage. "Mm. Coffee. Dylan, find something to do. I need to talk with your mother alone."

Dylan was crestfallen. "You said you'd watch my video."

"Later."

"You were gonna show me a picture of the **puppies.**"

Greg dug into his pocket and took out a small print.

"Oooooh," Dylan breathed as he adjusted the print so he could see. "They are sooo little and sooo fuzzy. Mom, look," he cried.

Deborah leaned over his shoulder. "Very, very cute."

"I want one, Mom."

"They aren't mine to give."

"Can I have one, Dad?"

"They're too little to leave their mother."

"But can I when they're old enough? I can **do** dogs."

"Looked to me like you could do basketball, too," Deborah said.

"Better 'n baseball. It's easier. I can compensate."

"Big word," remarked his dad.

"I know what it means," Dylan said. "It means I can focus on large shapes until I get close enough to see the small ones. It's like when you're outside in fog. You can't see anything until you get close." He looked from one parent to the other. "You'd understand, if you had eyes like mine." With that, he left the room.

Duly chastised, Deborah fixed Greg's coffee, and for a time they both sat silently nursing the brew.

Outside in fog. Deborah was there. **Can't see anything until you get close.**

"It was pouring that night," she began. "I couldn't bear the thought of dragging Dylan out in the car, so I left him here and went out to get Grace . . ."

Chapter 21

Deborah told him everything, right up through the shoplifting that had brought it all to a head. She refused to let him interrupt, needing to get out every last word. "I thought I was doing the right thing," she summed up in defeat. "I thought I was protecting Grace. I didn't understand what the lie would cost us. She's been choking on the guilt, and I haven't helped. Our relationship was nearly destroyed."

In the silence that followed, he stared at her. She didn't look away, didn't shift or fidget or offer more coffee.

Finally, he sighed and sat back. "You've made a mess," he confirmed quietly. "Why didn't you tell me sooner? It might not have gotten this bad."

"I wanted to handle it myself."

"Don't you always?"

"No, Greg," she insisted. "Not always. When we were married, it was expediency. Once you left, that changed. I was hurt. I felt like I'd failed. I needed to show you, me, the kids, all of Leyland, that I could do it myself."

"You left your father off that list. Didn't you need to show him, too?"

"Definitely. He always expected so much. But expectations can be dangerous. Grace feels the same pressure I did. She hates it. How could I have forgotten what it was like?"

"We want our kids to do well," Greg said. "Expectations are a powerful motivational tool."

But Deborah had thought about that. "There's a difference between expectation and hope. You hope your children will achieve certain things, knowing that what you wish for may or may not happen. Expectation involves demand. Your children produce, or else."

"Or else what?" Greg asked.

"Or else they lose your love, which is why Grace is so upset. She needs to know we still love her. The divorce hit her hard. She felt rejected." When he seemed about to argue, Deborah held up a hand. "I know. She hasn't given you a chance to explain, but try to understand. Her way of protecting herself from further hurt is to build walls. She's done the same thing now with her friends."

He sighed. "Tell me more about the booze. Two beers?"

"That's what she said."

"Has she been drinking with friends before?"

"At parties. She's never been drunk."

"Do you know that for sure?"

"No," Deborah conceded. "When she sleeps over at a girlfriend's house, I don't see her 'til the next morning. She comes home tired, but that's all."

"Do you ask?"

"If she was drunk? No. That feels like I'm making an assumption."

"Maybe you should."

She shook her head. "I know what you're getting at, Greg. You're thinking that we need to address her drinking by punishing her, but she has already suffered so much."

"She wants punishment. Isn't that what the shoplifting was about?"

"She wants to admit guilt."

"Publicly?"

Deborah sat back. "I don't know. That's the dilemma. I need your help here. What do we do?"

Grace was sitting on the floor with her back against the bed and her arms around her knees when there was a soft knock at the door. She said nothing. The door opened, and her father came in.

She couldn't tell him not to—didn't **want** to tell him not to. It was his turn to talk.

Putting her forehead to her knees, she waited until he crossed the carpet. She was surprised when he slid down to the floor next to her.

"I screwed up," he said.

"That's my line," she murmured.

"I screwed up before you did. I should have talked to you more about the divorce when it first happened. My leaving had nothing to do with you and Dylan."

"Only Mom," Grace said bitterly.

"Only me," he corrected, "and yes, I was selfish. I've been that way all my life. It's not a good way to be."

She shrugged. "You got what you wanted."

"At the expense of other people. That's not **good**."

She raised her head and looked at him. "Then why did you do it?"

"I didn't see the harm."

"And you do now?" she asked doubtfully.

"My therapist told me in no uncertain words."

That surprised Grace. "You see a therapist?"

"Rebecca made me. She said I would blow a second marriage if I didn't resolve certain issues. I need to understand why I can't focus on others. Why I can't do something someone else wants if it's not my own first choice." He grabbed her hand. "The problem is that even when you know what's wrong, it takes a while to fix it. Even though I know I should have talked with you, I didn't. I can blame it on thinking you weren't old enough. But if you can go out drinking with friends, you're old enough."

Grace pulled back her hand.

"Hey," he said with a smile, "that was a joke."

She tucked the hand between her knees. "You don't make jokes."

"Which explains why I'm bad at it," he said. He was quiet for a minute, then added, "I wasn't sure you'd accept what I had to say." He paused. "Would you have?"

"I don't know. But you're the father. You should have tried and **kept** trying."

"Well, I'm trying now. I do love you, Grace."

"But don't you hate what I've done?" she cried.

"Yes. But only the drinking part. And maybe the shoplifting part."

"What about the race I blew and the French test I tanked and the English paper Mr. Jones made me rewrite?"

"What English paper?" he said sternly, then abruptly smiled and raised a brow. "Was that better?"

"This isn't **funny**," Grace cried, though there was something to be said for his trying to be.

"I don't hate you for those things, Grace," he said. "I feel badly, because they didn't need to happen, but your mother and I are as much at fault for that as you are. As for the accident, your mother said you were driving perfectly."

"I had two beers."

"And you were wrong to get behind the wheel. But that's another issue. Right now, we have to decide what to do."

"What are our choices?" Grace asked nervously.

"I'm trying to figure that out."

He sounded into it. But Grace kept waiting for the other shoe to fall. "You don't seem angry."

He looked at her in surprise. "I thought we settled that."

She shook her head and stared at him, waiting. By way of answer, he drew her into his arms. Grace was no expert, but her gut told her this hug was real, especially when she started to cry and he continued to hold her. For an hour.

Well, maybe not an hour. Maybe only a quarter of that, but her old dad wouldn't have lasted more than five minutes.

Deborah, too, was feeling better. There was something to be said for sharing the responsibility. When Greg suggested taking both kids back to Vermont with him Saturday morning, Deborah didn't object.

They were gone by eight. By nine, Deborah was with patients. By noon, she was doing paperwork. By one, she was walking up to the house to see her father. He was in the backyard, raking the beds around Ruth's hydrangeas.

He gestured toward bunches of dried stumps that had the barest beginning of green growth in the middle. "Hard to believe these'll ever amount to anything," he said by way of hello. He wore old khakis and an even older flannel shirt with the sleeves rolled up. "Anything interesting growing on your end this morning?"

Deborah smiled. "Two streps, one bronchitis, two annuals, and more allergy complaints than you'd want to hear. How're you doing?"

"How do I look?"

"Chipper," she decided. His eyes were clear, his complexion healthy. He looked ten years younger than he was.

He resumed his raking. "How's Grace?"

"Less upset," she said. "Thank you, Dad. Whatever you said to her yesterday helped."

He combed a rakeful of dried leaves to the edge of the bed. "She was worried about seeing Greg."

"That wasn't all," Deborah said, wondering exactly how much her father did know. She hadn't grilled Grace. Yesterday, she had been more concerned with the outcome than the process. Today the process mattered.

He shot her a glance but kept on with his work. "No. That wasn't all. She's been carrying quite a load. I take it she told Greg everything?"

"In no uncertain terms," Deborah said.

"And what she didn't tell him, I did. It was time."

"Long **overdue,**" Michael corrected in a Dr. Barr tone, then seemed to catch himself and softened. "It's hard for a girl her age, halfway a child, halfway a woman."

"It's hard for **me.** I made a mistake."

"Oh, Deborah," he chided, "we all make mistakes." He paused. "Want me to talk to John?"

She smiled sadly this time, and shook her head. "The widow's already accusing the police of giving us special treatment. We'd better deal with John ourselves. I'm still not sure where this will end, but at least Grace is on the mend."

Michael bent to gather up leaves. A trash bag lay nearby. Deborah held it open. "For what it's worth," he said as he tamped the leaves inside, "I'd probably have done what you did. Don't know as I'd have let her off the hook for the beer, but I'm not the best authority on that score. She asked me some good questions about drinking, by the way, better ones than you've asked. Why'd you wait so long to open your mouth about that?" he asked, but in a gruff, face-saving way that demanded no answer. When he picked up the rake again and went at the bed, she felt an odd bit of peace.

Closing her eyes, she inhaled. "Ahhh. The smell of my childhood."

"Your mother loved spring. She loved these hydrangeas."

"Adinaldo will do this, y'know."

But her father didn't stop. "I'm doing it for Ruth," he said. "And for me."

"Want to take a break for lunch?"

"Nah. I'm feeling good. Don't you have to get home?"

"Actually, Greg took the kids back to Vermont."

"Grace willingly?"

"Uh-huh," she said with a smile. "But I am hungry. I'm going to get something with Jill."

"A sticky bun for lunch?"

"Try roast turkey on a croissant, with lettuce, tomato, mayo, and a thick slice of cheddar."

"Where?"

"At Jill's."

"Since when does she serve lunch?"

"Since they started serving lunch at Dunkin' Donuts." Deborah glanced at her watch. "I also want coleslaw, so I'm heading there now. They run out of that pretty fast."

He sniffed. "Your mother's recipe was the best."

"That's why they run out," she said and set off. Minutes later, she was in line at the bakery. When she reached the counter, she ordered sandwiches for Jill and herself, and took the only table left.

Her sister delivered the sandwiches and pulled a chair close. "I've been dying," she said, gently cross. "You couldn't call and tell me how it went?"

Deborah picked up half of her sandwich. "I couldn't until we finished talking, and then it was too late, and I saw patients this morning."

"Is Greg still here?"

"No. He took them back to the farm."

"Grace, too?"

Her mouth full, Deborah nodded.

Ignoring her own lunch, Jill sat back. "Where'd he stay last night?"

"At the house. In our bed."

"With you?" Jill asked warily.

"You're as bad as he is with the questions," Deborah said, but she wasn't angry. There was nothing to hide, nothing to feel guilty about. "Not that it's any business of yours, but he slept in our bed, and I slept in mine. We did not sleep together. He's married to someone else."

Jill was incorrigibly curious. "How'd you feel about that?"

"Fine."

"Were you tempted to tiptoe down the hall in the middle of the night?"

"Absolutely not." She took another bite of her sandwich.

Jill lifted a fork to poke at the coleslaw. "Was it awkward?"

Deborah finished chewing. "A little, actually, but only until I told him I had moved in next to the kids. I mean, I don't know what he thought. He knew there'd be a chance he'd sleep over. He brought a change of clothes—"

She stopped talking, because Jill was no longer listening. She was looking out the window. Turning, Deborah saw Michael in the same khakis and plaid shirt. Without missing a beat, like he did it every day of the week, he came in the door, looked around, and headed their way.

"Talk about awkward," Jill said.

Watching her father, Deborah was speechless.

"Hey, Dr. Barr," called a teenaged boy who was having lunch with his dad.

Michael put a hand on the boy's shoulder as he passed. "Hey, Jason," he said, but continued on. He was soon at their table, looking from one sandwich to the next. He pointed at Jill's. "What's in that one?"

She cleared her throat, her only concession to what had to be a wave of emotion. "Organic chicken breast, lettuce, tomato, and Dijon mustard on home-baked multigrain bread. Toasted."

"I'll have one," Michael said. "With coleslaw." He paused, unsure. "Where do I order?"

For a minute, Deborah feared Jill would simply point him to the ORDER HERE line. But her sister came through. She raised a hand in the direction of the counter and called a loud, **"Pete!"** Seconds later, her chief sandwich-maker appeared. "My father will have my special. Would you please bring it over when it's done?"

"Sure, Jill. Let me get you a chair, Dr. Barr."

"He can take mine," Deborah said, holding out her plate. "Would you wrap this for me?"

"Don't leave," Jill ordered quickly. She sounded alarmed.

She wasn't the only one. Deborah could feel the tension in her father's arm as she guided him to her seat. But they needed this time alone.

Besides, she couldn't have eaten another bite anyway. Her throat was too tight.

What to do then? For the first time in years, Deborah had no kids, no patients, no plans. Feeling oddly unsettled, she got in her car and headed out of town. She didn't want to go home. The house was empty. She might have driven to Grace's favorite boutique one town over and bought her something special for summer. She might have driven to the music shop where Dylan was eyeing a speaker for his keyboard. She might have gone to the mall and just walked.

But none of those things appealed to her.

Thinking of Dylan, she drove aimlessly along wooded suburban roads, crossing one town line, then another. The woods thinned; traffic picked up. When she reached the highway, she found herself taking the on-ramp and heading toward the city. Turning off the highway just shy of Boston, she crossed the river and entered Cambridge.

She wished she could pretend she was going to shop at her old student haunts, only they no longer existed. She wished she could pretend she was going to get a facial, but she wasn't a spa person. She wished she could pretend she simply wanted to walk along the river on a beautiful May day. Only it wasn't beautiful. Muggy and overcast, it looked like rain, which should have been reason enough for her to turn around and drive home.

Working her way through Harvard Square, she drove out Brattle Street, turning off onto a narrow street that was overhung with trees and lined with parked cars. One pulled out as she approached.

She pulled in. Then she sat and thought of all the reasons why this was not a good idea, one of which was the pending lawsuit, another the fact that Tom might have friends visiting. Or he might be out, in which case she could head back home with no one the wiser.

Deciding that heading home would be best, she was about to start the car again. But the thought of the way he had held her hand last Thursday stopped her. There had been comfort in his grasp.

Her father would tell her to drive off. Hal would say the same. Grace would be appalled, but Jill would smile crookedly and egg her on, and maybe Jill was right. Deborah had followed the rules all her life, and where had it left her? Sitting alone in her car on a side street in Cambridge, afraid to open her door.

In a burst of defiance, she got out, crossed the sidewalk, and climbed three steps to the door marked 42. His house was a free-standing brick one, tall but narrow, as were most on the street. The door was black with a shiny brass knocker and bell.

She rang the bell, at which point her defiance dissolved, but it was too late to leave.

"Yeah?" she heard from high above. She had to back down one step to see where he was on the roof. He stared at her for a minute, then disappeared, at which point Deborah felt a qualm. She imagined him up there with a woman, or the widow, or even the D.A.

She should have called, she thought. But she hadn't known she was coming.

He opened the door, wearing old jeans and a T-shirt. His hair was messed. He hadn't shaved. He looked as startled as she felt.

The ball was in Deborah's court. Taking a page from Jill's book, she grinned with mock brightness. "I was just driving around, when I saw your door and thought I'd say hi."

The corner of his mouth twitched.

Seriously, she said, "Bad timing?"

His eyes held hers. "No. Want to come in?"

Nodding, she stepped into a small front hall. On the right was a living room, on the left a corridor leading back, straight ahead a staircase that turned twice on its way up. "Doesn't look messy to me," she remarked. He had called himself a slob, yet a ten-speed hung neatly from hooks in the corridor.

He made an amused sound. "You can't see the kitchen."

"But the living room looks nice."

"I don't use it often. So it's neat."

"You were just on the roof?"

"That I do use. A lot."

"What's up there?"

Gesturing with his chin, he led her up the stairs. From the second floor landing, she saw three doors, one of which was open to his bedroom and a tangle of bedding and clothes. Up another staircase, the third floor had higher ceilings and was completely open, with columns placed for structural support. The walls were white, made even brighter by two pairs of skylights. She saw one desk with a computer, one without, and a table in the center of the room. Papers were strewn over every surface in sight.

The staircase to the roof was a free-standing spiral of wood. She went first this time, drawn to the open door. The rooftop was a small patio, complete with a table and chairs, lounges, and a grill. Shrubs grew in pots around the perimeter, and trees from the street were high enough to provide shade. A single section of wood fencing, cedar aged to gray, had been built for privacy, she guessed, but the rest was open to a leafy view, all of it bordered by a waist-high brick wall.

The grill was open; used cooking utensils, glasses, and plates filled an attached tray. The table here, too, was covered with papers. She wondered if he had been working and turned back to ask him, but the words never came. He was looking at her with such longing that Deborah was struck silent.

She might have come for this. She had refused to think about her feelings for Tom since their meeting in the park. But she knew that she was drawn to him.

Her own eyes must have said as much, and then some, because he said, "Not wise, huh?"

She shook her head. "I'm starting to wonder, though. We can be responsible all we want, then it's shot to hell when something happens that we didn't plan, didn't want, can't control."

"Like my brother."

"Like my daughter, my father, and my ex-husband."

"Not your son?"

"Him, too, only what happens to him at this age involves less an act of will than a pre-ordained physiological condition."

Tom looked at the papers on the table, then back at Deborah. "Do you think my brother's condition was a physiological one? Was he born with a chemical imbalance?"

She had no way of knowing for sure, but Tom needed a reason for Cal's behavior, and a chemical imbalance might be one. "Possibly."

He considered that, then went to the table and took a small envelope from the papers. Returning, he handed it to her. Inside were three childhood snapshots, taken in varying years. The boys were handsome, together in the first two pictures and with their parents in the third. The most obvious element of each shot, Deborah thought, was Cal looking away, leaning away, or turning away.

She pointed at one of the prints. "How old was he here?"

"Three," Tom said, sharing her thought. "I don't remember him being any other way. It's like he was born without the ability to relate to people. I've often wondered if he had a form of autism, only I always find things that don't fit the profile. He was a great student and a great teacher. But at home—in his personal life—something was missing. Selena swears he wasn't depressed, but how could she have known, if he kept it all to himself?"

"No note yet?"

"No. He was up to date paying bills, even ahead with a couple. Maybe a sign that he planned to be gone?" He answered with a shrug. "I'm still getting things from his P.O. boxes. They'll probably keep coming for a while." He looked at her. "I talked with the D.A."

"You did?"

"I told him I disagreed with Selena. He didn't back down. But I wanted him to hear an opposing view."

Deborah was grateful—and grateful that he had talked with the D.A. before this visit. That gave it more weight. Here, now, they felt like friends.

She had a wild urge to tell him everything about Grace and the accident, about Grace and Greg, about what she thought had to be done. She wanted his feedback, perhaps his advice.

But that wouldn't have been any wiser than falling into bed. There was still too much that had to play out, and, in that, they were opponents.

Seeming to read her mind, including the

part that held regret, he asked, "Are you hungry? It's late, but I haven't eaten. Want to walk into the Square?"

Deborah didn't have red meat often, but the burger she had at Mr. Bartley's was the best thing she had eaten in days.

"This is sinful," she said, mopping a ketchup drip with the last of her bun.

"Only one of the nice things about living here."

"Have you been here long?"

"Ten years." He sat back. "Selena claims Cal moved here to be closer to me. It would've been nice if he'd told me he was here."

"Maybe he just wanted to know you were close."

"Maybe. Anyway, I rented for the first few years, but I liked the area so much that buying was a no-brainer. If you went to school here, you know what I mean."

She did. "My friends are gone, though." She smiled. "Yours are taking their spaces." He had acknowledged half a dozen people since they had entered the Square.

He shrugged. "I'm at Starbucks every morning for coffee. I browse at the newsstand several days a week. I eat at local restaurants.

Even with students moving in and out, some familiar faces stay. You get to know people. And then there's my bike group. Lotsa road bikers in Cambridge. We meet most week-ends."

"You have a satisfying life."

He smiled sadly. "For what it is."

"What do you mean?"

"I have no family."

Deborah knew he wasn't talking about his parents or brother. She recalled wondering why he didn't have a family of his own. At that time, she couldn't ask. But they were friends now. "Do you not have a wife and kids be-cause of your own experience?"

"No. It just never happened." Seeming to catch himself, he looked troubled. "You're probably right. Some of the other, too. Ner-vousness. Fear I'd blow it."

"You're not like your parents."

"Can I be sure of that?"

When Deborah didn't answer, he gestured her up. "Let's walk."

They went to the river. The sky had grown darker. The grumble of thunder was distant and low. On her own, Deborah would have sought shelter. But Tom was quiet company. They walked slowly, stopping occasionally to watch a scull skimming the water.

Finally, she stopped and looked at him. "I didn't know your parents, Tom. I didn't know your brother. But you do communicate. Doesn't that make you different from them?"

"Maybe. I'd be taking a big chance, though."

"Not such a big one, if it's really what you want." She felt a raindrop. "I don't know what I'd do without my kids. And I don't mean just filling the time. They satisfy me. Of course, not everyone needs that kind of satisfaction." She felt another drop. "Maybe you don't."

"Who knows? Am I thinking of it now only because Cal's gone?"

"Did you think about it before?"

"Not the same way." He held out a hand. "Rain."

They had come a distance. Deborah was uneasy. "We'd better head back."

"Just when the conversation was getting good?" he asked with an indulgent smile.

It was, she decided, setting off. And suddenly she felt cross. "I hate rain. Why does it ruin everything?"

He walked beside her. "What does it ruin?"

"Clean cars . . . new shoes . . . **hair.**"

"This is a gentle rain."

"It still gets you wet."

His smile turned curious. "Is that bad?"

"The memories are."

"Then you need new ones," he said and, taking her hand, stopped her from moving.

"I think . . . we should . . . keep going," she sang.

Looking self-satisfied, he shook his head.

The rain picked up.

"Tom," she protested and tugged on his hand. She was starting to get wet.

"It's only rain."

"But I don't **like** rain," she said, laughing, and pulled free.

He caught her, this time wrapping his arms around her from behind. "Nuh-uh, no, you don't."

"I'm getting wet," she warned. Her hair was heavy, her jersey splotched.

"And how does it feel?"

"Wet." She tried to pry his arms loose, but they didn't budge.

"Think about it," he coaxed in that same patient voice. "Does it feel cold?"

Her face was wet now, too. "No. Not cold. Just wet."

"Does the rain hurt when it hits?"

No more than taking a shower, she realized. Actually, less than that. He was right; it was a gentle rain.

"What are you thinking?" he asked.

Of my mother, she wanted to say and if not that, **Of your brother.** Either was safer than thinking about Tom and how well he handled her.

"My hair," she wailed. "It's messy enough dry. Wet it's **unruly.**"

"Turn your face up," he urged softly.

She did, closing her eyes when the rain hit her lids.

"Now breathe, slowly and deeply. Just feel it, Deborah."

Again, she did what he said. She breathed slowly and deeply, slowly and deeply, thoroughly soaked now, but not minding it. Even when his arms loosened, she stayed with her face turned to the sky.

Finally, she righted her head, only then realizing that Tom had stepped back. She looked quickly around. He stood at arm's length, as drenched as she was. Dark hair streamed over his forehead, his shirt stuck to his skin. Despite it all, he retained a certain authority.

"How do you feel?" he asked.

Wet was one word, but that was pride speaking. **Free** was another. She went with the third, though, because it was the most surprising. "Cleansed."

It was also the most absurd, but that didn't keep her from thinking it again as she drove home a short time later in that same gentle rain. She didn't know how she could feel cleansed now that she had a whole other secret to keep. Grace would flip out if she saw Tom, and that, totally apart from Deborah's friendship with him—and **that,** totally apart from the fact that Tom's sister-in-law was suing her.

Bad timing? **Horrendous** timing.

But still she felt cleansed, which made an important point. Rain didn't make things messy. People did that all on their own.

Chapter 22

Greg returned the children to Leyland himself on Sunday afternoon, for which Deborah was infinitely grateful. Given what they had to do, having Greg there would make things easier.

First came a meeting with Hal. Greg set it up, and Deborah was grateful for that, too. Confessing to a lie was difficult, but even more so when the one deceived was a friend.

Once they were settled in the living room, Greg laid out the truth about the accident, and if Hal was disappointed in Deborah, he didn't let on. He barely looked at her, barely looked at Grace. Greg's presence modulated him, as Deborah had known it would.

"So," Greg finished, "how do we proceed? Clearly, we have to talk with John. What are the possible consequences for Deborah and Grace?"

Hal looked concerned. "Deborah filed a false police report. She could be charged with that."

"Penalty?" Greg asked.

"If she had a record, she could see jail time."

"Mom," Grace cried.

Deborah took her hand. "I have no record, Grace. Please, Hal."

He relented. "Likely probation. Maybe a fine."

Deborah could deal with that. "Who determines what happens?" she asked.

"The local police have jurisdiction over the issue of the false report, but not over a civil suit."

Deborah thought of Tom, but Greg rescued her with an impatient question for Hal. "I want to know what happens **now.** If we go to John, say, tomorrow morning, what are the consequences for Grace? Would she be charged with leaving the scene of an accident?"

"Possibly. Again, in this case, a misdemeanor. Likely probation."

"What does probation mean?" Grace asked in a nervous voice.

Hal's tone softened—but then, Deborah had never doubted his affection for her children. "It means, basically, that you go about your life as usual as long as you don't break another law, in which case there's trouble."

"She didn't do anything wrong," Deborah put in. "It was me. I sent her home. She wanted to stay."

"That would be taken into consideration," Hal replied. "Did she violate any permit requirements?"

"No."

"I was drinking," Grace reminded her.

"That's another issue," Hal said. "I'm not sure you need to tell John that."

Grace stared at him. "But I was **drinking.**"

"We may have to tell him," Deborah said quietly. "Grace needs him to know."

Hal didn't like being contradicted. "Fine, but trust me, his main concern is the other issues. I know John—"

"Knowing him doesn't justify special treatment," Deborah cut in. "Isn't that what the civil suit is about?"

Hal made a face. "Christ, Deborah, do you want him to throw the book at you simply **because** he likes you?" He turned back to Greg. "As for Grace, if there were no permit violations—and no civil infractions, like speeding—the RMV wouldn't impose sanctions. She'd keep on driving and be able to get her license. The danger is still the civil lawsuit. If you go to John now with full disclosure, he'll be required to tell the D.A. That'll complicate things."

"How public will it be?" Greg asked.

"That depends on how public the D.A. wants to make it. Actually, it depends on how the victim's family reacts. Grace is a minor, so her name would be kept out of the papers, but Deborah's would be there." He held up a hand. "This is all speculation. But you have to understand that there will be repercussions if you tell John everything."

Deborah was thinking that they might not have a choice, when the doorbell rang. Puzzled, she left the room and went to the door.

Karen stood there, clearly upset. "Is my husband here?"

"Yes." Deborah drew her inside. "What's wrong?"

"He said he was coming, but lately what he says has nothing to do with what he does." She was shaking. "I had a surprise visitor a few minutes ago, an Arden Marx. She wanted to return some of my husband's belongings. A pair of monogrammed cuff links. The engraved Montblanc fountain pen I gave him last year." Her voice rose. "Arden Marx claimed he had given them to her. She wanted to return them now, since it appears he's dumped her for someone named Amelia, another associate in his firm, which means," she was fairly shouting now, "that everyone in his firm knows he's been screwing around behind my back."

"Karen," Hal interrupted from the living room arch, "you're not yourself."

Karen turned on him. "Meaning that I'm not my usual deny-it-all patsy?" She gestured angrily. "How **can** I deny it this time, when it's shoved right under my nose? How could you, Hal?" she cried. "You're the first one to criticize clients who cheat on their wives. Did they give you lessons, or did it just come naturally?"

"Arden Marx has an axe to grind," Hal said, still calm. "She's just been fired."

"According to her, she quit," Karen argued, "and—here's something we can check out—she says she just signed on with Eckert Seamans, which is a more prestigious firm than yours, so if you're going to claim she was fired for poor performance, no one will believe you. She also says Amelia Ormant botched a case and got a sizable bonus for 'effort.' And what about the cuff links and the pen, both definitely yours. She might have taken the pen from your desk, but cuff links?"

She was breathing hard. "And what about Amelia Ormant, who is **married,** for God's sake."

"She's leaving her husband," Hal corrected.

"And that makes it all **right?** Hal, **you** have a wife. You also have a **daughter,** who's noticed all on her own that you're coming home late freshly showered or 'soaked by the rain.' Our daughter is seventeen. She isn't a child. She doesn't believe for a minute that you're playing racquetball, even though I defend you when she asks."

Hal was beginning to look uneasy. "This isn't the time or place, Karen."

"I think it is," she said. "If I don't say all this when I'm rip-roaring mad, I may lose my nerve, because we both know that part of me loves you enough to keep on denying the truth rather than risk losing my marriage. And Deborah and Greg have known us forever."

Hal looked from Greg to Deborah, waving a dismissive hand at his wife.

"That's **exactly** why I'm here," Karen argued. "I knew you'd try to make me out to be delusional. But Deborah and Greg know me. They know I'm right. Three years ago—**three** years, Hal—I got a call from our credit card company wanting to verify certain charges. When I asked you about the one from the Four Seasons downtown, you said it was for lunch for a large group, all eight hundred and fifty dollars of it, and I believed you. But there were other bills from the hotel on days you told me you'd be in Rhode Island or New Hampshire. Arden claims she was only with you for a year, and if it ended three months ago, like she says, that means you were with someone else before then."

"I think we should go home," Hal said, opening the door.

Karen followed him, but only to the threshold. "Did it start when I got sick?" she asked with a hand to her chest. "Were you turned off after my surgery?"

"I'm leaving," he said. "Either come or not." He glanced back at Deborah and Greg. "You got your free advice. If there's a civil case, I'll recommend someone to represent you." Leaving his wife at the door, he strode down the walk.

Karen stared after him.

Deborah waited, giving her a chance to follow, but Karen didn't take a single step as Hal got in the car and drove off. Only then did Deborah put a hand on her friend's shoulder.

Suddenly, all Karen't rage and bravado crumbled. "What did I do?" she cried softly and dissolved into deep, gut-wrenching sobs.

Greg and Grace had tactfully disappeared. Clasping her friend tightly, Deborah moved to sit on the stairs.

"He's gone," Karen said brokenly and pulled a tissue from her pocket. "I knew he would leave me." She pressed the tissue to her nose.

"Oh, I don't know," Deborah reasoned gently. "He was embarrassed in front of us."

"He was **caught,**" Karen said over the tissue.

"That, too. He'll lick his wounds and think about what he wants to do. The more important question is what **you** want to do."

Karen took a shuddering breath. "I don't know. I've asked myself that dozens of times. I can't keep on going this way. But will Hal ever change? I don't think he'll agree to counseling."

"He may, if he wants the marriage to last."

"That's a big if. He'll probably say that he can't stay with me after I've humiliated him in front of you. You know, I've fantasized about embarrassing him in public, because he's done it to me. Maybe that's why I came over today. Maybe I've deliberately goaded him to get

him to file for divorce because I don't have the guts to do it myself. I don't want to be alone. But I don't want to be married to someone who would prefer to be with someone else." She sagged against Deborah. "I just don't know. I don't know what I want. I wish I had a crystal ball and could see where I'll be in ten years. Between the cancer and Hal, I feel like I don't have a future."

Deborah smiled sadly. "If it weren't cancer and Hal, it'd be something else. We all want a blueprint that spells out what'll happen to us."

"I just want to know where it **ends.**"

"So do I, but we can't know. Dylan said it. It's like going through fog, feeling your way along until what's in front of you finally appears."

"That implies you do nothing at all along the way to determine your own future."

"But you get my point. Sometimes we just can't see far. People like you and me want to plan. But we can't. Not long-range."

"Then what do I do now, right at this moment?"

"Drive home. See if Hal's there. Talk with Danielle. Does she know about Arden?"

"She was listening. I didn't know it until Arden left. Dani heard every word."

Grace heard every word, too. She was in the living room, not hiding exactly but unable to leave. By the time Karen left, she was remembering the way Dani had crouched down beside her in school. **Something's going on with my dad. I really need to talk, Gracie. Please?**

Grace had refused, so obsessed with her own problems that she hadn't seen that her friend was in pain. And if Dani had been hurting before, it would be worse now. Grace knew what it was like to have her father jump ship—knew the creepy feeling thinking of him with another woman, knew the sense of betrayal.

Pulling her cell phone from her back pocket, where it had been tucked for the better part of two weeks, she pressed Dani's number. It wasn't like she knew what to say, especially when Dani picked up after a single ring and burst into tears. But this was a friend who was as close to a sister as Grace would ever have, and even if she could only sit there and listen, it was more than she'd done last week.

I'm not a good person for anyone to need, she had told Dani then, and it wasn't that she was suddenly a better person now. But she wanted to be.

Grace kept telling herself that. Still, she went back and forth all night, needing to tell John Colby the truth but terrified. Once it was out, there was no taking it back. It could totally change her life, just like that instant on the road in the rain.

Unable to sleep, she curled up in bed with her mother. Deborah wasn't sleeping either. They lay together for a while, staring into the darkness. Grace couldn't be sure what her mother was thinking, but her own thoughts didn't stray.

"Are you sure we can't talk to Chief Colby here at the house?" Grace finally whispered. There was a jail at the police station. That made her nervous.

But her mother shook her head. "We're better off going there. That way no one can claim we're pulling strings. Don't try to predict what will happen, sweetheart. Imagination is often worse than reality. Tell me about Vermont."

"I can't think about Vermont."

"Your father came through, didn't he?"

"Yes."

"Do you feel better?"

"A little."

"Want to talk about it?"

Grace did, but it was awkward. "Do you really want to know that Rebecca's a great cook?"

There was a moment's silence. "Is she?"

"Yes," Grace said, "but she freaks out at the sight of blood. She cut her finger chopping veggies and nearly fainted. I had to put the Band-Aid on."

"Was she appreciative?"

"Totally."

"Is she good with Dylan?"

"I guess. He spent all his time with the pups."

"I may lose that battle."

But Grace didn't want to talk about Dylan, or her father, or Rebecca. "What do you think John'll say?"

Her mother was quiet. "He's fair. He's compassionate. He cares about us."

"That's favoritism."

"It's fact. He'll do what he feels is best."

"That's no answer."

"What can I say? I wish I had answers for everything, Gracie. Clearly, I don't. Clearly, I make mistakes."

"I drank. I drove."

"I lied."

Grace knew her mother was tense, could hear it in her voice. But Grace was the one urging them to confess. Maybe she was wrong. "Maybe going to John is a mistake, Mom. Maybe we should wait."

Her mother sighed, seeming resigned. "The outcome won't change if we wait, and the longer we do, the harder it will be." She stroked Grace's hair. "I'm sorry, sweetie. I didn't realize the effect my lie would have on you."

"I won't try to shoplift again," Grace promised. "That was really dumb of me. Like, I didn't even want the shoes."

"You did. Just not enough to steal them." Deborah tucked a long curl behind Grace's ear. "I try to protect you, but there are limits. That's one of the things I've learned from this. I can say you did nothing wrong driving that night. The state investigators can say the same thing. But what happened is part of you now. You need to own it."

Chapter 23

Deborah was having second thoughts of her own by the time they left the house Monday morning. The drive into town was too short and every face at the police station too familiar. She was feeling totally awkward. When John closed the door to his office, there was some relief, but it lasted only until the chief lowered himself to the chair behind his desk and sat frowning at the papers there.

Deborah cleared her throat. "I need to correct something on the crash report I filed," she began.

But John had his own confession. Without looking up, he said, "A funny thing happened last week. I drove Ellen home from school, only she'd forgotten to have me stop at the market on the way, for salad or whatever for dinner. We agreed she'd go back there herself, so I got out of the car. She walked around and got in my side and leaned forward to adjust the seat." He raised troubled eyes to Deborah. "Seeing her do that, I remembered the night of the accident when I asked you for your registration. You slid in behind the wheel, but you had to adjust the seat."

Yes, Deborah would have done that. Grace's legs were still shorter than hers.

Grace was one step ahead. "You **knew?**" she asked John in a half whisper.

"No. I didn't question it at the time. Your mother had to reach across to the glove box. It would have been natural for her to want more room for that." He shifted a paper or two around on his desk. "Then things started going wrong for you, Grace—school, track— and I knew it could be guilt. I also knew it could be nothin' more than a reaction to the accident. But when the D.A. started talking cover-up, I had to take a close look at my part of the investigation."

Deborah held her breath. She guessed that Grace was doing the same, because Greg was the one who had to ask, "What did you find?"

"Holes," John said. "Actually, only one. But it was gaping." He turned to Deborah. "I never asked if you were driving. I assumed you were. We all knew you. We knew you were a good driver. We just assumed . . ." His voice trailed off.

Deborah finished the thought. "You assumed I'd tell you if Grace had been the one at the wheel."

"No. It wasn't your job to tell. It was my job to ask, and I didn't do that. Yes, I assumed. Would I have assumed if it had been someone else? Someone I didn't know? Probably not. So maybe the widow was right. Maybe I did give you a free ride because I know you so well."

Impatiently, Greg said, "But isn't that what it's **supposed** to be like when you live in a small town? You know everyone. You trust everyone."

"I abused that trust," Deborah broke in, but turned at the bold sound of Grace's voice.

"I was drinking," she said, staring at John.

John recoiled. "Were you. That I didn't know."

"Neither did my mom, so don't get mad at her. The accident was all my fault. I had two cans of beer."

He was a minute taking it in. "I thought you were studying."

Grace was silent. Deborah knew she didn't want to implicate her friends.

"Were you debilitated?" he asked.

"You mean, like drunk? No. But if I hadn't had anything, I might have seen Mr. McKenna."

"Grace," Deborah begged, because they had been through this so many times, "**I** didn't see him and I had **nothing** to drink."

"Don't condone it, Deborah," Greg warned.

"I'm not condoning it," she reasoned. "I'd never condone it. She's underage. She shouldn't have been drinking, period. But that isn't what caused the accident."

John was looking at Grace. "When your mother came to pick you up, did it occur to you not to drive?"

"No. I felt fine. But if I'd been drinking, my judgment about how I felt would have been warped. Wouldn't it?"

"You tell me."

She said an unhappy, "Yes."

"And you couldn't tell your mom you'd been drinking, not even after Mr. McKenna died?"

"**Especially** not then. I mean, she already knew I was the one driving, so I'd gotten us in enough trouble. Adding the thing about the beer would have made it worse. She would have been **really** upset."

"When did you finally tell her?"

Grace shrank into herself. "Thursday. In the alley by the bakery, after I tried to swipe those Pradas. That was the first time she knew."

John thought about that, then turned to Deborah. "The night of the accident, when Grace got in the car to drive, did you see anything different about her?"

"Absolutely not," Deborah said. "She seemed in control. I was amazed at how calm she was driving in that storm. In hindsight, maybe the beer gave her false confidence. But I couldn't fault the way she drove. Nor did the state police," she reminded him.

John leaned back, brows knitted. From the outer offices came muted sounds of business—the scrape of a chair, an indistinct voice, the ring of a phone. Here, all was silent.

Deborah felt suspended. In his unprepossessing way, John Colby wielded huge power.

Finally, he looked up. Clearing his throat, he focused on Grace. "What are your thoughts here?"

Grace seemed unprepared for the question. She was a minute searching, then said, "I'm scared."

"About what?"

"Knowing Mr. McKenna's dead. Living with it for the rest of my life. It doesn't matter what anyone says about my driving, I'll always wonder."

"You weren't drinking alone."

"I was the one who hit a man."

"But your friends were drinking, too."

"And, see, that terrifies me. Now you know, and they'll hate me for that."

"Sounds like it's already pretty bad for you at school."

Grace nodded.

"What'll make it end?"

Her eyes welled. "I don't know."

John grew quiet. After a minute, he asked, "Do you feel like you need punishment? Is that what the shoplifting was about?"

Grace hung her head. "I guess. It's like I've done all these bad things and gotten away with them, and maybe there are some kids who can do that and still sleep at night. But I can't." She looked up. "I lie awake thinking about it. I keep wondering who knows."

"So you're here today because you can't live with the fear of being caught?"

"No. It's not that." She seemed to struggle. "Well, maybe a little. It's that what I did was wrong. It doesn't make me feel good about myself. It doesn't make me feel like I can **be** someone someday."

Proud despite the circumstances, Deborah wanted to reach for Grace's hand, but resisted. Grace needed to do this on her own.

John sat staring at his desk while their lives hung in the balance, the only sounds muted ones from the outer office. Finally, he looked from Deborah to Greg. "This is one of those times when I wish we still had stocks." He glanced at Grace. "Know what those are?"

Pale, she nodded. "Like in **The Scarlet Letter.**"

"We could set you up on Main Street for a morning and be done with it. Very simple. Very effective. Nowadays, things are more complex." Again, he looked at Deborah and Greg. "Too complex for an instant opinion. I think I need to talk with the D.A."

Deborah was thinking that they couldn't wait, that they **did** need an instant opinion, and that involving the D.A. would only prolong the agony—when there was a knock at the door. It opened only enough for John to see someone and rise. "Be right back," he said on his way out, closing the door after him.

Deborah did take Grace's hand then. It was icy. She rubbed it between both of hers.

"What'll he **do?**" the girl asked.

Deborah looked at Greg, who shrugged with his hands.

"Going to the D.A. will be bad, won't it?" Grace asked.

Greg came forward and touched her shoulder. "It may not be. It could be as simple as John thinking of the civil suit. If the D.A. is part of any decision now, charges of a cover-up become null and void."

The problem, Deborah knew, was that if the D.A. was involved, a joint decision might be tougher, precisely to avoid the smell of a cover-up. Greg knew this. She could see it in the look he gave her.

In the ensuing silence, there were more muted voices from without. This time, above that, Deborah heard the ticking of the large clock on John's wall. The seconds seemed endless. She was about to scream, when the door finally opened.

John closed it and stood for a minute. He was holding some papers and seemed startled. "Well," he finally said. "That's something." He rubbed his neck, then looked at them. "It seems Cal did write a note."

Deborah glanced quickly at Grace, then back to John. "A suicide note?"

Nodding, he handed her a sheet of typing

paper, loosely folded in thirds. He stood nearby, arms folded over the swell of his middle. One hand still held the envelope.

Deborah unfolded the paper and, heart pounding, read what was inside. As suicide notes went, it was neither eloquent nor enlightening, in many ways as cryptic as the man himself. **By the time you get this, I'll be gone. I'm sorry. I just can't do it anymore. For every good minute there are five bad ones. I'm tired.** It was written in the same precise script that Deborah had seen on Grace's history papers.

Feeling a swell of emotion—overwhelming relief, pervasive sadness, amazement at the timing—she handed the note to Grace, who read it with Greg over her shoulder.

"How did you get this?" Deborah asked John.

"Tom McKenna just brought it. He got it this morning, forwarded from a P.O. box in Seattle." He passed her the envelope.

"It's addressed to Tom."

"Yes. Postmarked the morning after the accident. Cal must have put it in the mail slot shortly before he went running in the rain."

"But Tom lives here," Deborah pointed out. "Why would Cal have mailed this to Seattle, rather than directly to Tom?"

"I asked Tom that. He says it's how Cal's mind would work. He knew Tom'd get it, since he'd be the one collecting his effects."

Greg took the letter from Grace. He straightened and reread it while a wide-eyed Grace asked Deborah, "What does this mean?"

Deborah deferred to John.

"It means," he said gently, "that you can't blame yourself for what happened. Calvin McKenna deliberately ran in front of your car."

"**Knowing** it was us?" Grace asked in alarm.

"I doubt it. He just needed a car, and yours was the one that came by."

"But people are hit by cars all the time, and they don't die. How did he know he would?"

"He was on Coumadin," Deborah said. "He figured he would just bleed to death."

"That's **horrible,**" the girl cried.

"Suicide is."

John took the note from Greg. "Let me bring this back out. We have to make a copy. Tom wants to take the original back to show Cal's widow."

"Tom's still here?" Deborah asked.

John nodded and left. Deborah followed. She spotted Tom standing by the front door of the station. A lone figure, his back was ramrod straight, his eyes dark and filled with pain.

"I'm so sorry," she whispered when she was close enough not to be heard by the others. She wanted to touch him but didn't dare.

His voice was low and tight, his mouth barely moved. "What in the hell possessed him to do that?"

It struck Deborah that he was furious. "Mail it to Seattle?"

"Throw himself in front of a **car.** Didn't he know that whoever was driving that car would suffer? You could have gone into a tree and died, too. And yeah, why did he send the note to Seattle? If he'd sent it straight to me, we'd have known this ten days ago. He was a selfish bastard."

"He was in pain."

"So he sends me that note that explains nothing at all, and now I have to tell his wife?" He took a short, angry breath. "Y'know, maybe he'd have found meaning in life if he'd been able to get over self-pity long enough to see the **good** stuff that he had."

Deborah did touch his arm then. She couldn't not do it, perhaps the same way she couldn't not have driven to see him Saturday. "He's gone, Tom. The best we can do is to hope that he's in a better place."

Focusing on her, Tom softened. "You didn't deserve what he did."

"It wasn't personal. My car just happened to be there."

"And you can forgive his using you?"

"I can. You will, too." When he looked doubtful, she gave his arm a tiny shake. "You will, Tom. First, you have to grieve."

"Here you go," John said, coming up from behind and handing Tom the envelope with the letter refolded inside.

Deborah took her hand from Tom's arm. John gave no indication of having seen it, simply turned and headed back to his office.

"Gotta go," Deborah whispered. "Can we talk later?"

Tom stuck his hands in his pockets. "Are you sure you want to after this?"

She scolded him with a look. "You could have burned the letter."

"No. I couldn't have done that. Not to you."

She felt the words deeply, along with a dire need to tell him all he didn't know about the accident, but this wasn't the time or place. "When'll you be home?" she asked softly.

"One or two, I guess."

"I'll call." She looked at him a second longer before returning to John's office. Taking a seat again, she ignored the curious looks coming from Greg and Grace. Her relationship with Tom was hers alone and would stay that way until she figured out what it was. Another lie? No, she realized. Simply no one's business at this point in time but her own. "What happens now?" she asked John.

He scratched his head. "Good question. A suicide note changes things. Once Tom shows it to his sister-in-law, he'll get it back to us so that we can validate the handwriting."

"It was his," Grace said in a shaky voice.

"Tom agrees. We'll just make it official."

"So . . ." Greg urged him on.

But John was silent. He was clearly grappling with this unexpected twist at a time when his own judgment had been called into doubt. Deborah could almost sympathize.

Finally, he shook his head. "I can't press charges. What we have here is a situation where the victim caused his own injury by throwing himself in front of your car."

Deborah had suggested that herself— **Who** is **the victim here?** she had asked the detectives—but hearing the words from John made her truly accept them.

"Then it's over?" Grace asked, sounding afraid to hope.

"I'll have to consult with the D.A. But I'd suspect yes."

"What about the beer?" the girl asked.

Wincing, John ran a hand around the back of his neck. "The problem is if I do something public about that, I'll have to go public with the rest." He eyed Deborah. "That's where I'm torn. Do we want the student body dealing with another suicide, this one a teacher, an authority figure?" He looked at Greg. "All things balanced, is full disclosure necessary? What would it accomplish?" He turned to Grace. "The note does exonerate you. The world does need to know that Cal McKenna came out of the woods and ran out into the path of your car. But the accident reconstruction report will say that, anyway. So what if we conclude that Mr. McKenna was disoriented in the rain? It's certainly not a lie. A person wanting to kill himself is disoriented. Don't you think?"

Grace considered that. "Yes," she finally said.

"As for the beer, we have no way to prove it this long after the fact. What if I put it into a memorandum here in my file cabinet, to be taken out only if you break another law? If, say, three years go by and you're clean, we destroy the memorandum. So you'd basically be on probation for three years, which is what a judge would likely do. Are you comfortable with that?"

Grace nodded. Quietly, she asked, "What about the shoplifting?"

"In my file as well. You never did make it out the door with those shoes."

The girl made an embarrassed sound, but she was sitting straighter. Deborah suspected that nine-tenths of the battle had been won simply by telling the whole truth to John. Feeling lighter herself, she asked, "What about my filing a false report?"

"Same thing. Locked in my cabinet. Probation there, too."

"And the civil suit?" Greg asked. "Do we assume it'll be dropped?"

John gave a tentative smile. "That's up to the D.A. But a suicide note puts a whole other slant on things. Don't you think?"

Chapter 24

Standing in John's office, Deborah held Grace for the longest time. Words weren't needed; there was relief and love aplenty in the embrace. When John left, Grace drew back and turned to her father. Deborah felt her hesitation. Urging her on mentally, she was pleased when the girl hugged him, too. Greg had come through for her. He had come through for them both.

Father and daughter went off for time by themselves, allowing Deborah to return to work, but her eye was on the clock. She had a phone call to make.

Impatient, she barely made it to one before trying Tom's line. When he answered, she smiled. "Hey. How are you?"

"Been better," he said gently, but he sounded tired. "I just got back from Selena's.

She's having a hard time with this. Seeing the note means she can't pretend anymore."

"Pretend?"

"That Cal wasn't unhappy. That something wasn't wrong with their marriage. When I showed her the note, she didn't question its authenticity. It's like she half expected it. She kind of buckled and grew sad. The fight left her." The fight seemed to have left him, too. His voice was quiet. "I went to get her a drink, and when I came back, she started to talk. But it wasn't the wild talk I'd heard before. She sounded defeated, wanting to understand what had happened by telling me what she had seen."

Tom was a good listener. Deborah knew that firsthand.

"She talked about how they met," he went on. "The actual events were much the way she had first told me, only this time she talked about his moods. They frightened her, but she loved him, so she went ahead with the marriage. Then she saw it full-time—the silence, the brooding, the pacing at night in the dark. Remember how I said he compartmentalized?"

"Yes."

"That was what she saw. He was great at school. Really another person. And there were times when he was great with her. But then there was the dark, silent side. He would never talk about it. She asked me what I knew, but what could I say? I don't know what depressed him. He had demons none of us understood."

"Had it been worse lately?" Deborah asked. She wanted to understand, too.

Tom didn't answer immediately. Finally, sounding defeated himself, he said, "Apparently, yes, it was worse. She couldn't reach him at all. It was like he had less of a reserve of goodwill, she said—like he used it all up at school and had nothing to draw on at home. When she told him to see a shrink, he didn't talk with her for three days."

"Do you think he was seeing someone and just not telling her?"

"I can't find any record of it. If he was in therapy, he was paying in cash and leaving no trail. He wasn't on medication for depression—and yes, you're thinking he might have stopped taking it, which would explain why he reached the breaking point."

"And why it didn't show up in an autopsy."

"But I've combed his medical file. There's nothing." He paused briefly. "I can't fault Selena in this. She tried. She was—is—legitimately grief-stricken."

Deborah accepted that. She still resented

Selena's having gone to the D.A., but, for all she knew, she might have done the same herself, had the tables been turned. "Well, you were good to listen," she told Tom.

"Oh, nothing altruistic there. I needed to hear what she said."

"Did it help?"

He was quiet. Then, "Some, I guess. I still blame myself for not being more on top of what Cal was going through. I might have gotten him to a psychiatrist. With proper medication, he might have lived. But this does explain things a little. Selena isn't a bad person. She knew Cal had problems. She thought she could help."

"Many women do," Deborah said. She didn't ask about the lawsuit. It was irrelevant just then. She wanted to know more about Tom. "You were angry at the police station."

"I still am. I understand more about his reaching a tipping point, but he had no right using innocent people as his suicide tool. I think John got it as soon as I showed him the note. Was that your ex-husband with you in his office?"

"It was. He came down to help with Grace. She's had a tough time with all this. We actually worked out some of the hard feelings relating to the divorce."

"That's good."

"Very." She wanted to tell him more—about the divorce, about Grace, about the accident—but the time wasn't right. Until the civil suit was dropped—until she knew what she and Tom **were**—until Grace was comfortable with his knowing that she'd been the driver that night, Deborah couldn't say anything. There were a lot of **if**s to get past. She simply had to let the future play itself out a bit.

Not that she couldn't give it a nudge. "Tom—"

"Deborah—"

"What?"

"Dinner? Later this week?"

She smiled. "I'd like that."

She had just finished the last of the day's paperwork when Greg showed up. She looked past him, expecting to see Grace as well.

"I dropped her at the bakery," he explained. "Had a SoMa Shake with Dylan, and here I am. I'm heading back now. Thought I'd say goodbye."

Deborah was pleased he had come. She did want their new relationship to be better. The calm she felt now was in part related to the scabbing over of the open sore their divorce had left. "How did it go with Grace?"

"Up and down. But increasingly up. She's still asking why I left and what my life in Vermont gives me that this one didn't. And she asks lots of questions about my relationship with Rebecca. I'm trying to explain that there are no comparisons between you and Rebecca. Rebecca could never do what you do here. She could never be the kind of mother you are."

Still you left me, Deborah thought, but in a knee-jerk way. She had a better understanding now of why he'd left. The bitterness passed.

Taking the papers and her bag, she joined him at the door and flipped off the light. Walking him to his car, she said, "Thanks, Greg. Your being here has really helped."

"For me, too. Coming back was like a sword hanging over my head. Now I know I can do it. And it is good for the kids, integrating our lives a little."

She nodded. When they reached the Volvo, they hugged. It was an easy, comfortable gesture, a step forward in and of itself.

Deborah cooked dinner on the grill that night. She and the children needed to eat, and this night, Lívia's offering wouldn't do. Working together—Dylan wielded a **mean** spatula—they produced grilled chicken and garlic bread, a big fresh salad, and for dessert—a celebration—s'mores. Deborah had grown up making s'mores over a fire, and while a gas grill wasn't quite the same, it came close. The marshmallows melted well, in turn melting the chocolate squares just enough so that, pressed between graham crackers, the tastes blended. Hot marshmallow oozed out the edges and fell to the flagstones. But that was fine. By the time the s'mores were gone, a slow rain had begun to fall to wash the drippings away.

"You go inside," Grace told her mother, quickly stacking plates. "I'll bring everything in."

A week ago, Deborah might have let her. Today, she was in no rush. "I'm okay," she said, gathering the lemonade pitcher and empty glasses.

"You hate rain," the girl reminded her.

Deborah stopped what she was doing and straightened. Setting the pitcher and glasses back on the table, she took Grace's hand. "Come."

Grace shot her an amused look. "Where?"

Deborah didn't answer, just led her deeper

into the backyard. Turning so that they faced the house, she wrapped her arms around Grace's shoulders from behind.

"Mom," Grace protested, putting her hands on Deborah's arms.

"Shh," Deborah said softly. "Listen." Raindrops were landing on the forest's leaves, creating a gentle, cushioned sound that city-dwellers wouldn't hear. "Very soft," she whispered.

"What are we doing, Mom?"

"Making new memories."

"Of what?"

"You. Me. Life." Slowly, she let her arms drop. Coming to Grace's side, she slipped a hand into hers and, closing her eyes, turned her face to the sky. "What do you feel?"

"I feel like my mother's flipped out," Grace said, but her fingers clung.

"Seriously. Do you feel the rain on your face?"

There was a brief pause, then an indulgent, "Yes."

"What else do you feel?"

"Wet."

"Okay. Just breathe, slowly and deeply." She waited a minute. "Slowly and deeply?"

"I am."

"What do you feel now?"

There was a long pause, then a tentative, "Free."

"Anything else?" Deborah asked.

"Yeah."

"What?"

"If I tell you, you'll think I'm the one flipping out."

"No. I won't. Tell me."

It was another minute before Grace said a bemused, "Cleansed," at which point Deborah hugged her tightly. They had gone through so much in the last two weeks, and there was more to go through yet. The D.A. had to decide on the civil suit; Grace had to find her place back in school; Dylan had to deal with his eyes; Deborah had to feel her way along with Tom. Calvin McKenna's death would always be a part of their lives. But so much else had been resolved, and they survived.

She hugged Grace again. "Definitely cleansed. We start fresh."

Grace returned the hug. "I'm not you," she warned.

"So I've learned. But your heart is so in the right place."

The words were in tune with the sound of the rain, but then other music drifted from Dylan's window. It was the boy at his key-

board. After listening a minute, Deborah began to sway.

Grace joined her, humming. Soon, laughing, they sang along. **"I'd be sad and blue . . .
if not for you."**

Acknowledgments

I am deeply indebted to Bob Delahunt for information on law; to Ellen Gilman for information on eyes; to doctors Sherry Haydock and Lynn Weigel for information on practicing medicine; and to my son, Andrew, for information on track. Many thanks to my assistant, Lucy Davis, for exquisite organization; to my agent, Amy Berkower, for brilliant management; and to my editor, Phyllis Grann, for bold direction.

To my whole family, always, my thanks and love.

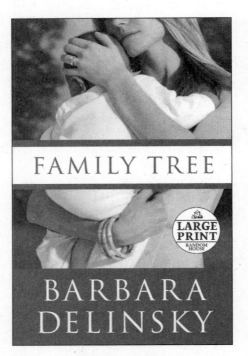

About the Author

The author of more than sixteen bestselling novels, Barbara Delinsky was a sociologist and photographer before she began to write fiction. A lifelong New Englander, she and her husband have three sons, two daughters-in-law, and a cat. There are more than twenty million copies of her books in print. Visit www.barbaradelinsky.com.